EVERYTHING ASIAN

EVERYTHING ASIAN

SUNG J. WOO

THOMAS DUNNE BOOKS
ST. MARTIN'S PRESS
NEW YORK

This is a work of fiction. All of the characters, organizations, and events portrayed in this novel are either products of the author's imagination or are used fictitiously.

THOMAS DUNNE BOOKS.
An imprint of St. Martin's Press.

Illustrations by Dawn Speth White

Book design by Susan Yang

www.thomasdunnebooks.com
www.stmartins.com

Library of Congress Cataloging-in-Publication Data

Woo, Sung J.
    Everything Asian / Sung J. Woo.—1st ed.
        p. cm.
    ISBN-13: 978-0-312-53885-9
    ISBN-10: 0-312-53885-5
    1. Teenage boys—Fiction.   2. Koreans—Fiction.   3. New Jersey—
Fiction.   4. Domestic fiction.   I. Title.
    PS3623.O6225E94   2009
    813'.6—dc22

                                                          2008037673

First Edition: April 2009

10   9   8   7   6   5   4   3   2   1

For my mother, Young Sook Woo,
my sisters, Sunny Woo and Chung Woo,
and the memory of my father, Han Jin Woo

ACKNOWLEDGMENTS

How do I thank thee? Let me name some names.

Claude Amadeo took away *The Red Badge of Courage* and replaced it with *The Dead Zone*. Carol Tistan showed me that some needles can be good. Bob Beers told me to get up an hour earlier. Suzanne Ruffo and Beth Siegrist gave me the gift of time. Dave Torok answered my questions about Great Adventure. Caroline Hwang guided me to write the perfect query letter.

These fellow NYU MFA workshoppers provided insights and encouragement: Humera Afridi, Elizabeth Chey, Alisha Davlin, Bradford Demarest, Paul Gacioch, Steve Horwitz, Arun John, Alisa Klevens, James H. Lee, Marco Fernando Navarro, Sophie Powell, and Alycia Ripley; Leila Binder, Olivia Birdsall, Shamar Hill, John Kurita, Rebecca Lane, Andrea Luttrell, Cleyvis Natera, Sara Padilla, Leeore Schnairsohn, Chastity Whitaker, and Marlene White.

Renée Zuckerbrot, agent extraordinaire, brought out the best writer in me. Diana Szu, my editor, believed in this first-time novelist. Helen

Chin made me consider the importance of commas. Jessica D. White found what couldn't be found.

Suzan Cole and Susan Jarosiewicz, my ESL teachers, taught me how to read, speak, and write this language. Elaine Flynn and George Ripley introduced me to T. S. Eliot and William Faulkner. Chuck Wachtel reshaped the first half of this novel.

Stewart O'Nan—teacher, mentor, friend—read the first draft of this novel and was kind enough to read the second.

Dawn S. White offered her editorial acumen, deft strokes, and enduring love.

GRAND OPENING

 IT'S MY SISTER ON THE PHONE. She's talking, I'm sort of listening.

"So anyway, on the way down, I drove by Peddlers Town," she says.

Words carry information. Some words carry memory. And some words, like Peddlers Town, carry a life, my life, my first year in the States. I was twelve then, and even now, a quarter of a century later, I can go back in an instant to that sad sack of a strip mall. What I see most clearly is our own gift shop, Father sitting behind the register, Mother helping a lady try on a kimono, my sister and I manning the showcases, sliding open those beat-up wooden doors at least a hundred times a day.

"Hey Junior, did you hear what I said?"

"Sorry," I say. "No, I missed that."

"They tore it down. It's gone."

———

can leave directly from my house to Peddlers Town, but I don't. Instead I head back to our old apartment first. It's a fine day for a drive, not a cloud in the sky, the crisp autumn wind whipping through my car. The detour adds a good hour to the trip, but I don't mind.

I turn into the entrance of the apartment complex, which is nothing more than a couple of balding flowerpots sitting in front of a tombstone-gray block with ROBERTSON MANOR carved in sharp black letters. The yellow and red bricks of the apartments themselves don't look any better or worse than when we lived here. Back then, Reagan was maybe only one can short of a six-pack, the collective cloud of aerosol hairspray poked holes in the ozone, and girls had very cold legs, as they all wore leg warmers, even over jeans.

I park at the end of the street and walk up to our old apartment, 282B. We were on the second floor. Below us, a single mother and her son lived in near-total anonymity. Even though we were upstairs/downstairs neighbors for more than ten years, we only discovered their names through misdelivered mail. I don't remember them as being particularly surly or shy, but for whatever reason, every time we encountered one another (which happened with great frequency, as we shared the same outside entrance), we would both look askance and go quickly about our ways. This wasn't as awkward or uncomfortable as it may sound; there was an elegance to this dance of avoidance, our bodies never touching, repelling each other like magnets.

What I recall most about the people downstairs is their balcony, whose neatness was in stark contrast to ours. At one point, in preparation for the upcoming Christmas season, Father used ours for storing overflow inventory, stacking brown boxes right up to the roofline. One floor below, our quiet neighbors had three simple objects on their deck, like normal people: a round table with a parasol staked through the center, a green chaise lounge, and a folding beach chair latticed with yellow and blue straps.

Which is, as I scan the patio in front of me, exactly what the current tenants have. I suppose it's possible that the same mother-and-son team is living there, but does it really matter? Would I ring the doorbell so I could look away and walk past them one more time?

Up above, it's obvious no one lives there right now, as the balcony is clear and the window leading to the living room is without blinds or curtains. I can't see too much from down here, but every angle shows me white, the walls as blank as an empty canvas, the floor probably cleaner than it's ever been.

Even if it is only a temporary vacancy, I'm glad that on this visit, my old home remains unoccupied. That's the way we'd left it, and I can almost make myself believe that no time has passed since our departure.

I walk up to the front door, then turn around. From here, the community pool that we hardly used sits in the far right corner of the complex, the silver rungs of the diving board glinting in the sunlight. To the left is a thin line of evergreens failing to hide the beige-bricked back of the neighborhood A&P, whose loading dock is like an open mouth, with a trio of apron-wearing workers smoking in a triangle.

I follow the concrete path that leads from the entrance of the apartment out to the parking lot, the same route we took as a family every Saturday and Sunday. Father and I would lead, each of us carrying boxes of merchandise from the apartment. Mother and my sister would be a few steps behind with the day's lunch and dinner in grocery bags. Kids in school were doing fun things on the weekends, going to amusement parks or watching movies, and here I was, trapped into going to the store. It didn't take long for me to resent it, yet when I look back at my teenage years, what I remember most clearly are those days and nights I spent in Peddlers Town, convincing a grandmother that her clawlike feet looked beautiful in a pair of open-toed, red satin slippers, and running the register while Mother stood by my side and bagged the purchases.

A black chicken-wire fence runs around the perimeter of the strip mall, but there's no mall, just a dusty parking lot.

There isn't a drivable entrance, so I park at the Dairy Queen across the street. It's not exactly ice-cream weather, but I get a twist of chocolate on a sugar cone anyway.

I lean against the hood of my car and lick the rich chocolate, surveying the scraps of wood and metal and concrete behind the fence. The vessel of my childhood, obliterated. I didn't visit this place often, but it was never far from my mind. People say that when you lose an arm or a leg, you continue feel the phantom limb, sometimes for years. As I gaze beyond the fence, I can still see what used to be there, the beige rectangular slab of a building with a ridiculous giant rooster weather vane at its center, the backlit yellow-and-black sign that always had a few bulbs missing. Business was never great, and every year seemed like it could be the last, but we managed to stay afloat and so did Peddlers Town. I didn't expect this building to last forever, but frankly, I never expected it to be gone, either.

I should've been here when the building was demolished, should've borne witness to the wrecking ball and the yellow bulldozers, the noise and the dust. This place was my second home, and I feel like I've abandoned it.

A long silver Lexus pulls up next to my ancient Honda. This was not what Sue was driving last time, but I know it's my sister.

She turned forty this year, and no matter how many times I say it to myself, I don't believe it. She certainly doesn't look like she's middle-aged, not when she's wearing a sweatshirt and frayed jeans that make her a closer kin to a college student than a vice president of a bank.

"Whaddyathink?" she asks.

"Nice," I say, and it's true, it's a lovely car, though it doesn't do much for me. I see automobiles as machines designed to transport humans and cargo from point A to point B, nothing more, but for Sue, luxury cars are her designer drugs, and she happily feeds the addiction with a different model every year.

With a click of a button and an ensuing chirp, the car's rear lights wink and the doors unlock. Inside, everything is wood and chrome, a magnificent blend of old-world grace and bleeding-edge technology. It has a combination GPS and DVD player that pops out of the dashboard like a James Bond gadget.

"Let's take it for a spin. You gotta ride in this thing to really appreciate it."

I agree, but only if we ride around the ruins of Peddlers Town first. My sister sighs, but she realizes that I'm giving in to her whim, so she gives in to mine without too much fuss.

We circle the remains of Peddlers Town at a crawl, much to the chagrin of the cars behind us, driving by a cracked kitchen sink, an upturned toilet, a metal chair mangled into a modern-art pretzel. As I gaze at the wreckage, I hope for some kind of closure, but it's not there. All I feel is pity—for the place or for me, I'm not sure. Probably both.

As we complete the loop, we see a sign that announces a future grand opening of a brand-new exciting store, the white letters and orange background looking all too familiar. Next year, this will be a Home Depot.

"Happy?" Sue says.

"No."

She guns the gas and we peel off. I know she'll make fun of me if

I look back, so I stare straight ahead. For about five seconds—until I turn around for one more glance.

"Still there," she says.

"What remains of it."

"Lunch will make you feel better," she says.

"You think so, huh?"

"Remember when I bought you lunch for the first time? At Hometown Grill?"

I did. And she was right, I did feel better.

Sue darts around a cluster of slower cars, ignoring the smattering of annoyed honks, until the empty highway stretches ahead of us. I sit back, close my eyes, and remember.

EVERYTHING ASIAN

 I WAS WAITING TO USE our apartment's only bathroom, shifting from foot to foot, when the door burst open and my sister walked out, her eyes raw and puffy, followed closely by Mother, arms tautly alert, ready to catch her if she fell, if she melted, if she died.

My sister had chosen this day, my twelfth birthday, to try to kill herself, or at least to pretend to kill herself. Looking back on that day now, I can see it was merely a stunt to gain attention, and even then I think I knew she was bluffing, but still, I couldn't ignore the blue dish and the paring knife sitting on top of the toilet seat, its tip pointing toward the bathtub like a compass needle. On the dish, a pile of white pills sat like an offering. I put the dish and the knife on the floor and flipped the seat up. As I peed into the bowl, I stared down at the silver edge of the blade, wondering how close it had come to my sister's wrists.

When I finished, I walked the stuff back to the kitchen. I let the pills roll onto the faded Formica countertop and counted twelve of them. I arranged the tablets on the dish in a circle, placed the paring knife in the center, and mouthed the words "Happy Birthday" in English. I wheeled the knife around until it pointed five past seven, the exact time my head would have poked out of Mother's you-know-what, twelve years ago to this day, the twenty-eighth of February, my squishy eyes slowly unsticking, wondering just why the world had gotten so cold.

I called my sister *Noona,* Korean for "sister." Her full name was In Sook, and her American name was Susan. She wouldn't know this until later, but there was another name in waiting, Sue, one she would eventually grow into.

Noona, almost sixteen, had days when she didn't say a single word, not to me or to anyone else. Then there were days when she wouldn't shut up. I would ask her if she wanted another ice-cream bar and she would start cursing like you wouldn't believe. When Father wasn't at the store, he was in New York, striking deals with wholesalers and vendors, so he wasn't around to see these strange fits. Luckily, Mother was home to handle her. When my sister became deaf-mute, Mother spoke to her like there was nothing wrong. And when Noona became irate, Mother listened calmly, and when there was a break in the yelling, she took her into her arms, where, for a moment, my sister would sink and disappear. When she resurfaced, silent bright rivers ran down her cheeks.

Noona was not taking the move from Seoul, Korea, to Oakbridge, New Jersey, too well. Unlike me, she actually had friends to miss, especially her boyfriend. She wanted to call them all, but Father wouldn't let her because it was too expensive, and besides, with a half-day time difference, it was next to impossible to get anybody at a reasonable hour. Noona called anyway.

"I only called four times," she said to Father when the phone bill arrived.

"Three hundred dollars!" he screamed, the first time I'd heard him scream. Before then, he was nothing but nice to us. "Where am I going to get three hundred dollars?"

"It's the least you can do," Noona said. Her voice stood at the edge of a cliff. Father had no rebuttal. He looked hurt, he looked tired.

That was the first month, the first phase of Noona's loneliness, soon to swell heavy and round like a full moon.

The very next day after their fight, Father came home with the biggest tape recorder I'd ever seen. "Here," he said, showing Noona how to use it. It was the kind that you'd find in high-school language labs, the black rectangular monsters with one giant woofer on top. The buttons were so big, you almost had to use two fingers. When Father pressed EJECT, the lid sprang up like a catapult.

Noona put the tape recorder to work immediately. She spoke intensely, her long black hair falling around the unit like a cape, her lips floating over the tiny triple slats on the built-in microphone. The first day, she sat in her room and made five ninety-minute tapes in a row, seven and a half hours of her fragile voice laid out on thin magnetic ribbon. How could anybody have that much to say? It was a miracle she was able to keep the phone bill under a thousand dollars. When the tapes were ready to be mailed, she insisted on accompanying Father to the post office with as much nervousness as a mother sending her child off to school for the first time.

The reply didn't come for three long weeks. When Noona saw the package from Korea with her name on it, she ripped into it with animal ferocity. There was a quick scribble on an index card and a tape that looked too professional to be an amateur recording. The note read:

Sorry you can't be here
This band is really good
We miss you

My sister listened to the tape once, slipped it back in its case, and buried it deep in her drawer.

She wasn't eating well, and she was losing weight. She chewed her food slowly and carefully, as if her mouth were full of broken glass. If her eyes weren't puffy or red, they were black and sleepless.

Mother was worried. I knew this because she came up with ridiculous suggestions.

"Maybe you two should sleep in the same bed," she said. "You know, like when we were in Korea."

"I'm too old now," I said.

"Says who?"

"Mother, we're in America," I explained. "In America, brothers and sisters don't sleep in same beds."

Mother nodded, stared at her hands, sighed. Her few stray grays had multiplied since our move. She looked old and scratched up like my secondhand dresser.

It was hard enough being Noona's roommate, let alone sharing the same bed. Nights were the worst. From the other side of the room, I heard her lingering sobs, how they seemed to come automatically, without any provocation. I tried not to be rude, but after a week of running short on sleep, I had to push off the covers and yell, "Can you please stop crying?"

She stopped. I couldn't believe it worked, just like that. "That's better," I said half-jokingly, but no response was forthcoming. I felt bad for yelling at her, but in an instant I was dreaming of sitting plush in a candy-striped La-Z-Boy on a soccer field, munching on barbecue potato chips, my new favorite food.

The next day was my twelfth birthday, when she did the knife-and-pill thing, so suffice it to say, I was not pleased with myself.

When Father returned from New York that day, Mother merely told him that Noona was a *noon-mool bah-dah,* a sea of tears, and that's all she would say. But Father was no dummy. He knew heartbreak when he saw it.

"Tell me, Joon-a," he said, cornering me in the kitchen, the refrigerator cold on my back. He resorted to using my nickname whenever he wanted something.

"Why don't you ask Mother?"

"Good son," he countered in English. "My good son."

He knew I liked hearing these words from him, but he was using them too frequently. Six weeks ago, Father had been nothing more than a picture in Mother's album of black-and-white photographs, a man who stood beside her in various poses behind various backgrounds. He'd left five years ago to make us a new, better life in America, and now here he was, in the flesh. In the pictures, he looked taller than he actually was, maybe because Mother was sitting down while he hovered over her, but everything else was exactly the same: his hair still short and parted to one side, his dark-framed eyeglasses too big for his face. He seemed harmless enough, but then I'd catch him on the phone talking to his wholesalers, looking sideways at me as he spoke, giving me a wink—and suddenly he looked like a different person, a fake.

I pointed to the dish that was still sitting on the counter. "That was in the bathroom," I told him. "Noona was in the bathroom with that."

He noticed the pills I'd arranged. "You made a clock out of it?" he asked.

"It's a cake. It's my birthday."

"Happy buss-day."

"Do you know the song?"

"I forgot it was your birthday," he said.

"It doesn't matter."

"How old are you now?"

"Twelve."

"I know the song," Father said. "Happy buss-day to you," he sang, running his fingers through my hair, "happy buss-day to you. Happy . . ." His voice cracked. I continued singing. ". . . birthday dear Da-vid, happy birthday to me."

He quickly wiped his eyes with his sleeve and cleared his throat. "What can I buy you?" he asked.

I wanted to take my time to compose a thorough list, but looking at Father's desperate face, I had to offer him something. "A Frisbee," I said, telling him the first thing that came to mind and regretting it immediately.

"Wait here," Father said. He returned moments later with a white round disc approximately the size of a coaster. In the center was the familiar McDonald's golden arches. "I'll get you a real one tomorrow," he said, handing it over. "Happy buss-day."

So tomorrow I'd have two Frisbees that I didn't want instead of one.

We never went out to eat anywhere, so when Father told us we were going out, I knew something big was up. I was hoping for Friendly's, but we headed toward a Korean restaurant managed by one of Father's friends, Mr. Lim. This didn't make any sense to me. Weren't you supposed to go out to eat food you couldn't get at home?

"Be quiet," Mother said. "This isn't about you."

When we returned from busting our bellies with oxtail soup and pepper-laced rice cake, a piano had joined our living room. It stood upright and had a splotchy look to it, maybe because its two front legs were varnished a darker brown than the rest. Noona went to it like a person possessed, lifting the creaky keyboard cover, and tracing the nicked rectangles of the ebony with her delicate fingers. The ivory keys were the color of Mr. Lim's teeth, but Noona didn't seem to mind. She sat down and played a couple of riffs.

"It sounds wonderful," she said.

Standing between Father and Mother, their hands resting on my shoulder, on my head, I watched my broken sister give love to her piano. I didn't know it then, but she was playing Beethoven's *Für Elise,* a tune she could play with perfect execution from memory alone.

That evening, I listened to Father and Mother arguing. Apparently there was some confusion about where Father got the money for the piano. Mother thought he had it saved up, because that's what he told her. Actually, he borrowed the hefty sum from Mr. Lim.

"That's why we went there for dinner, to thank him," Father said.

"You son of a bitch," Mother said. "You lied to me."

"You saw how much she needed it," he said. "What're you complaining about?"

"Don't turn this around. You're always turning everything around."

"Come on. You can't fault me for this. Not this."

My parents' voices and Noona's piano were intermingling, becoming oddly sing-song. It wasn't beautiful and it wasn't ugly. It just sounded like my family.

ather was right, of course; the piano turned Noona around. Often I
stood next to her as she played, watching her fingers flutter over the
keyboard, her bare feet jamming the pedals below. With every note
triggering the rise and fall of a hammer, how could you not feel better?
Noona's negativity fled in droves as notes dashed out of the piano.

Financially, the piano was a horror. Within two weeks, we lost our
telephone. A nice black man knocked on the door and said, "Good eve-
nin', good sir," to Father and slipped our rotary phone into a little canvas bag. We almost lost electricity, but somehow Father managed to
sell enough merchandise at the store to get everything back before the
end of the month.

It must've been difficult for Mother to live with Father again, constantly living on the edge of disaster. He was a smart man in a lot of ways,
but not when it came to money. To this day, I'm unable to figure out exactly what he was doing wrong. I don't think he ever could, either.

he best vantage point from which to see all the cars in our apartment's back parking lot was out the kitchen window, standing on a
chair, looking down and to the right. This was how Noona and I decided that Father drove the ugliest car in the neighborhood. It was a '77
Ford station wagon in a shade of green that felt doomed. In the summer
the car held a fishy stench. In the winter it shook while idling.

There's a story that goes with the purchase of this car.

July to August, 1980. For six consecutive weekends, torrential rain
soaks coastal New Jersey. This is great for business because Father's
store is half an hour away from the beach and when people can't head

for the shore, they head for the store. Each weekend he sets a new sales record. Mr. Lim has been kind enough to carpool with Father, the detour adding a good forty miles to his trip, so it's time for Father to get a car of his own.

At the end of six weeks, he has enough money to buy the black '78 Mustang from Bill Moreno, the scruffy guy in 14A. Since the beginning of the summer, a fluorescent FOR SALE sign has adorned its rear window. Father knows it's a good buy because he's seen the way Bill Moreno makes his turns like an old woman, and the car wash and wax that happens on every Saturday without fail.

On the day that Father decides to approach Mr. Moreno, Mr. Lim comes looking for him. "My car just died," he says. "I don't know what I'm gonna do. I'm sorry, but I won't be able to give you a ride anymore." Father lends Mr. Lim a sizable part of his money—enough to fix the busted transmission—and dejectedly goes to a Ford dealer, hoping to get maybe a '75 or a '76 Mustang, then comes hobbling back with the station wagon.

"Why did you buy the car?" I asked Father.

"I don't know," he told me. "It didn't seem like I had a choice. I was gonna get one that day, so I was gonna follow through."

"You couldn't wait?"

"I wish you were here that day," he said.

It was just what I wanted to hear.

The day that Father and Mother decided to have me and Noona begin working at Father's store ("Our store, not my store," Father repeated until I got it right), Mother drove for the first time. She'd been taking lessons from Father, but it was obvious they weren't going well, for after each session, Father would knock back a double shot of his Cutty Sark and Mother would run into their bedroom, slam the door shut, and crank up her Korean lounge music to near-deafening levels.

I'm not sure why Mother drove that day, but I'm sure it was Father's idea. "You can do it," I can almost hear him saying to her, coaxing her. "Honey, you can do it. It's the beginning of our new life here." Her hand squeezing the car key until it left an indentation in her palm, thinking, *Yes, yes, I can do this.*

Mother twice swerved into the curb with her extreme right turns, twice almost hit the same car on Route 35 (the driver of the other car, a tiny Spanish woman, screamed with buggy eyes, twice), and ran over an already flattened squirrel. She cried after she did that, waiting at the traffic light, just hid her face in her hands and wept.

But when the light turned green, Mother stepped on the gas. And when the next light turned red, Mother stepped on the brake. After all, she was driving. She had a job to do.

At our store, we sold everything Asian. That should have been our name, Everything Asian, but instead we were called East Meets West. Our store was one of "One-Hundred and Eighteen Fine Stores" of Peddlers Town, a depressed, second-class strip mall in Mannersville, New Jersey. A quick sampling of our shop: From Japan, we featured flowing kimonos, cloisonné bonzai trees, cone-shaped patchouli incense in tiny red sacks with gold drawstrings. From China, ceramic figurines of happy bald monks, shrieking dragons carved out of soapstone, silk pajamas with tiny Chinese eyehook buttons. And from Korea, a round black plaque accented with mother-of-pearl flowers, a guitarlike instrument that intoned sad and lonely vibes, a tall, regal vase with glassy cracked skin.

Despite all these beautiful things, Father was ashamed, maybe because there were no real doors to this store. Instead, he had to pull down on a loop of cable to roll up thick canvas curtains. It was like drawing up a gigantic window shade.

"Can I help?" I asked.

"It's heavy," he said, out of breath.

I grabbed onto a cable, lifted up my feet, and let my weight bring me down. It was fun.

"Is this okay?" Father asked.

"Okay?"

"Working here. You don't have to do anything you don't want to."

"What am I supposed to do?"

Father took off his eyeglasses, wiped the lens on his shirt, and put them back on. He surveyed the store. It was pretty large, much bigger than our apartment. Compared to the surrounding neighbors, we occupied the largest space. I thought Father should be proud. It's a fine store.

"There," he pointed, referring to some customers struggling with an item. "That music box—nobody can figure it out. You know how it works; it's the one that Noona has."

I felt nervous. "So I show them how?"

"Yes. But do it nicely."

I didn't know how to do it nicely, but I got up my courage and walked up to the two women, probably mother and daughter.

"Hello," I said.

"Hi!" the mother said. "Can you help us with this contraption?"

I had no idea what she said after "Hi," but I didn't let it frighten me. I reached over and pushed in the little silver button on the base of the pagoda-shaped music box. Tinny-tiny music, uncoiled at last, came to life.

"It's 'Moon River,' Mom," the girl said. Her eyes were very green and a little scary. Her skin was white to the point of translucence, and she had brown freckles everywhere. She smiled and I quickly looked away.

"Thank you! What's your name?" the mother asked.

Name—I knew that.

"David," I said.

"David, you've been most kind."

"Thank you, David," the green-eyed girl said.

Feeling somewhat triumphant at surviving my first customer assistance, I turned back to where Father had been, but he wasn't there; he was at the register, ringing up some other sale, Mother wrapping and bagging next to him. In his place stood Noona, who watched me with a rueful smile.

My sister had unusually large eyes for a Korean, and her face was almost perfectly round. Or at least it used to be. She seemed not just thinner but older, and prettier, too, her cheekbones pronounced, her arms somehow longer and more graceful. Never again would she look the way she did in Korea. I don't know how I knew that, but I did.

"Good work," she said.

"No sweat," I said.

We sat inside the fortress of showcases in the middle of the store, she on the aluminum stool and me on the wooden one.

"Do you like it here?" she asked, and I didn't know if she meant this store or this country or this planet. I was going to ask for clarification, then I stopped myself when I realized my answer would have been the same.

"Could be worse," I said.

She nodded slowly.

"It can always be worse," she said.

IN SOOK KIM

 THE MOTHER AND DAUGHTER were still fidgeting with the pagoda music box, laughing it up as they stood close to one another, and what In Sook hated most about these two Americans was how relaxed they seemed. They were the ones who should be out of place in this store full of Oriental merchandise, but no, it was she who didn't belong.

The mother was pretty in a way Korean women could never be. Everything about her was long—legs, fingers, even her eyelashes—and she was tall, taller than most men. The girl was also gangly, but it didn't quite fit her, at least not yet. In Sook could see how she might grow to look like her mother, but for now, her body was stretched beyond the limited boundaries of beauty.

American women were big, no doubt about it. Apparently their vaginas were larger, too, because all the Maxipads In Sook had bought—three different brands—were unnecessarily wide. Back in Korea, her breasts had been considered normal, but here they were often dwarfed by girls her brother's age.

Which made sense. This country was all about glorious excess, super this, mega that, so why wouldn't its people reflect its principles?

The mother and daughter approached the register, the girl holding the pagoda music box.

"Hello, Harry," the woman said, and In Sook's father greeted them with a ridiculous, clownlike grin.

"Did you hear that?" In Sook said to her brother. "She called him Harry."

"I think that means he has a lot of hair."

For a second she imagined smacking him on the back of his head. She could almost see it, her hand rearing back, her palm landing flat and loud, her brother furrowing his eyebrows and rubbing his head, looking up at her with his mean face, which wasn't mean at all but just a younger version of Father's: a bump for a nose, tiny bright eyes, ears that stuck out like handles.

"No, you idiot, that's his American name. Did you know that's what it was?"

Dae Joon shook his head.

As her father rang up the sale, she heard snippets of their conversation. He was giving the woman a discount, and she was saying something about another store. Even though In Sook had taken two years of English in high school, she found that most people spoke way too fast. And even when they slowed down, they used too many words she didn't know or slang that wasn't in the dictionary.

From the front counter, her father pointed to them, and now everybody was walking over to the showcases, including her mother, who'd been busy arranging the new stock of Chinese umbrellas at the far end of the store.

"Hi," the woman said. She held out her hand. "I'm Sylvia. And this is my daughter, Mindy."

It was irritating to have to say hello, but In Sook complied. Sylvia then shook her brother's hand, and then her mother's, and still she wasn't through. She proceeded to hand out her business cards to everyone.

ANIMAL ATTRACTION, the cards read, silhouettes of a cat and a dog bookending the store's name.

"Please stop by," Sylvia said very slowly. "We are just seven stores down."

"Yes," In Sook said.

"Do you like animals? Dogs, cats?" Sylvia asked. And when no one spoke, she proceeded to bark like a dog and meow like a cat, complete with faux scratching gesticulations to simulate a feline in action.

"Dog, cat, yes, I know," In Sook said. She hadn't meant to say it in such a derisive manner, but that's the way it'd come out.

There was so much she missed. Not just her friends, but everyday things she'd taken for granted, like *ja-jang-myun,* her favorite dish, sweet black bean sauce spread over a bed of noodles. In Korea, *ja-jang-myun* was purported to be part of Chinese cuisine, but she'd been to a pair of Chinese restaurants here in the States and neither had it on the menu. At the last place—some restaurant called Golden Dragon or Happy Dragon or Golden Panda, they were all named stupidly alike—she'd mustered up the courage to ask a waiter, who went into the kitchen and reported back that neither of their two chefs, both from Shanghai, had heard of it. And the Korean restaurant owned by her father's friend didn't serve it, either.

She came home that night and began a list in her diary of all the things she missed. After filling three pages, she noticed a disturbing trend. Things she'd despised, like her ugly high-school uniform and the stinky movie theater—she longed for them the most. It was an unsettling revelation, to suddenly want the things you thought you hated. It made you question everything and trust nothing.

Still, the past was preferable to the present, so that's where In Sook spent most of her time, especially when the store was quiet, like it was now. Since Sylvia and her daughter left, not a single customer had walked into their shop, so she closed her eyes and saw herself in that old school uniform of hers, the white blouse with a ring around the collar, the black skirt with the rusty zipper that required weekly lubrication with beeswax. On Thursdays after school, she and her friends would bus over to the theater that smelled of fermented soybeans from the factory next door, and although they would complain about the awful sweaty-sock scent that filled the darkness, they were happy.

She used to be happy. But now she wasn't, spending all her free time at this stupid store, dealing with impatient shoppers and, even worse, with her father, who was clearing his throat loudly to make sure she knew he was walking over.

"Hi," her father said. He stood beyond the glassed surface of the showcase like an uncertain customer.

She knew it was hard for him, to have his family back after five long years, but she didn't care. They were now well into the second month of reunification, and she hated him just the same. He was an easy target, and a willing one, as if he knew he deserved to be punished.

Of course he did. It's all his fault. If not for him, I wouldn't be here.

But he did get her the piano, that was something. Did she ever thank him, actually tell him those words, *Thank you, Father?* The thought filled her with guilt and hate again, because if not for him, she wouldn't be feeling any of this negativity.

She looked up at him and said nothing.

Five years ago she was ten years old, two less than her brother now, and she'd watched her father leave. Watched him wave with his briefcase in hand, the scene in Kimpo Airport growing fuzzy as tears softened her vision. How she loved him then. How she loathed him now.

She'd become a woman in those years, but he'd stayed the same. He wasn't any grayer or heavier or anything, just the same guy who'd disappeared. It was almost as if he'd preserved himself inside an ageless vacuum as he waited for his family to arrive, so that when they were together again, their lives would magically resume.

It was an incredibly heartless, selfish notion. He'd uprooted her from everything that mattered, her life, her fucking life, and he just expected her to accept it all? Smile and hug and tell him what a wonderful father he was?

He did. That was his little stupid dream, and In Sook had taken it upon herself to wake him up, because no one else would. She'd never intended to kill herself last month, but she knew the drama of a supposed suicide attempt would serve as an effective alarm. The knife, the pills, the locked door, they would send him the message, especially when it came secondhand from her mother, who had a tendency to go overboard when it came to her children's well-being.

He was smiling, his hands folded behind his back.

"I have a surprise for you," he said. "You got this in the mail."

When she looked up, he was holding an international envelope, blue and red rectangles alternately running around the edges. She snatched it.

"Is it from one of your friends?" he asked.

He made her say the most obvious things. Who the hell else would be sending her mail from Korea?

"Uh-huh," she said.

The last letter she'd gotten was two weeks ago and she'd begun to lose hope for more, but now here it was, the return address bearing Kyung Mee's name. There were people In Sook had been closer to, but now this made it four letters from Kyung Mee, while the two girls she'd considered her best friends had only written once each. It was odd how relationships changed when you moved away, how when you started writing letters, you were actually creating a wholly different bond. You almost became a different person.

In Sook drew the letter to her nose and took it in, but all she could smell was paper.

"Aren't you going to open it?" her father asked.

This was the problem with the store being slow, the stupid questions, the needless talking. She rose from the stool and told him she had to go to the bathroom.

"Okay," he said, keeping his happy face on, though she could tell he was hurt. He shuffled back to his chair behind the front counter and hid behind the open pages of a Korean newspaper.

In Sook walked away with the letter in her hand. Just feeling the envelope between her fingers filled her with joy. It was only eight o'clock, still a whole hour to go, so she'd use her letter judiciously. She'd meter out one paragraph at a time every quarter hour.

Their store wasn't the only one dead; the entire mall was deserted. The reason became clear when she walked by a window and saw snow coming down. Nothing serious, just a dusting, but it kept customers away, and it was probably the reason why she heard the argument on the other side of the walkway, one booth down from where she was standing.

Sylvia and Mindy, again. It seemed as if she couldn't get away from these people today, but actually, things were getting interesting at Animal Attraction. In Sook approached their incredibly bright store—everything was gleaming there, from the silver frames of the pet cages down to their shiny chrome bowls.

"Stop," Sylvia said. "Don't do this anymore." Then she turned, and In Sook saw a man who looked tall enough to play professional basketball.

"Do what?" he said.

"I know you think you're doing the right thing, but it's not."

The man looked like he was going to cry, then he did.

"Jesus, Russell, get a hold of yourself," Sylvia said, handing him a Kleenex.

"Mindy doesn't mind me coming around," he said, his voice sounding boyish, small.

"But I do," Sylvia said. "You're her dad, but you're not my husband. Not anymore."

In Sook picked up a few of the words and watched their body language to fill in the missing pieces, the man's slumped shoulders, Sylvia's defiant stare. Sylvia wrapped her arms tightly around Mindy, who looked vacant. Her face was numbness, her eyes far away.

She didn't remember seeing a ring on Sylvia's finger, so In Sook figured the man to be the ex-husband. Maybe it was a bitter divorce, the two parents screaming at each other, Mindy in her room with her pillow squeezed over her ears. Wasn't that how it was always shown in American movies?

Whatever. It was their problem, not hers. In fact, she had no problems right now because she had a letter to open. She stopped at Hotdog Heaven, got herself a Coke, and found a booth in the back where no one would disturb her.

The letter felt thicker than usual, so In Sook expected to find pages full of Kyung Mee's delightful tales of their mutual friends, but it wasn't the case. Instead, all she found was one scribbled sheet and another bulky envelope.

> *Dear In Sook,*
> *Didn't I promise you that I'd send your next letter to your store? That way, it would be a sort of a surprise. Okay, maybe not much of one, so here's another: a photo! I'm sure it's one*

you haven't seen because it was from an old camera, from two autumns ago. I put cardboard in there so it doesn't get bent, so I hope you like it. I would write more, but it's exam time and I need to brush up on trig functions, especially tangent. I have no idea what that's all about. Anyway, I'll write soon.

Much love, Kyung Mee

She tried not to be disappointed, but she couldn't help it. Last time her friend had thoroughly recounted the winter dance held at the school's gymnasium, describing how she and her friends had found matching dresses at a consignment shop and how during a slow dance, she'd pretended to lose her earring, and while her clumsy partner got down on all fours, she made her escape. *We laughed so hard,* Kyung Mee had written, and even though she was half a world away and a month late, In Sook had shared in their laughter. But this time, there was nothing here except for a photograph.

In Sook slurped down the rest of her Coke and rose. She wanted so badly to peek at the picture, but she made herself wait. It would be her reward for making it through another day.

She walked around the rest of Peddlers Town, going all the way down to the pharmacy in the new wing of the building, but there was nothing she wanted to see or hear or touch. With the lack of customers roaming the walkways, it seemed less like a mall and more like a museum, the place too quiet. A few of the merchants seemed to recognize her, but none of them bothered to say hello, which was actually fine because she wanted to be left alone.

But was it, really? Wouldn't it be nice if somebody knew her name, called her over, wanted her to stay?

She didn't want to go back to the store, but there was nowhere else to go, so she marched onward, and then she heard a scream. It wasn't just a short shriek of sudden pain or distress; this had legs, it went on and on and on, and it was coming from the rear of her store, in the furniture section.

Nobody was at the front counter or behind the showcases. In Sook made her way to where her parents were, standing a good ten feet away from Sylvia, who stood next to the large rosewood table. Underneath the table was Mindy, her hands gripping a table leg.

"What's going on?" In Sook asked.

Her father held up his hands as if in surrender. "I don't know. The girl was here with a tall man, and then her mother came, then he left, and now here they are. She"—and here her father surreptitiously nudged toward Sylvia—"just tried to pull her out."

"Why is she under the table?"

Her father shrugged. "Joon-a went to get Mr. Hong, so maybe he can help."

Mr. Hong was a friend of his, the only other Korean man in Peddlers Town. He owned a luggage store and often stopped by and chatted with her father during the day. He spoke better English than anyone in her family, though that wasn't saying much.

"I'm sorry," Sylvia said. She kept rubbing her hands together, as if she didn't know what to do with them. "I— I don't know what to say but say I'm sorry."

"I'm not going anywhere until Dad comes back," Mindy said from below.

Sylvia crouched down, furious. "You scream again, and I swear . . ." But then she trailed off and looked utterly baffled, and it was obvious why. What could she possibly say? If the girl didn't want to leave, what could her mother do? What could anyone do, really? It was actually kind of funny, so In Sook laughed, which got everyone staring at her, especially Sylvia, who seemed more embarrassed than ever.

Her brother arrived with Mr. Hong in tow, and he didn't waste any time. He walked right up to Sylvia and asked her why her daughter was acting this way.

"She won't move until I call her father," Sylvia said.

"You call him?" Mr. Hong said.

"No. That's not going to work. We're not—we're divorced," she said, ashamed at having to reveal a part of her personal life. "We have a visitation agreement, and we have to stick by it."

"I see," Mr. Hong said.

The two Korean men walked off to the side, where they could talk by themselves and make all the decisions, as usual. Since Sylvia couldn't understand Korean, they spoke at normal voices.

"So?" her father asked.

"Family problems," Mr. Hong said. "Divorces can be ugly."

"I see. Of course."

"I don't know what we can do. Call Reggie, the head security guard, that's one thing."

Her father shook his head. "We could wait it out."

"But the mall closes in ten minutes."

Her father looked over in their direction. "Joon-a," he called.

If only her brother could see himself. It was almost comical, the fear that gripped his little face. He sort of looked like one of the Three Stooges, the one with the helmet-shaped hair that was always punching everyone else.

"Better go," In Sook said, and gave him a push.

"What do you think he wants?" he said. Unlike his sister, Dae Joon was wary of their father. Her brother had been seven when their father left for America, so he should have had some memory of him, but curiously, Dae Joon had none.

Behind, her mother sat in the severe-looking Japanese armchair that was on sale for half price, the one made of a single contiguous piece of wood.

"I heard you got a letter," she said.

"From Kyung Mee."

"That's good." Her mother looked tired, as she often did nowadays, especially in the eyes. Her makeup masked it to a degree, but her fatigue went deeper than that. The transpacific move wasn't agreeing with either of them, but her mother was a trooper, a noncomplainer.

In Sook sat down next to her on the floor and, as expected, her mother's fingers began running slowly through her hair. It was like an automatic response, one of the few things that could be counted on, and she reveled in it while in front of her, like a play, the drama unfolded. Her father was telling Sylvia that he and his son would stay as long as necessary.

"No," Sylvia said, her guilt obviously mounting. "I can't ask you to do that."

"No problem," her father said, then repeated it twice more.

The men came over and told them what was going on. Mr. Hong would be driving the women home.

"I think this is the best way," her father told her mother. "Don't you?"

"Sure," her mother said. "Just come home as soon as you can, but watch the road, it's snowing."

And that was it, the end of her day. In Sook looked back at the dismayed face of her brother and couldn't help but smirk.

"Have a nice time with your daddy," she said.

On the way to the parking lot, Mr. Hong confessed his car was a mess. "But I can clean it up real quick," he said.

"Please, we can do that," her mother said.

A mess was an understatement. Greasy burger wrappers lined the floors, cigarette butts crawled out of the overflowing ashtray, a window was spattered brown with dried-up cola.

"Asshole," In Sook said as she and her mother filled two grocery bags full of garbage while Mr. Hong stood by the mall entrance, enjoying a smoke.

"Watch your language," her mother warned.

Her fingers were so cold they hurt. She wished she'd brought her gloves, but In Sook hadn't thought she'd need them. To keep going, she thought of all the things she wished she could do while sitting behind Mr. Hong on the way home. Slap him on his bald spot, spit into his ear, grab hold of his ugly comb-over and give it a good yank.

"Thank you so much," Mr. Hong said, getting into his pristine car. "Crazy American girls should scream in your store more often, huh?"

What kept In Sook from screaming herself was the photograph in her pocket. Halfway home, there was a stretch of the highway where it was lit up bright enough for her to take in the picture and transport herself to Seoul. What could it be? One of Kyung Mee's cousins was into photography, so it was probably from his 35mm. In the letter, she'd written that it was during the fall two years ago. Back then, she hadn't even known she would be leaving her home, her life no different than those of her girlfriends.

And look at me now, In Sook thought. *No, don't look at me, please nobody look at me.*

"Are you okay back there?" her mother asked from the front passenger seat.

"Yeah, I'm fine," In Sook said, but her voice betrayed her words. She quickly wiped her eyes with the sleeve of her coat.

Up ahead, she saw the yellow glow of Route 35, and it looked magical under the falling snow, a hazy tunnel of light. She tore into the envelope and leaned against the window.

It was in front of their school, six girls sitting on the grass and holding hands, forming a human line of everlasting friendship. She remembered this day, the earthy scent of the surrounding pine trees, the gentle warmth of the afternoon sun. Everyone in the picture was smiling into the camera.

But no, not everyone.

How could this possibly be? Her tired, sick-of-this-world face stared back at her, no different than her reflection framed in the bathroom mirror this morning. In Sook thought hard back to that day, trying to recall anything unpleasant that might've happened, but she couldn't come up with anything.

Maybe it wasn't this new country that made her miserable. Maybe the misery had always been inside her.

Strangely enough, this realization didn't depress her. Instead, it gave her hope, because if it was indeed inside her, that meant she owned it. She could continue to wallow in the pool of her own pity, or she could go on. Her choice, no one else's.

In Sook tried to take another look at the photograph, but it was once again dark in the car, the lights of the highway now behind them, fading into the night.

GO FISH

 AT QUARTER PAST NINE, the overhead lights went dark. Not all of them—it looked like every fifth fluorescent bulb stayed lit.

"Don't worry, Joon-a," Father said. "It won't take long."

I certainly hoped it wouldn't.

To pass the time, Father suggested we play cards. I turned on the gooseneck lamp on the front counter while he rooted around the desk drawer for a *hwat-toe* deck. Unlike American playing cards, these rectangles were made from thin hard plastic sheets about half the size of business cards, but they were far prettier. Father passed four cards down to me and to himself, then placed three cards between us. He flipped them over one by one, and each revealed a nature scene: a full moon on a hill, a deer in an autumnal forest, and a trio of roses in full bloom. The moon was worth twenty points, and if I held the card that featured the same hill but no moon, I could've taken it, but all I had were three scenes of wheat fields and a cardinal perched on a cherry-blossom branch.

Before we could start the game, we heard footsteps approaching us. Sylvia and Mindy were holding hands and looking much more mother-and-daughter-like. Though it seemed as if they'd been crying, they didn't act sad.

"I think we're good," Sylvia said.

"Good, good," Father said.

"Unfortunately, before we go, I think Mindy needs to stop at the bathroom."

"No problem," Father said. "I go, too."

He got up and extended a hand to Mindy, who took it eagerly.

After they left, Sylvia took Father's seat and looked like she wanted to say something.

"Your father's a very nice man," she said.

I nodded. She must've known there would be little comprehension on my part, but she didn't care. She kept talking, probably lavishing more praise on my father, and when she realized that she was making me feel uncomfortable, she stopped and took in a breath.

"Thank you, David."

These words I understood, and for that I was grateful.

"You're welcome, Sylvia," I said.

What we found outside when we finally left the store that night was snow. Not a whole lot, at most an inch, but the parking lot looked vast and still, the lights from the lampposts casting soft yellow ovals over the blanket of white. There were just four cars left, our station wagon two spaces away from a minivan.

Father held the mall doors open for Sylvia and Mindy, and the four of us carefully made our way down the short staircase to the pavement.

"Thank you again, Harry," Sylvia said, and she leaned in to give

Father a quick peck on the cheek. And before I knew what was happening, Mindy planted a similar kiss on my own forehead. It felt damp and I wanted to wipe it off, but I didn't want to be rude, so I thrust my hands into my jacket pockets.

Because the snow was fresh, it was simple to brush it off the windshield. All it took was a few broad swipes and we were set to go.

"Nice job!" Father said with more enthusiasm than was necessary.

As we pulled out of the lot, he said, "These American women, you know," then made a *tsk-tsk* sort of sound. I didn't know, so I said nothing. Then we were silent for quite some time, and I wished he would turn on the radio, but every time I stole a glance at him, Father seemed quite content listening to the occasional swoosh of the passing vehicle and the droning hum of the road.

I was avoiding him. I had been for a while, and I thought maybe he hadn't noticed, but obviously I was wrong. As I sat in darkness, watching pairs of headlights brighten and disappear, I replayed the discussion we had when Mindy wouldn't leave the store. *Joon-a and I will stay,* Father had announced to everyone while standing behind me. Then he placed his hands on my shoulders and pulled me close enough for me to get a whiff of his Old Spice. *This is a job for men.*

I didn't mind being with him when Mother or Noona were around, but when we were alone together, he was like a different person. His voice would drop lower, he'd suddenly break out a fake grin for no reason at all, and sometimes when I caught him looking at me, it was like staring at the face of a starving man. I knew he wanted something from me, but what? Things were easier when we were still just feeling each other out. Now that the initial rush of meeting each other had run its course, all that was left were these moments of awkwardness.

I loosened the seat belt around my chest and shifted in my seat.

"You all right?" Father asked.

"I'm okay."

"Have you ever gone fishing?"

At first, I questioned whether I'd understood him properly, but I was certain that's what he'd asked.

"No," I said.

"I think we should," he said. "Just you and me."

Those last four words were like an icicle driven into my heart. "What about Mother and Noona?"

"Fishing," he said, more than happy to supply the answer, "it's what men do together."

My brain ran into overdrive, scrambling to squirm out of this future appointment with torture. "But it's too cold to fish, isn't it? I mean, you fish in the summer. When the weather's warm. When there isn't snow outside. Right?"

"Nah," Father said, with an easy dismissive wave of his hand. "Plenty of winter fish in the ocean. Like winter flounder. You know what a flounder is?"

I had no idea what a flounder was, and I really didn't care, but that didn't stop Father from elaborating on the subject. Apparently, its summer counterpart was the fluke. "The difference between the two is that the fluke has both eyes on its left side, while the flounder has them on the right. Kinda strange, huh?"

"Yeah," I said, sinking into my seat. "Kinda strange."

Look at that," Father said on the following Monday, scanning the crisp blue sky from our balcony, shading his eyes from the sun. "It's gonna be a great day for us to catch some fish, Joon-a."

Mother got up early to roll us Korean sushi, which was like its Japanese brother except the raw fish was replaced with slivers of cooked beef.

"What are you and Noona gonna do?" I asked as she sliced the seaweed roll into bite-sized wheels. Both my sister and I were off from school because of a statewide teachers' meeting.

"Not much of anything, I figure. Just clean up around the house and watch some television."

I would've happily volunteered to scrub the toilet with a toothbrush if I didn't have to spend the day with Father. What would we do for the next eight hours, what would we talk about? He already had the day mapped out: driving down to Neptune to get fresh bait, then heading over to the piers at Long Branch to fish, a two-hour round trip in the car. The prospect of being stuck with him by myself in the passenger seat made me ill.

That was it. Maybe I wasn't feeling so well. Maybe my stomach hurt and I'd have to stay home. "Oh," I said, holding on to my tummy with both hands. "I don't feel so good."

Mother paused in her slicing and stared at me. It was a long, silent gaze that made me drop my act.

"You'll have fun," Mother said. She picked up two rectangular panels of dried seaweed and placed them onto the bamboo mat.

To make up for my attempt at deception, I scooped a spoonful of rice for her. "I don't think so."

Mother spread the rice onto the seaweed and added soy-marinated spinach, strips of fried eggs, pickled daikon radishes, and dropped little clusters of beef and caramelized onions on top. Then with few efficient and graceful turns of her wrists, she rolled up the mat like a scroll.

"He just wants to get to know you."

"But why can't you guys come? Doesn't he want to get to know you, too?"

With a snap, the sushi spun out of the mat and onto the chopping board. She handed it to me as is, so I could eat the roll like a banana.

"Maybe that's something you guys can talk about," she said.

I chewed viciously as I made my way back to my room. In Korea, Mother would have done everything in her power to protect me, but now? Now she was practically pushing me into the horror that awaited me. I plopped onto my bed and wanted to chuck something breakable against the wall.

"Are you still here?" my sister said from beneath her covers, her voice heavy and thick from sleep. She had her sheet pulled over her head, so I was about to converse with a mound of purple.

"It's a day off from school and I have to get up even earlier. It's not fair."

"You know what's really not fair? You waking me up, that's what."

I grabbed my pillow and flung it at her, aiming for her head.

"Hey!"

"It wasn't me."

The mound straightened and stretched momentarily, then curled back to its original position. "Don't be a baby. Go and spend quality time with your daddy and leave me alone."

I did leave, but not before opening up the curtain to let the morning sunlight shine right on Noona. It wasn't much of a victory, but it did cheer me up, especially when I heard her cursing me out.

In the bathroom, I washed up and changed into a pair of jeans and a red sweatshirt. I combed my hair and paused at the face in the mirror staring back at me. I thought of all the terrible things that could happen to someone—like blindness. I couldn't even imagine what it must be like to live out the rest of my life without sight, to never see my own face or anybody else's ever again. I turned and tilted my head to the left and tugged at my right ear. What if I suddenly went deaf? I stuck out my tongue and examined the tiny red bumps that made up its surface. I was sure there was some disease out there that eliminated the ability to taste.

So that's how I steeled myself for the day ahead, by thinking of how much worse things could be. Compared to losing my senses of sight, smell, and taste, going fishing with Father wasn't so bad.

What I didn't realize then was that Father was just as nervous about this day as I was, if not more. When I got out of the bathroom and carried our lunch down to the car, he was checking off a list on a notepad, making sure we had everything for our outing.

"Are you ready," he said, then in English, "my good son?"

I nodded. Mother had forced me to wear my winter jacket, but I could see it wouldn't be necessary. Even though it was early March, it was an unusually warm day, almost springlike. I started to take it off, but I stopped, wondering if he would have anything to say about it.

"You wear what you want to wear," he said. "It's just you and me, Joon-a." He held open the car door, sunlight reflecting off the green vinyl seat.

"Is there oil or something on there?"

"It's Armor-All," he said, holding up a spray can. "Makes it look brand-new."

I slid in, and he slammed the door behind me with a huge, crazy grin; I had to fight the urge to jump out and run back inside. As I watched him hurry around the hood of the car, I still hoped for some sort of a miracle, like him tripping and breaking his ankle. But no, he got in, closed the door, and we were once again alone in the car.

"I have a surprise for you," he said, and I was genuinely terrified.

Without warning he leaned toward me, flung his arm between the space in our seats, and thrust a foiled bag in front of my face.

Potato chips. On the label, a black rod ran through the letters BBQ, skewering them over an open-flamed grill. I was surprised he knew they were my favorite.

"Thank you," I said. Father looked and waited, and it became clear to me that he wanted me to open it, which I did. The familiar smoky, greasy scent immediately filled the car, and I extracted a chip. Mother never would've let me eat junk food in the morning, and that was his point.

"Hey," Father said, "that's a big one!"

"Uh-huh." I bit into the salty sweetness and said, "It's very good."

He flashed another eager smile and slid the car into gear.

As we drove to the bait shop, Father asked me about school. Both Noona and I had been attending for almost two months now; she was in tenth grade, I was in sixth. I spent most of my time with Ms. Dennis, who was my English as a Second Language instructor, so for six excruciating hours each day, she tried to convince me that the madness of the English language was worth learning. I was no easy convert—English seemed to have no rhyme or reason, the way the past tense of *play* was *played* while *go* was *went* and *buy* was *bought* and so on and so forth. Compared to the sensible rules and structure of the Korean *hangul*, English seemed like a bunch of half-complete jigsaw puzzles haphazardly glued together.

"English is crazy," Father agreed. "What purpose does *the* serve? It makes no sense why you say *the sky is blue*. Why not just *sky is blue?*" Our car screeched to a sudden stop, and a long, loud horn sounded from behind. "Oops. That was the street we wanted." He lazily spun the steering wheel with one hand, making a wide U-turn in the middle of the road, which seemed a little dangerous, but his mind was elsewhere, his face looking as if he was trying to find something. "Oh, have you made any friends at school?"

I grabbed another enormous chip and nibbled on it. "Not really," I said, which was sort of true.

"Don't worry," Father said. "You'll have lots in no time."

I thought of the three kids I hung out with at lunch. Billy's face was squished and he made strange sudden movements with his hands. Marty, when he wasn't drooling, slurred all his words to the point of incoherence. Petey, afflicted with a mild case of Down Syndrome, looked like he could pass for my brother.

On the very first day of school, I got to know the word *retard*. Every few minutes, somebody would come over and yell "RETARD!" to us. I didn't have to look up this word in my trusty dictionary—I knew what it meant. These kids were all mentally challenged, slow-thinking misfits of society. There was a name for them in Korea, too: *baa-bo*.

We parked beside a yellow cement block of a building. Above the steel door was an ancient-looking sign made out of strips of iron, JACK'S BAIT SHOP, the letters bleeding rust onto the wall. Next to the entrance was a clearance table of what I supposed was fishing paraphernalia: black rubber boots that came up to my chest, reels of lines in all colors and thicknesses, and a plastic box with a handle on top that hid three hinged trays that opened up like steps.

"Go right in," Father said. He pointed at the phone stand off to the side of the building. "I have to make a call."

"All right."

"A wholesaler," he said. "I can't be there today, and there's an order I was supposed to pick up, so I should let them know."

I didn't know why he felt like he had to explain that to me, but I just nodded and went inside.

A bell rang as I opened the door, but neither the large bearded man behind the counter nor the shopper buying a six-pack of beer noticed. The store sold more than just fishing stuff, also carrying small grocery items like 7-Eleven did. As I walked down the aisles, I caught Father through one of the smaller round windows. Although I couldn't hear what he was saying into the telephone, he looked like he was having an argument. He was no doubt late with a payment; he often talked like that to his wholesalers.

A minute later, the bell rang again, and Father bounded in. "Come on, Joon-a!" he said. The clownlike grin was back on his face. "Let's buy us some bait!"

Father drove, and I talked. Mother wasn't kidding when she said he wanted to get to know me. By the time we got to the piers of Long Branch, my throat was sore. Father asked me one question after another, about the last five years of my life, like what happened on my eighth birthday. Who was there? What did I eat? What presents did I get? Did the Bugs Bunny figurine he sent over arrive in time? It was exhausting to recall every detail of something that happened years ago, and I couldn't wait to get out of the car so I wouldn't have to listen to my own voice for one more second.

"This is great. I really feel like I'm catching up, you know? Five years is a long time."

"Uh-huh," I said, and drained the remains of my can of Coke.

We rode over a pair of speed bumps, and I could hear the silent asphalt road giving way to the crunch of sand. Father slowed and shifted the car into park. "I know you've been doing all the talking, so on the ride back, you can ask me whatever you want."

"All right," I agreed, though with reluctance. Is that what he expected, for me to reciprocate by querying him incessantly on the return trip? I picked up the clear plastic container of worms and watched their squiggly struggle, inching around the curved surface of the neverending wall. I couldn't think of a single thing I wanted to know about Father's life. What was there to know? He worked at the store, he lived in the apartment. How was his life any different before we arrived? While we fished, I was going to have to come up with something. Lots and lots of something.

My mood brightened considerably when the car doors opened and we stood up looking at the ocean in front of us. The salty scent of the sea hit me first, followed by the hypnotic call of the waves as they crashed onto the beach. I remembered the last time we were on the coast in Korea, Mother and Noona and I sitting together on a large towel as we watched the sunset, the bright disc turning redder as it dipped under the horizon. This was two summers ago, but my memory of that entire day was as strong as if it had happened yesterday, my sister and I running on the beach, stamping our bare feet into the wet sand, Mother peeling fresh apples for us to munch on.

I felt Father's hands on my shoulder. "Isn't this great?" Father said. "It's so beautiful, so peaceful."

It was colder by the ocean, and windy, too, my hair quickly whipped into a shaggy mess. Mother had been right to outfit me with both my winter coat and a wool cap. I wanted to get the cap from the back seat, but Father's hands were still perched on me, so all I could do was wait it out. The entire beachfront was deserted except for a man walking his dog. To the left was the pier—a strip of rocks where we were supposed to fish.

Father finally let go of me when we heard the sound of another car behind us. It was a black Jeep, and emerging from it were a Latino man and a boy. He seemed to be about my age, though taller and tanner and wearing a Yankees baseball hat. The man acknowledged us with a quick nod, which is how Father should have responded, but instead he raised his hand and bellowed, "Good morning!"

They walked around their Jeep and picked up their fishing gear.

"Looks like we're not the only ones today, huh, Joon-a? Let's get going!"

Father led me to the back of our car to pop the trunk, but it wouldn't open. Every once in a while it would get stuck, and the only way to get it working was for me to hold the release switch next to the driver's seat while Father turned the lock. As I trudged back to the front of our car, I wished we had a cool Jeep like them instead of this ugly station wagon. And while I was at it, I wished I had the Latino guy for a father; he seemed like the strong, silent type, unlike my own.

"Okay," I yelled back, pulling on the release.

"My good son," he said again in English, and when the trunk sprang up and I saw Father's face through the body of the car, I had a funny thought: What had he been like when he was my age? In school, some of the bigger kids made fun of me and the retards, but they also went after the ones who smiled too much, the ones who desperately wanted to be liked. If I had met Father as a classmate, I probably wouldn't want to be friends with him.

Father armed me with a white bucket and our lunch while he carried the poles and the tackle box. From afar, the pier seemed flat, but close up, huge rocks jutted out in various angles. It wasn't difficult to negotiate, but there were some places where the surface was slick.

"Here we are," Father said, handing me a fishing pole. The one he gave me was new, the yellow enamel polished, the rubberized grip almost sticky, while the one he held looked like it might not make it to the end of the day. When I tried to trade, Father held up his hand.

"Nothing but the best for my son," he said. "Besides, this one's fine, it's just old and beat-up, like me." That was a joke, and to make sure I got it, he laughed.

The used pole was from Mr. Hong, one of his spares. Father said they fished together all last year, from late winter to late fall.

"You know, it would be fine with me if you invited Mr. Hong next time." I wasn't exactly a fan of his, but at least he and Father could gab and I could sit in the back seat with minimal participation.

From the bottom of the tackle box, Father brought out a pair of reels. Again, he gave me the new one and kept the old, and I mirrored his actions as he clasped the reel onto his pole and threaded the nylon line through the rings. I couldn't figure out how to tie the hook and the sinker, so Father did that for me.

All that remained was for us to put on the bait, so we each took a worm out of the canister. It felt like a cold, wet noodle between my fingers.

"It's my least favorite part," Father said, looking forlornly at his brown worm. "But it's for a good cause, so no regrets." He pierced one end through the hook, twirled it around, and pierced the other end, creating a pretzel around the metal. The worm squirmed a little, but didn't seem to mind too much. My bait didn't look as neat as his, but it was done, and we were ready.

Casting was simple: hold the line with the index finger, grasp the pole with both hands, pivot ninety degrees to the right, then fling the pole back to the front, releasing the line at the same time. It took me a couple of tries to get it right, but in no time flat, I was plunking the sinker a good distance away.

"It's all in the hips," Father said, and then proceeded to twirl his behind in an exaggerated circular motion, as if he were hoola-hooping. Again, it was supposed to be a joke. I glanced back at the Latino family, to see if they were watching. Fortunately, they weren't.

In fact, they weren't doing anything but fishing. As I cast and waited for my line to tug, I noticed how quietly they were interacting with one another while Father kept up a steady stream of small talk, forcing me to discuss the weather, the store, and everything else that meant nothing to me. I envied those two, the ease of their silence, their immobility. They seemed like a pair of bronze statues, something out of an artful photograph.

An hour passed without a single bite. I thought maybe we weren't doing something right, but the other guys weren't faring any better. And then Father almost lost his pole.

"Whoa!" Father yelled, grabbing it with both hands. We had been sitting down, but now we were both up, and Father pulled the pole to his chest, the end bending into a u. I couldn't believe it hadn't broken.

In the excitement, I blurted out, "Your hips, use your hips!"

Father laughed. "Right!" He pulled and reeled and pulled and reeled, and whatever that was on the end of the line was putting up a hell of a fight. And then just as suddenly as it had come, the line went slack.

"Oh shit," Father said.

"What happened?"

"Sometimes they manage to wriggle out of the hook." He reeled in the line dejectedly, but it stopped again and the pole bowed. I started to get excited again, but Father's reaction was now one of annoyance. "Christ, it's stuck."

We followed the taut line and sure enough, it looked like the sinker was jammed in the crevice between a pair of rocks.

"I can get that," I said.

"It's all right," Father said. "We can just cut it off."

"No," I said, surveying the path down to the point. It got me close to the water, but it didn't look dangerous. "I think I can."

"You sure?" Father said. "I guess we can use that sinker. I bought plenty of hooks but not too many sinkers."

I was getting bored of sitting around anyway, so I welcomed the activity. As I'd suspected, finding purchase between the pieces of rock was simple. I climbed down slowly, and at the halfway point, I looked back and gestured a thumbs-up to Father.

"You don't have to do this, Joon-a," he bellowed from above.

"Almost there," I yelled back.

As I got closer, I got wetter. I tried to evade one particular swell, but it still got my feet, my sneakers soaking the water like a sponge. But that was the worst of it, as I found the hook and yanked it free from the crevice.

"Okay!" Holding the sinker in my palm, I felt triumphant, as if I'd scaled down the face of Mount Everest. I flung it back to Father with all my strength, and suddenly found myself slipping backwards, unable to stop.

I didn't even have the chance to scream. I was floating in air one moment, and next, there was water everywhere. The long-sleeved cotton shirt I'd been wearing became a wet second skin, and even though the water must've been cold, what I felt most was the heat of panic. I flailed my arms, kicked my legs, and did all I could to stay above the surface.

"I can't swim!" I yelled. I didn't know where Father was, where the pier was. Seawater rushed into my mouth and I spit out the salty contents, only to have more of it funnel back in.

Father said something back to me, but I was beyond hearing. My head dipped under completely, but somehow I managed to rise, and when I was able to take in another lungful of air, I thought about how angry Mother would be if I died.

Stand up. That's what I thought I'd heard.

"Stand up!"

It wasn't Father's voice. My eyes were blurred, but I could make out the Latino man as he stood at the edge of the pier, his hands raised out toward me, like a god welcoming his children.

He yelled it again, and this time I listened. I stopped my thrashing and stood up straight, surprised to find ground beneath my feet. The water was only as deep as my neck.

On the return trip home, the car's heat was on full blast, all the vents pointed toward me. I could use it, as all I had on was my underwear and my winter coat. Everything else was in the trunk, stuffed into a garbage bag and ready for the laundry.

"It's really kinda funny, huh?" I'd said.

Those were the first and last words spoken in the car. Father's eyes remained glued to the road, and his hands were choking the steering wheel at ten o'clock and two o'clock.

I thought he should lighten up. There I am, thinking I'm going to die, and it turns out that all I had to do was stand up. If that's not funny, what is? Of course I could've drowned, and no doubt he was feeling bad about letting me go down there in the first place, but still, I didn't think it was fair for him to be acting this way.

When Father finally broke the silence, he said, almost offhandedly, "You swam just fine."

What was he talking about?

"You don't remember," Father said.

"Remember what?"

"You used to swim just fine. I never learned, so I always wanted you to."

"When was I able to swim?"

Father laughed, but it was the mirthless kind. "Your sixth birthday, the year before I left, we had a party for you at Uncle Chan's house."

The name was somewhat familiar, but I couldn't place him. My life before eight was like feeling my way around a dark, familiar room. There were times when I would run into something and know it immediately, but those occasions were rare.

"He moved to Austria of all places the same time I left, but he was very rich. Had an indoor pool that was heated, and that's where you swam. Your mother was by your side the whole time, but you hardly needed her help. You were a natural."

Father didn't say anything further. As we turned off at the ramp and neared our home, I felt a mixture of confusion and anger. It didn't seem right that I'd lost something I didn't even know I had, and a part of me resented him for revealing my shortcoming.

Our apartment loomed ahead, the yellow-bricked building looking especially ugly at this time of day, the late afternoon sun exposing the cavities of missing bricks, the rusting gutters. A handful of turns later, we were back where we started from.

"Stay here," Father said. "I'll bring down a blanket for you."

"All right."

As he slid over to exit from the driver's side door, something fell from his back pocket and onto the seat. It was his little notebook. After the door slammed shut and I saw him disappear into the apartment entrance, I picked it up.

Everything he'd asked me earlier in the day was in here, and more. For someone who never finished high school, he had fine penmanship, better than mine. On the last page, he'd written:

Ask him if he remembers me
Ask him if he is going to call me "father" or "dad" in English
Or "pop" or "papa" maybe

From where I sat, I looked up and saw him at the kitchen window, talking to Mother. She moved to her left and disappeared from view, then returned in a moment holding something blue in her hand.

Father strode through the back door, the bundle of blanket in his arms, ready to bring me home.

MR. HONG

IT WAS NOW HALF PAST ONE, and the burger in front of Kim only had one single bite.

"Right," Hong said, barely listening to his friend's verbal diarrhea. He was still harping on the fishing trip he took with his son, about how the boy almost drowned, even though nothing bad actually happened, even though it was now over three weeks ago.

"I had this dream last night," Kim said. "Everything was under water, you know, like Atlantis or something, and I see my son . . ."

Hong didn't want to be rude, but he saw no other choice. "You gonna eat your hamburger, Kim, or what?"

"Huh?"

Hong pointed at the round sesame bun.

"Oh," Kim said, looking down at his plate, almost surprised at the food in front of him. "You in a hurry, Hong?"

For a moment, Hong wished he were a more impetuous man, the kind of person who'd stand up so fast that his chair would kick out behind him. Then, without a word, he would stomp out of Hometown Grill, leaving Kim with his jaw wide open, not caring that every eye was on him.

"No," Hong said, "no hurry."

"You want some?" Kim grabbed his burger with both hands and began the messy process of tearing it in half.

Hong held up his hand. "No, no, Kim, I'm fine. You eat."

While his friend ate his burger, Hong picked at the few French fries left on his plate. All the whole ones were gone, so only the rejects remained, slivers burned black, stumps oozing grease. He knew things would change once Kim's family arrived, but he hadn't expected their weekly Saturday lunches to be ruined like this. They used to talk about politics, religion, important things about the world, but now the only thing on Kim's mind was his family, especially his son.

"Hey, guys," the voice above him said, and Hong was glad to see Jake, glad he could still be counted on. Even though he was busy cooking in the kitchen, he always took time out for a quick chat. He held a pair of white coffee mugs in his left hand while his right gripped the orange-handled pot of decaf.

"Thank you, Jake," Hong said. "You growing mustache, huh?"

Jake placed the mugs in front of each of them and poured up to the rim for Kim while leaving room for Hong. He rubbed the dark fuzz of hair underneath his lip. "A beard, actually. What do you think, would I look good with a beard?"

Hong considered the question seriously. He tried to envision a full, bushy beard on Jake, and thought it wouldn't look good at all. On some men, beards awarded them the illusion of age and wisdom, but on others, they made them look more animal than human, and Jake unfortunately fell in with the latter. But it was obvious the guy wasn't looking for the truth, so Hong told him he would look hand-some.

"Handsome, yes," Kim mumbled in agreement, his mouth full. "Very."

"Well, thank you, gentlemen," Jake said. "You guys have a nice day now."

Not likely. Hong picked up the small cow-shaped ceramic pitcher by its tail and watched as the cream poured forth from its open mouth, di-luting the deep darkness of his coffee into a lifeless beige. He should be happy for Kim, and he was, but at the same time, he couldn't help feeling left out. Before Kim's family came, they did things together all the time. Kim came over for dinner, they watched television afterwards, they played cards. And the two of them went fishing all last year. Nineteen times, twenty-seven fish caught between them, each of their outings me-ticulously logged in Hong's spiral-bound notebook with the time of day, the temperature of the water, the state of the sky.

"Man, this is a good burger," Kim said, now halfway through.

Hong met his eyes, but only for a moment. If he stared, too many feelings came up: anger, frustration, and a potent combination of jeal-ousy and shame. How he wanted to yell at Kim right at this moment for failing to warn him. Yes, that was it. Kim should've informed him that he was nothing but a substitute for his son, that once his precious name-sake made his decorated arrival, Hong would be on his own.

He ripped a packet of sugar and stirred it into the mug in tight, clockwise circles, troubled by his thoughts, his feelings. What the hell was wrong with him? Hong focused his attention on his coffee, the sil-ver spoon as it rotated inside the rim, the rich scent of the dark roast. He had to get a hold of himself.

"I almost forgot," Kim said, down to his last bite. He talked with his mouth half full. "Remind me to return the fishing pole you lent me. I finally brought it in."

Hong pulled out a twenty out of his wallet, dropped it onto the table, and stood up.

"Hong?"

This time, Hong was unafraid to meet his friend's eyes, to thrust the fullness of his fury. It wasn't the content of what Kim had said but his delivery, so completely nonchalant and criminally unaware, just like the way he'd originally asked for the gear, with a smile on his face and a spring in his step.

My son and I are going fishing, he'd said.

And all Hong could say was: *That's great. Good luck. Happy fishing.*

"I gotta go," Hong said, and left without looking back. Perhaps this meant the end of their friendship, but considering what it had become recently, maybe it wasn't much of a loss.

Thankfully, the walkways of Peddlers Town were bustling with people. It felt good to meld into the generous anonymity of the crowd, the gaggle of their collective voices soothing him like white noise. He paused at the stereo shop, HiFi FoFum, and saw that Dmitri was striking a familiar pose, one ear plastered against a gigantic speaker, struggling to reach a red slide switch on the amp. The crazy Russian, always tweaking with his equipment.

"Good afternoon," Hong said.

"Hello there, my friend," Dmitri said. "Come here and listen to this, okay?"

Like the Russian, Hong placed his ear flat against the black mesh of the speaker cover, the thin cloth soft against his skin. The classical music that was playing was louder now, and being this close to the woofer allowed Hong to individuate each instrument. When the piece suddenly quieted from the orchestra to a violin solo, Hong almost felt as if he could see this musician, a girl, the rise and fall of her shoulders as she moved with the music. He'd always wondered why some people bought Dmitri's ridiculously expensive equipment—this speaker here was a thousand dollars, for just one, not even a pair—and now he could see why. It wasn't so much the quality of the sound but the clarity of the dream that it evoked, that one could close his eyes and see the orchestral ensemble surrounding him, a king graced with a private performance.

"This is good," Hong said. "Amazing."

They chatted for a while, the Russian showing off the twelve-band equalizer on the amp, and as Hong listened to his animated demonstration, he remembered why he didn't come in here too often. Talking to Dmitri was usually a one-way affair, with him doing the talking and you doing the listening. All he cared about was his precious audio equipment, especially the four speakers at the corners of the store. He even had names for each of them. Who in his right mind names merchandise he plans to sell? He was a strange man, and when Hong saw a break in the conversation, he mumbled an excuse and got out of there.

As he made his way back to his own store, Hong resented Kim more than ever. Wasn't it Kim's fault that he'd gone into Dmitri's store in the first place? Absolutely. If not for the way their lunch had ended, Hong wouldn't have felt the need to connect with someone else. He would have just waved at the Russian and passed him by, with his stomach full of Jake's hamburger and his mind full of Kim's sunny take on the current state of Korean politics. Things were still shitty back home, the new president just as corrupt as his ousted predecessor, but his friend always had a way of looking at things in a positive light.

A hard round object rammed into his shoulder blade from behind.

"Damn it!" Hong said.

The object turned out to be a head belonging to a boy, Kim's boy, who looked and sounded out of breath. The boy bowed his head.

"I'm sorry, Mr. Hong," he said.

"You should be," Hong said, his voice louder he expected it to be, the strolling shoppers turning their heads. "This is no place to run."

"Yes, sir," the boy said, his head still down.

Kim often referred to his son by his American name, but Hong refused to go along. The boy was born as Dae Joon, so that's how he addressed him now, lecturing him on how a person is supposed to behave in a public place. Hong knew he was going overboard, fabricating a ridiculous tale about how he once witnessed a kid at a Korean fish market break both of his arms when he ran wild and fell over a cart, but he couldn't stop himself. It was gratifying to exert power over this boy, to hold him prisoner with his words.

To his credit, Kim's son listened quietly without fidgeting. When Hong finally let him go, he thanked him and walked away in small, measured steps, but Hong had a hunch it was all for show. Hong made it look like he was walking the other way, but a few steps later he looked back, and sure enough, the little bastard was taking off like a rocket.

Were kids always this rotten?

Back at his own store, Hong was greeted with a child ten times worse than Dae Joon. This mini-monster was a blond blur, sprinting down the accessories aisle, almost knocking over an elderly lady as he bolted between the spinning rack of belts and the cardboard display of wallets.

"Yabba dabba doo!" he yelled.

"Jerry," a woman said as she considered the heft of a brown leather purse, "stop it."

She was no doubt the mother, and from the look of her, it was not surprising why the kid acted the way he did. She was dressed like a gypsy, in layer upon layer of multicolored shawls and scarves, one of which dragged on the ground like a tail. As she moved from purse to purse, dandruff drifted out of her poofy red hair like confetti.

"Yabba dabba doo!" the kid screamed.

Hong walked past the boy's mother and sat down behind the counter next to his wife, Jhee.

"Can you believe this? What the hell is happening to kids these days? I swear . . ."

He stopped when he saw the way she was looking him. Like an angry dog, her upper lip stretched into a thin sneer. She was in one of her moods again, and Hong braced himself for the oncoming onslaught.

Why was he so late? Did he forget that she had to eat lunch, too? Didn't he care about her well-being, especially when she wasn't feeling a hundred percent today? And did he remember to ask Kim about his wife, because Jhee wanted to get to know her?

Did he? Didn't he? Did he?

It was bad enough listening to his wife barking at him, but seeing the manic kid run back and forth in the background, with his idiotic mother whining for him to stop—this was more than he could handle.

"Just stop," he told Jhee, but she wouldn't. Her mouth kept moving and discordant sounds continued to flow out, and if he were a lesser man, he would have slapped her straight right then and there. Instead, he thrust his palm over her mouth, maybe with more force than necessary, but it was better than what he really wanted to do.

"I hear you," he told her surprised, still eyes. There was a brittle edge to his voice as he struggled to keep calm. "I do. But these people are driving me crazy." He removed his hand slowly, his wife nodded, he nodded, and an understanding passed between the two of them. He couldn't remember the last time they were able to communicate so well without words.

Hong rose from his chair and approached the woman, the mother. "Excuse me," he said.

"Yeah," she said, in the same vacuous tone she used on her son. She was too busy fingering a patch on a brown suede handbag to actually look at him.

"Excuse me," Hong said again, a little louder.

"Okay, just walk by me for chrissakes," she said, still oblivious. She took the handbag off the hook and brought it right to her eyes, like a jeweler examining a diamond.

Her boy, meanwhile, was on the other side of the store, and Hong couldn't believe what he was seeing. He had already looped four handbags around his neck, laughing as he kept pulling more off the rack.

This menace had to be stopped, and Hong knew he wouldn't get any help from the mother. His intention was to ambush, to grab the boy from behind, and to stop this nonsense once and for all, but as he neared him, the boy took off on another run, and seeing him take off so suddenly and so freely zapped whatever reserve Hong had remaining in his system. The boy's tiny face was frozen in smug satisfaction as his necklace of purses flailed about, and the only thing Hong wanted from his life right now was to wipe away that smile. As he quickened his pace, Hong knew what he was about to do, and for the first time today, he felt happy.

What actually took less than a few seconds seemed to happen in slow motion. Hong crouched behind the three-piece Samsonite luggage set, and the boy didn't have a chance. Hong stuck out his right foot with impeccable timing, and he felt the boy's foot jam against his ankle, then watched his small body launch forward. A green glossy purse with a round brass closure—which Hong had marked down to 50 percent off last week—gracefully slipped off the boy's neck and landed half a second before the first part of his body, the left elbow, struck the carpeted floor.

The boy tumbled completely twice and ended up sitting on his butt, facing Hong a few feet away. He expected the boy to scream out in pain, but that was not the case. Instead the boy stared at Hong's black loafer, still in its protruded position. Hong retracted it immediately, and that's when the boy's blue eyes snapped up to meet his own. For a second there was no expression, and then it was like watching glass shatter: Every part of his face broke into shards of misery.

Hong trotted back to the counter, his heart beating hard. There were no customers outside of the boy and his mom, so as far as Hong could tell, nobody had seen what happened. Behind him, the crying became a wail, and the wail was soon punctuated with tearful calls for his mother. Hong sat down and picked up the newspaper and pretended to read, taking deep breaths to calm his shaky hands. He was about to say something to his wife, something innocuous and distracting to force the noise emanating from the corner of the store into the background, but he stopped when he saw the empty chair beside him.

Left for lunch, probably.

Or maybe left him for good.

It was a strange thought to have, to think that his wife had stepped out his life forever, but it helped him stay an arm's length away from the situation at hand. The mother crossed in front of him and hurried over to her child.

What the hell had he done? What kind of a monster was he, hurting a little boy, even if he was acting up? He could've died. He could've landed on his head, snapped his neck, and died. Jesus.

And how about the way he handled his wife just before, shutting her up with his hands like that, shoving his palm hard against her mouth? Never in all their years together had he ever touched her inappropriately. Never struck her, never pushed her, not even during their worst fights.

From the far end of the store, he heard faintly:

"What happened, baby?"

"It hurts, Mommy, it hurts!"

"Oh baby, you're bleeding."

"Ow! That hurts!"

More wailing, more screaming, and then nothing. Seconds, then minutes, and still nothing. They were gone, but Hong couldn't make himself look away from the newspaper in front of him. There was safety here behind this black-and-white wall.

He dreamed of the boy. Not nightmares, but what disturbed Hong was the consistency of his appearance, now four days in a row. Last night the boy ate an orange without peeling it, chomping at it like some animal. For some reason Hong found this incredibly sad and woke up at four in the morning with tears soaking into his pillow.

This would be the kind of thing he would've talked to Kim about, but since their lunch, he hadn't gone to see him and Kim hadn't come to his store. His wife knew that there was something amiss, seeing how Hong no longer left for his twice-a-day visits to East Meets West, but she knew better than to prod into his business. Hong had made it clear to her long ago that certain parts of a man's life were his own, and that he had no desire to discuss them with her, though that never stopped her from trying.

"I think I'll go for a nice walk," Jhee said. "You'll be here, right?"

It was four o'clock, the time he usually went to see Kim, and it was an obvious attempt to bait him into talking. Maybe he was just tired from not being able to sleep after waking from that strange dream, but it got on his nerves.

His reply to her was curt: "I'll be here."

"Good," his wife said. She wisely said nothing further as she stood up, stretched her arms, and winced, her hands going to her back. "God, that really hurts."

If she was waiting for concern or pity, Hong had no intentions of giving her either. He just wanted her to leave, but when she finally did, he wished she'd never left. He went up to a couple of customers and asked them if they required assistance, but they declined politely. Back behind the counter, Hong stood up, sat down, stood up. He stared at the numerous bags he sold at his store—a three-piece luggage set, a rack of black school backpacks, a throng of purses shaped to look like jean pockets—and all he could think about was how empty they were inside. Some of them had crumpled tissue paper to provide structure, but most just had air trapped within their zippered confines, these poor bags, so vacant, so alone, and if the phone hadn't rung, Hong was sure he would have succumbed to a fit of tears, but then the telephone rang.

He grabbed it in the middle of the first ring and held the receiver like a talisman, as if it possessed the power to save him. For all he knew, it was a telemarketer on the other line, wanting to sell him a vacuum cleaner, and that was just fine. He'd buy the damn thing, he was so grateful.

"Mom? Is that you?"

Hong stayed silent. Of all the millions of people with telephones in this damn country, the one who had to call at this very moment was his son. He pulled the earpiece away and listened to the tiny munchkin voice as it pleaded: "Mom? Dad? Hey, is anybody there? Hello?"

Realizing the absurdity of his behavior, Hong cleared his throat and attempted to speak in a neutral tone. "Hello, son. Good to hear from you."

There was noise in the background, faint snare drums and a few guitar riffs. Yun Sae was calling from the student union at his college, letting them know that he wouldn't be coming home for spring break this weekend like he said he would. He had three huge projects that were all due on the same day, including a twenty-page research paper on the Japanese occupation of Korea during World War II. He honestly didn't know how he was going to get them all done, and there was palpable concern in his voice.

Hong initially found it difficult to concentrate on the conversation, but once engaged, he found it comforting to listen to his son's problems. Hong was able to soothe him by doling out a mixture of advice ("It's better to get some sleep than none") and compliments ("You make us proud by just being who you are"), and then Yun Sae surprised him by asking about Kim.

"Why do you ask? Did you hear something? Did you talk to your mother?"

His son laughed. "Jeez, Dad, you're sounding kinda defensive. I was just curious about his daughter, In Sook or Susan or whatever her name is. But what's up? Is anything wrong?"

Was it right to burden his son with his troubles? Even though he knew Yun Sae was certainly old enough to be a man, Hong couldn't get past the toddler he used to be, the one who fell asleep beside him in his easy chair, his little hands tugging at his father's shirt like a blanket. But it was time, wasn't it? Time for his son to grow up, and Hong, too.

"Son," he said. "Yes, there's something on my mind. It might help if I can talk to you. Would that be okay?"

As expected, he heard his son turn serious, and proud, too, Hong could tell. "Of course, Dad. Please feel free to say whatever is on your mind."

So he told him everything. There was something profoundly safe about professing his story over the telephone, and Hong ended up saying more than he ever thought he would. Like how deeply hurt he was that Kim cast him aside, and the undeniable flash of joy he received from seeing the little boy tripping onto the ground. And Yun Sae turned out to be an astute listener, saying just the right things to keep the conversation flowing and sometimes staying silent for minutes at a time.

"This is a lot, I know," Hong said, his throat parched. He gulped the last of his tea and waited for his son to speak.

"Dad," Yun Sae said, and paused. And the pause elongated into something uncomfortable, and Hong wondered if he'd revealed too much. "First of all, I can't tell you how honored I am that you chose to confide in me."

His son was being sincere, but instead of feeling reassured, Hong felt as if he'd lost something. Whatever he was suffering from had been his and his alone, but now it sat between him and his son, out in the open, naked and ugly. Yun Sae spoke at length about how he saw the situation, talking in analytic, almost clinical terms. He was taking psychology classes, and he diagnosed Hong as suffering from a neurosis called projection.

"See, Dad, projection is the opposite defense mechanism to identification. We project our own unpleasant feelings onto someone else and blame them for having thoughts that we really have."

"I see," Hong said, though he didn't see. His son was learning so much from the university, more than Hong could ever know. How would he see his father years from now? As a weakling, an imbecile, someone who suffered from mental diseases.

"So theory aside, what you need to do is deal directly with the core of your fear. That is, to make peace with not Mr. Kim but his son, because he's the one you're really mad at. I recommend you spend some time with him."

There was no one in the store, but he was tired of talking and even more tired of listening. "I better go. There's a customer I gotta take care of, so I better go."

"All right. Any time you want to talk, just call. Really."

When the conversation finally came to its merciful end, Hong stared at the telephone. The longer he looked, the less it looked like what it was supposed to be. It was a sleek plastic thing, all curves and black as midnight, and he remembered the last time he and Yun Sae talked, his son had explained to him that black wasn't really a color. It was the absence of color, and that was another concept Hong hadn't fully understood.

For some reason he kept thinking the phone would ring again. If it did, he would just let it go, let it ring for an eternity.

Next morning at the store, more sleep-deprived than ever, Hong drained his third consecutive cup of coffee.

"You look like hell," his wife said. "Did you get any sleep last night?"

"Two, maybe three hours," Hong said. His teeth felt tingly and tight, and no matter how much coffee he drank, he couldn't get rid of the metallic taste in his mouth, as if he'd been sucking on a roll of nickels.

Lying awake in bed the previous night, with his wife snoring away beside him, he'd replayed his conversation with Yun Sae. *I recommend you spend some time with him,* he'd said, like a doctor dispensing advice. Hong didn't know if he believed his son, but at this point, he was ready to try anything.

"Are you okay?" his wife asked.

He stood up from behind the counter and announced, "I'm going to Kim's. There's something I have to do."

"What? What do you mean? What are you gonna do?" Jhee was practically frantic, but the funny thing was, it didn't bother Hong. Maybe it was his overwhelming sense of fatigue, which had a muting effect on just about everything, even his wife. To diffuse the situation at hand, he simply stated the truth.

"I'm going to spend some time with Kim's boy," Hong said.

"Dae Joon?" Jhee said. "But why?"

"Because he's the son of a friend and I don't know him very well."

His wife slowly sank back down to her chair. "Okay," she said, "It's just that you're so, I don't know . . . quiet."

He reassured her he was fine and that he'd be back shortly. As he walked over to East Meets West, he considered where he could take the boy. Perhaps the arcade, a place he knew Dae Joon frequented.

The Kim clan was busy with their morning chores. The kids were spraying Windex on the showcase windows and wiping them down with paper towels; Kim and his wife were at the clothing section of the store, securing an extension cord near the ceiling. His wife steadied the ladder while Kim held a hammer in one hand, lining up the head to strike.

Hong hesitated for a moment. It was awkward the way they'd parted last time, but he knew Kim. He wasn't the kind to hold a grudge.

"Good morning," Hong said.

"Hong!" Kim said, surprised but happy. He pointed his hammer at Hong. "Long time no speak, my friend."

"I haven't been feeling well."

"Better now, though, huh?"

"You could say."

Hong watched as Kim drove three white nails neatly into the wall to hold the cord in place. His wife handed him a barrel-shaped spotlight, and Kim clipped it onto a nearby shelf.

"Would you help me align the beam, so it would shine on the rack of silk kimonos there?"

It was Kim's way of telling him everything was all right between them, so to show his appreciation, Hong guided his friend to make several exacting adjustments until the lamp was placed perfectly.

"The gold embroidery looks nice with the light," Hong said.

"Exactly," Kim said, climbing down the ladder. "So, you wanna grab a cup of coffee or something?"

"Actually, I wanted to take Dae Joon out, if you don't mind."

There was an awkward pause. "You want to take him . . . out? Out where?"

"The arcade. I figure he likes the arcade."

"He goes there all the time. Joon-a!"

The boy hurried over. When he saw Hong, he slowed down a bit, no doubt remembering his last encounter with him.

"Mr. Hong wants to take you to the arcade," Kim said.

"Just for an hour," Hong said. "So let's go." He didn't want to give the boy a chance to say no, because he probably would. He grabbed his hand and marched forward. "We'll have a good time, don't worry," he said, loud enough for everyone to hear.

As they walked down together, Hong wondered how he could engage him in conversation. They had nothing in common except for their Korean heritage, and that was hardly something kids wanted to talk about anyway.

"Do you like baseball?" Hong asked.

"No," Dae Joon said.

He didn't like football, either, and Hong's other questions were answered with one-word replies or shrugs. After another prolonged bout of silence, the boy cleared his throat.

"So just an hour, right, Mr. Hong? After that I can go?"

They were only four stores from the arcade, but Hong felt as if someone had dropped an anvil on him. He slumped into a nearby wooden bench. What was he trying to do, torture the poor kid? This is what he got for listening to his son's cockamamie ideas.

"It's right there," Dae Joon said, pointing to the neon sign surrounded by a rectangle of multicolored bulbs, ARCADIA.

"Here," Hong said, reaching into his pocket. He brought out a fistful of quarters and offered them to him. "You go play all you want. Let me rest."

"All this?" Dae Joon said, incredulous. "All this is mine? To keep?"

Hong nodded, and the boy didn't hesitate. He shoved the change into his pocket and sprinted to the arcade without looking back.

Hong closed his eyes, opened them, closed them again. He sat for what seemed like a long time but when he looked at his watch, only half an hour had passed. He considered going back to his shop, but didn't see the reason for doing so.

"Hey!"

He saw Dae Joon waving both arms at him from the entrance of the arcade. The boy was jumping up and down and screaming at him to come. He walked over and followed Dae Joon into the darkness of the arcade.

"You have to see this. He's about to beat Pac-Man!"

There were at least a dozen people crowded around the machine, all kids. Hong stood back and watched the player, a boy with thick glasses wearing a baseball cap backwards, move the joystick with superhuman dexterity. Hong had seen this game before, but never at this speed, the ghosts racing up and down the blue-lined maze like pinballs, the Pac-Man a yellow blur. It didn't seem possible that anybody could play the game at this obscene rate, but this kid was doing it, and even though Hong believed like many others that video games were a waste of time, it was awe-inspiring to see someone so good at something.

At some point, half of the screen filled with weird, random characters, and everyone cheered. Apparently that was the end of the game, because the kid took a few bows and went to the next machine, a shooting-flying thing called Defender.

"One hour," Dae Joon said, tapping at his wristwatch. "Time to go, right? Otherwise, my mom will get worried."

He wasn't a bad kid. In fact, he was a very good boy. He didn't have to come out and get Hong when the Pac-Man thing was happening, but he had. He'd wanted to share the experience with him. It was something Kim would've done.

Outside the arcade, the boy presented the remaining quarters in his pocket for Hong to see, giving him the opportunity to reclaim his change. "I still have a lot."

"And they're still all yours."

They walked back together. Hong asked him about the fishing trip, his supposed near-death experience.

"It was stupid," he said. "I just had to stand up."

"So I hear."

"Do you think," the boy said, "you might come with us next time? You like to fish, right?"

This was the magic of children, wasn't it? To see the simple in the complicated. Maybe instead of getting worked up, all Hong had to do was just tell Kim that he wanted to go with them on their next fishing trip. Was that so hard?

"Yes," Hong said. "I like to fish."

They returned to East Meets West together. Kim was at his desk, a bemused look on his face.

"You guys have a good time?"

"Of course," Hong said.

Hong watched the boy walk to the back of the store. He was a small kid, but he looked like he'd grow tall. Probably as tall as his own son, who towered over his old man. But it was the job of old, little men like him and Kim, the fathers, to take care of their young. To give them love and care so they'd grow up strong.

"He's a good kid," Hong told Kim.

"I think so," Kim said.

Instead of heading back to his own store, Hong decided to loop around Peddlers Town, stopping at the candy shop for a quarter-pound bag of malt balls. The new wing of Peddlers Town had looked sparse a few months back, but now it had filled out nicely, only one empty booth left, and it didn't look like it would stay that way for long. A heavyset woman with long red hair was directing a pair of burly men where to place her merchandise. One guy was holding a big blue vase that looked identical to what Kim sold, and the other rolled in a clothing rack packed with red and blue Chinese satin dresses.

A TOUCH OF ASIA

 **IT WAS SPRING**, it was April, yellow flowers lined the highway, white flower petals drifted down the sidewalk, and Father was mad as hell, mad enough that the hair inside his ears puffed out like tiny gray smoke.

Of course, it was money, always money, failing to grow on trees, flowing down the drain like water, extending its long legs and sprinting away. It was a bright, feather-light morning when Mr. Hong mentioned the new store in the new wing of Peddlers Town, but of course, it was really about money.

"You haven't seen it?" Mr. Hong asked, sitting on the edge of the front desk, his stumpy legs dangling, his back to Father. This was their normal way of conversing, Mr. Hong talking to the air around him as Father replied to the back of his friend's head.

"Seen what?" Father said, leaning back in his chair.

"I thought you knew." Mr. Hong extracted a chewed-up pen from his breast pocket and gnawed on it. "They hung up the sign this morning, A TOUCH OF ASIA."

Father sprang forward in his seat. "A touch of *what*?"

I followed Father and Mr. Hong as they marched down the walkway. As we passed the Peddlers Town main office, Father slowed down enough to look in the window. Sitting with his feet up on the desk was Jason DeLeon, the owner's brother-in-law, staring into the television. On the screen, Smurfs marched through their mushroom village while singing their silly "La-la-la-lalala" song.

"Son of a bitch," Father muttered under his breath. "He's the one, I know he's the one." We moved on.

Except for the whiter paint and new ceiling tiles, the new wing of Peddlers Town didn't look much different than the old wing. However, the stores in this section were more eclectic than in the rest of the mall: The Future Is Now, where an old black lady told fortunes with a bunch of yellow sticks; Beads Forever, which carried everything from beaded dresses to beaded toilet seat covers; and We Wear the Masks, where nothing but masks of all kinds—clown, African, Chinese, whatever—were sold. The latest arrival was A Touch of Asia, in the far right corner, Booth 113.

As we neared the store, Father turned around and asked me to stay back. "Duck in there, Joon-a"—he gestured at the comic-book store, Comic Relief, which stood catty corner—"and whatever you do, don't show yourself."

I briefly entertained the idea of asking why, but from the way Father was acting—speaking too fast, moving too fast, his eyes wide and unblinking—I thought it best to keep quiet. So inside Comic Relief, hiding all but my eyes behind the latest issue of *The Incredible Hulk*, I watched Father and Mr. Hong make their approach. The proprietor of A Touch of Asia, a round-faced and overweight woman, waddled from one end of the store to the other, trying to put the place in order, her braided rust-red hair whipping around like a dog's tail.

By and large, she sold identical merchandise as our store, but there was something special about the way she displayed them. Each of her small vases had a single tiny rose, exponentially increasing their individual loveliness. Her kimonos were not hung on rigid hangers but on haphazardly placed hooks, giving the robes a loose, homey feel, like they were already hanging on the back of your bathroom door.

She was a better decorator, but the store was maybe a tenth of ours in size, so we had nothing to worry about. But Father's face told a different story.

"Why, hello there," the woman said, seeing for the first time the two men standing in front of her store. She had a Southern accent. I'd never heard one before, and I liked it immediately, especially how it elongated and softened every word she spoke. "I apologize for the mess, but I just opened. You're free to come in and look, if you don't mind a little dust."

For a second, I was afraid Father would walk up and clear all her vases with a single swipe of his arm. Instead he smiled broadly at her, somehow stuffing all his rage between his stretched lips, and that was truly unnerving. If he could hide his anger so completely, what else did he have back there?

"Beautiful," he said. "Store beautiful."

"Why, thank you," she said, almost curtsying. "If I may be so bold, it means a lot to me to hear that from you, to hear you approve."

"Another Oriental store, here?"

"You mean in the building? I'm not sure. I just got here a week ago. I don't think there's another one here, though."

Father nodded, satisfied by her answer. "Very beautiful," he said again, then left. He passed me without a glance, like I wasn't even there. I didn't know what to do, so I waited until the woman got busy again and darted away at my first chance.

On the way back, I saw Father and Mr. Hong in the main office, talking to Jason DeLeon. It sounded more like shouting than talking, and strangely delayed at that, with Father yelling at Mr. Hong in Korean, who then yelled at Jason in English, then Jason replying, and Mr. Hong translating back.

Father explained it to Mother because she was his wife, his confidante. Mother told Noona because Noona was the firstborn. And I got it out of Noona because I begged and pleaded and annoyed her until she grew tired and spoke deliberately, like a drunk recounting his binge from the night before.

When Father first signed his lease, it was agreed that no existing shops could sell Asian gifts or clothing. Furthermore, it was agreed that no new store carrying these items would be allowed into the mall. This wasn't sealed with a handshake—it was actually written that way in a legal and binding contract.

So why was A Touch of Asia now sitting in Booth 113, selling our merchandise? This was what Father and Mr. Hong found out that day: George DiPalma, the owner of Peddlers Town, was in Florida. It was his son's fifth birthday, so he and his wife flew down to Disney World to introduce their boy to Mickey and Minnie, Goofy and Donald, leaving his brother-in-law Jason, who was apparently as bright as a busted lightbulb, in charge. Jason, trying desperately to impress his sister's big-shot husband, single-handedly brought in a whole new store while George was gone, wasn't he smart, wasn't he the best assistant manager?

"So why can't they just kick out the new store?" I asked Noona.

"Because they sign contracts, too, dummy. You can't break a contract, not unless you want to get sued."

"Well, then why can't we sue?"

"I don't know. It costs money. And besides, that's something Americans do, not us."

It seemed like something anybody should do, but it wasn't my choice. When all the arguing was said and done, Mr. Hong had negotiated a two-hundred-dollar discount on the monthly rent, so that was something.

Our business did not suffer. If anything, there seemed to be more people roaming our store than before, but Father was not convinced. He'd see somebody pick up a figurine, look at the price stuck on the bottom, put it back, and assume A Touch of Asia had it cheaper. Another sale lost—that became his favorite new phrase. He uttered it in the car, at church, during meals, and especially at the store.

"This is not good," he said, sitting behind the counter, watching another customer walk out empty-handed. "Not good at all." His chair squeaked as he rocked back and forth. "None of them are buying. They're all comparison-shopping."

"Is there anything we can do?" I asked.

It turned out that he knew exactly what to do, from the very beginning, when I followed him and Mr. Hong down to A Touch of Asia and he commanded me to hide. He was merely waiting for the right moment to ask me, the perfect time to pounce, which was now.

"David, my good son," he said in English, then continued in Korean, "I have a job for you. But only if you want to."

I turned and faced him.

"I want you to go down there and check the store out. You know, see what they're selling, how much, things like that. Can you do that for me? For us?"

It would feel like spying, but I couldn't refuse those pleading eyes of his, the eyes of a puppy.

prayed that the store was busy, so I could travel unseen while taking mental notes of prices. Of course it was empty.

The owner stood over the shoe table in the front part of her store, tagging a row of wooden Japanese clogs with a pricing gun.

"Good afternoon," she said.

"Hello." She was a short woman with bright green eyes. If not for her fatness, she would have been stunning. She looked to be in her mid-thirties, so I tried to imagine her husband, but nothing came to me. I had the distinct feeling that she was alone.

"Please, feel free to look around," she said.

So that I wouldn't be found out, I pretended to shop seriously, picking up a vase, scrutinizing its intricate flowered pattern, and stealing a glance at the price as I placed it back on its stand. I repeated this four more times: with a pair of Chinese slippers, a roll of sumi paper, a skinny box of rosewood incense, and a pair of lacquered chopsticks. When I glanced back at her, our eyes met and I immediately looked down. I hated Father for making me do this. He should have given me money so I could buy something to ease any suspicion.

"Find anything you like?"

The chopsticks I was holding jumped out of my hand and onto the floor.

"Yes," I said, picking them up quickly. "Sorry."

She came over and bent down carefully, balancing herself by latching onto the display table. She retrieved the price tag, which she stuck back on the pair of chopsticks. She pressed on the sticker but the second she removed her finger, it curled up like a wet stamp. "I'm the one who's sorry. I shouldn't have startled you like that. And these stickers—they're just terrible."

Up close, her words fell like slow, steady rain. I was mesmerized. I don't even remember how I replied. I walked out dazed, returning to our store on automatic pilot, and debriefed Father.

"Slippers."

"$4.95."

"Chopstick."

"$1.95."

When I finished running down the list, he shook my hand ceremoniously and told me how proud he was, how difficult it must have been, and how important it was I do this again next week.

"Next week?"

"We're at war here, Joon-a," he said, his voice bumping down a pitch. "And wars only end in one way: there is a winner and there is a loser." He cut off my protest with a forceful chop of his hand, like a cop stopping traffic. "She's going to try to outprice us. She's doing it already, can't you see? Her incense is *ten cents* cheaper! That makes us look bad, and when we look bad . . ."

"I know," I said. "Another customer lost."

"Exactly."

"Why can't Noona go?"

I shouldn't have even bothered to ask; we both knew Noona was moody and unpredictable. Besides, Father added, this was a man's job, this is what men do, we are men, we do these kinds of things that women don't do—which apparently included talking like an idiot.

took in a deep breath and raced through the story I'd concocted; my parents owned a luggage store in Peddlers Town, much like herself. In the Bag was its name, which was actually Mr. Hong's store. I had all this ready in my head and waited for her to pop the magic question: "So, what brings you back?"

Instead, she surprised me.

"Well, look who it is, it's my little friend."

"Hi," I said, not knowing what else to say, her Southern accent lingering in my ears.

"Let's do the names, huh? I'm Stacy." She was eating a bag of potato chips.

"David," I said, eyeing the shiny bag. They were barbecue.

"Want some?"

"Okay." Normally I was shy with strangers, but Stacy didn't seem very strange. I scooped a handful and stood there, munching away.

"Ladies first," she said, and started to tell me who she was. This wasn't easy, as I still had only a basic understanding of the language, but spending six hours a day in my ESL class was apparently helping. With patience and my pocket dictionary, I learned that Stacy Brooks had lived in Knoxville, Tennessee, all her life, having moved to New Jersey only a month ago, all by herself. She'd been in love with Asian culture since she was a child. "Mama bought me a Barbie, so I ran a black magic marker over her blonde hair and made a little Chinese dress by sewing up one of my father's old neckties."

So I told her who I was, delivering my carefully laid-out story, feeling a little guilty for lying but not too terrible. It helped that I had practiced it a whole lot, the repetition lessening the fiction of the tale. My English was badly broken, but Stacy was patient.

"In the Bag, huh? I like that. It's mighty creative. I'll have to come and take a look at it one of these days."

Because I had thought of her only within the confines of this space, it never occurred to me that she could leave, that she had another life outside this store. What if she tried to find me in Mr. Hong's store? "But of course," she added, "I can't because I have to be here to sell, sell, sell. Maybe you can watch the store for me one of these days and I can actually see the other shops around here."

"Sure," I said, lying again, getting used to its rhythm. It wasn't all that different from telling the truth.

I began to lie to cover up my other lies. Father wondered where I was going all the time, so I told him that I met a friend. A guy named Martin, but, of course, Martin was Stacy. Was I ever going to bring him around? Sure, I said. And so on. All my little fibs held one another's hands, quickly forming a chain of dependencies.

It was simple to keep them all running. Father was still distracted by Stacy's store, so I fed him more prices. Of course, these, too, were now made up, since I couldn't keep spying on her. She was a friend after all, and just trying to make a buck like everybody else. Besides, even though Father would have disagreed with me, I knew that Stacy wasn't hurting our store. Her customers were few, which actually had me worried.

"They'll come," Stacy said, but she was losing hope. I suggested we retool the store, move and switch sections around.

She agreed, and after we were done we knew it looked better, but it meant nothing to the shoppers, who just kept passing by. I secretly hoped that my presence would be able to somehow increase the "Orientalness" of the store, but I made no difference, either. Stacy just kept eating a lot.

"Bad food," I told her, pointing to her platoon of potato chips, candy bars, chocolate-chip cookies, and cheese curls. "Not good." She'd put on a couple more pounds since I met her.

"Cravings," Stacy said, pointing to her stomach. When she saw I didn't understand, she put my hands on her tummy, which felt as tight and round as a beach ball.

She wasn't just fat, she was pregnant.

"Boy or girl?" I asked.

"I don't know."

"Father?"

"He doesn't know I'm pregnant."

When I was with her, time disappeared; when I wasn't, it refused to budge, but when I saw her again, all those hours I didn't see her shrunk down to a tiny dot. Sitting next to her, I suffered surreal visions of the perfect married life: Stacy in a little apron and frying up a stack of pancakes while I read the newspaper; us sashaying hand in hand across a grassy hill dappled with dandelions. Even as a twelve-year-old, I knew these were ridiculous fantasies, and they always broke when reality banged me awake, like when Stacy's ever-expanding stomach came into view. I wondered who the father was, if he was still in Tennessee, if this was the reason why she left home.

There's a saying in Korea about long-term deception, and it goes something like this: Every lie you create lengthens your tail of lies, and sooner or later, either you will unwittingly step on your own tail or somebody else will trip on it.

I was at our store, sitting behind the island of showcase counters with Noona, when Stacy tripped on my tail. At first, I thought it was just somebody who looked like Stacy—the mind always hopefully rationalizes—but of course it was her. She didn't stop in; she merely passed by, our eyes meeting briefly, then she quickly disappeared from view.

"What's wrong?" Noona asked.

"Nothing," I said.

"Bullshit. I saw you. You've been acting weird lately. Who was that woman?"

It came out in a flood, out of control. Once I started telling her, the story took over my tongue and refused to give it back. I told her about the spying, the shared potato chips, and the fabrication of prices for Father. I even told her that last week, I took a pair of ceramic elephants from our store and put them on Stacy's shelf.

"Are you serious?" Noona asked. "Why?"

"Because her business is doing so badly. I was just trying to help. I didn't mean to hurt anybody, it just happened . . ."

"Keep your voice down," Noona said, seeing Mother nearby.

The only part I left out was how I felt about Stacy. "Now I'm afraid to go back there."

Noona held my hands. She usually felt cold—Mother said it was because she was born in the year of the snake—but now she felt like the coal stove we had back in Korea, her warmth spreading in waves.

I didn't see Stacy that Saturday, but I did the next, not because I was brave but because I missed her. As usual, there was nobody in the store, just her, flipping through a magazine with one hand while digging into a bag of Doritos with the other.

"Well, look who it is," she said, "it's my little friend."

"I'm sorry."

She slid off her stool and took me in her arms. I buried my face into her bosom and didn't realize my tears were soaking into her dress until it was already happening. Usually I felt stupid whenever I cried, but not in front of Stacy. It seemed like the right thing to do.

"Oh, David," she said, "what's the matter?"

"I lie, big liar."

"Because your family owns East Meets West, not In the Bag? And because you took these"—pointing to the elephants now on the counter—"from your store and put them here?"

I chanced a peek at Stacy and found her on the edge of laughter. "You have to admit, it *is* funny," she said, and couldn't hold it in any longer. She let out a laugh that turned heads, complete with piglike snorts that were quite unattractive.

"I feel like such a failure," she said when we sat down next to each other, stool to stool. "I mean, you brought those elephants here and I didn't even see them until this morning. What kind of a store owner am I, not even aware of my own stuff?"

"I am spy," I admitted, and began to tell her about my price-war-inspired espionage, but she shushed me.

"I know all that. I knew when your father walked in for the first time. When I saw you later, I knew who you were. You look like your father, David. Why, anybody can see you two are father and son. The resemblance is unmistakable."

I didn't like what I was hearing. If I looked like Father, that meant chances were I would grow up to be like him.

"Oh, stop pouting," she said, and pinched my cheek. "You're such a sweetie-pie."

Sweetie-pie: it was my first American nickname, and I treasured it like gold. As we shared the bag of Doritos, Stacy recounted childhood stories from Knoxville and my eyes caught on a short figure standing across the aisle in Comic Relief. He held up a copy of *Batman* over his face, but I'd know those stumpy legs anywhere. When he knew he was recognized, Mr. Hong lowered the comic and revealed himself.

"Oh shee-it," I said.

"That's not very nice," Stacy said. "I hope you didn't learn that from me."

I told her what I'd just seen.

"Oh shee-it," she said.

Father was waiting for me when I returned. I looked at his ears and sure enough, they were there, the puffs.

Father stood up from his chair and said, "Joon-a, my good son." I stared at my feet, afraid to look up. "I sent Mr. Hong over there to see how you were doing."

This I didn't expect. I thought it was just a coincidence that Mr. Hong caught me. "You sent him to spy on my spying on her?"

"I told you it was war, didn't I? And what of it? Was I wrong to send Mr. Hong?"

"Yes."

"Have you been giving me prices like I asked you to?"

"No."

"Then why was it wrong?"

I didn't like the way this was going, so I tried to put the blame back on him. "You never should've sent me over there."

"Did I force you?"

"No, but . . ."

"Mr. Hong said he saw two elephants on the counter."

"I can explain that."

"Great," Father said. "Why don't you?"

"No," I said. "It's stupid."

He stared me down without a word. Then he returned to his seat, spun his chair around, and went back to shuffling his pile of invoices.

For two weeks I stayed away from Stacy. She never came by. I never stopped thinking about her, replaying our time together in montage, complete with segues: when Stacy was six she fell off her bike and broke her leg and that was like when I was seven and I broke my arm trying to climb a tall oak tree, like the one Stacy had in her backyard when her brother had a treehouse where he played silly military games with his friends, like the pretend game Noona and I used to play when we were young and I became the North Korean dictator and she the nurse who was also the general.

I knew I wouldn't last, and I didn't. The following Saturday I found myself walking back to the new wing of Peddlers Town. When I reached Stacy's store, somebody else was with her, an older lady.

"Sweetie-pie!" Stacy said, lumbering over. She was even larger now. She hugged me the best she could and told me that she was leaving. "The father," she said, rubbing her ripened stomach. "I have to go back. I was just afraid all this time, but I'm not afraid anymore." She'd be gone a little over a month, she said, then she'd return. She'd stay with her mother while she recuperated.

"With father?" I didn't want him to come. I didn't want to know who he was, what he was like. I didn't even want to know his name.

"I don't know," Stacy said. "We'll see how it goes when I see him."

She introduced me to Eleanor, a distant cousin of hers who lived not too far away. She'd mind the store while Stacy was in Knoxville. Eleanor offered her hand and I took it; it was cold and damp like a basement wall.

"No long goodbyes now," Stacy said, and told me she'd write, let me know how she was doing. She kissed me on the forehead and gave me a box, which I opened later in the privacy of the men's bathroom and found the two elephants and a hurried note.

Put these back in your store, silly, the scribble read. *I'll bring back a real gift. Yours, Stacy.* I could almost hear her voice.

———

A month later I received a postcard with a picture of Elvis on the cover, a black-and-white still from *Jailhouse Rock*, the King in stylish prisoner stripes. It was the first real piece of mail I'd received from anyone. It read:

> *Congratulate me, sweetie-pie, I'm now a mother of a beautiful baby boy. I'm gonna call him Nathan, like the hot dogs you like so much. It also happens to be my favorite uncle's name, but just between you and me, I named him after the dogs.*
>
> *Things are complicated down here in K-ville. Hope to be back soon.*
>
> *Yours, Stacy*

It took me half an hour to translate it, and afterwards, as I kept staring at the words she had written, I wondered when she would return.

With the postcard in hand, I walked over to A Touch of Asia, hoping Eleanor could provide more information.

When I got there, a Chinese woman I'd never seen before was minding the store. She had no idea about anything; she told me her husband bought the store from some silver-haired American woman the week before.

"Eleanor?"

The Chinese woman peered at me. "Who are you?" she asked, suddenly suspicious.

It was in the same space with the same merchandise, but this store felt nothing like Stacy's.

"Nobody," I said.

———————

For a while I was miserable. I moped around, kept to myself, spoke only when spoken to. I carved a hollowness out of my grief and thought this concavity would stay with me for the rest of my life. And this made me happy in a twisted way, latching on to this conjured permanence, but it, too, proved short-lived, for I couldn't deny that with each passing day, Stacy faded further away from me.

"Hey," Noona said. "Hey, I said."

"What?"

We were sitting on our usual stools, behind the showcases. My sister jumped off hers. "Let's go."

"Where?"

"Come on," she said, and then clapped her hands together. She pointed a finger at my face as she spoke: "I'm buying you lunch." She was full of energy, and it put me on guard.

"Why?" One-word questions seemed to fit my mood.

"Because I'm your big sister and you're my little brother, that's why."

She told me she made reservations at a restaurant. She told me to put on my windbreaker. We left the stale mall air and ventured outside, where the sky was the color of steel and steady rain was falling.

Everything about the day was melancholy. A procession of black umbrellas marched in and out of the main entrance of Peddlers Town, the faceless crowd shuffling along as if attending a funeral. A family of doves had nested inside the o of the giant sign above, but they were nowhere to be found. A busload of senior citizens pulled in, walkers and wheelchairs and cane-leaning grandmothers doddering up the ramp.

"Where are we going?"

"Right here," Noona said. All we had done was circle the building.

We were, however, now in front of the outdoor entrance of Hometown Grill.

"Oh," I said.

In response to my obvious display of disappointment, Noona smacked the back of my head.

"Ow! What the hell was that for?"

"I'm trying to cheer you up."

I rubbed where she'd hit me. She had tiny hands, but somehow she could make her slaps smart like nobody else. "If you hadn't noticed, I want to be miserable."

"Oh, I've noticed," she said, opening the door. "That's why we're not leaving here until you're back to normal." She meant it as a joke, but it came out more like a threat.

I stood at the threshold. "Are you going to be nice to me? Because if you're not, then I'm going back."

"Can you please quit being a baby for just one second?" she said, and I turned around. "Okay, all right, I'll be good, I promise."

For the first time that day, she sounded sincere. And I was hungry, and to my knowledge, my sister had never bought me lunch. So I walked on through, passing from the grayness of the day to the darkness of the restaurant, and was greeted by a bearded man in white, his blue apron cinched around his waist. I'd seen him around Peddlers Town and knew him to be the chef.

"Welcome," he said. "I'm Jake. Please follow me."

On the way to our table, we saw Sylvia and Mindy from Animal Attraction sitting in a booth. There was a chocolate cupcake in front of Mindy, a single lit candle protruding from the frosting.

"Hi, David!" she said.

"Hi, Mindy," I said.

"It's Mindy's birthday," Jake said. "Twelve, right?"

"Thirteen," Mindy corrected.

"Happy birthday," I said, and Mindy beamed at me.

Jake led us to a corner table next to a crackling fireplace. He pulled the chair out for Noona, then for me, then handed us leather-bound menus with the words HOMETOWN GRILL embossed in gold on the cover.

"Your waitress will be out shortly. Great to have you both here."

Then he left, and I looked at Noona beyond the white tablecloth, across the sets of shiny silverware.

"I feel so special," I said.

"I hoped as much," Noona said. "I haven't seen you smile in like forever."

Was I smiling? I was. And it felt okay.

"I think that girl kinda likes you," Noona said.

"I think that girl is kinda crazy," I said. "She'll probably scream any minute now."

My sister looked over the menu. "Just order the burger. I only have twenty bucks."

IN YOUNG KIM

 AS IF HAMBURGERS WEREN'T BAD ENOUGH, In Young Kim was now being subjected to a thin, triangular piece of bread covered with melted cheese and tomato sauce. She picked it up like the way she'd seen her husband do it, folded it in half by the crust, but she hadn't counted on the orange-colored oil dripping off the crease and plopping onto the paper plate.

Her kids had called it *pizza,* an unpronounceable word. The best she could do was *peejaa* because there was no such sound as *ts* in Korean, but this was not important. When it came to food, only one aspect mattered, and this particular dish tasted greasy and salty and just plain awful. If only she could chase each fatty bite with a mouthful of *kimchi*—but that wasn't a possibility.

In Young placed the slice back on the plate, and as if alive, the piece slowly unfurled back to its original flatness.

Her husband said they couldn't eat *kimchi* at the store because it stunk. Americans found the smell unappetizing, though nothing disgusted In

Young more than to walk by the cheese aisle in the supermarket. How anyone ate something so rank and continued to live was anybody's guess.

Usually she brought discreet Korean meals from home to the store, but the little refrigerator in the stockroom was broken, so she was stuck with disagreeable American meals for one more day. Her husband would drive into the city tomorrow and return with another fridge, probably used and in need of cleaning, but as long as it worked, In Young didn't care.

"Hi," a male voice said from above.

She was sitting at the front counter where her husband usually sat because he'd taken the kids for ice cream. He promised they'd be back in fifteen minutes, so if anybody asked anything she didn't understand, she was to tell them to wait. Before leaving, her husband had made her say the usual phrase, to make sure she remembered it.

"Fifteen minute please," she'd begrudgingly repeated for him. It seemed like a silly thing to do, but now, looking at the people in front of her, a man and a woman who were about to say words that meant nothing to her, she was glad he'd made her practice.

"Hello," she replied.

She thought she'd seen the man before, and his white shirt and pants and dirty apron provided confirmation. He was the chef at the restaurant where her husband and Mr. Hong met for their Saturday lunches. The last time she'd seen him, which was maybe a couple of weeks ago, he had started to grow a beard, and now it was a big, bushy thing. He was a large man to begin with, and the beard somehow made him appear even larger.

"I'm Jake," he said, offering his hand. "Hometown Grill? This is Martha, my wife."

"Yes," In Young said.

"I need your help," he said, then scratched his beard. Tiny follicles fell from his cheeks, and as In Young tracked their descent down onto the counter, she caught his wife watching, too, and her obvious disdain. When Martha turned away, In Young noticed she was pregnant. Very pregnant, probably eight months.

"I'm looking for a lantern," Jake said, "kind of a small one, about yay big."

He gestured an open circle with his huge hands, but In Young remained clueless as to what he wanted. Yet, instead of uttering the rehearsed phrase that asked the customer to wait fifteen minutes for her husband's return, she found herself wanting to help this couple, and maybe help herself, too. She was going to have to learn this language if she wanted to make her life here, and the only way to do that was to just do it.

"Lantern," Martha said, also gesturing a circular object.

"Lantern?" In Young said. "I don't know lantern."

"Oh," Jake said. "Jeez."

"Over there," Martha said, pointing at the back right corner of the shop. There were a few round-shaped objects there, but the one that stuck out was a threesome of lighted orbs hanging in a line off the ceiling.

From afar they looked like flawless spheres of light, but standing directly below them broke their smooth illusion. The lanterns were actually made of many thin aluminum rings, glued half an inch apart to the inner curved surface of the rice paper. A green sticker stuck at the bottom of each reported their size: twelve, twenty-four, and thirty-six inches.

"That's it! The twelve is what we need," Jake said.

Twelve. Numbers she understood.

"Okay," In Young said.

This was a part of the store she didn't know well, but she'd seen her husband root through a box behind the eight-paneled screen, and sure enough, that's where the lanterns were, collapsed into flat round discs and stacked vertically, like LPs in a record shop.

"Okay," she said again, pointing to the box.

"Fantastic!" Jake said.

"One, two, three?"

"Huh?"

"She's asking if you want one, or two, or three," Martha said. "Come on, Jake, I'm tired, let's get it and go."

In Young looked twice through the box to make sure, but unfortunately, it was the only size they didn't have in stock.

"No twelve," she said.

"No problem," Jake said. "Thanks so much for looking. Maybe when you get them in again, you can let me know? Our restaurant is at the end of . . ."

"Christ, Jake," Martha said, cutting him off. "She hardly understands anything, can't you see?"

The woman was obviously running out of patience. Without another word, Martha turned and stormed out of the store.

"Sorry about that," Jake said. "I think it's the hormones. But wait a minute, you probably have no idea what I'm talking about."

They walked back toward the front of the store together, In Young quickening her steps to keep up with Jake's gait. The only word she heard for sure was *sorry,* but she knew what he'd meant. He was apologizing for the way his wife was acting, which was probably something he did often.

"Thank you again," he said.

"Okay," she said.

She watched him go, hoping he'd duck past the string of wind chimes he was walking toward, but no, he ran right into them and flooded the store with a chorus of metallic tinkling.

"Oops," he said, and when he turned back, as large as he was, he looked like a little boy who'd done something wrong.

"Okay," she told him for the fourth time, wishing she could say something other than that stupid word, but he waved and she waved and that was the end of her encounter, because her husband and her two kids came sauntering back, each with an ice cream cone in hand.

"Did we miss any excitement while we were gone?" her husband asked.

For a moment she considered telling him what happened.

"No," she said.

He'd left her behind. No matter how many times she tried to convince herself otherwise, that was the truth. Even though she had ample warning of her husband's departure to the United States—after all, his emigration process took a year—the fact was, one day they were a happy family of four, and the next day, they weren't.

The first year had been the hardest, not only because of her husband's absence but because of money. He tried his best to wire cash every two weeks, but sometimes it was three weeks and sometimes it was half as much as the one before, which made life harder than it already was. Every time either of the kids came down with something, it literally made In Young's stomach churn, and she hated how she could never get them anything worthwhile on their birthdays or Christmas.

But that was all in the past. Her family was together again, so she should be happy, but she wasn't. Obviously being in a foreign country had something to do with it, but it was more than that. The fact was, even though she was no longer the one left behind, she still felt like she was.

Maybe it was because her husband had changed. It wasn't anything big, like the way he made love (still the same, still awkward and sweet) or his favorite dish (*bulgogi,* thinly sliced beef marinated in soy sauce), but it was the littler things, and what she had never realized was that a significant portion of a person's identity was an accrual of miscellaneous traits such as these:

He never watched movies back in Korea, but now he watched them all the time.

He used to sleep on his back, but now he slept on his side.

She'd never seen him wink, ever, but now he winked on a daily basis.

In Young knew it was foolish of her to expect her husband wouldn't change. After all, it was his life that had been turned upside down, not hers. He was the one who had come to this country first, slaving over dry-cleaning machines in the morning and attaching heels to countless shoes in the evening, living with three other Korean men in a grungy Jersey City apartment, saving every penny so he could start his own business.

She felt a hand on the small of her back.

"Now what are you thinking?"

This was another new facet of his character, asking about her thoughts. Perhaps it was what sensitive American men asked of their wives, but In Young found the question tiresome and, frankly, frivolous. Thinking about things never got you anywhere; it was doing that mattered. But here was her husband, his tender eyes magnified by his eyeglasses. Lately she had to make things up just to appease him.

"I was just thinking about how healthy our daughter is looking."

She followed this up with a long, thoughtful gaze toward In Sook, who was indeed feeling better—eating more, frowning less, even taking her brother out to lunch—but her husband wasn't buying it.

"Yeah," he said, "yeah." He sank farther down into his chair and nodded vaguely to no one.

Fortunately a few customers walked up to the counter, so while her husband rang up a couple of sales, she stood next to him to bag while she searched for something more compelling to say.

When things quieted down again, In Young said, "I was also think-ing about what you said to Dae Joon last night."

He almost jumped out of his chair.

"You know," he said, "I was just thinking the same thing!"

In actuality, nothing could've been further from the truth. The pre-vious evening, their son had gone to great lengths to describe a game you hooked up to the television, some machine called Atari. After his presentation, her husband told him to leave the living room, so he and his wife could discuss the subject in private. As soon as Dae Joon left, he wanted to know what she thought, what their plan of action should be.

If In Young had her way, her choice would've been to say she had no opinion whatsoever. For five years, she had made all the decisions, and that was fine because that's what a single parent did. And now that they were reunited, she had looked forward to letting her husband take up the patri-archal reins, let him make the choices she had made for all those years.

But no, he had to ask, he always wanted to talk, just like now. Was this torture ever going to end?

"I'm beginning to think it wasn't a great idea to have Dae Joon saving up half the cost and us footing the rest," he said. "I mean, he wants this thing, right? And it's not for school or learning, it's a game. Maybe 75–25 would've been the smarter thing."

Now it was her turn to nod vaguely while scanning the store for a possible escape from yet another dialogue on this subject. And there, she had it.

"*Yeuh-boh,*" she said, still a surprising delight, using the Korean term of endearment for a spouse. She'd missed that word far more than she'd imagined. "Hold that thought. Looks like that old lady over there can use my help with those Chinese slippers."

"Oh, sure," he said as she headed over to the customer. "You know, you're really good at selling shoes."

"Yeah," she said. "Kinda funny, isn't it?"

It was funny because it was true. Even though she could hardly communicate with these Americans, she somehow made them feel good about buying shoes. Maybe the secret was the reverence she felt for the least appreciated part of the human anatomy. Here and in Korea, feet were seen as generally dirty and unpleasant, but In Young never felt that way. She'd always considered a person's feet as the core of his being, the living bedrock, and every time she saw a pair, she felt great compassion for the amount of abuse they took every day.

The ones in front of her now were no exception. Having sat down and slipped off her leather flats, the old woman wriggled her toes and looked at her own two stockinged feet. For her tiny frame, they were enormous.

"Ronald McDonald, my grandkids tell me," she said with a chuckle.

Her hair was as white as a Q-Tip and her thick glasses reduced her eyes into brown pinpricks, but this lady was full of life. It was good to see someone so old still so happy. Most of the older folks she'd known in Korea seemed bitter, probably because their bodies hurt more. Medical care was so much more advanced here, just like everything else. Even though leaving her country was the hardest thing she'd done, In Young was glad to be here. Once her kids became Americanized, which they would sooner than they knew, they would be happy, too.

In Young crouched down and helped the old lady try on a pair of black velvet slippers, the fancy ones with sparkly dragons on top. The lady put her feet together and tilted them in various angles, the detailed embroidery glittering.

"Do you like them?" the woman asked.

"Looks good," In Young said, one of two phrases she used to make a sale. Then she said the other: "Very pretty on you."

"Yes," the old lady said, "I think so, too."

She bought not only one pair but two, both in black, probably wanting to have a spare. It was something In Young often did, buying two or three of the same shirts if she found one to her liking, an act her husband had always found strange. Because he was the kind of person who would opt to buy not only different colors, but different shirts altogether. They were different people, but they still made a good couple.

"My wonderful shoe-selling wife," he whispered to her when she walked up to the register with the old lady in tow.

She stood by and watched him punch the keys on the register. She watched him take the old lady's money, watched her own hands slide the slippers into the brown paper bag.

This was her life now, and what her life would most likely be for the foreseeable future. Selling shoes to people, giving them a quick bow and thank-you and goodbye. It wasn't such a bad life, was it? Her kids were right there, sitting behind the showcases, waiting for the next customer just like she was. She knew they wouldn't always be there, that they would grow up, and go to college, and get a job someplace far away—this country was way, way too big—but the important thing was that they were here now, and she was with them.

"Joon-a," her husband said, calling their son to the counter. "Can you come over here?"

The boy came, though with a hint of reluctance. She wished they would get along more easily, like the way the little black kid named Arnold and his rich foster father got along in that TV show, but that was make-believe and this was reality. It would just take time, like anything else worthwhile in life.

"Yes?" he said.

Her husband pointed to a large box that was sitting next to the desk. "Wanna find out what's in the box?"

Like most kids, her son liked to open things up. Her husband handed him the box cutter, and the boy sliced the tape down the middle and flung open the flaps wildly, making a handful of packing peanuts fly through the air.

"Good job!" her husband said, overenthusiastic as usual.

The two men of the family proceeded to unearth the contents of the box, which were a bunch of smaller boxes. One of them had a drawing of a lantern on it, and it looked small enough. She picked it up and opened it to make sure of the size.

"I'm glad those finally came in," her husband said. "I ordered them a while ago."

"I'm glad, too," In Young said, and when her husband looked at her quizzically, she told him she'd place them into stock.

As she walked the box to the back of the store, she thought of why she didn't want to tell him about Jake and Martha. Was it because he would insist on taking over the transaction? What was the big deal? Why did she care?

Because it's mine. I started it, and now I'm going to finish it.

In those five years of loneliness, she'd learned to do things by herself, for herself, and it was strange to realize that she missed these solitary moments now that she was back with her husband.

Making sure no one was looking, In Young took a lantern out of the box, slid it inside her T-shirt, crossed her arms, and began to walk toward the exit. She'd almost made it when her husband hailed her.

"Hey," he said, "where are you going?"

"Just the bathroom," she said, hoping it didn't sound like a lie.

"Okay," he said, and he and their son were back at it, forming a pillar of bamboo coasters on the desk. They had made restocking into a make-shift game, taking turns to see who could stack one more before it all toppled over. Her husband worried about being a good father, but seeing the two of them like this, she knew they would be just fine.

As soon as she was out of sight from her family, In Young pulled out the lantern. The white disc felt warm but still looked fine, none of its wires bent out of shape.

It was half an hour before closing time, the walkways of Peddlers Town virtually clear of shoppers, her footsteps clicking loudly against the floor. She'd been by Hometown Grill before, but never at this time of night. Restaurants usually had stragglers who stayed beyond their meal, so as In Young looked into the window, she expected to see a couple of late diners, but the place was empty. She tried the door, but it was locked, which was strange because she was certain the restaurant actually stayed open later than the mall.

She was about to leave when she saw someone walking through the swinging door to the kitchen. All she caught was a blur of white, most likely Jake. So he was still here, probably closing up.

In Young knew there was a back door to the restaurant, so she exited the mall and walked around to the rear of the building. Outside, the night was cool, the late April moon hanging low against the line of far-away evergreens. She wondered if she was being too obsessive with the delivery of the lantern. After all, she could easily do this tomorrow morning, too, but she'd come this far. It seemed right to finish it.

As she walked past the giant green Dumpster and navigated around a slapdash cluster of milk crates, she heard Martha's rising voice.

"It's *exactly* the same thing. Yes, your body is yours, but because we are *married*—this ring here, Jake, that means we're married, right?— you have to think of somebody else besides yourself, and that's something you're gonna have get through your thick skull before our baby is born."

She sounded extremely angry. Then In Young heard Jake.

"You don't understand. Just let me say what I have to say."

"No, I don't think *you* understand what the hell is going on here. A very, *very* fragile creature, who has no ability to live on her own, is going to be *our* responsibility."

If this was an argument, from the sound of his voice he was losing badly. Martha continued.

"This is not one of your many hobbies, not something you can abandon like your workshop in the garage, the model airplanes in the basement, the fucking coin collection, God knows what else. You, Jake, you're gonna have to grow up!"

Then silence. Considering how loud the voices were, she knew they were close. Two steps from where she was standing, there was an open window, but she didn't dare move.

Jake spoke once again. "I'm not shaving my beard."

"You think this beard gives you something, but it gives you nothing. Makes you nothing!"

More silence, then footsteps moving away from her, and now returning.

"You want my beard gone so bad? Well, go right ahead. Have a fucking blast."

In Young began to step away slowly, but what she heard next made her stop. And when the sound continued, she found herself quietly creeping toward it.

It was the unmistakable noise of a pair of scissors cutting human hair, and that's exactly what she saw when she peered at the corner of the window. In the back of the restaurant's kitchen, Jake sat on a stool while Martha sheared off his beard. In Young knew it was wrong for her to witness this private moment, but at the same time, she couldn't pull herself away. What was it about human misfortune that was so endlessly fascinating? Why did people slow down to gaze upon car wrecks and burning buildings? As she watched Martha snip her scissors with surgical precision over her husband's cheeks, In Young considered the possibilities and came up with what had to be the simple and cruel truth: because the tragedy was happening to someone else.

After Martha had razed half his face, Jake said one more word, almost a whisper.

"No," he said.

Martha stopped and dropped the scissors, then sank down to the floor, sobbing.

Jake made no move to stop her. Instead, he stared blankly at the random clumps of hair around him.

In Young placed the lantern next to the back door and hurried back to the mall, her face hot with shame. It felt as if she'd seen them naked.

She wanted to rid herself of the experience, but an image of Martha refused to fade. It was her ring finger wrapped around the handle of the scissors, her diamond catching the lights above, flashing gaudily as she cut away at her husband. That Martha—she was a piece of work. She was an American. In Young tried to imagine doing something like that, and couldn't. It was beyond her. This country was beyond her, these people, these weird, weird people.

When she returned to her store, they were in closing mode, her husband starting in the rear right corner of the store, her kids in the rear left, turning off the spotlights one by one as they worked their way to the front. In Young stood in the center of the store and watched the gradual darkening.

It was good that a day ended, that there was morning and there was night, and it was good that her children were now walking toward her.

THE MISERABLE
MONTH OF MAY

CHILDREN'S DAY WAS THE ONLY saving grace in May. Otherwise, it was a terrible collection of thirty-one days, and there was great potential for it to get worse now that we were in the United States. What kind of a demented country was this? Bugs Bunny and Mickey Mouse were born from this soil, but no Children's Day? The fifth of May was a national holiday in Korea, but here there was no such thing.

Parents' Day followed three days after. It used to be called Mother's Day, but then the fathers got mad and demanded a day of their own. Nay, declared the Korean government. You'll have no such day. Instead, we'll just dump you in there with the mothers and let the children decide who's more important. In Korean, the day is called *uh-buh-ee-nahl,* which literally translates to Moth-Fath-Day. When Koreans say they're going to merge something, they don't mess around.

And finally, there was May 23, Noona's birthday. She wanted gifts, two of everything, because under the Western zodiac, she was a Gemini. "Gemini is a twin," she told me. "So now there're two of me to celebrate."

"You're a snake," I retorted.

"A twin," she said with such vengeance that I lost all desire to argue.

If it was a ploy to double her number of gifts, it wasn't a bad one. I made a note to increase my birthday loot next time by leveraging my own zodiac sign, Aquarius, the water carrier.

Sick," Father said into the phone. "David Kim sick, Susan Kim sick, everybody sick. Yes yes, thank you." He hung the handset back on its cradle and turned to Noona and me. "Today we'll have Children's Day," he said, "even if we have to lie a little." Then he winked at us and I wished he hadn't, because I still had a hard time with that wink. It dripped of an oiliness that made me want to run the other way.

He had one more call to make, to a wholesaler to let them know that he wasn't coming in. On Mondays, Father drove to New York to shop for new things to sell, but not this day. "Whatever you want to do, we'll do," he said.

"Nothing too expensive, though," Mother added quickly.

"Great Adventure," Noona and I said together. The night before, we'd agreed on a plan of action. If we didn't speak with one voice, we'd probably end up doing nothing.

Neither Father nor Mother knew what we were talking about, so we threw our best pitch. Great Adventure, we told them, was an amusement park filled with roller coasters and Ferris wheels and games and shows and it wasn't just for kids . . . no way, it was for grown-ups, too. Plenty to do for everyone, so can we please please please go?

"How much?" Mother asked.

Neither Noona nor I wanted to answer this, but of course we had to.

"Fifteen dollars? Per person?"

Start high, Noona had said last night. Start high then tell them the real price. Then we'll have 'em. We brought out our coupons and displayed them on the table, each neatly cut on its perforated edges, each offering a five-dollar savings.

"But," Noona said, "as you can see, it's much cheaper on Mondays, thanks to these coupons we found."

Father nodded to Mother, giving his okay. Mother looked at the coupons and then at us and said, "On one condition: We take lunch." That was Mother, who'd never been to an amusement park yet instinctively knew that food there would cost an exorbitant amount. Mother was shrewd like that when it came to money, and so was Noona. When I think back to these times now, I'm positive they should've run the store instead of Father, or at least he should have enlisted their help in some way, but of course that just wasn't the way things were done. Invisible walls existed everywhere in our household. I wanted to help with lunch but Mother shooed me away, citing the unwritten law that kitchen work was for the women of the house. She and Noona went to work for the next two hours, wrapping roll after roll of Korean sushi.

By eleven we were off in Father's ugly green station wagon ("*our* station wagon," he corrected again, but I didn't want any part of that thing). Noona and I sat in the backseat, excited beyond words. We'd only seen pictures of this wild place that was full of precipitous roller coasters and free-falling elevators, their sole purpose to test your nerve, to make you scream as the wind rushed into your mouth. The drive down I-195 to Jackson Township, New Jersey, was an hour of agonizing anticipation. Noona and I hardly talked, our bodies readying for the heavy-duty gyrations to come.

"We're the first ones here!" I said. There would be no line for us, the early birds.

"There's nobody else here," Noona said.

"I know. Isn't that great?"

"No. I don't think so."

When we got out of the car, we realized we were one of about twenty cars in the huge parking lot that seemed to have no end. We trudged to the entrance and saw the horrible truth: because it was so early in the season, the park was open only during the weekends. In a couple weeks it would be open every day, but that wouldn't do us any good today.

"We should've called them," I said, but more to myself than anyone else. Nobody thought of it because we were all afraid of the telephone, of having to muddle through with our broken English as the distant American voice on the other end of the line grew impatient. Father's vocabulary was by and large limited to sales-related words, Mother could count and knew a handful of phrases, and although Noona and I had been learning with ESL classes for the past three months, we ran into trouble unless people spoke slowly and carefully. I felt angry at my family for being so stupid, at this country for speaking a language we didn't know, at our fear and pride for handicapping us.

"We're here, let's see what's out there," Father said.

"Why bother," I said, kicking a loose stone across the pavement.

"So when we come next time, we'll know where to go," he said.

"When will we come back?" I said. Father promised a lot of things and didn't follow through. Like the new vacuum cleaner he promised to buy a month ago, where was that?

"I don't know exactly when, but we'll be back, I promise."

Then he winked.

We walked the park's periphery and admired the rides we couldn't enjoy. There was Lightnin' Loops in the distance, a short roller coaster that took you down, looped you around, took you up, then did it all over again . . . backwards. I'd heard one of my classmates, Jimmy, talk about that one, how everyone just lost it when it reversed. I saw the tippy-top of the Buccaneer, where you climbed aboard a ship and it swung you around like a pendulum. Jimmy said people threw up, and that change fell out when it goes really far up. And in the far corner, you could see the twisty-turny skyways of Rolling Thunder. Jimmy got sore shoulders after riding in it just once. I wanted sore shoulders. I wanted to throw up.

"We'll be back," Noona said. Lately her mood needle had swung over to the nice part of the scale, and for that I was grateful. She could be so nice when she wanted to be, like a young, sprightly version of Mother.

When we walked back to the front of the park to return to our car, a man called to us. He was a young guy in a blue uniform, probably the security guard. He stood behind the barred gates and yelled, "Hey!"

"Yes?" Father said.

"What're you guys doing here?"

"Go in?" Father said, pointing to all of us. For a second my hopes rose; if anybody could let us in, it would be this man.

"Not today," the security guard said. "We'll be open on the week-end, though."

"Children's Day," I blurted out. "Today."

He eyed me suspiciously. "Children's Day? Never heard of it."

I walked up close, my face pressed against the cold metal bars. "Korea, today Children's Day."

"Not here," the security guard said. "No day for children in America, bud."

I said to Noona, "We should take them somewhere they really want to go and when we get there, it should be closed." Three days later and I was still bitter.

"That's not very nice," Noona said, setting a new record for most consecutive good-mood days. She was just getting sweeter, if that was possible, and it was beginning to get on my nerves, but it was only a matter of time until she'd be back to her mean old self, so I decided to appreciate this miraculous downtime.

For Parents' Day, we agreed to give service-related gifts since we had no money. We had a hard time figuring out just what to offer because Friday was a workday and they were gone from nine in the morning until nine at night. I was hoping we could wash their car before they left, but it was still too cold in the morning, and besides, it was lame. About the only thing we could do was prepare a late dinner for them.

"What are you going to make?" Mother asked, nervous. She had a hard time with American food. After forty years of eating *kimchi* and rice, her body couldn't handle grease- and fat-laden dishes.

"Spaghetti," Noona said, remembering the one time we had it in a diner when a friend of Father's was visiting. Even though Mother hadn't loved it, at least she was able to eat it.

"Spaghetti is okay," Mother replied that Friday morning as she readied for work. She packed up lunch for the day, chopping this and boiling that, putting the *bahn-chahn,* the side dishes to be eaten with the rice, into little glass jars that used to contain strawberry and concord grape jelly. Watching her, I recalled the same routine back in Korea, when she worked at a bag factory on the outskirts of Seoul. She had run the machines that made and pressed paper bags of all kinds and colors—yellow shopping bags for Lotte Department Store, plain brown bags for the neighborhood grocers, long thin ones for the flower stores around the city. She'd liked that job, and was going to be promoted to an assistant manager position before we flew in a plane for eighteen hours and arrived at this strange place.

When we returned from school, Noona and I laid out our plans. "I'm sure I can make spaghetti," she said.

"Really? Have you ever cooked it before?"

"No, but I've seen it on TV."

I was excited at the idea of cooking something. I knew so little about it. "I can help, right?"

"Of course," Noona said. "You can do the chopping, dicing, stuff like that."

Father left us ten dollars to buy the ingredients, which was plenty. We had to get spaghetti and spaghetti sauce, and maybe a loaf of some nice Italian bread, which would definitely cost less than ten.

"We should get a treat for ourselves," I said.

"We'll see," Noona said, sounding more like Mother every day.

The A&P was a block away from our apartment. We didn't talk much as we walked, just chatted about television shows. We were both fond of the sitcom *Three's Company,* mainly due to John Ritter's physical comedy. It reminded us of the variety shows we used to watch in Korea, where the humor of the body dominated over the humor of the word. Actors were always falling down, slipping on something, though never on banana peels because bananas were very expensive and slipping on one would hardly be funny.

Noona and I had watched these shows together, looking up at the nine-inch black-and-white screen, sitting on the floor. And here we were, in a different country, still sitting together and watching and laughing. As we approached the A&P, it occurred to me that this wasn't the way it was always going to be. Noona wouldn't always be next to me, watching TV or strolling to the supermarket, because soon she would grow older and go to college and get a job and move away, just like everybody else. And sadder still was the fact that once she left, things would go on. The hole in my heart would remain, but I'd find a way to look somewhere else.

"What's the matter?" Noona asked as we stepped through the automatic door. I looked into her dark pretty eyes and saw the tiny reflection of my own face. I should've said something poignant, or maybe even something stupidly sentimental, anything but what actually came out of my mouth.

"Nothing," I said.

Inside the supermarket, as we walked around gathering the ingredients for our Parents' Day dinner, I held her hand, and she didn't mind.

We didn't start cooking until eight-thirty, since our parents weren't due back until half past nine. In the kitchen we spread out on the counter a box of spaghetti, a jar of sauce, a bunch of scallions, four eggs, and an English-Korean dictionary to aid us in figuring out the directions.

While we waited for the water to boil, I set the table. Noona insisted that we have forks and spoons instead of chopsticks. On TV, families ate their spaghetti by spinning the noodles against the spoon, keeping the rotation tight to create a nice, even mouthful. "Don't worry, we'll teach them," she said, happy about this idea. Mother would probably opt for chopsticks, but it was worth a shot.

Noona cracked open four eggs, diced the scallions, mixed them all together, and panfried the mixture. I chopped the fried eggs into thin little strips while she warmed up the sauce. When I'd finished, she slid the eggs into the sauce and lowered the range temperature. The clock read 9:25. "Almost there," Noona said.

Using a pair of scrunched-up dishtowels, my sister and I lifted the steaming pot and emptied the noodles into the colander and what came out was one big sticky pile of goo, a deformed giant ball of pasta.

"What happened?" I asked.

"I don't know," Noona said. "Maybe it cooked for too long." She glanced directions again and pointed at a word. "There. I think we were suppose to stir it as it cooks. And use more water."

"What do we do?" I asked, panicking. It was 9:35, our time was up.

"Plan B," Noona said. She found a box of Japanese noodles and boiled two pots of water to save time. These things took three minutes to cook, so by the time the door opened and Mother and Father walked in fifteen minutes later than usual, we were ready.

"I'm glad you're late," I said.

"You can thank Mr. Hong," Mother said. "I never thought he'd leave."

Father removed his coat and threw it on the couch. "He just wanted to make sure you and his wife are gonna meet up next week."

"I don't like her," she said. Mother often made up her mind about people in advance.

"Come on," Father said, "you hardly know her."

On the dinner table, our parents found plates of quasi-genuine spaghetti waiting for them.

"Mmmmm," Father said, taking in the aroma.

"This is better than the spaghetti we had at that restaurant," Mother said. "The noodles are much softer, like our Japanese noodles."

They ate fast. Obviously they'd skipped their usual dinner to wait to eat our food.

Afterwards, as Noona washed the dishes and I dried them—much to Mother's chagrin—we dreamed of ways of becoming rich and famous with our daring gastronomic invention, Japanese Spaghetti. "You can be the chef and I'll be your assistant," I suggested. Noona would wear the puffy white hat and I'd wear the dirty apron, and that's how we would stay together after she grew up and left. We'd work together in our kitchen. She'd boil the water and I'd chop the scallions.

By the time her birthday rolled around, Noona's irrational rage was back in full force. Not a trace remained of the sweetheart that I wanted to be with for the rest of my life on Parents' Day. She was mean, she was vicious, and she wanted to go bowling.

Originally, she'd also wanted to go to a French restaurant, where she was determined to gobble up caviar and frog legs. "And soufflé," she added, having just learned the word in school. "It's this thing that puffs up and you have to eat it real fast or it sinks down, deflates, like a leaking balloon." Amazingly enough, Mother talked her out of it, enticing the wild beast with her favorite food, *mahn-doo,* bite-sized Korean dumplings filled with ground beef, vermicelli, spinach, onions, and tofu. I loved it, too, but obviously you had to throw an epic tantrum to get these things made around here.

"Fine," Noona agreed, "we'll stay home and eat. But we are going bowling."

Why bowling? Nobody questioned Noona when she got into one of her moods—we just went along the best we could.

We found some lanes nearby at a faded pink block of a building named Bowl-O-Rama. Father had gone bowling before, so he knew the routine of borrowing the shoes and picking out the ball. Mother initially said she didn't want to play but changed her mind, curiosity playing a part.

"These shoes feel funny," I told Father when we sat in our lane.

"They're supposed to feel like that."

"I think there's something in there." More in my left foot than the right.

"You're probably just nervous. It's no big deal," Father said.

"Shut up, Junior," Noona said. That was the nickname she used when she was trying to get under my skin. "Shut up and just bowl."

Father went first, so we could see how it was done. "It's all in the wrist," he told us; then he aimed, brought back the ball, stepped forward four steps, stopped, slid, and launched the black bowling ball, all in one fluid motion. The collision was thunderous and complete. "Strike!" he yelled in English. "That's how it's done."

Mother was next, and she used both hands, shuffling toward the lane with the ball swaying dangerously between her knees. Though her delivery looked nothing like Father's, she also knocked down all the pins. "Oh, oh," she said, and looked to Father, who laughed and said, "It can be done like that, too."

I glanced at Noona, wondering if she wanted to go next, but she wasn't even looking in my direction, staring instead at the rest of the alley. Three lanes over, a group of boys were bowling away, high-fiving each other after every turn. Concentrate, I told myself, and aimed my burgundy ball like Father and pitched it like Mother, a two-handed effort. It seemed to roll forever, and it started out centered but ended up in the left gutter.

"It's all right," Mother said. "You'll do better with your second ball."

That one was even worse, sliding into the right gutter not even halfway down the lane.

"This game is stupid," I said.

Before we could say anything else, Noona got up from the lime-green molded chair, clawed her lime-green ball, and whipped it down the lane so hard that she almost lost her balance. It was as if the pins fell down to avoid her fury.

"I don't want to bowl in this lane," Noona said.

"What?" Father asked. "Why?"

"Because I don't like it. And it is my birthday, isn't it? I should get what I want."

"Listen," Father said. "This doesn't make any sense." He looked to Mother for help, but she just shrugged.

And with that, Noona took her ball and walked two lanes away and started flinging. The sound of the impact between ball and pins was deafening.

"Hey," the guy behind the shoes counter yelled at her. "You can't bowl there."

"I pay," Father yelled back, holding up his wallet. "I pay."

"Well, then pay now," he said. While Father sighed and walked up, Noona picked up a spare and another strike.

"Whoa, girl," one of the boys in the third lane said, a tall and gangly sort. "You sure can bowl."

"Yeah, you're really good," another one agreed, this one with a crew cut so short he almost looked bald.

Noona paid them no attention. She floated her hand over the air vent, picked up another ball, and knocked down more pins. She never looked at me or anyone else as she continued to roll.

Mother attributed most of Noona's tirades to her periods, but I didn't buy it. There had to be something else to her madness, something more singularly Noona than a trait shared by every woman who walked the Earth.

"She's just this way," Mother said to no one in particular, rubbing her belly and grimacing. Mother swore that on our birthdays, she felt intermittent pain in her lower stomach, nature's reminder of her struggle with our births.

"Has she always been like this?" I asked.

"Not always," Mother said, waving off Father who gestured it was her turn. "You bowl for me, my stomach hurts." Father threw the ball with two hands, which made Mother laugh.

"As long as I can remember, she's been like this," I said.

"She was a lovely baby," Mother said. "Never cried, not like you anyway. Even as a little girl, she was always happy."

"So what happened?"

We watched Noona hurl another fireball down her lane, this one going down the left gutter. Her beginner's luck had run out, but she didn't seem to care.

"She's just your sister," Mother said finally. "This is who she is now, and you should be happy and thankful that you even have one."

I wasn't happy but I was thankful, thankful that I only had one nutty sister and not more.

Back at our apartment, Noona blew out two cakes, one vanilla and one chocolate. Maybe what she needed was a sugar fix, because after having a piece of each cake, she was all smiles.

She received a pair of matching gold bracelets from our parents, which she immediately put on her wrist, admiring their glitter as she twirled them under the kitchen light. I gave her my present, silver earrings with green snakes that dangled like worms on a fishing hook. They had cartoonish bug eyes and were wearing oversized black-rimmed glasses and a big pink nose with a mustache, and Noona loved them. She gave each of us a hug, even me, and as she held me close, she whispered in my ear, "Thank you," the earnestness of those words so sincere that they raised goosebumps on my arms.

"You're welcome," I said, though what I wanted to say was: "Please don't hurt me."

JHEE HONG

SOMETIMES SHE FOUND money on the floor. It was inevitable, working in retail, especially if you saw how people carried their cash. There was one customer yesterday who shoved his hand into his jean pocket and excavated a fistful of his life: a torn matchbook, a shopping list, two M&Ms (red and yellow), a used Kleenex, a movie ticket stub, and finally, a pair of crumpled ten-dollar bills. People kept their money in their front pocket, their back pocket, their shirt pocket, and sometimes in their hands, the bills turning soggy from their sweaty palms. Women were better than men, but not always. Jhee Hong had met enough frantic purse diggers to know that when it came to monetary organization, neither sex was immune to disarray.

So when she found the twenty-dollar bill lying underneath the rack of leather wallets, the money folded in half, splitting the face of the man in the oval down the middle, Jhee wasn't surprised. What did alarm her, though, was how when she picked it up and held it in her hand, she felt nothing. This was free money, money she could buy anything with. Granted, it wasn't a huge amount, but still, you could get plenty of things for twenty dollars. What, though? What was there to buy, really?

She unfolded the bill and gazed at the portrait. Probably a president, but she wasn't sure. She recognized Washington and Lincoln on the smaller denominations, but this man with his high forehead and wavy gray locks, he was at best a familiar stranger. She'd seen his face a thousand times, and she knew his name to be Jackson because that's what it said below his portrait, but his identity remained a mystery.

At the front counter of the store, a young woman walked up with a tiny red leather purse with a long spaghetti strap. It was about the size of two credit cards, but she was gladly forking over eighty dollars for it. This year marked the fifteenth anniversary of their store, and if there was one thing Jhee had learned from all the time wasted here, it was this: There was a buyer for every product. The key was having patience, waiting for that destined customer to walk in, fall in love, and leave with the bag of their dreams.

"Thank you!" she heard her husband say, sliding the item into a brown paper bag. "Thank you very much!"

She had been patient. Fifteen years ago, she was happy, and her husband had promised her the American Dream, and it was true, he didn't twist her arm to emigrate, but where were they now? Still stuck in an apartment where the people upstairs woke them up on Saturday mornings with their ear-splitting Spanish music, still barely making ends meet selling knock-off Gucci purses at this cut-rate flea market of a mall. The last vacation they'd taken was three years ago, and they hadn't even left the state, spending their savings on a mosquito-infested motel by the Jersey shore.

Jhee walked back to the counter and sat beside her husband, wincing as a sharp jab of pain bored into her lower back.

"You okay?" he asked.

She said nothing.

Her husband continued anyway. "Mr. Paik's gonna help you, I know he will. Kim says he's the best acupuncturist in New York, and he makes house calls to Jersey all the time." Then he kept talking, about how difficult it was to get the appointment because he's so popular, how Mr. Kim had friends who'd made amazing progress, but Jhee was only half listening. Instead, her mind was on last night, at the dinner table, when her back had ached so badly that she could scarcely breathe.

"Maybe," her husband had suggested, in between long, loud slurps of his red miso soup, "it's your period."

She laid both hands on her back, trying to let the heat of her palms soothe the beast underneath her skin. It seemed as if there was something alive in there, a red-eyed monster with an unshakable grip, twisting her spine like toffee. But Jhee couldn't decide what was worse, this physical pain or that her husband hadn't realized she was no longer menstruating. She'd become menopausal half a year ago, hadn't he noticed? Or did he not even know what that meant?

Jhee put her head down on the table. The lacquered wood felt cool against her cheek, and somehow it felt better to look at the world sideways, the half-empty glass of water transformed into a crystalline tower, the silver salt and pepper shakers gleaming like rockets, and behind it her husband's oblivious face.

"I'm sure it's nothing," he had said, and only her silent tears finally clued him in to the severity of her discomfort.

So all morning, he'd been on the phone with Mr. Paik, making sure he was talking loud enough for her to hear.

"Yes, her back is very sore. Very sore.

"That's right, she's forty-four, but she looks at least ten years younger.

"Money is of no issue, Mr. Paik, none whatsoever. I just want you to get my wife well."

For his attempt at forgiveness, she'd given him the silent treatment, but her husband knew it wouldn't last for long. Jhee liked to talk, and she had no one else to talk to, though perhaps that would change today.

As if reading her mind, he paused in his praise of the master acupuncturist and said, "Hey, this is your big day, right?"

When she looked up from the Korean newspaper she'd been pretending to read, Jhee was caught off guard at the earnestness displayed on her husband's face. She knew it wasn't a handsome face, tiny black beads of eyes too close together, a nose not so much flat as rather haphazardly deflated, yet there were times, like now, when this unattractive conglomeration reassured her and gave her strength. Immediately, the feeling that rose up from her was guilt. The only way she got Mrs. Kim to agree to do anything with her was by falsifying her husband's birthday, which in actuality had come and gone a month ago. At some point her lie would be exposed, but Jhee didn't care. The only thing that mattered now were these few hours ahead of her, these hours she would spend pretending to shop with Mrs. Kim, whose first name she still did not know.

Jhee didn't know her name because in Korea, mothers referred to one another by the name of their firstborn child, a custom she never could accept. There were many things about her native country that annoyed her, actually—such as the automatic respect extended to anyone older, even if they didn't deserve it, or how most wives acted like little girls in front of their husbands, often addressing their counterparts as "Daddy." That was just plain disgusting, but the last thing she wanted was to be ostracized as the neighborhood freethinker, so Jhee kept her opinions to herself, smiling and nodding while secretly hoping for an overseas escape. One of the reasons she'd married her husband was because his brother, a naturalized citizen in the United States, had offered to invite him to be a permanent resident.

What was Mrs. Kim's story? Why was she here? As she stood beside her in A Second Chance, the used bookstore in Peddlers Town, Jhee wanted to know, and she didn't understand why Mrs. Kim wasn't curious about her. They were the only two Korean women in this entire building, and yet it had taken Jhee months to get her to come to this outing.

"That's a lovely scarf," Jhee said.

"Thank you," Mrs. Kim said, putting her hand on the red-and-blue hand-knitted fabric wrapped around her neck. In actuality, it was ridiculous for her to have this on, considering it was May and already feeling like summer. "My daughter made it for me."

Of course, she was one of *those* people, all about her kids, everything about her kids.

"Yun Sae's Mother?" Mrs. Kim asked.

"Jenny," she reminded her. "Please call me Jenny. That's what I call myself now, here, in America."

"All right," Mrs. Kim said, clearly uncomfortable. "Why are we here?"

Finally. For a bit there, Jhee had wondered if Mrs. Kim would ever ask, but now that she had, Jhee could relax somewhat. Mrs. Kim had taken the bait, and now the conversation was going the way she'd intended.

"Look at all these books," Jhee said, sweeping her arm dramatically, feeling a little like an actress delivering her lines. "Each of them has a story just waiting to be discovered. Isn't that exciting?" She pulled out a hardback from the shelf, the worn jacket barely hanging on to the covers, and flipped through the pages.

"You can read these books?" Mrs. Kim asked, astonished.

No, of course not, Jhee was about to say. She'd intended to talk about the books she read in Korea when she had been a private tutor, which she hoped would lead Mrs. Kim to share her own past. But then she saw Mrs. Kim staring at her with eyes full of reverence. She was a taut ball of a woman, her arms crossed tightly, as if to keep herself from opening up to the world. From the moment they met, Jhee knew she wanted to get to know her, but she hadn't known how. Now she stood in front of this locked door with a key.

"Yes," she said, not quite believing what had just come out of her mouth, the audacity of this fabrication.

But it was the right thing to say, because what lay on the other side of that door was Mrs. Kim's bright blossom of a smile.

"It must be so nice. I can't read a damned thing. I mean I know the letters, but I don't even know how they sound." She glanced at the book in Jhee's hand and attempted to sound out the title. "Duh . . . Goo-ra . . . Goo-ra . . . ?"

The words were written in dark blue, in the sky above the blue mountains and the desert-colored earth. In the foreground of the cover art was a family, Jhee gathered, the father standing and the mother and son sitting on a hill, all three people with their backs turned, gazing at the desolate landscape below. In front of them was what looked like a very old car, its trunk packed with junk.

Lucky for Jhee, she knew these words, at least the first three. *"The Grapes of,"* she said, and explained to Mrs. Kim that grape in Korean was *poe-doe.*

"Poe-doe? Isn't that strange. *Goo-ra-ip.* It's not even close, is it?"

They laughed together. "And this," she said, pointing at *Wrath,* a word she had never seen. She rifled through her small cache of vocabulary, thinking of grapes, what goes with grapes, it wasn't *summer,* she knew that—then she had it. "This word, *woo-rae-tuh,* it's the name of the town. It's a town in California."

Mrs. Kim nodded understandingly. "So you read this book?" Mrs. Kim opened it to a random page and gazed at the English words staring back at her.

"Not the whole thing," Jhee said, settling into her lie, "the first half of it was good, but then it slowed down a lot."

What Mrs. Kim didn't realize yet was how little she actually needed to know to survive in this country. Jhee remembered when she first arrived, the fear and hopelessness that tugged her at every sign she couldn't read, every conversation she failed to understand. But then it turned out that words on signs were often accompanied by descriptive pictures (an x through a lit cigarette) or revealing colors (green for yes, red for no), and there weren't many phrases you needed to know to sell handbags to customers. *Looks good on you. Very pretty. Nice, strong bag. Big enough, fit everything.*

In time, Mrs. Kim would find this to be true, but for now, Jhee was grateful for her ignorance. Maybe she was taking advantage of the disadvantaged, but there were worse things you could do in this world. All she wanted from this fellow countrywoman was her friendship. And one other thing.

"So," Jhee asked, perusing through another book, a burgundy paperback without cover art, "what is your name?" She'd kept it as casual as possible, but she knew she hadn't succeeded, as Mrs. Kim glanced at her with unease. There was an agonizing pause, and Jhee fought herself several times from recanting her question.

"Well," Mrs. Kim finally said, and to Jhee's surprise, it was she who was apologetic. "It's just In Young. I don't have an American name, like you."

Jhee replaced the book on the shelf, held her friend by her shoulders, and spoke with fierce determination. "Then we'll get you one."

"My husband calls himself Harry," Mrs. Kim said. "I think it's silly, but he likes it."

"A name," Jhee muttered to herself, scanning the various colors and sizes of spines lining the back wall of this bookstore. On the topmost shelf, a large brown volume caught her eye, the author's name in gold: SHAKESPEARE. Of course! When the idea came to her, she literally jumped for joy, never mind her creaky back. She felt wonderful, creative, energized—the opposite of the way she usually spent her days, and it was all because of this woman who stood next to her. Jhee wished to hug her, but no, not yet, there would be time for that.

"Here," she said, and took Mrs. Kim by the hand, which was unexpectedly small, almost childlike. And she related her idea to her as they walked among the shelves. They were in a bookstore after all, and the name of the author of each and every book was ripe for their picking.

"Oh!" Mrs. Kim said. "That sounds like fun."

And it was, like a treasure hunt. Jhee had chosen Jenny because her Korean name started with a J, so she advised Mrs. Kim to do the same, but none of the names seemed right. Ida, Iris, Ilene.

"How about this?" Mrs. Kim said, holding a book titled *Out of Africa*. On the back was a profile of the author's face, but she was named Isak, which Jhee knew to be for a man.

"I think it's a mistake," Jhee said.

"Too bad," Mrs. Kim said. "I like that name, *eye-sack*."

When they ran out of the I's, they tried the Y's, but they were even fewer in number.

"Yolanda?" Jhee said.

Mrs. Kim shook her head. "Too many sounds."

In the end, it was Mrs. Kim who found her American moniker. She held up a dog-eared paperback to Jhee, the cover an old painting of a beautiful white woman from the neck up, her skin as pale as rice, her thin lips pink and pursed. There was something inherently weak about her, though, maybe even unhealthy, the way her cheeks sunk in slightly, her eyes masking a sorrow only she knew, but Jhee thought this potential vulnerability only added to her beauty.

"She's pretty, don't you think?"

"I guess," Mrs. Kim said. "So . . . is this okay?"

"Sure, Jane's a great name."

"Oh," Mrs. Kim said, hesitating. "Yes. Okay."

"Wait," Jhee said. "You don't like it?"

"I like this more, I think. *Ehm-ah,* am I saying that right?"

It was the title of the book, printed below the author's name: *Emma.*

"Yes," Jhee said, a little annoyed that Mrs. Kim wasn't so linguistically challenged after all. "You sounded that out? That's good."

She chuckled. "No, not really. The only word I know by sight is Mommy, and it looked like that. And if it sounds like it, too, that's even better."

"Uh-huh," Jhee said. Mrs. Kim was so Korean, a good little mother who lived for her children. Jhee had hoped she'd found someone with attitudes similar to hers, and it was disappointing to discover that she was just like everybody else, but maybe she was being too harsh. In time, she'd show her another way to live her life, that there was more than just doting after children. There had to be. The separation between children and their mother was an inescapable fact of life, but for immigrant parents like them, it was worse. She could remember her own son coming home from elementary school, eager to share his newfound knowledge with her; but as the years rolled on and the happy boy turned into a sullen teenager, she saw how glad he was for the language barrier between them. It broke her heart.

They had to stick together, she and Mrs. Kim. There was so much Jhee had to teach her. She snatched the book away from her and smiled, not only because she was about to do something nice, but because she now had something meaningful for the twenty dollars she'd found.

"I love it, In Young. Emma is the perfect name for you, do you know why? Because it's the one you chose. And I'm going to buy it for you." She knew Mrs. Kim would decline once, and again. Then she would say thank you and let her buy it, because that's how it was between Koreans. Did no one else see the inherent inefficiency of these silly customs?

At the front desk, Jhee greeted Ralph, the owner of the bookshop. He was flashing his biggest, warmest smile, which in actuality was like seeing the widening of an open wound. Jhee heard Mrs. Kim draw in a quick breath behind her.

"Good afternoon, ladies," Ralph said.

The man was, in every sense of the word, ugly. His nose was enormous, his eyes were off-center, and these unfortunate components were embedded on a face that was long and horsy. Who could love a man like this? Hopefully a woman equally as unattractive, or one that simply didn't care. For his sake, Jhee hoped there was somebody out there for him. He seemed like a nice enough man, always greeting her whenever they saw each other in the mall, and the few times they met at a door, he held it open for her.

He just had to be patient. Somebody would come along, just like the woman who came in and bought the little red purse from their store this morning. If she could speak better English, that's what she'd tell him—though maybe not. It was easy to think in such terms when the possibility didn't exist, like somebody saying they'd donate a heap of cash if they won the lottery. In reality, they'd probably keep all the winnings to themselves, and Jhee wouldn't say anything.

She handed the book to Ralph and pointed to Mrs. Kim. "My friend. Emma Kim."

"What a coincidence," Ralph said, "just like the book. It's great to meet you, Emma." He extended his hand to Mrs. Kim, who shook it. Then she gave him a quick bow, probably out of habit. Seeing it reminded Jhee of the more elaborate bowing that went on during the Korean New Year, when the children honored their parents with a ceremony known as *jurl*. Standing straight with your arms by your side, you silently got down to your knees. You never made eye contact, you always looked down, because that's how you showed respect. Then as your head dipped forward down to the floor, you drew a studied arc with both arms, and if you were doing it correctly, you finished with your forehead resting on the backs of your hands. Sometimes this sequence of motion was repeated three or four times in succession, though Jhee couldn't remember why. Mrs. Kim probably knew.

"Goodness," her friend said as Ralph rang up the sale, "this man is just hideous."

"Oh yes," Jhee said, feeling bad for what she was about to say, but only for a moment. "Isn't he just the ugliest person you've ever seen?"

Ralph, oblivious to their Korean conversation, leaned over and plucked a plastic Snoopy bookmark, complete with a yellow Woodstock-inspired tassel, from the bin on the other side of the register. He tucked it behind the front cover and handed it back to Jhee. "Just a little present from me. A gift."

They both thanked him and giggled together as they left the store.

"Hah-mah," Mrs. Kim whispered, "hippopotamus" in Korean. "That's what he looks like."

Their laughter had the weightless quality of schoolgirls, but then Mrs. Kim peered at her wristwatch and it broke the spell.

She cleared her throat. "We should find your husband's present," she said, back to her stern, boring self.

What Jhee ended up getting was a portable cassette player, which now sat underneath her seat. It was the least expensive thing she could find at HiFi FoFum, which was still too much—Dmitri, who owned the stereo store, only carried name-brand merchandise—but time had been running out. The way she'd wanted this day to end was to treat her new friend to dinner, and it had taken a great deal of convincing to get her to Hometown Grill. The amount of guilt Mrs. Kim exhibited over a simple meal away from her kids was downright embarrassing.

"They'll survive without you," Jhee had said, but Mrs. Kim hadn't even gotten her sarcasm.

"I guess so," she said, and as they sat in the cozy dimness of the restaurant, she kept up the annoying habit of looking behind her. What did she think, that her two children were going to come begging for her return? They were probably glad to eat something American for a change, which is how Mrs. Kim should be approaching this opportunity.

The key was to distract her with questions. Her drive to learn was as demanding as a child's, and as she answered her queries, Jhee was happily reminded of her tutoring days in Korea, the rush she received from imparting knowledge to another person.

"Now that little black cap on his head," Mrs. Kim asked, referring to Dmitri's yarmulke. "What is it?"

It had been too long since Jhee experienced this connection between a teacher and a student. She'd forgotten how it was like giving a gift, how it made you feel generous and superior at the same time.

"It's because he's Jewish, Emma. Some Jewish men wear it."

"I'm amazed it stays on. He was moving around pretty fast in that store of his."

"Well," Jhee said, and she paused here, relishing the moment, "they stick bobby pins around it so it doesn't slide off."

Mrs. Kim nodded, and Jhee saw how she wanted to ask something else, but she stopped. Instead, she stared into the votive candle lit in the middle of the table and spoke quietly.

"I know I'm asking too many questions."

And instead of being gentle, Jhee was firm in her reply. "There's only one way you can offend me, and that is to not ask what's on your mind. Understand?"

"You're too kind," Mrs. Kim said.

"Next question," Jhee said, and Mrs. Kim smiled.

"Does he wear it every day? The hat?"

"It's called a *yah-mah-ka*."

"*Yah-mah-ka,*" she repeated.

"It's a show of devotion to his god," Jhee said, not certain about this part but saying it with confidence, with authority.

"Isn't that interesting," Mrs. Kim said. She seemed so youthful whenever she learned something new, her eyes opening up a little wider. "And what about this on the table?" She pointed to a printed card on a miniature brass easel.

Jhee explained to Mrs. Kim about the special of the day, which she was glad to see was something she recognized: steak.

"*Stae-kuh,*" her friend said, unsure. "Is that good?"

"Oh yes, very good, especially with hot sauce."

Jhee and her husband had eaten twice at Hometown Grill, and on both occasions, they'd been serviced by the same waitress, but today it was the chef himself, Jake, who'd seated them and handed out the menus. Perhaps the waitress on duty was late or was attending to some emergency, or maybe they were just early. It was a quarter to five, not exactly prime dinner hour. Jhee usually saw him from behind the chrome counter of the open kitchen in the back, his face occasionally illuminated by the flare-up of the grill flames. He looked tired today, a slow shuffle to his step, but there was something different about him, too, and when he returned to take their order, Jhee realized what it was.

"Hair," she said to him, pointing to her chin. "No hair."

Jake stood with his pen poised over his notepad. Their eyes met, and it was strange how his smooth face made him look younger and yet at the same time older, like the feeling you got looking at a midget.

"Yeah," Jake finally said after a lengthy pause, "yeah." Then he asked them for their order.

"We will have the special," Jhee said, a phrase she'd memorized yesterday. She'd also remembered, "Grilled chicken, please," and "Grilled steak, please," but she'd hoped to order the special, because it sounded very American.

"Very good," Jake said, and took away their menus. "It'll be out shortly."

As Jake left for the kitchen, Mrs. Kim stared after him with concern. "Do you know him?" Jhee asked.

"No," Mrs. Kim said, and when she saw Jhee examining her, she blushed. She adjusted the napkin on her lap and changed the subject. "I hope I can speak as well as you can one day."

Jhee was about to reassure her that she would indeed, with time and with her guidance, when something thin and hot seared deep into the small of her back. It came with such intensity that she let out a small gasp.

"Jenny," Mrs. Kim said, alarmed, "are you all right?"

It was the first time Mrs. Kim called her by her American name, and Jhee knew she should praise her for doing so, but she couldn't form the words. Instead her entire being was consumed by this excruciating sensation, and it seemed to Jhee that time was moving very slowly. She saw Mrs. Kim rise up from her chair in slow motion, then crouch down a centimeter at a time next to her. Her friend's hand floated to her forehead and rested there for an eternity.

"Are you okay?"

What if it never left? What if she felt like this for the rest of her life? The purity of this pain was exquisite, but it was already fading, ebbing away, and a strange thought crept into her mind. She could see how a pain this true could become a source of strength, how you might come to depend on it like the chiming of a clock or the setting of the sun.

"I'm fine," Jhee said, but now that the ache was gone, in its place was a feeling of profound uselessness. Why had it been so important to befriend this woman, a woman she didn't really even like, a woman she'd lied to from the very beginning? Suddenly she felt very stupid.

As if on cue, Jake appeared and clanged a pair of white dishes in front of them. Shredded carrots and broccoli florets outlined the perimeter of the plate, but the thing in the middle didn't look like steak. It looked like a mound of raw ground beef, mashed together with chopped onions and a gooey yellow paste that resembled egg yolk.

"Steak?" Jhee asked him.

"Right, steak tartare," Jake said. "Bon appetit."

And once again they were alone, the two Korean women of Peddlers Town.

Mrs. Kim poked at her bloody cake with a fork. "Is this cooked?"

Jhee Hong sectioned off a wedge and stared at the clump of meat in front of her. It almost looked alive, glistening in the candlelight.

FIRE SALE

 MR. HONG SAT on our front desk, his back to Father, talking about what it was like to be without his wife for the last few weeks. She was visiting her relatives in Korea, and he had the whole apartment to himself.

"Toilet seat," Mr. Hong said. "I leave it up all the time."

"Oh yeah," Father said, full of nostalgia. "I remember what that was like."

"And when I pee, I leave the door wide open."

It was eight-thirty, half an hour before closing time on a Saturday, and I was barely awake. Listening to their conversation wasn't helping, but it was better than fixing up the kimono section with Mother and Noona. Half the robes were scattered on the floor because kimonos, especially the ones made out of silk or rayon, weren't meant to be hung on hangers. I watched Mother pick up a shiny red one and slide it back onto its pink plastic frame. Then it was Noona's turn, then back to Mother. Pointless.

A deafening popping sound, like the snap of a giant whip, woke me right up and silenced everyone else.

"What the hell was that?" Mr. Hong said.

It had come from the far west end of the mall, near Hometown Grill. Everybody, including the few customers in the store, came out to the walkway to investigate. Our neighbors, Mr. and Mrs. McManus of the mirror store Cimmetri, joined the group. We waited a couple of seconds but saw nothing.

"FIRE!" Mr. Hong yelled. He didn't have to yell—everyone was within earshot. "FIRE!" he yelled again.

Through the two large windows of the restaurant, yellow and orange flames blazed, some as tall as the ceiling. I was witnessing my first live fire, outside of a struck match or a flicked lighter. People ran away from it screaming. A woman was yelling as she almost tripped on her way to the exit. As she ran by, one of the windows at Hometown Grill burst and shattered, the shards falling in a shower of light.

"My store!" Mr. Hong yelled. He dashed up and cut a dramatic hard left, a long wing of his comb-over hair flying.

Father turned to Mother and said, "I'll be back."

"What?" Mother said.

"Hong may need some help."

"What if *our* store catches on fire?"

"We're pretty far away from it," Father said, looking down at Hometown Grill. "Besides, I'm sure the fire trucks are on their way."

"We *all* should get out of here right now," Mother said.

"Hong's wife is out of town, he's got nobody. I'll be right back."

Mother started to say something, then stopped. I knew what she was going to say—it was what she said about Father to Noona behind closed doors. "We always come second," I heard her say bitterly on more than one occasion. "His friends, the store, everything else comes first."

Jason DeLeon, the useless assistant manager of Peddlers Town who nobody liked, lumbered up to us. "I just ran *all* the way up here from the office," he said, as if it were some kind of an accomplishment.

Mr. McManus said, "Why aren't the sprinklers working?"

"I don't know," he said, tugging at his beard. "I'll have to get back to you on that." It was the same line he gave Father whenever he was asked about the leak in our ceiling. "I'll need to use your phone," he told Mother. Mother nodded, though not without suspicion. Jason dialed 911 and reported the fire.

"He hasn't done that yet?" Noona said. "How stupid is this idiot?"

The greatest advantage of speaking a different language was the things you could say about people while standing right next to them.

"Shit for brains," I said.

Things weren't looking good at Hometown Grill. The fire had spread to the next store over, HiFi FoFum. Black smoke that smelled of burning plastic wafted over our way.

"The fire department already knows," Jason said. "A truck'll be here in less than a minute."

"We've stayed around long enough," Mother said. She herded Noona and me outside, but not until she gave a long and disgusted look back at Father's trail to Mr. Hong's store.

We stood outside in the parking lot and watched the west wing of Peddlers Town light up the sky. Though it was early June, it was rather chilly, which seemed strange because the fire raged in front of us. A caravan of siren-wailing fire trucks came, one after the other, three in all. Following closely behind were two ambulances and a police cruiser. Dressed in yellow slickers and thick rubbery black pants, the squad of firefighters jumped off their vehicles, attached three white hoses to three different hydrants, got into their places and formations, and proceeded to put out the fire. They chopped down the pair of large oak doors that led directly into Hometown Grill and sprayed white jets of water into the heavy flames. Black smoke escaped through the restaurant's broken windows and drifted downward, a dark shadow that glided across the tan cinder-block walls of Peddlers Town.

"Jake!" Mr. McManus said. "You all right?"

Jake was a big guy, but tonight he seemed smaller than Father, his head hanging down, his shoulders drawn together. "Everybody's fine. One of the gas stoves blew, I don't know why."

"Hey," Mr. McManus said, "the important thing is that nobody's hurt."

Jake nodded, though he hardly seemed convinced. He reached for his chin but stopped halfway, and looked more dejected than ever.

The fire, which seemed powerful and threatening before the trucks had arrived, was beaten down in less than ten minutes. The only one who needed medical assistance was Dmitri, the Russian guy who owned HiFi FoFum, who'd suffered a cut on his forearm from the look of his bandage. He walked over to where we were standing.

"Everything okay?" he asked.

"Yes," I said.

"What's wrong with Susan?"

And that's when I realized that Noona was nowhere.

"Where's Noona?" I asked Mother, but she hadn't noticed her disappearance, either. Sensing our distress, Dmitri cleared his throat and pointed to the ambulance in the middle of the parking lot. Sitting in the back of the open truck was my sister, and standing in front of her was an EMT guy.

Mother and I looked at each other in confusion. "I'll get her," I said.

I made my approach slowly. The guy had slicked-back, wet-looking hair, and he was shorter than Noona.

"Take a deep breath," he told my sister, so she did. He had a stethoscope plugged into his ears and was apparently listening to her heartbeat, but he didn't look like a doctor and Noona didn't act like a patient. In fact, they were both smiling, like they were playing a funny game.

"You'll be just fine," he said.

"Thank you, Dr. Ramon," Noona said. She sounded coquettish, childlike—but not entirely unfamiliar.

"You're welcome."

"You saved us," Noona said with such sincerity that it was almost laughable.

Ramon chuckled. "And what's your name?"

Noona offered Ramon her crazy dark eyes. I knew they were crazy, but of course Ramon didn't. He would've thought they were beautiful and terribly mysterious. When she answered, her lips reaching out to him as she formed the word "Susan," it all came back to me. This was exactly how she acted back in Korea when she was with her Boyfriend of the Month. How could I have forgotten it? The lilt in her voice, the showering of sweet compliments; it was all there, with nothing lost in the translation from Korean to English.

"Susan. You pretty cool," Ramon said.

"Hey," I called out to Noona. It made them both turn around. "What're you doing?"

Noona jumped off the truck and greeted me with a stinging slap on my arm. "None of your business, Junior."

"You talking Chinese or something?" Ramon asked. "Where you going?"

"See you," she said, and blew him a kiss as we walked away.

"I hope so," Ramon said, making an exaggerated pretend-grab at her toss.

We found Father propped up against the nearest lamppost when we returned. His shirt was soaked with sweat and his hair was a mess.

Mother, silently stewing all this time, tore into him. "Where have you been? And what happened? Don't tell me you've been with Hong all this time."

Father held up his hand, trying to catch his breath. "We moved maybe half of Hong's bags outside. Hong's hurt," he managed to say. "They took him in the ambulance." He pointed, but we didn't see any ambulances, just the one remaining fire truck and its blinking red lights. Seeing our confused faces, Father shook his head. "No, no, it left already. Come on, everybody in the car, let's go." Nobody protested, not even Mother.

We rode in silence. I felt bad for Mr. Hong, all alone and suffering in a hospital room. With his wife out of town, all he had was his son, and he wasn't nearby, attending a college in Connecticut.

Mother broke the silence with a quiet, demure question, obviously feeling guilty for being so confrontational with Father. "Is he burned badly?"

"He slipped and broke his leg. On the way out. I think it was an ice-cream bar."

"*Broke* his leg?"

"He said he broke it. Couldn't put any pressure on his ankle. Screamed like a baby when he tried."

After a lengthy pause, Mother continued. "He has a son."

"Who's three, four hours away. Come on, this is the least we can do."

"Our store almost burned down and you're worried about Hong and his stupid ankle." Father started to say something but Mother interrupted him. "I'm done listening," she said, and leaned her face against the window, staring out at the fields of corn blurring by.

I wondered how long this fight would last. Whenever Father and Mother argued about nonmonetary matters, they typically managed to work things out within twenty-four hours. If it was money-related, the awkward silence could blanket an entire week. I wasn't afraid of their fighting, but seven days of them avoiding eye contact and saying the bare minimum to each other wore me down.

When we arrived at the hospital, Mother opted to stay in the car. "Just leave me here," she told Father. "Go and see your friend and leave me here." She dug into her change purse and fished out two dollars for me and Noona, all in quarters, in case we wanted to get something to eat. If there was a vending machine in there and it wasn't a total ripoff, that translated to eight Twinkies.

We entered the hospital through the waiting area and saw the misfortunes that had struck ordinary people. In the corner a kid sat holding a hand towel over his right eye. Next to him was a black woman whose legs were covered with fuzzy white dots. At the receptionist's desk, Father found out Mr. Hong's whereabouts and we wasted no time pushing through the double swinging doors and into the bright clinical lights of the hospital corridor.

Mr. Hong was in a room that wasn't a real room, just a space sectioned off by a pair of blue curtains. He lay on a narrow bed, his bad leg propped up on two pillows.

"Hey, Hong," Father said, giving his shoulder a firm squeeze.

"What are you doing here?" Mr. Hong asked. He saw Noona and me lagging behind and greeted us.

"Just thought I'd stop by, see how you're doing."

"My son is on his way."

"That's good," Father said. "Well, I'll just stay here until he comes."

"You don't have to do that," Mr. Hong said, though he was obviously pleased.

That was the high point of their conversation. It soon degraded into the fire, about insurance, about what route his son had taken to get over here, then spiraled further into boredom as they talked about the currency exchange rate between the Korean won and the U.S. dollar.

"Ugh," I muttered to myself, turning to Noona, finding no one there. She'd done it again. "I'll be back," I told Father, who nodded vaguely.

A quick peek outside Mr. Hong's room offered no trace of Noona. I walked carefully, sidestepping an incredibly old man slumped in a wheelchair—I couldn't believe he was still alive. I almost tripped as I avoided a stampede of doctors with their scrubs on and their masks hanging on one ear. Following them were two burly men rolling a gurney at full speed, their eyes wide and alert and staring straight ahead. The hospital was not for the slow-footed. I hugged the inner curve of the wide hallway and stuck close to the wall.

"Susan," I heard, then laughter. It was coming from Radiology, a darkened room illuminated by a low reddish glow. I peered into the room and saw Noona flat against the wall and someone in front of her, their faces maybe a foot apart and the distance shrinking quick.

"You're hot," the man said, and their lips met. It was the same guy from the ambulance, Ramon.

Across from me was a tall woman who wore a name tag (ROSEY) and had the look of someone in authority. She scrutinized a chart on the wall. I tiptoed away from my peeping position and tapped on her lower back, as I couldn't reach her shoulder.

"What do you want?"

I flinched, then waited. Usually this was an effective maneuver to soften up adults, but not this lady.

"I said, what do you want? Can't you see I'm busy?"

"Kiss kiss," I said, and puckered up. Then I pointed to Radiology.

"What in the world you talking about, child?"

I grabbed her hand and she followed willingly. She was a pushover after all—just talked a mean game.

After bringing her to the threshold, I slunk away and hid behind the nearby water cooler. Rosey stomped into the room and said, "Ramon, what you think you're doing?" She pried him off Noona by his ear and dragged him away.

"Ow, stop it, Rosey!" Ramon yelled. When she let go, he straightened up and slicked back his hair. "I was gonna get me some, you understand?"

"The only thing you be getting is my foot kicking your sorry ass," Rosey said. Ramon waved her off and walked away in a huff. Rosey walked back into the room and stared Noona down.

"And you," Rosey said, "should be ashamed of yourself, child. What you got to say for yourself?"

"I don't know," Noona said, and started crying. I knew they were fake tears, but she had Rosey convinced. She threw her soft, dark arms around my sister to comfort her.

"There, there," Rosey said, "it's okay. Just be careful, you hear?"

"Okay, thank you," she said, feigning a couple of sobs. Such an actress, she almost had me fooled.

When Rosey left, I casually walked over to Noona and said, "Hey, I've been looking for you." I braced myself for the onslaught of insults, but it never came. Instead, Noona hugged me and wept and wept and wept.

"It's okay," I said. "It's all right."

"No, it isn't," she mumbled, clutching me harder.

She had cried like this on the night before we left Korea, she and her boyfriend sitting on our white sofa, holding hands, shedding enough tears to fill an ocean. Noona's eyes were still swollen when we boarded the plane the morning after.

And now here she was, months later, and her wounds still just as fresh. I didn't know what to do, so I waited until she was finished.

"Come on," I said, "we have to go."

Noona nodded and let me lead her back to Mr. Hong's room. His son was there now, sitting next to Father and looking bored. When he saw us, he jumped up and greeted us both.

"What's wrong?" he asked Noona. She didn't bother to reply. Ever since Yun Sae first laid eyes on my sister at Newark Airport, the very first day we arrived in the United States, he'd been in love with her. Of course, this meant that Noona wanted nothing to do with him.

We said goodbye and wished Mr. Hong a quick recovery. "Take care," Yun Sae said to Noona, but again, she pretended not to hear.

Back at the car, Mother hadn't moved an inch. The radio was tuned to the oldies station, Frank Sinatra belting out "My Way." He was Mother's favorite American singer. She turned it off when we got in the car.

"He'll be fine," Father told Mother, even though she hadn't asked him. It was a quiet ride home, both of the women looking far into the dark—brooding into the moonless night.

As we drove up to Peddlers Town the next morning, we saw the black hole that used to be Hometown Grill.

"Oh my God," Mother said, the first words she'd spoken since last night.

"I'm sure it looks worse than it is," Father said.

He was right. After we drove by Jake's restaurant, we saw that the rest of Peddlers Town was just as we'd remembered it. None of us was ever thrilled with the faded beige walls or the dirty brown trim of the building, but that morning, we couldn't have asked for a more beautiful sight. Our store looked untouched.

"Hey, Harry," Reggie, Peddlers head security guard, greeted Father. I still wasn't used to hearing Father's American name, but he seemed to like it fine, shaking Reggie's big hand. Everything about Reggie was big except his face, which was long and oval and shrunken like a raisin.

"Good morning, Reggie," Father said. "We go in?"

"Sure. Got electricity back this morning."

They'd sectioned off the first three stores closest to Jake's due to damage, and since there were three rows of stores, that meant that nine stores were affected, including Dmitri's HiFi FoFum and Mr. Hong's In the Bag.

Though the fire hadn't spread over to our store, we were not exempt from its effects. Our bad luck came in the form of smoke damage and soot, nasty black flakes that had settled on half the store. This wasn't much of a calamity when it came to vases and jars and such—a quick wipe with a wet rag would bring things back good as new—but there was no such easy solution for the clothing.

"Maybe I can wash them," Mother suggested.

Father shook his head. It was okay to wash the cheaper stuff like kiddie pajamas since they were made out of cotton, but the kimonos were out of the question. "Silk or rayon," Father said, going around and checking tags. One of our most esteemed possessions, the Japanese winter kimono crucified against the far wall with four spotlights igniting its gold-threaded embroidery, was made of silk. Fine black dust had left a pattern that resembled a mountain range. I thought it looked kind of cool. Nobody else did.

"What do we do with all this?" Father said. None of us could think of anything useful to say. I felt helpless and afraid. This store was all we had to bring money into the household—if we couldn't sell our merchandise, how would we eat?

Father phoned Mr. Hong at home to find out how he was doing. I heard him warn Mr. Hong to brace himself when he came in.

"Hong's doing fine," he relayed to us, as if we cared.

"Look," Mother said, pointing to our window that faced the parking lot. "What is going on out there?"

It wasn't even ten o'clock yet and the lot was already half filled. On Sundays, Peddlers Town opened at eleven.

"It's like Christmas," Father said. "They all came early last Christmas Eve, lined up in front of the entrances, and when Reggie unlocked the doors, it was like a flood." Father snapped his fingers. "They must've heard about the fire!"

We followed him as he walked to the front counter, dipped underneath, and came back up with a large white piece of construction paper. From the coffee can that housed all the pens and markers, he fished out a red, an orange, a yellow, and a black.

"You're good at drawing," Father said to Noona. "Can you draw me a sign that reads FIRE SALE?"

She nodded and went off by herself to the back corner. Father and Mother looked at each other and smiled, the official gesture that signified the end of their latest fight.

While my sister busied herself with her pens and markers, the rest of us cleaned up. Sharing a spray bottle of Windex and two rolls of paper towels between the three of us, we attacked shelf after shelf, our hands quickly becoming filthy. It felt nice working together as a family. As we cleaned, Mother and Father recounted a story about me and strawberries. Way back when, Mother's family had owned a strawberry farm in the Korean countryside, and every June, we'd all drive down for a visit.

Supposedly when I was three, I'd inexplicably become enamored with strawberries. When we got there, I bolted out of the car, ran to the strawberry field, and started picking and eating everything in sight. Before anybody could catch me, I'd eaten so many strawberries that supposedly my face had turned a very real shade of green.

"Do you remember how he looked?" Father said.

"It wasn't so funny then, but yes. Like this," Mother said, picking up a green-colored bowl. "You looked just like this, Joon-a."

I'd heard this story before, but this was the first time I heard it from both of my parents, and I didn't like it. They were using my story of innocent gluttony to ease the tension from their latest argument. Their cruel laughter sounded forced, but they kept on laughing.

"I'm done," Noona said behind us. She held up the sign in front of her.

"Wow," Father and Mother said together. First, I was in awe, then I was filled with jealousy. Noona had all the talent in this family. She could play the piano like Beethoven and draw signs like this. All I was good for was gorging on strawberries.

FIRE SALE, the sign read. Little tiny flame-creatures jumped off each letter, their spindly legs and arms in wild motion. The whole thing had a real animated look to it. She'd done it all with just three colors: black, orange, and red.

Once again, Father crouched underneath the front counter and this time brought out a bunch of hollow aluminum sticks. (What else did he have under there?) He slid the sticks together and like magic, he erected an easel.

He leaned the sign on it and stepped back to admire it. "It's perfect," he told Noona. "Thank you."

It was eleven. We heard Reggie announce, "Welcome to Peddlers Town!" He said this every time he opened up the mall, even if there was no one waiting. Now that he had a sizable audience, his voice boomed. "Welcome to Peddlers Town!"

Father pushed the easel right out in front. He looked at me, and Mother looked at Noona, and we listened to the stampede, felt the feet of hundreds. Then they came, they came in waves, they drowned us with their bodies and their voices.

DMITRI POPOV

IN THE CAR, DMITRI SAID, "Yahoo."

Pitiful. He wasn't even trying. What would his wife say if she heard such a feeble attempt? He bit into his onion bagel and sipped his bitter coffee.

"Yahoo," he said again, this time with feeling.

No, it was gone, it just didn't work anymore. Ever since the fire had burned up his store last month, he'd been in poor spirits. It disappointed him to think that he could be saddened so easily, a thought that depressed him even further. He should have just stayed in bed. He should have never opened his eyes.

But wait—wait. Things weren't so bad. After all, he did collect enough insurance money to replace most of the merchandise, and wasn't the store now at least two-thirds back to normal? And what was this on the dashboard radio? He placed his bagel on his lap and cranked up the volume. It was! Vivaldi's *Four Seasons,* or, in Italian, *Le quattro stagioni*. "Winter in F minor," the first movement, *allegro non molto*. He was catching the last minute of it, the violins in heat. He pulled into the parking lot of Peddlers

Town, yanked on the emergency brake, and yelled, "Yahoo!" This was more like it, this was just what he needed. He jumped out of his Nova, and the bagel flew off—and into the hands of young David. Parked next to him and unloading were the Kims, the quiet Korean folks who owned the big Oriental store.

"Yours?" David said, pinching the bagel carefully between two fingers.

Dmitri bowed dramatically and said, "Good catch!"

"Thank you."

"No, thank you!" Dmitri ruffled the boy's helmet-shaped hair.

The world was a wonderful place. America was a wonderful place. Look at these four people, nicely dressed and ready to make money. Before they had immigrated to the United States, surely the Kims were just barely scraping by in Korea, probably North Korea, eating one meal a day and hoping to avoid the insidious evil of the oppressive Communist regime. They were lucky and so was he.

As he walked up the gray concrete steps leading to the mall entrance, Dmitri planned out his day. In the morning, he would tweak his four Bose Pro Loudspeakers set up at each corner of his store. He drew pride and confidence from merely gazing at his tall obsidian monuments. He'd lost the original quartet in the fire, but last week the replacements had arrived. Just like before, he named them after his brother's beautiful daughters: Svetlana, Natalia, Nina, and Anna. Marusha made fun of him: "Tell me you can tell them apart." His wife was a smart woman, but she was no audiophile. When he'd told her that the four speakers were like four distinct species of birds, she shooed him and kissed him and said, "My Dmitri, who hears better than Laika." Laika was their poodle.

Reggie greeted Dmitri at the front entrance. "Have a great day," he said, and Dmitri replied, "Yes, I will," with such conviction that Reggie flinched.

As usual, he was one of the first ones in the building. He and the Kims were probably the only ones there besides the restaurant owners; it was always the immigrants who tried the hardest. Granted, he didn't exactly fit the bill of an immigrant anymore—it was back in 1961 when he, his brother Stepan, and his parents escaped the Soviet Union with an amazing string of good fortune—but the immigrant spirit had yet to leave him.

He loved the smell of Peddlers Town before it opened. Each morning he was surrounded by the sharp scent of sauerkraut from Hot Dog Heaven, the yeasty aroma of Eatza Pizza, the sweet buttery fragrance of Marty's Bakery. Put together, it smelled like money, hard-earned money, good happy money.

Dmitri unbuckled the ring of keys from his belt and drew out the key labeled #1. He was crouching down to unlock the first of four locks when he noticed something peculiar. He touched the thick canvas curtain and felt it give like there was nothing there. He pushed further and saw what had happened: Somebody had cut a very neat door close to the floor, big enough for a man to crawl through.

Dmitri sank to the floor and threw down his keys. What had he done to deserve this? How had he offended God? He wanted to get up and dust off his pants and walk out to his car and drive down Route 35 South, drive all the way until Seaside Heights where he'd rent a boat and a fishing rod and catch flounder and bluefish and blackfish until the sun went down. What a dream that life would be. What a nightmare this life was.

When he lifted the flap and looked into his beloved store, his eyes drilled the four empty corners. Svetlana, Natalia, Nina, Anna. Who had you now?

————

The owner of Peddlers Town held his monthly merchants meeting at Hometown Grill. Now that Jake's restaurant was being rebuilt, the meeting had relocated to Eatza Pizza, the only other place in Peddlers Town able to seat fifty people, though that was overkill. Usually only twenty or so people showed up, and out of that twenty, ten were regulars.

But today it was standing room only because the day before, Peddlers Town was robbed. Reggie began the meeting by reading off the list of things that had been taken. From East Meets West, the thieves had taken the white vase that was worth over a grand. Dmitri remembered it well, the detailed etching of a pair of doves on its curved surface, their eyes and beaks filled with real gold. The vase had sat inside a glass case and was lit by a pair of spotlights, and now the case was empty and the lights shone on nothing. Dmitri walked over to Kim and his boy, who'd come late and were standing at the periphery of the crowd.

"Sorry, Harry," Dmitri said.

"Thank you," Kim said.

"From HiFi FoFum," Reggie read, "four Bose speakers."

"Special Edition Bose Pro Loudspeakers!" Dmitri said. Everybody turned around to look at him, but he didn't care. The least Reggie could've done was to announce his loss accurately. "They are the best speakers money can buy, and now they are no more."

Reggie walked up to the table where the owner of Peddlers Town, George DiPalma, sat. He unpinned his gold security guard badge and dropped it in front of George. "I take full responsibility," he said. "I don't deserve to wear this no more." He also turned in his flashlight, a chrome cylinder long enough to house a dozen D-cells.

"Please, Reggie," George said, sliding the items back to him. "We don't blame you for any of this. The robbers somehow got around the alarm system. That's the problem we need to address."

Reggie didn't seem convinced, but he continued to read the extensive list of missing items anyway. The two jewelry stores in the mall had safes, so they hadn't lost any of their merchandise, but over thirty other stores had been hit. The robbers had good taste—they took only the most expensive items they could find. The total estimated loss topped sixty thousand dollars.

"But don't worry," George said. He stood up from his chair, clasped his hands together, and gleamed a toothy smile. The owner of Peddlers Town was a handsome, tall man who talked a great game. Dmitri couldn't stand him. "We're fully insured, so you'll receive the wholesale value of all your stolen goods."

To Dmitri's amazement, his fellow merchants cheered at hearing this news. Hong from In the Bag sidled up to Kim and translated for him, and Kim, too, was now clapping. What was wrong with these people? Didn't they realize this was the *least* management could do?

"Excuse me!" Dmitri yelled, silencing the room. "I do not agree this is a happy time. Bad people stole from us. How is this happy?"

"Now, now, Dmitri," George said. "Let's keep our heads here. Let's stay calm." George often addressed him this way, as if placating a silly child.

"From day one, everybody should have steel curtains, not canvas, I said. From day one."

"Oh, my friend," George said, shaking his head slowly, as if Dmitri was disappointing him. He was a crafty one. In Moscow, he would have gone very far in politics. "We've discussed this before. It doesn't make economical sense, do you understand? It's far more financially efficient to provide protection for the entire building than the individual stores. Which, by the way, is exactly what we are doing."

On cue, Reggie passed around a stack of pages. Dmitri reached over and got three copies, for himself and for the Koreans. At the top left corner of the brochure was a knight in black armor, and above it was a word he couldn't pronounce, but underneath the picture he read ALARM SYSTEM. The document sang its praises in bullet points, how it was the fastest, the most secure, the best.

"And how will this," Dmitri said, trying to figure out how to say the word, "piss . . . piss . . ."

"The bathroom's over there," George said, and the room erupted in laughter. "Sorry, Dmitri, I just couldn't resist." He cleared his throat and stared at the crowd importantly. "The word you're looking for is Psion, the name of this esteemed security company. Our Russian friend makes an excellent point: How will this little black box help us when the current alarm failed to protect our valuable assets? Well, how about this: It's used by our red, white, and blue, our very own U.S. government."

Excitement rumbled through the crowd. Dmitri knew bullshit when he heard it—probably it was some tiny pencil-pushing office in the middle of nowhere that utilized the alarm system—but who would listen to him now, after George made a fool of him? While George continued to highlight the amazing features of the new system, Dmitri scrutinized the brochure. There were a few words he didn't understand, but he refused to let that faze him. He kept on, getting right to the end where the name and number of the salesperson was blacked out with a magic marker. He tilted the paper against the light in various angles to see if he could make out the letters, but it was no use.

When he looked up to speak once more, chairs were sliding back and everyone was rising. The meeting was over.

Hong patted him on the shoulder. "Just twenty dollar."

"Twenty what?" Dmitri asked.

"Small price. Rent go up twenty dollar for new alarm."

"Small price," Kim agreed.

Unbelievable. So not only were they robbed by thieves, they were just robbed again. Dmitri crushed the brochure in disgust, crumpled it into a ball. He wanted to chuck it as hard as he could, preferably at George DiPalma's head, but the only person who was paying him any attention was Kim's boy, who looked concerned when he saw Dmitri's fist.

"Don't worry," he said. "Not for you."

David approached him carefully. "This is you," he said, and held up his brochure and tilted it up and down, mimicking Dmitri from a moment ago.

"Yes? So what?"

The boy handed him the sheet and pointed at the bottom. Unlike his brochure, somebody had forgotten to black out the name of the salesperson from this one. BENJAMIN DIPALMA, it read, with a phone number.

"Thank you, David," Dmitri said. "May I keep this?"

The boy nodded and went back to his father, who was in conversation with Mr. Hong. One table over, Ted McManus, the owner of Cimmetri, motioned Dmitri to join him, but Dmitri shook his head.

"I have to go," he said.

"Right now? Come on, Dmitri, sit. I'm gonna have a slice. My treat."

Dmitri stared at Ted evenly. "Your treat? You are now rich after the robbery?"

Ted snorted a laugh. "Never mind," he said. "I can see you're not in the mood."

It was nearing noon at Eatza Pizza, and hungry customers were crowding into the restaurant for a quick bite to eat. Four fresh pies slid out of the oven and filled the air with their heavenly tomato scent, but Dmitri was already on his way back to his store. He had a phone call to make.

————

The following morning, Dmitri arrived at Peddlers Town half an hour before it was set to open. Instead of finding the parking lot empty, it was already almost halfway full.

His poodle, sitting up in the backseat, whimpered.

"Down, Laika," Dmitri said, and to his relief, she quieted herself and plopped down.

He'd wanted to come in early so Laika could have the run of the building with minimal distractions, but now that wasn't going to be possible. He could almost hear his wife's warning from the morning.

"It is a bad idea, Dmitri," Marusha had said as she poured coffee into his thermos. "Our girl has a good nose, but she is no tracking dog."

During their evening walks, Laika sometimes got distracted when a large group of people passed by, either pulling hard toward them or away, depending on her mood. Loud music spooked her, though not always. His wife was right, this wasn't going to work—but then Dmitri thought of George DiPalma at the meeting, how he swindled everyone into getting that alarm system.

With her leash firmly in his hand, he let Laika out of the car and found Reggie by the main entrance.

"What is going on?" Dmitri asked him.

"No idea," the security guard said. "I guess they read about the robbery in the local paper."

A family of shoppers walked past them and into the mall.

"The door is open for customers already?"

"George thought it was a good idea to let them in and look around."

What was it with people? The mall was packed like Christmas after the fire, and now this. Maybe they should suffer some catastrophe on a weekly basis to boost business.

"Cute dog," Reggie said. "Yours?"

"My daughter," Dmitri said. "Laika, Reggie. Shake."

The poodle approached the man in uniform, sniffed his shoes, and lifted her right paw.

"What a smarty!" Reggie said.

Unfortunately, Laika's good behavior was short-lived, as she started barking and lunging at various passersby the moment they went into the mall. Dmitri tried to contain her, but she was a standard poodle with sixty pounds of muscle. A few powerful jerks later, his satchel and Laika's dog bowl and treats lay scattered on the floor while he desperately held on to her leash. Luckily, he saw Kim's boy walking toward him.

"David!" Dmitri yelled, and the boy stopped. He looked conflicted, and he almost turned around. "David, please help me!"

He came, though reluctantly. While Dmitri held on to Laika with both hands, the boy picked up his belongings. "Father say no talk," he said.

"Just help me to my store, okay? Please?"

David looked around, sighed, and followed.

"Why does your father say 'no talk'?"

David shook his head. The boy didn't say another word as they trotted to HiFi FoFum.

When they arrived at the store, David piled Laika's belongings next to the register.

"Thank you," Dmitri said. "You did a good thing."

He had fully expected the boy to run off at this point, but surprisingly, he didn't. Instead, he ruffled Laika's head and said, "Good dog."

"She is a smart dog," Dmitri said, "and we are going to get evidence."

"Evidence?" David said.

Dmitri led Laika to the four corners of the store, to the exact locations of the stolen speakers. Whoever the robbers were, they must've spent some time disconnecting his equipment. It wasn't easy taking off the wires and brackets, so they had perhaps sweated in these areas. After sniffing the final spot, Laika raised her head.

The dog suddenly stood up straight, her nose in the air, black nostrils flaring. She circled the store a few times, then slowed. Her head snapped in one direction and another, and then suddenly, as if a switch had been thrown, Laika sank her nose to the floor. She retraced her steps to the four corners, and then pulled Dmitri out into the walkway of Peddlers Town.

"You come with, if you wish," he said to David before being yanked forward.

Laika led, Dmitri held on, and David followed. The boy kept his distance, especially when the dog brought them to East Meets West.

"Good morning," Dmitri said. Before Kim could answer, Laika pulled him past the counter and through the ceramics aisle, her tail barely missing a stack of bowls on the corner shelf. Dmitri shortened his leash and tried to remember the exact location of the white vase, but he didn't have to. Where a giant Buddha now sat, Laika pointed her scruffy snout to its shiny bald head, then turned her gray mug to her owner. Why did people sometimes wish dogs could talk? Laika said everything she needed to say without ever uttering a word. If humans could communicate this easily, there would be no wars, no grief.

"Goodbye," Dmitri said to Kim as Laika tugged him away. When he glanced back, he saw the Korean hurrying in the opposite direction, toward Hong's luggage store, no doubt to report on what he saw.

"She knows," David said.

The boy had returned. Any doubts he had about Laika were long gone, as he now stared at her with respect.

Laika seemed to feed off David's approval, as she dove back to her tracking with even greater fervor. She ran them through four more stores before encountering a pair of black loafers that stopped her from entering the fifth.

Ted McManus stood in front of his store with his arms crossed. The morning sun shone in from the side window, its golden glitter reflecting off the mirrors against the back wall, making Ted look like a guard in front of a room of vast treasure.

"Ted," Dmitri said.

"Your dog can't come in here, Dmitri."

"Why?"

"She'll leave wet noseprints everywhere. It's what dogs do."

It sounded logical, but Dmitri didn't believe it for a second. Across the walkway, he caught the sight of the two Korean men hanging out in front of In the Bag, pretending not to watch. He glanced behind him, and sure enough, David had disappeared once again.

Laika's ears perked up, and she suddenly barked harshly at Ted and lunged at him. Most of the time, his dog looked like something out of a Disney movie, what with her teddy-bear-like curls and soulful brown eyes, but when she wanted to be mean, she was a frightening sight; if she stood on her hind legs, she was almost five feet tall. Ted took a step backwards, and a scene played through Dmitri's mind: his hand dropping the leash, Laika launching herself, Ted on the ground whimpering as bared canine teeth, dripping with saliva, hovered over him. It made him smile, and now Ted did look nervous.

"Look," he said, pleading. "What's the matter with you, Dmitri? Why can't you just leave this alone?"

"Will you let me in here? Or not?" Dmitri said. Now it was his turn to play tough.

"Jesus H. Christ," Ted said, and stepped out of his way.

But it was no use. For some reason, Laika was no longer interested in following the trail, and just as Ted had predicted, she ended up smearing her nose on a number of low-hanging mirrors. When she started barking at a warped image of herself on the funhouse-styled mirror, Dmitri knew it was time to go.

"I will come back and clean those up, with Windex," he said. He felt like Jackie Gleason at the end of a *Honeymooners* episode, all apologies and nowhere to go.

Ted shook his head. "Just get your dog out of here. Please."

On the way back to his own store, David sidled next to him.

"Laika not good?" he asked.

"No," Dmitri said. "Laika not good at all."

But was he being fair? There was no doubt Ted broke her concentration. Maybe that was his intention all along, not to stop him from coming in but to interrupt the flow of their investigation. This wasn't over. With or without Laika's help, Dmitri was going to get to the bottom of this.

The film that came to his mind was *Murder on the Orient Express*, when it turned out that all thirteen suspects on the train car had participated in the murder. Dmitri couldn't remember why Detective Poirot let them go, but that's what happened. Somebody died and no one was punished. If it happened in Russia, he could understand, but here, in the land of the free, the home of the brave?

"Everybody is involved," he told Marusha.

"You are being ridiculous," his wife said. "Why would you say such a thing?"

Because for the rest of the week, he had been treated like a disease by his fellow merchants. For years he waved at Harry Kim and the man would wave back, but now Kim averted his gaze, pretending he hadn't seen him. Dmitri could understand why Ted McManus wanted nothing to do with him, but why Kim? What had he done to him?

"George DiPalma set up the robbery. I believe he had help. Definitely Ted, maybe others."

"And where is your proof?"

"I have the brochure," he said.

But that piece of paper meant nothing. How was it that in movies, a single inconsequential clue led to so much more, the first domino that made the rest of them fall? Because they were works of fiction, that's why. In reality, the brochure was nothing more than an advertisement for an overpriced alarm system. Sitting behind the counter of his store on Friday morning, Dmitri stared at the sheet of paper until a voice broke through.

"We need to talk," Ted McManus said.

Dmitri wasn't surprised. After all, this was the day the insurance agent was suppose to pay his visit, a day of great importance.

"I am ready to hear the truth," Dmitri said.

Ted walked around and sat in the folding chair next to him. He sounded tired. "I think you have the wrong idea."

"My idea is that George DiPalma and you are involved in the robbery," Dmitri said. "You and others."

"Look at me," Ted said. "At my face. Is that what you really believe?"

Dmitri looked, he stared. It was the same friendly face he's always known, the face of a good man who had led him to the ambulance during the fire, when Dmitri fell and scraped his arm. The longer he looked, the stupider he felt, and he finally dropped his gaze.

"Do I need to get everybody who had their stuff stolen to come here, so you can look into their faces, too? Come on, Dmitri, we're all in this together."

Dmitri said nothing. "Then why the silent treatment from everyone? What did I do?"

"Because you're not happy that your speakers are gone."

Dmitri stood up. "What is this? Of course I am not happy! Why should I be?"

Ted sighed. "That mirror the robbers took, it's been there since day one. They did everyone a huge favor. They stole things that had no chance of selling."

"No," Dmitri said. "We are here to sell our goods to customers. I am not here in this country to play games with thieves."

Ted rose. "You're wrong. Because we are in America, we are getting paid for our losses. This is as American as apple pie."

Dmitri picked up the brochure and pointed to the name. "I call this number few days ago, and who answers? Benjamin DiPalma, brother of George DiPalma."

Ted took the sheet and glanced at it. "You scratch my back, I scratch yours."

"I am not into back scratching," Dmitri said.

"That doesn't mean George engineered this robbery. It just means George is a sleazy guy who'll take advantage of a bad situation, but we've always known that. Besides, the monthly security fee is tax deductible for us, Dmitri. It's a win-win."

"Lose-lose," Dmitri said.

Ted nodded and walked away. At the entrance of HiFi FoFum, he turned around.

"Everybody's afraid you're going to say something when the insurance guy comes. You have to understand, these guys would love to have a reason not to pay us. If you tell them your theories, this will drag on and on, and nobody will see any money for months. I don't know about you, Dmitri, but I can use the cash. This would really help me out."

At half past noon the agent came, a man who introduced himself as Bob. He wore a blue suit and jotted things down on a clipboard.

"So that's all you lost, just these speakers?"

"Special Edition Bose Pro Loudspeakers," Dmitri said. "They are very expensive."

Bob whistled when he found the item on his list. "I see that, wow." He checked it off and verified Dmitri's personal information. "So is there anything else you want to tell me?"

Dmitri glanced at the brochure on his desk. After Ted left, he'd made up his mind to speak freely to the insurance man, but as the day went on, Dmitri considered his friend's words. His thoughts drifted to his life back in Russia, living in the outskirts of Omsk with his brother, selling sugar and grain at the local market. They were lucky, as nobody in his right mind wanted to filch huge, heavy bags of flour, but he saw plenty of other comrades whose goods were stolen, sometimes in broad daylight. And what reparations did they receive for these injustices? Nothing, not a thing.

"Is there an investigation?" Dmitri asked.

"Well, I'm sure the police are looking into it. You know, they'll do their job. I'm just trying to do mine."

"I see," Dmitri said.

"Great, just sign here, and here," Bob said, offering his pen.

"I am signing what?"

"Just standard stuff about how you understand everything I just told you, just legal junk."

Dmitri took the pen but signed nothing. Instead he asked the agent to go over each page with him.

Bob laughed, thinking it was a joke. "Wait, are you serious?"

Half an hour later, Dmitri signed the document.

"I don't think I ever had to do that with anyone before, ever," Bob said.

Next on his list was East Meets West, and Dmitri offered to take him over there himself. "I know a shortcut," he said, which was true. Five booths down and through the silk flower store put you right in front of it. On the way, they passed by Cimmetri. Ted looked up, and Dmitri gave him a thumbs-up sign.

At East Meets West, Dmitri introduced Bob to Harry Kim. When he saw how lost Harry was with what Bob had to say, he offered to get Hong.

"Yes, thank you," Harry said.

Seeing the two Korean men in action reminded Dmitri of his own life, many years ago. His brother Stepan had been the smart one, playing Hong's role of interpreter until Dmitri stepped up and learned the language for himself. And there was no other way to make it in this country but to learn it yourself, as evidenced by Hong, who didn't ask Bob for any explanation. Didn't he know how dangerous it was to sign these things without understanding them?

After Hong and Bob left, Dmitri approached Harry.

"Twenty years ago, I took night classes, every night for two years. That is why I speak so good now, you see? That is why I am here today. You must learn, Harry. You and your family." Dmitri saw there was uncertainty in his eyes, so he repeated the important portion of his speech. "English night class. Ask Hong. English night class."

"English night class," Harry said.

"Bingo!" Dmitri said, and slapped him a hearty clap on the back. "It will be hard, but it will be worth it. Believe me."

"Thank you," Harry said. "I go."

And he would, too. Dmitri could see it in his face, that immigrant determination curing like cement.

COMMUNICATING IN ENGLISH

JOHN REEVES WAS A LITTLE MAN, shorter than Father, with curly brown hair and a neatly trimmed goatee around his puckish mouth. His startling green eyes darted from Father to Mother to Noona to me, then settled on Mother.

"Welcome," he said, even though we were late. "Welcome to ESL 012. Please sit anywhere you please." He had a pleasant voice and a measured way of speaking, enunciating every word like a sharp pair of scissors cutting crisply through paper.

There were four other people in the class, an East Indian woman, a black man, and a young Asian couple. Looking at them in their T-shirts and jeans, I felt horribly overdressed. Father had insisted that he and I wear suits and Mother and Noona wear dresses. "You have to show these teachers respect," he'd said. "Nothing shows respect like a suit and a tie." We let him talk us into it back at the apartment, but now I fully disagreed—wearing a suit and a tie in the middle of the scorching summer for night classes showed nothing but pure idiocy.

There were twelve chairs in this small classroom, three rows of four chairs. Nobody sat in the first row or the last row. Much to my chagrin, Father led us to the front.

On the blackboard Reeves had printed his name and his office phone number, big enough to take up half of the board's real estate. His penmanship was precise yet flamboyant, the straight lines dead straight and the curves dramatic.

"Our class just doubled in size," he said jauntily, snapping his finger, "just like that. Let us go around the room and say again who we are"—here, he pointed to himself—"where we are from"—here, he pointed to the map of the world next to the blackboard—"and what we do for a living." Reeves liked to talk with his hands. It was probably a necessity when teaching people who hardly understood what you were saying.

The Indian woman was first. "My name is Aarti Choudhry. I am from India. I am a supermarket cashier." She had trouble pronouncing the last two words, but she managed.

"Good job!" said Reeves.

The black man spoke next, his thick accent rendering his answer almost unintelligible. "My name is Demeke Okunsende. I am from Mali. I am a restaurant dishwasher."

"Wonderful!" said Reeves.

"I am Yan," the Asian man said. "And I am Xiu," the Asian woman said. Then in perfect, practiced harmony, they announced together, "We are from Taiwan, and we own a shop."

"Great!" said Reeves.

Before I could stop him, Father stood up. Nobody else had stood up.

"My name is Harry," he said. "I am from Korea, and I own a shop."

"Top notch, Harry! You can sit down now," Reeves said, extending his index finger at Father and wagging him down.

I stayed seated and said, "My name is David, I am from Korea, and I am student."

"I am *a* student, David," Reeves corrected. "I am *a* student. Say it."

"I am *a* student," I repeated.

"Way to go!" said Reeves.

"My name is Susan," Noona said. "I am from Korea, and I am a student."

"Fantastic!" said Reeves.

"My name is Emma," Mother said. "I am from Korea, and I own a shop."

"Beautiful, Emma," he said, his gaze lingering on Mother. I looked to Father, but he was staring down at his desk, scrutinizing the various graffiti carved into its wooden surface.

Sometimes I slept until noon. If my sister was feeling generous, I'd wake up to the smell of spaghetti sauce simmering, every slow burp of the thick tomato paste like a puff of a smoke signal, telling me to open my eyes, to stretch out my arms, and to get out of bed.

My first summer in America was wonderful in many ways. Unlike Korea, I had two and a half months off instead of two and a half weeks, and more important, I was in the luxurious comfort of industrial-strength air-conditioning. In our apartment we had a monstrous pair of Westinghouse units that could freeze the rooms in fifteen minutes, and according to Reggie, all of Peddlers Town was kept at a shopper-drawing temperature of seventy-two degrees.

The best part of this prolonged summer of freedom was that I was no longer forced to learn. I didn't despise school, but I wasn't exactly in love with it, either. Given the choice, I preferred to learn by osmosis rather than through the rigors of academia, by watching *The Smurfs* and *The Fall Guy* instead of writing a vocabulary word and its meaning fifteen times in a notebook.

As usual, Father was in New York on Monday, trying to get the best merchandise for the cheapest price from his wholesalers. He returned at dinnertime with his car full of kimonos and vases and a boatload of energy.

That evening, Mother prepared her patented *mee-yuk-gook* and *bi-bim-baap,* beefy kelp soup and Korean fried rice, but neither tasted right; the soup was too salty and the rice was burned. Whenever Mother's cooking wasn't up to her usual level of excellence, it meant she wasn't feeling well, but I couldn't see anything wrong with her, at least nothing physical. She did seem distracted, and when Father sat down at the dinner table, she avoided his gaze.

As we ate, Father described scenes of New York: life-threatening driving maneuvers by cabbies, posh people shopping on Fifth Avenue, the corner saxophonist playing for loose change. He was getting us relaxed with these pictures of New York, the way a used-car salesman might soften up a customer by sharing a funny joke about his witchy mother-in-law. As soon as there was a lull in conversation, Father pounced.

"We can start tonight," he said.

From his briefcase, he brought out the Monmouth County Community College schedule of classes. He spread out the paper in the center of the dining table and pointed his chopsticks at one particular entry, circled in red marker:

ESL 012—Communicating in English I

The night ESL program is designed primarily for adult ESL students who hold daytime jobs and whose ESL goals are largely nonacademic. The classes attempt to meet the special needs of students in a concentrated course of study that emphasizes the practical application of class material and its relevance to the students' lives. Mandatory P/Z grading. [MTW 9:00PM–10:30PM, Room 10-B]

"Nine o'clock? But our store closes at nine," I said.

"I can close early on those nights. Business is dead by eight o'clock anyway," Father said. "And it's just a couple of months."

For a class whose intended audience was people who hardly spoke English, its description was saturated with difficult words and phrases. *Emphasize? Practical application? Relevance?* I barely understood what it was trying to say, and told Father so.

"That's why we should go, so we can understand what this says. Who's with me?" His eager eyes scanned the table: I said nothing, Noona stared out the window, and Mother sighed.

"Aren't you tired?" Mother asked. "You were out all day."

"Sure I'm tired, but I'll always be tired."

Mother was about to say something—something crucial, from the way she looked—but she caught me looking at her and stopped. "Do what you want," she finally said, and carted the empty dishes from the table to the kitchen sink.

We drove by a warehouse building without a single intact window. We drove by a house without a roof, another without a door, and one that looked as if a slight wind would cause it to collapse. We drove by people who didn't want to be stared at.

We tried not to stare back, but it was hard because we were supposed to keep an eye out for Billerica Avenue.

We were lost.

"Lock your doors," Mother warned from the front seat.

I checked mine and Noona's, who, as usual, couldn't be bothered with anything. She wasn't enjoying this excursion, her lips in full pouting mode, her hands clenched into icy fists. "All locked," I announced.

"Maybe we should turn back," Mother said. "We're already half an hour late."

"We're close, I know we are," Father said.

"Billerica!" I screamed. We'd just passed it.

"Ow," Noona said. She slapped me on the head. "Don't be so loud, Junior."

"Don't hit me," I said, and kicked her leg.

"Good job, my good son," Father said in English as he steered into a U-turn.

Monmouth County Community College looked like it had been built in the seventies, a two-storied gray concrete box of a building with clashing pink and blue stripes running between the windows. Outside the entrance two men milled about, smoking cigarettes and chatting between puffs.

Father parked the car and we stepped into the heat of the night. Sweat rolled down my back as we carefully trudged toward the entrance. The parking lot was like a minefield, potholes and cracks threatening to trip us at every step.

The inside of the building was no better. Many of the black-and-white linoleum tiles were either split or missing, and all the windows were barred with rusty iron prongs. Every door was an identical slab of metal. The place looked like a decrepit mental institution.

As we searched for room 10-B, I muttered, "This tie is choking me," but nobody was listening. I started to loosen the knot when Father stopped me.

"Da-bid," Father said, "no," again speaking English. This was going to be annoying, hearing him speak English all the time. I'd turn into Noona in no time.

We climbed the stairs and found the room at the end of the second floor. A door labeled 10-B in thick blocky black letters stood closed in front of us. The instructor's voice came through loud and clear, then the sound of chalk scratching against the blackboard. Father straightened his suit, took in a lungful, exhaled slowly, and put his hand on the door-knob.

This was probably the first classroom he'd be in since . . . when? Many years ago, in a different country. All he was trying to do was make things better for himself and the rest of us. But did he have to drag the whole family to this thing? Noona and I were doing just fine, learning at school and through television, and Mother couldn't care less. If Father wasn't afraid, wouldn't he just go by himself and leave us in peace?

Who knows. He turned the knob, pushed open the creaky door, and there we stood, a Korean family in America, ready and willing to learn, and impeccably dressed to boot.

"Welcome," John Reeves said. "Welcome to ESL 012."

In our second ESL class, we were each given a big softcover workbook titled *Communicating in English*. John Reeves's name was on the cover. "Look, he's written a book," Father whispered.

I flipped through the book. It was hard to read most of the pages because they were photocopies of photocopies of photocopies. A closer look revealed that none of it was original—it was all copied from other books.

"He didn't write this," I whispered back to Father, but he shushed me. John Reeves was telling the class that for the next fifteen minutes, we were going to converse with one another with what he defined as "small talk"—a method of spoken communication composed of current news, the weather, and anything else that was strictly informational. "Small talk is very important," Reeves had said at the beginning of class. "It is how strangers become friends." Reeves split us into groups: me, Father, and Aarti the Indian woman; Noona and Xiu; Demeke and Yan. "Emma," Reeves addressed Mother, the one left without a group, "I'll be your partner." Again I looked to Father, and again his attention was elsewhere, busy making small talk with the Indian woman.

"For some ideas, turn to page fifteen," Reeves announced. He and Mother were sitting side by side on his desk, and he said something to make her laugh, but it hardly sounded like her. It was a higher-pitched girlish laughter that reminded me more of my sister than my mother.

Father found the page and loosened his tie. There were better ways of standing out from the crowd than putting on a black suit in the middle of a heat wave, but I kept quiet. I was just glad he didn't force me to dress like him.

"Nice wae-dah we ahh habing," Father read to Aarti.

"I hear it is going to rain," Aarti read back in her sing-song Indian accent. In the background Mother laughed again, and this time Father had no way of avoiding my gaze. For a second Father's face exhibited spectacular anger—then it let go, like a tight rubber band suddenly snapping back to its loose loopy form. He smiled wanly and gestured for me to participate. I turned to page fifteen to recite my line.

"I am glad I brought an umbrella," I said.

On Wednesday, I was standing inside our store's island of showcases and straightening out the cloisonné necklace section, my mind turning over the events of the night before, trying to form a plan of action.

My sister was sitting on the stool and doing her nails, clipping and filing and buffing, currently at the brown-side-of-the-emery-board stage. Spread out on top of the silk purses showcase stood six bottles of nail polish, looking like miniature missiles waiting for their launch. She was still deciding on the color; she eventually settled on a deep burgundy labeled AUTUMN PLUM.

"Speak," Noona said, her arm extended and her fingers flat and together, admiring her handiwork.

I asked her about Reeves and Mother, and she said, "Duh." When I told her I didn't like what was going on, she shrugged me off, nonchalant.

"We should do something," I said.

"It's their business. Besides, what's there to do?"

I told her my plan, which was greeted with a snort.

"What, are you joking?" When she saw my sincerity, it made her even meaner. "That's television, Junior. That's not real life. What's happened to your brain?"

"I don't know," I said, more depressed than ever. Something bad was happening between Father and Mother, and I wasn't smart enough to think up anything better.

Noona slowly raised her eyes from her nails. She stared at me for a good long while, looked back to her nails, and said, "All right, fine."

"You'll do it?"

Noona nodded. She could be a good big sister when she wanted to. "I like getting dressed up, anyway."

"I'll buy you a bottle of nail polish."

That evening, as we drove out to MC3, Noona looked more than ready to play her part. Her makeup was perfection: just a hint of rouge on her cheeks, and her lips and nails matched in a deep dark black-rose red. She was wearing a long-sleeved shirt, but once we got to class, she would say how hot the room was and reveal a tight, spaghetti-strapped tank top to woo Reeves with her perky set of "cha-chas" (her words) and the world's cutest belly button (her delusion).

Reeves, in his usual getup of a pressed white shirt and khaki pants, told us at the start of class that tonight was "listening night." He brought out a giant children's book—*Goodnight Moon* was its title—and set it on an easel. "My mother read this to me for many, many nights when I was a child," said Reeves. "Not this one, obviously—this is a special large edition for teaching. As I read, I will point"—and here he pointed—"to the pictures that match the words. We'll move onto more adult books in future classes, but I always start with this, a kind of a tradition, you could say."

He flipped to the first page, which showed a green room and a bed with a rabbit in it. "In the great green room," he started, and proceeded to go through page after page. Why was there a rabbit in a human bed? What did mush taste like? And why were we told to say good night to all these inanimate objects? It was a strange book. I tried to remember any comparable Korean children's stories, but the only thing I recalled was the tale of the precocious flying monkey. His name escaped me, but he was forced to wear a gold crown on his head and he caused mischief everywhere he went. Mother had read that story to me, sitting in the rocking chair, her whisper lulling me to sleep. That was at least six or seven years ago, and it was one of the few moments from early childhood

I could still recall with great clarity. I could see why Reeves enjoyed reading *Goodnight Moon*.

Unfortunately, Reeves being all wrapped up in his childish nostalgia negated Noona's efforts. She'd already taken off her shirt, but Reeves just kept on reading and pointing. Noona hiked up her skirt some and dramatically crossed her legs—which caught the eye of just about everyone in the classroom, including Father, who gaped at Noona with a combination of shock and shame—but that also had no effect on Reeves. Frustrated, she said, "Excuse me," interrupting Reeves as he was bidding good night to a pair of mittens in the voice of the book's narrator.

"Yes, Susan? Do you have a question?" Reeves looked at Noona and waited, without a trace of recognition of my sister's attempted sexiness. She'd been right; this was a really stupid idea.

"No," Noona said. She put her shirt back on and slumped into her chair. She wouldn't even look at me, which was bad sign. It meant she blamed me, and there weren't enough bottles of nail polish in the world to save me from her wrath.

In between pages, Reeves glanced at Mother, and I couldn't believe I hadn't noticed it all along; her eyes were locked with his. Mother smiled for him, laughed for him, focused her entire being on him. The reason why Reeves kept on was because my mother was reciprocating his advances. Why would she do such a thing? As far as I knew, Father hadn't made any financial blunders lately, but I didn't know for sure. Even so, if Mother were getting back at Father for some monetary fiasco coming down the line, her actions here seemed like an unreasonable way to retaliate.

At the end of class, Reeves bid everyone a wonderful weekend. He assigned homework for the next meeting: watch two shows on TV and see a movie in the theater. "I want you back here next Monday," he told everyone, though I knew he really only meant it for Mother.

F ather and I were watching *Diff'rent Strokes,* starring that oh-so-hilarious and chubby-cheeked Gary Coleman and his entourage of soon-to-be-criminal siblings. About fifteen years down the line, Willis would serve time for coke possession and Kimberly would be dead of a drug overdose, but then and there, they looked like the happiest family in the world. Their father was filthy rich, they lived in a palace, and they had a wise-cracking maid. If only I could jump into television and join the Drummunds—I could fit right in as the Korean orphan boy who saves Arnold's life when he's surrounded by a gang of nogoodniks in the heart of Koreatown. There I would be, named Chu or Ping, karate-chopping the hell out of the thugs and having Arnold say his catchphrase: "Whatchoo talkin' about, Chu?"

Father wasn't gung ho about doing the assignments.

"I don't know, Joon-a," he told me. "Do you like the class?"

He wanted a way out. Maybe he felt embarrassed for dragging us over there and then giving up so quickly, but it looked like the goings-on between Mother and Reeves were finally getting to him.

I told Father, "No, I don't like the class."

"Me neither."

Then he waited, maybe for me to suggest a course of action. I said nothing.

On Friday night, before we closed up shop, Mother asked me if there were any movies I wanted to see. "Do I?" I answered. I was dying to see *Raiders of the Lost Ark.* It looked like a winner—a guy named Indiana Jones whipping Nazis, finding treasure, and getting the girl. I guffawed every time the television played that bit where the Arabian guy is showing off his spectacular swordsmanship and Harrison Ford just shoots him.

I shouldn't have supported Mother in this venture. I should have stuck by Father and told her that there was nothing worth seeing, but I was feeling opportunistic, like the way those old explorers must have felt when they stood at the edge of a primitive civilization and saw all they could take. Greed overcame my good sense.

"It's late," Father told Mother. "And I think we're all a little tired."

Mother fired back: "Sure we're tired, but we'll always be tired. It's no excuse for not learning."

Father was going to say something then decided against it. Flanking Mother were Noona on her left and me on her right. Outnumbered, Father sighed, and gave me a look worthy of a Caesar betrayed.

Watching the movie was like riding a roller coaster. Starting with the boulder-chasing-Indiana intro, the film never let up. The theater was packed, a great rowdy Friday night crowd that ooohed and aaahed with every cliff-hanging scene. I missed a lot of what was going on, and the ending was a mystery to me, but it was still fun. As the credits rolled and the lights slowly returned to brightness, I sat back and reveled in the magical moment. The big screen, the big sound, the captivated audience. It was all that I'd hoped for.

"Can we go?" Father asked me sharply. I'd completely forgotten about him.

"Did you like the picture?"

He stood up. "Yes. Let's go."

The morning after, in an attempt to alleviate my guilt, I got up early and made Father his favorite breakfast: two scrambled eggs and three strips of bacon. "Thank you," he said, though he still sounded mad. As he ate, we watched *The Smurfs* and I explained the show to him. "The guy with the glasses, he's Brainy, he's smart. And the guy with the tattoo, he's Hefty, he's strong."

"And Handy," Father said, "is the builder. The one carrying a T-square who has the pencil stuck in his ear?"

"This is a great show," I said. "It's really good for us, because the people's names are what they do."

"It is a fine show," Father agreed. "They're very blue."

"I was thinking, maybe instead of going to that class three times a week, we can watch *The Smurfs* and I can teach English to you and Mother." It sounded ridiculous, but Father looked as if I told him we'd won the lottery.

"You really think so?"

"*The Smurfs* and *Diff'rent Strokes,* that's a great show, too. When school starts up again, I can bring home whatever I'm learning and show you guys so you can learn, too."

"That would be wonderful, Joon-a," Father said, not only thankful but proud. "Look at you, already taking care of your parents."

Taking care of them? I hardly thought that was true. Father busted his butt at our store six days a week, and on the only day he had off, he went to New York. Unlike most of my friends, whose fathers worked at companies that paid steady salaries, Father had no such fixed luxury. And he did all that with his broken English.

On Monday evening, after Father returned from New York with another carload of goods, Mother made dinner, washed the dishes, and got ready for class.

"I thought we weren't going anymore," I asked Father.

He got up and went into their bedroom. He came back out a minute later, slump-shouldered. "She says she's going."

"Why?"

"I don't know what's wrong."

"You're going to let her go?"

"Listen," Father said. "I want you to go with her."

"What?"

"Yes."

"No way."

"Please, you have to."

After being embarrassed in the last class, I knew Noona wasn't going. She wasn't even talking to me. "Why don't *you* go with her?" I said, and was immediately sorry. "Fine, I'll go."

"My good son," he said in English, a phrase I'd come to despise.

The door to my parents' bedroom opened and out came Mother. The hair, the face, the nails, the shoes—I'd never seen her so dolled up. She looked at Father defiantly. "I'm going to class."

Without a word, Father stepped around her and walked into their bedroom. He slammed the door, the whole apartment shaking from the impact.

I had no idea what was going on. I was afraid, but I said it anyway: "I'd like to go to class, too." I'd wanted it to come out strong, but instead it came out shaky. She was ready to deny my request, but the mixture of fear and courage in my voice softened her up. She nodded.

In the car she didn't say a word. I sat next to her and stared out the window as we passed by Oceanview Mall, the Mobil gas station, and rows and rows of trees. This was my favorite part of the drive, before we headed into the ugly city of Neptune, and this was where I heard Mother cry. Mascara-streaked tears ran down her cheeks.

At the intersection of Pine Street and Route 35, she pulled over. She was practically bawling at this point, and I was terrified. I sat next to her like an idiot, my hands stuck under my thighs, and not knowing what else to do, I started to cry myself. Call it a sympathetic response, but there we were, mother and son on the shoulder of the highway, weeping away as if it were the end of the world.

"Why are you crying?" Mother managed to ask in between sobs.

"I don't know," I said, and that made both of us cry even harder.

Eventually we stopped, probably because we were just tired of it. Mother flipped down the visor and peered into the tiny mirror, trying her best to clean up. She had all kinds of stuff in her handbag, including a small jar of Ponds cold cream that turned her into a kabuki player then back to the mother I'd always known.

"Are you feeling better?" she asked me.

"Are you?"

"Yes," she said. And they weren't empty words—she did look better, cleaner, lighter, like she'd somehow purged herself of whatever was bothering her. At least for now.

"Me too."

"Is it okay if we don't go to class?"

"Yes."

Mother signaled, pulled a U-turn, and we were on our way back home. She told me I could turn on the radio, so I found a station that played the oldies. I wanted to ask why she'd been so upset, but I knew she wouldn't tell me. "It's not your place," she would say, like she'd said countless other times.

"It's nothing you should worry about," she said when I finally broke down and asked her. "I'm sorry I upset you."

"I'm not upset. I'm fine."

"You're just not old enough to know about certain things."

Whatever, I said to myself. If I told this story to Noona, she'd probably end up talking to Mother, then Noona would tell me. Unless she somehow got all hoity-toity and agreed with Mother that I should be left in the dark.

At home we found Father watching a strange movie where ants got huge and started attacking people.

"Did class end early?" Father asked.

I waited for Mother to answer, but she didn't.

"We didn't go," I said. "We changed our minds."

"Oh," Father said, and seeing that he wasn't going to get any more information, went on staring at the TV.

Mother went into my room to talk with Noona. Father got comfortable on the couch and invited me to sit. "Good job, Joon-a," he said, ruffling my hair. "I knew I could count on you." Then he winked.

What happened in the car must have had something to do with this man sitting next to me, this man who was my father, who called me his good son and winked like a crook. Who was he? And for that matter, who was Mother? I'd known her my entire life and had known him for six months. Together, they were an inscrutable puzzle.

"You're right, Joon-a," Father said. "We can learn from television and from you, but you know what we really need?"

I was afraid to ask.

"What we need are American friends. Friends who'll talk to us, friends who'll teach us."

"Who?"

"I haven't figured that out yet, but you know, Joon-a, there are plenty of Americans in Peddlers Town, aren't there?"

Yes, there were. And none of them, not one, wanted to befriend a screwed-up family like ours.

TED MCMANUS

THINGS COULD BE WORSE—that's what Ted McManus was thinking when the vacuum vomited something black and metallic.

"Oh shit," he said, and stepped on the power button, which had been broken for a month. He ran for the plug, but the vacuum, already smoking up a burnt rubber stink, came to a squeaky halt on its own.

"What happened?" Eileen asked. She yanked at the cord and it came at her like a whip.

"How many times do I have to tell you not to pull out the plug like that?"

"I don't care about the cord. Is that smoke?"

"That's how things break. Here"—Ted pointed at the accordionlike joint between the plug and the cord—"this is the relief joint. You're going against the physics of the product when you pull it out like that."

"Oh, I see. So I broke the vacuum, right? I broke the physics of the product. That's why it's stinking up the whole store."

Ted choked the cord around the vacuum, avoiding looking at his wife. When he finally did look up, he found her staring into the giant round mirror that was Cimmetri's centerpiece. A year ago, they had paid twenty-five hundred dollars for that mirror. Twenty-five hundred dollars just hanging there, doing nothing but reflecting their naiveté.

"I think we got a great deal," he'd said.

"It's expensive, but it's so gorgeous," she said.

"It'll sell within a month. Or I have no business sense."

After a year, Cimmetri was barely breaking even, and both of them were to blame.

Ted turned the Hoover on its side. He pried open the bottom panel and peered carefully. "I think the belt came off."

Eileen came over and perched over his shoulder. Ted did the best he could, but he eventually had to say it: "You're blocking the light, honey." Without a word, she went back to cleaning the crystal figurines displayed inside the bi-leveled hexagonal showcase.

"But honey," Ted said, "you were."

She'd finished buffing the top level, the mammals, which included a dog, a cat, a bear, and two pandas, all made out of tiny crystal balls glued together. The bottom level was a family of clowns—laughing clown, juggling clown, fat clown, and baby clown, complete with a microscopic pacifier. Underneath the showcase was stock—two of everything, untouched.

Only one figurine had sold, an octopus, the one that the wholesaler had begged them to take. Who'd want to buy an octopus? They bought it as a joke, but the joke was on them: After they sold their one and only, they had five more requests for it. It drove them crazy. Nothing made sense in the retail world.

Watching her polish the crystals, Ted wondered if Eileen missed her old job as hostess at Thirsty Pete's. At least at the restaurant, there was logic: People wanted seats as quickly as possible and all she had to do was act pleasant even if they were crabby.

Ted wiped the sweat off his forehead with the back of his hand, careful to keep the grime off his face. He looked down at the vacuum, its innards splayed on the floor. His hands were as filthy as a mechanic's. At AT&T, where Ted had worked for over twenty years behind a desk, the only mess he encountered was in the form of copier toner. He'd also reported to four demanding bosses, met ridiculous deadlines week after week, covered his ass before a project blew up—but really, had it been any worse than this?

As his fingers jammed into the guts of the machine, Ted regretted buying this dump of a store from the previous owner. He and Eileen had considered two other possibilities before plopping down a good part of their nest egg on Cimmetri, a café and a candy shop. They never should've chosen to sell something as frivolous as mirrors. Everybody drank coffee and ate sweets, and although people used mirrors on a daily basis, how often did they actually buy one?

"Damn it," Ted said as a thin silver rod sprang up and bounced away from him.

"Let me try," Eileen said, picking it up. She placed it back into the cradle, but she couldn't make it fit, either. A closer examination of the dark crevice revealed a smell not unlike rotting garbage. "Oh, Lord," she said.

"It's awful," Ted said. "Like something threw up and died."

"Look," Eileen said, pointing at East Meets West, the Oriental gift store across from them. Mr. Kim was running a vacuum that looked remarkably identical to their Hoover, at least from afar. "I've seen him fiddle with his. I think he's good at fixing stuff."

"You know he doesn't speak English very well," Ted said.

"Oh, come on, this isn't rocket science. Just go up and ask, what's the hurt in that?"

"All right. You stay here and mind the store."

Ted thoroughly scrubbed his hands in the bathroom, ran a comb over his almost-bald head, and stuffed in a loose shirttail. Although Mr. Kim had been his cross-hallway neighbor since he moved in a year ago, he'd hardly said anything beyond a simple greeting. Mr. Kim always said "Hi," never "Hello." He'd heard somewhere that Asians had trouble pronouncing "L" words. Was Mr. Kim avoiding all words that had the "L" sound? What kind of a conversation would they have if it excluded L's?

Mrs. Kim, busy dusting the vases in the corner, stopped and stared at Ted as he walked in the store. When he tried to meet her eyes, she immediately looked at her feet. The two kids who usually sat behind the showcases were nowhere to be found. "Mr. Kim," Ted said, his voice a little high. Oblivious, Mr. Kim kept vacuuming. "Mr. Kim," Ted said again, this time louder and more normal.

"Hi," Mr. Kim said, turning off his vacuum. He pushed up his black-rimmed glasses with his thumb. "You need?"

Still no "L" words, Ted thought. "I think you and I have the same vacuum cleaner, and there's something wrong with mine. Can I . . ."

"Sure," he said, and flipped his vacuum upside down with some effort. "I see. Here," he said, and let Ted have a good look. "You see?"

Ted tried, but it was impossible to figure out the problem. "I'm sorry, but no."

"Get vacuum," Mr. Kim said. "Let me look."

"Okay," he said, and hurried back.

"Are things okay?" Eileen asked.

"Sure. He wants to help."

"So he *can* speak English after all, huh?"

"Yeah, yeah," Ted said, and returned to the waiting Mr. Kim, who looked back and forth between the two machines a number of times. Mr. Kim's sideburns were inching toward grayness, and Ted wondered why a man his age—probably in his mid-forties—would leave everything he knew and come to a whole different place where he would have to start all over again. He didn't know whether to admire his courage or question his foolhardiness.

Mr. Kim crouched down to look at the back of the vacuum. As he examined the chassis, he asked, "You like my name?"

"Excuse me?"

"Harry, my name."

Ted laughed, but seeing Harry Kim's face, he immediately regretted it.

"What's funny?"

"Nothing," Ted said.

"Not like Harry?"

"No, I didn't mean that . . ."

"I pick Harry. Dirty Harry. I like gun." He cocked his finger and pointed it at Ted. "Bang!" he yelled.

Ted flinched. He didn't know what to say. Then Mr. Kim laughed. "Kidding," he said. "No gun."

Ted laughed out of surprise more than humor; the idea that Mr. Kim could be joking never crossed his mind. Mr. Kim pulled a chair up for him, pushed his cash register aside, and put the two vacuums on his large metal desk. He turned on the desk lamp and bent its gooseneck to gain maximum luminance.

It didn't take them long to figure out the problem: Ted had put the belt on the wrong spoke. Mr. Kim crawled under his desk, plugged in Ted's vacuum, and it came back to life.

"Good," Mr. Kim said, then crinkled his nose. "Stinky."

"I think I need to change the bag," Ted said. "Listen, thank you very much. You just saved me a lot of grief. And a lot of money."

"No problem."

"Maybe I can buy you a drink or something," Ted said, although he hoped Mr. Kim would decline. What would they talk about over beer? Vacuums and Clint Eastwood?

"No pro . . ." Mr. Kim started to say, then stopped. Ted saw a glint of something behind those eyeglasses. ". . . blem," he finished. He offered the vacuum's handle.

"Thanks again," Ted said, and rolled the vacuum back to his store.

"Next time . . . ," Mr. Kim said, then trailed off.

Ted turned. "Yes?"

Mr. Kim waved him off. "No, no. No problem."

"No," Ted said. "What did you want to tell me?"

"Next time," Mr. Kim said, "you help me, maybe."

"Sure," Ted said. "You just let me know, okay? Harry?"

"Okay, Ted," Mr. Kim said, and returned to vacuuming his rug.

What could he have in mind? There was something embarrassing about the way he'd asked. He was about to tell Eileen of his encounter with Mr. Kim when he saw his son standing beside her.

"Billy?" he asked, trying to remember if he forgot why he was here.

"Dad," Billy said, giving him a quick hug. The last time Ted had seen him was over Easter weekend. He looked different somehow, older, maybe.

"What are you doing here? Why aren't you at work?"

Billy turned to Eileen. Eileen looked down. "Oh Christ, Mom," Billy said, on the verge of tears, and ran out of the store. Seeing the back of Billy's head, Ted realized what was different about him: He was going bald.

"Eileen?" Ted asked. She sat down and bit her fingernails. "Eileen?" Ted asked again. "Why is Billy here?"

"Oh, Ted," Eileen said. "I didn't want to worry you. With your high blood pressure and all. I wanted to tell you, but you're always so busy with things."

Ted let that one go. He took a deep breath, sat down in front of her, and waited. A young couple came in and pawed at a couple of full-length mirrors, leaving their fingerprints everywhere. They held hands and laughed, looking at each other's reflections.

The routine was a familiar one for Ted; after Eileen finished biting her fingernails, she filed them down. This was how she talked to him about difficult things, cutting around her cuticles, clipping the ragged ends clean.

"Billy's been out of work since May," she began. Ted blinked a couple of times. He thought of all the obvious replies he could provide with justifiable anger, but instead of blowing up, he grabbed the Bic pen lying nearby. He noted the blue cap, the gnawed-off clip, the tiny man with a big black ball for a head.

"What has he been doing for all these months?"

"What do you think he's been doing? Looking for a job. But it's hard to find one right now, with the economy the way it is."

"Don't blame the economy."

"Oh, Ted, you know it's hard for Billy. He's not exactly the outgoing type."

Ted got up and stretched. He had read somewhere that you should pretend to reach for the stars to really stretch, not only physically but also mentally. Ted reached hard, but all that came to him was an unwelcome invasion of superhuman tiredness that spread all the way down to his toes.

"He couldn't pay last month's rent. He's got no money. His unemployment doesn't pay for half of his expenses."

"So he's going to stay with us. Where is he going to sleep? On our loveseat?" After Billy had gotten his assistant editor job with Henry Holt, they had sold their house and moved to a two-bedroom condo. The spare bedroom was still more like a warehouse, with mountains of unopened boxes filling every corner, so the living room was the only option.

"It's only going to be for a while. You still have that army cot, don't you?"

Ted's last memory of the cot was Billy taking it out of the attic and loading it into the trunk of his Honda for some camping trip with his artsy-fartsy college friends, the ones who wore black turtlenecks and smoked long, thin cigarettes.

Billy came back an hour later with a pot of yellow chrysanthemums for Eileen and a small box of chocolate-covered cherries for Ted. "I'm sorry I blew up like that," he said, and asked them if there was anything he could do around here to make their lives a little bit easier.

Ted looked at the red digits of the alarm clock and saw that it was ten past one. Was it the heat that was keeping him up? It was another scorching night, their central air running a constant hum. He couldn't remember the last time he couldn't fall asleep, but here he lay, sleep as far away as China, which was strange because things were looking up for everybody. The store was doing a little better, Billy had a couple of interviews lined up with some publishing houses, and Eileen was happier with their son around. Seeing them together again for the past month reminded Ted of just how little he and Billy actually talked, but he shrugged it off. Some sons were closer to their mothers than their fathers, and at this point of their lives, there was nothing he could do about it. He was just glad to have Eileen laughing again.

Lying in bed, Ted wished for a hard-on. As he stroked himself, he thought back to when they had just married, when they woke each other up in the middle of the night to screw. He looked over to his wife, and he started to feel the beginnings of fullness when he heard the doorknob of their bedroom turn.

"Ummm," Eileen said. The doorknob stopped turning. Ted waited. Eileen shifted around and started snoring lightly. Slowly, somebody pushed the door open. Ted pretended to be asleep. He thought of the baseball bat in the closet; he wondered if he'd have time to get to it. Slowly the door was . . . being pulled closed?

Ted crawled out of bed and crept over to the door. Somebody was walking around—and then he remembered Billy. Was he all right? He heard the flick of a cigarette lighter. Soft, uneven light seeped in from under the door—candlelight. Then a snapping, like a rubber band. Ted pulled the door open with steady hands, just a crack, so he could peek out.

Billy was on the couch, his legs spread apart. There was something shiny on his legs, and it took Ted a couple of seconds to realize that it was pantyhose. Billy's left hand pulled the waistband down below his testicles while his right hand made a fist around his erection and started a slow pumping motion. Billy had his eyes closed, his neck muscles taut like cables.

Ted closed the door. He stood there, thankful for the darkness that engulfed him, trying hard not to think of what was going on beyond his bedroom.

I n the morning, he avoided Billy. The only time they were in close proximity was in the car. Ted managed to completely bypass the rearview mirror during the drive to the store.

How was he going to approach this with his son? He'd heard of men wearing women's clothes, but only on TV. It was an episode of some soap opera that Eileen was watching, where the husband was caught wearing the wife's slinky evening dress . . . which brought up another question: Whose pantyhose was Billy wearing? The thought of Billy going into Eileen's drawers and fishing out a pair of black stockings made Ted uneasy. His son buying a pair from a lingerie store wasn't exactly better: standing next to faceless mannequins wearing garter belts and lacy panties, selecting pantyhose that'd fit him best. What had he told the saleswoman at the counter, that he was buying them for his girlfriend?

Maybe his son was gay, which had been in the back of Ted's mind throughout most of Billy's high-school days, when he didn't go on a single date with a girl. All that changed his senior year, when he went steady with that flag twirler. Not that Ted would have disowned him or anything stupid like that if he was homosexual, but it just would've made things harder for everyone, Billy especially.

At the store, Ted was glad UPS came by early to drop off a shipment. Ordinarily, the prospect of putting out more mirrors he couldn't sell depressed him, but today he was grateful for the distraction. There were three boxes in all, and each contained two dozen smaller boxes of various handheld mirrors, the kind barbers and hairdressers used to display the backside of haircuts to their customers.

Ted gave the price gun to Billy and showed him how to use it.

"Why does everything end in '99'?" Billy asked. "You know, like why '$4.99' instead of '$5'?"

"It makes it look cheaper," Ted said. "It's psychology."

As the day wore on, Ted became sure about one thing: He wasn't going to tell Eileen about last night. It was a given that if he were to tell her, she'd immediately talk to their son herself. Maybe this was a blessing in disguise. By handling this crisis himself, a bond that never existed before might form between them. After all, what bond was stronger than one forged with guilt?

"Hi," Mr. Kim said.

Standing next to him was his son David, who seemed distracted by the multitude of reflections Cimmetri's mirrors offered.

"Hey, guys," Ted said.

"Busy?"

"No, what can I do for you?"

"Remember?" he said, gesturing a vacuuming motion. His voice sounded strained, forced.

"Yes," Ted said, and looking at Mr. Kim, Ted realized what he really meant. "Yes, I remember, Harry."

Mr. Kim nodded. "Next Sunday, seven o'clock. Dinner my house."

Ted didn't know if he understood. "Dinner . . . as in you want me to . . . come to dinner?"

"You, your wife, your son."

"To dinner?"

"Busy?"

It would've been easy to say just that, but Ted couldn't do it. Maybe if Mr. Kim had come alone, but there was something sinful about lying in front of both him and his son. "No. It's Sunday night. We usually eat McDonald's on Sunday nights."

"Hamburger we make. Hamburger or spaghetti?"

"Hamburger."

"Okay," Mr. Kim said. "Thank you."

Mr. Kim was gone before Ted could ask him why and what for. At the threshold of East Meets West, his wife was waiting for him. He spoke to her, she nodded, they both looked over.

"Thank you, Mr. McManus," David said with perfect pronunciation. Ted had forgotten that he was still there.

"What's going on with this dinner? Why does your father want us to be there?"

The boy stayed quiet.

"You don't want to tell me?"

"I don't know all English well," David said. It was an excuse, Ted could tell.

"You speak fine."

"Thank you. See you Sunday," he said, and ran back to his store.

When David left, Billy came over and asked, "What was all that about?"

"We're going to have dinner with them next Sunday."

"Why?"

"I don't know."

"What?"

"Never mind," Ted said. He met Billy's eyes for a moment, still not sure how to talk to him. "Hey, have you eaten yet?"

"No."

"Let's go to Jake's, you and me."

"What about Mom?"

She was busy spraying and wiping picture frames with Windex. "Just bring something back for me," she said, which meant the usual— chicken Caesar salad.

Hometown Grill was still being rebuilt, but a small portion of the restaurant was now open. Sitting at their table, Ted ordered two quarter-pounders and a basket of onion rings for an appetizer. Billy told Ted about the two interviews that he had coming up. Springer-Verlag, a scholarly publishing house, was located in the Flatiron Building near Madison Square Park. "I think I can get that one," Billy said, "but I'd rather work for Knopf. More challenging."

Ted listened blankly, his mind preoccupied on the proper mechanics of bringing up what he had seen last night. No time seemed like the right time, and lunch was quickly coming to a close: The burgers were gone and only two onion rings remained, the napkin inside the basket translucent with overlapping oily circles.

"I'm going to run to the men's room," Billy said, and Ted was momentarily relieved. He walked over to the bar and ordered two bottles of Heineken and drank almost all of his by the time Billy came back.

"Billy," Ted said in the softest, kindest voice he could muster. "Why are you wearing women's pantyhose?"

Billy took several big gulps of beer and belched quietly. Neither spoke for what seemed like a long time. He finished his beer and tried to peel off the front label. He got halfway when it ripped jaggedly.

"Are you ashamed of me?" Billy asked.

"No," Ted said immediately. *Be truthful,* he told himself, and made himself say, "Well, I don't know. Maybe."

"Does Mom know?"

"No."

Again, they were silent. Ted began to regret not involving Eileen in this mess. Maybe this was not the right thing to do. Maybe a secret this shameful needed to be spread between two people.

"Do you want to know why?" Billy asked.

He wanted to look at Billy, but he couldn't. Instead, he stared at his empty green bottle and nodded.

In his third year of college, Billy took up scuba diving to fulfill a phys-ed requirement. The worst thing about the class was putting on the wetsuit, which was made out of neoprene and almost painful to put over dry skin. This was when his instructor, Monica, suggested that he wear a pair of pantyhose.

"I remember laughing about it with her. Should I get the sheer-to-waist variety? Perhaps I should get Silken Mist in Pearl so I'll have that zip in my step. She got me a pair, my first pair, a black sheer one from L'Eggs, the kind that come in a little egg." Billy had the look of someone remembering a kiss, a dreamy, faraway gaze. "When I put them on, I felt a tingle. Like my skin was alive, and I . . ." He stopped. "I'm sorry, Dad, I can't tell you this."

"No, it's fine," Ted said, even though it wasn't.

"It's something I can't explain. I never thought I would get turned on by it, but once I put them on, I just didn't want to take them off."

"So that pair you were wearing last night . . . is it the same pair?" It was a stupid question, but Ted didn't know what else to say.

Billy laughed. "No, of course not. They don't last that long. Even the ones that advertise they're long-lasting."

"They're not your mother's, right?"

"Jesus, that's disgusting, Dad!"

They looked at each other and burst out laughing. "Whatever you say, Billy," Ted said.

After they settled down, Billy got serious again. "You going to tell Mom?"

"I will if you want me to."

His son hesitated for a moment, but then made up his mind. "No. I'd rather she didn't know."

"That's fine." He looked into Billy's eyes and smiled. There was something new there, he was sure of it, a brightness like a star, a star only he could see. "Let's get back to the store."

"Okay. Let me go back to the bathroom, though."

"Again?"

"I need to . . . adjust something."

"You're wearing . . . ?" Ted asked, incredulous.

"Sometimes I like to wear them underneath. I'll be back."

Ted waited. He tried not to think about it. He failed.

Ted looked at his watch. It was 10:14. He still had two hours left.

On the king-sized bed was a pair of Eileen's pantyhose, the sheer flat legs crisscrossing each other over the pink sheets. He tried to find black ones; the darkest ones in Eileen's underwear drawer were the color of chestnuts.

He was naked except for a shirt. His clothes sat in a small, neat pile on the top of the dresser. He felt hot, maybe from the continuing heat wave that was grilling the tri-state area, more likely from what he was about to do.

He looked at his watch again. Eileen and Billy were at the movies, due back around midnight, and this was nuts. What would she say if she were to walk through those doors right now? Ted couldn't even imagine her response. The most pizzazz they'd attempted in the bed-room was having her on top. In all their years together, he'd never cheated on her, but this felt something like that.

He held the pantyhose and sniffed them. They smelled like Eileen, a strong baby powder–like scent. He stretched a leg between his fingers and peered at the bedroom lamp through the network of thin fibers, the light shimmying through in an orange haze.

He rolled up one leg like the way he'd seen his wife do many times. His fingers, being much rougher than hers, caught the pantyhose, but he managed to roll it up between his index finger and thumb.

He slipped the shiny fabric over his left leg, then he put on the right leg. He stood up and carefully pulled a little at a time, so all of his lower body was covered under a soft brown shine.

He walked around. On one step, it felt like being trapped. On an-other, he felt freer than ever. He ran his hands over his legs and felt a smoothness he'd never experienced on his own body. He lay on the bed and stared at his tight thighs, which glistened like fish. An erection grew so hard that it hurt. He spread his legs and pushed down the pantyhose.

When he was through, when the shame had ebbed away, he tried to think about why he had done this. There were two possibilities: Either this was his way of somehow getting closer to Billy—or it was just pure sexual curiosity. Neither of these explanations seemed entirely healthy.

Eileen and Billy returned to find Ted sitting in his La-Z-Boy, watching the Phillies-Mets ballgame. Ted hoped that Billy would somehow know what had transpired during their absence, but of course, he seemed to sense nothing. He thought about telling Billy but decided against it. Keeping all these secrets to himself got him more excited than he wanted to admit.

That night, he and Eileen made incredible love. Just thinking about the pantyhose got Ted wild. Eileen, short of breath, told him in the middle, "My God, Ted, you're going to give me a heart attack."

"I'll go slower," he said, also out of breath.

"No way," she said, and dug her fingernails into his back.

Afterwards, Eileen wanted to know what was going on, but she didn't press it. She was too happy to question and fell asleep quickly. Spooning her body, he knew he'd tell her someday, but that day wasn't here yet.

Next morning, while Eileen was cooking breakfast, he slipped on the brown pantyhose and pulled his pants over them. Every step he took felt airy and full of energy, just like those commercials on TV where the stockinged women galloped and sashayed across the city street.

It was a fairly busy Sunday, a surprising number of customers keeping him hopping from the register to the stockroom and back again, and at times Ted forgot that he was even wearing them. Every time he did remember, he felt a pleasant tingle.

At seven o'clock, as he and Billy lowered the canvas curtains and threw on the locks, Mr. Kim came over. He said hellos to Eileen and Billy, then turned to Ted.

"You follow?" he said.

"I'm sorry?"

"Remember?" Billy said. "We're going over to Mr. Kim's for dinner tonight."

He had forgotten, and under normal circumstances, after a tiring day at work, this would have gotten him in a foul mood, but all he had to do was think about what he was wearing underneath to perk himself up.

"Yes, I'll follow you," he said to Mr. Kim, who nodded quickly and gathered up his family.

Mr. Kim was one of those nightmare drivers who seemed to brake for no reason, so Ted kept a safe distance. Ted looked back at Billy in the rearview mirror and tried to catch his eye, but he always semed to be looking away.

The Kims lived in an apartment complex, on the second floor. At the top of the stairs, Mr. Kim opened the door and let in his wife and kids. It was like an oven in there, and the first thing the boy did was run to the air conditioner and turn it on. Ted, Eileen, and Billy followed. The kids were taking their shoes off, and so was Mr. Kim.

Ted looked at Billy, but Billy was busy taking his shoes off as well. He had on a pair of white athletic socks.

"What's the matter, Ted?" Eileen said, removing her shoes.

"Nothing," Ted replied, doing his best to keep calm. In the morning, he'd slipped on dress socks over the stockings, but a couple of hours later he took them off because his feet were sweating too much. In the stockroom of Cimmetri, Ted had laid those socks on the topmost shelf so they could dry, and that's where they still were, two black socks like commas, pausing in the darkness.

Everyone else was already in the living room. Ted took a deep breath; the lights were dim enough that maybe no one would notice his sheer, glistening feet. Billy and Eileen sat on the loveseat while Mr. Kim and his two kids sat on the sofa. In the kitchen, the sound of running water stopped abruptly. The smell of sizzling meat began to permeate the apartment.

Ted scurried to the rocking chair and sat down. He crossed his feet underneath the seat and stayed still. Eileen and Billy looked over with the same expression on their faces: What the hell are we doing here?

"I like your place," Ted told Mr. Kim. "It's very homey." Actually, it was anything but. The living room was like an annex to their store at Peddlers Town, decorated with vases and figurines. Behind the television, a large round plaque depicted an ancient country scene with farmers and fields and mountains, which was magnificent except for an unsightly crack that ran from the top right edge of the plaque to the center. In one corner of the room, a pyramid of brown boxes rose from the top of the beat-up piano to the ceiling. What a strange way to live; the last thing Ted wanted from his home was to be reminded in any way of his store. He wouldn't last ten minutes in this place if he had to live here.

"Thank you," Mr. Kim said. "Nice weather we are having."

For the week so far, if it wasn't a hundred degrees outside, it was showering sheets of blinding rain. Ted nodded, not knowing what to say, and the longer the silence continued, the more he was certain he was somehow disappointing Mr. Kim. He wished for Eileen and Billy to rescue him, but they were talking intently with each other, chatting like best friends like they always did.

Mr. Kim cleared his throat. As if on cue, David, sitting beside his father, suddenly leaned forward and asked, "How is business, Mr. McManus?"

"It's okay. Could be better, of course, but it's been decent. How is your business going?"

And now it was the daughter's turn. "Business is okay," she blurted out, then slower as she tried to recall what Ted had just said, "it is slow also, this time of year, for us, too."

"Yes," Mr. Kim said, delighted. "Very slow business, this time of year, for us, too."

"Uh-huh," Ted said, and he realized what was going on. They were practicing their English on him. That's why he and his family had been invited tonight, so the Kims could brush up on their conversation skills. Were they their first American guests? It seemed like it, from the way they were acting, sitting tight and straight in their seats with their hands politely interlocked at their knees. Ted felt both pity and tenderness toward these people. All they wanted was to be Americans, and they'd asked him to show them how.

Ted smiled, and all three of them smiled back, his students. He'd teach them how to relax, to put their feet out and lean back, let the words flow out naturally. That was the key to any successful dialogue. There was no better way to educate than by example, so Ted loosened his shoulders and settled into his rocking chair. As expected, Mr. Kim mimicked his movement. Ted started to slide out his feet—but then remembered his stockings and stopped short. All three sets of eyes gazed down, and Ted felt blood rushing to his face.

Mrs. Kim emerged from the kitchen. In a tiny squeak of a voice, she said, "Dinner."

The dining room was brightly lit, so Ted knew he had to beat everyone. He jumped off the rocking chair—and slipped. He fell with flailing arms into the chair, then both he and the chair slammed backward to the floor. He closed his eyes on impact.

When he opened them again, he saw everyone looking down not at him but at his legs. Both cuffs of his pants had slipped all the way to his knees, exposing two hairy white legs wrapped up in brown pantyhose.

A giggle escaped from Mr. Kim's daughter, but it was cut short when Mrs. Kim elbowed her.

Eileen crouched down next to Ted and helped him to a sitting position. She was shocked, but her mothering instincts took over. "Are you all right?"

"I think so," he replied. He slowly got up and dusted himself. "Can I use your bathroom?" he asked Mr. Kim.

"Yes," he said, not looking at him, just pointing to the hallway.

Ted glanced at Billy and saw nothing but confusion on his son's face.

In the bathroom, he locked the door and sat down on the toilet. He sat there for a while. He had to take this stupid thing off. He unzipped his pants and dropped them to the floor. On the door was a full-length mirror, and for the first time, Ted looked at himself, his legs and ass looking like rotting summer sausage. What happened? Why was he in the bathroom of somebody he hardly knew, having dinner with people who barely spoke any English, and to top it all off, wearing his wife's stockings? If he had any guts at all, he would fill up the tub and throw himself facefirst into the water.

A knock. "Ted?"

"Hold on," he said. He peeled off his pantyhose, rolled it into a ball, stuffed it in the trash, and put his pants back on before unlocking the door. Eileen entered and closed the door behind her.

"Sit," she said, pointing to the toilet seat, so he did.

"Let me see your head," she said, so he tipped his head down.

It was just what he needed, to be told what to do. She felt around his scalp and touched a painful spot. She'd brought a sandwich bag of ice cubes and held it against the bump.

"Thanks," he said.

Eileen knelt down next to him, using her free hand to pat his thigh. "I think I know what's going on," she said, and Ted wanted to stop her. He hoped she didn't think he was some kind of a closet fruitcake, but before he could speak, she kissed him. "This has to do with Billy, doesn't it?"

Ted didn't know what to say. He stuttered and stumbled until he was able to ask, "How did you know?"

"Billy told me about his whole pantyhose thing," she said. "Right after he talked to you."

"He did, huh?" Ted said. His legs felt heavy and his toes were cold.

"So you just wanted to see what it was like . . . is that it?" Concern crossed her face, and Ted suddenly felt the urge to lie to her, to tell her that he had been wearing pantyhose for the last twenty years, that he and Billy had been wearing them together behind her back—but when he looked into his wife's eyes, whatever irritation or resentment he'd briefly experienced faded away.

"Yeah," Ted said, "that's it." He could see she was relieved, thankful that it wasn't anything horribly strange.

"Like son, like father," Eileen said. She rose from her crouch. "Come on out when you're ready. The food's getting cold."

Ted nodded, watched her leave, waited.

Outside, he heard chairs sliding on the hardwood floor. He heard the muffled sounds of conversation. He heard laughter. The smell of French fries seeped under the door and he realized he was famished. It helped to think about basics of life, like eating, taking a bite of a hamburger, the ground beef and the bread and the dollop of ketchup meeting in his mouth. And maybe there would be tomato slices and lettuce leaves, too, if the Kims had gone all out.

PERSON WHO HAS
LARGE NOSE

 ON THE LAST DAY OF SCHOOL before my first American summer vacation, Mr. Conklin, my math teacher, was lecturing about something I didn't understand, but this was
nothing unusual. I just had to wait until he drew his enormous dia-
grams.

Chalk dust puffed off the blackboard as he sketched two examples,
the first one being football. Mr. Conklin was a big guy, and he'd
probably played the sport as a kid because he often relied on pigskin
metaphors. "Let's say Team A is on Team B's ten-yard line. Team A's
quarterback throws a pass, and let's say he threw it off by one degree.
Does the wide receiver catch it in the end zone?"

Somebody in the back yelled out, "YES!"

"You better believe it's good!" Mr. Conklin bellowed, raising both of
his arms upright. On to the next example, the space shuttle, another one
of Mr. Conklin's favorite subjects. I think his dream was to become the
first pro-football-playing astronaut, half Jim Brown and half Neil Arm-
strong. On the board, he began a white line from the shuttle and drew it

across as he spoke. "Now think of the long way the space shuttle has to travel to reach the moon. If the engineers back at NASA are off on their angle of trajectory by, let's say, one tenth of a degree, does the shuttle reach the moon?"

"NO!" the entire class yelled out, including me. Mr. Conklin often asked loaded questions like this.

"No good!" he said, his arms waving back and forth. "A small mistake becomes humongous over the long haul. And that is why it's so important to have precise angular calculation when great distances are involved."

As my summer vacation was running out and seventh grade loomed ahead, I thought it was my family in that space shuttle, Father and Mother at the helm and Noona and me in the back, and somewhere way back, a crucial calculation had gone slightly awry and we were now inexorably off course, heading toward the planet of Unhappiness.

Nobody was happy. Father was disappointed after the dinner debacle with the McManuses, where Mr. McManus came to our apartment wearing pantyhose underneath his pants. Maybe Mother was right; all Americans were bizarre. Father wanted to make American friends so he could learn the language and be more successful in business. So far, it wasn't working.

And ever since the crying fit in the car, Mother had not been the same. She seemed to be on the verge of anger or depression, snapping at me or turning strangely silent for no reason at all, much like Noona. It was no longer a mystery where my sister got her moody streak.

And Noona? She was always pissed about something. The air, the sun, the moon. I asked her about why Mother was upset, and she said, "You wouldn't understand."

"Why not?"

She huffed out a long, tired sigh. "See, this is why you wouldn't. If you understood why you wouldn't understand, then you would understand it in the first place."

Then she donned her headphones and buried her face in her fashion magazine, her head bopping to the synthpop beat. This was her newest way to annoy me, this headphone-magazine combination.

And me. I wasn't exactly unhappy, but being surrounded by these malcontents inevitably brought down my spirits. I never thought I'd say such a thing, but I couldn't wait until school started.

It was the last weekend in August when Father tried to steer the family space shuttle back on course. We got to Peddlers Town an hour early and sat down at Marty's Bakery, the only store that was open at eight on a Saturday morning. Father got us a dozen donuts and a quart of milk. As I filled up on sugar and grease, I braced myself for whatever was going to come out of his mouth. It would be something harebrained, probably unpleasant, but before I could get too uptight, he came right out and said it.

"Three potential candidates will be coming by the store today."

"Candidates?" I asked.

"I thought it would be a prudent move on our part if we were to hire a professional salesperson." Then he paused dramatically. "A *kho-jeng-ee*." *Kho-jeng-ee* was the slang for a white American, which literally translated to "person who has large nose."

"Why do we need another salesperson?" Mother asked.

"It's not just another salesperson. It's a *kho-jeng-ee*. This is the link that we've sorely needed. Can't you see? That well-spoken American will be a gateway to many people who might be afraid to shop in our store. He'll be the link that binds the two cultures together."

Was he talking about an ambassador or a retail sales clerk? I didn't like the sound of it. A total stranger, a total *American* stranger, working with us? The store was a family affair. I considered it a second home, and I had no desire to share it with anybody who was not a Kim.

"I don't know," Mother said.

"Me neither," I chimed in. Two against one.

Father turned to Noona.

My sister, ever the beauty queen, was buffing her nails. *Please*, I prayed to myself, *please say something rude and take yourself out of the voting booth.* "There is one thing to consider," Noona said, using her grown-up voice. My heart sank. She tapped the emery board a couple of times against the edge of the table, tiny white clouds bursting with each rap. "I don't plan to work at the store for the rest of my life. And at some point, you will require third-party assistance. Before we came along, how did you manage?"

Father told us about a guy, one of Mr. Hong's friends. Apparently he didn't do much, just made sure nobody stole anything and told people to wait five minutes when Father left for a bathroom break. "But this was before the store was large like now. A month before you all came, it was only half as big."

"That's right, I forgot," Noona said.

"It was? I didn't know that," I said, sounding more hurt than I had intended.

"In Sook makes an excellent point," Father told Mother. "Neither she nor Joon-a will be working here forever, and it makes sense for us to find more permanent employees."

"But that's not for a while," Mother replied. "She isn't leaving anytime soon. Are you?"

"I suppose not," Noona said and yawned, like it meant nothing to her.

"I'm not going anywhere, either," I said.

"Yeah, we know," Noona said.

"I could get a job somewhere else if I wanted to."

"Nobody's going anywhere and nobody's getting another job," Father said. "I know I might be acting a bit hasty, but let's just give this a try. What do you say?"

Father looked to me and I looked to Mother. Mother, her hands clasped together on the table, looked at Father and said, "Do what you want."

"It's not what *I* want, it's what *we* want," he said.

"If it makes you feel better to believe that, then go ahead." Before Father could respond, Mother got up and left for the store, and Noona followed behind her.

There was a time when they had the decency to argue behind closed doors, but we were now apparently at a new level of intimacy. I longed for Father to be a stranger again, for this new home to feel foreign and uncertain. We were much nicer to each other before we got to know one another.

"It really is what we want," Father said. The way he said it, I thought he was thinking out loud, but then he nudged my arm. "Isn't it?"

"Right," I said, tired of everything. I looked at my watch. 8:32. This was going to be a long day.

The first guy was a fat middle-aged man named Norm Butler. He probably broke three hundred pounds, the thin belt around his waist like the equator around his planetary mass.

It was too bad he was so obese, because that was the only thing wrong with him. Norm was a born salesman. As Mr. Hong and Father conducted their interview, I watched his wide moony face express every possible emotion, full of pain when he talked about his last job ("the owner died of a heart attack"), bursting with joy when he told us about his daughters ("my beauties, my life"), unadulterated admiration as he described his sales philosophy ("honesty with sugar on top"). That evershifting face of his had the ability to engage you, to suck you in. Coupled with his sweet personality and flawless, accentless English, I could easily see why he was voted Salesman of the Year four times with his last company.

"How much?" Mr. Hong asked, the all-important question.

"I was getting paid eleven an hour, but I worked up to that," Norm said. "To start off, I'd accept nine." Nine dollars an hour! I couldn't believe my ears. Father was paying me five measly dollars *a day*. On Saturdays we were open from nine to nine, twelve hours, so that worked out to less than fifty cents per hour. I knew I was no salesman of the year, but this was ridiculous.

The interview was conducted at the back of the store, in the furniture section. Earlier we had moved things around, pushed our cluster of little lacquered decorative tables to one side and temporarily relocated our wooden chests, the kind with a hundred tiny drawers, to the wall. Above us hung one of our bestselling expensive products, a four-panel mother-of-pearl plaque of the four seasons. In the center of each plaque was a dancing lady, who looked exactly the same to me in all four pictures, though Father swore there were subtle yet defining differences that pointed specifically to a certain period.

In the midst of the ornate furniture were four folding chairs, two of which were Mr. Hong's. We sat around Norm in a semicircle, which seemed predatory, but that's what Mr. Hong recommended. If their plan was to make Norm nervous, it was working: Sweaty half-circles seeped out of his armpits. As he squirmed, I saw his enormous behind spilling around the seat, his flesh overhanging like a thick tablecloth.

After Norm departed with a firm handshake for everyone, Father and Mr. Hong looked at each other.

"Fat," Mr. Hong said.

"Really fat," Father said.

"Too fat."

"Way fat."

"He was nice, though," I added.

"Nice, sure, but fat," Father said. Father's goal was to have the typical American representative, and Norm was hardly typical. Still, it didn't feel right, and I told Father so.

"Life's tough," Father said. "What do you think, Hong?"

"He shouldn't eat so much," Mr. Hong said.

"Life is hard, so don't get fat," Father concluded. "Life is hard enough as it is."

Richard Caruso was also on the chubby side, but compared to Norm, he was as emaciated as a supermodel. Richard was in his early thirties and talked like a New York City Italian. "From Brooklyn," he told us. "Know what I'm sayin'?" Not really, but we all nodded, drawn helplessly to his caterpillar eyebrows. Richard would be a very different kind of a salesperson than Norm, a hard seller, the kind of guy who'd intimidate you into buying something.

"Let's see," Richard said when Mr. Hong asked what experience he'd had in selling. "I sold cars, new and used, in Manhattan and Middletown. Rugs. Men's clothing. Women's clothing. A shitload of stuff. Whatever you want me to sell, I sell. You'll see."

His asking price was a whopping thirteen dollars an hour. "And worth every penny," he assured us. "I ain't known as Slick Richie for nothin', know what I'm sayin'?" He must have asked us if we knew what he was saying a dozen times during the interview.

"Sees yous later," Richard said, high-fiving each of us. The interview only lasted fifteen minutes but it seemed like an hour had gone by. Nobody was sorry he left.

"This Alex better be good," Mr. Hong said, referring to our final candidate, Alex Moyer. He looked over his resume with much apprehension.

"Norm wasn't that fat, was he?" Father asked. I felt sorry for him. Nothing was working for him lately. Mother was mad at him for some unknown reason, business was slower than last year, and any attempts at bettering himself ended up badly, with the likes of Fat Norm and Slick Richie. Did he deserve any of it? No doubt he was asking the same question, and like me, had no answer.

Alex, our last candidate, our hope and savior, was twenty-two and fresh out of college. The thing I immediately noticed about him was his huge red head. You couldn't miss it—it was way out of proportion from the rest of his tall, thin body, and it stuck out like a cherry-flavored lollipop. It was mostly his hair that was taking up so much space, like he'd been grooming for a red Afro ever since he was five. When he scratched his head as he attempted to recount his past sales experiences (he had none), his hair submerged his entire hand.

But he had a good disposition, and he spoke like an American. And he was cheap, willing to work for five bucks an hour. You take what you can get, so we took him, enormous head and all. Father thrust out his hand and Alex shook it.

"When you work?" Father asked.

"Whenever's fine. Tomorrow, if you want," he replied. He didn't exactly seem overjoyed about getting hired. He'd probably never worked for a non-American boss before, and I'm sure it had him worried. I doubt this was his dream job—especially after spending four years for a college degree. When it came down to it, he was the best loser of our group of applicants, and I'm sure we were the only people who'd offered him a job so quickly.

Alex started the next day. We got to the store at ten-thirty, half an hour before Peddlers Town opened on Sundays, and he was loitering outside. He had done something to his hair because it didn't seem as freakishly large, looking as if he'd combed it down a bit. "Good morning, Mr. Kim," he said. He wore a blue button-down shirt, pressed khakis, and a thin black tie.

I thought he was overdressed, but Father obviously approved. "No Mr. Kim, Harry," he said, slapping him on his back. He handed Alex the ring of keys to open up all the locks to the canvas curtains.

"You trust him with the keys?" I whispered to Father.

"It's not like I'm going to let him keep them," Father said. "Relax, Joon-a. It's no big deal."

But it was a big deal to me, seeing this stranger open up our store. What was wrong with everybody? Didn't they feel the icky intrusion of the red-headed American?

"No," Mother said. "It'll be all right."

"No," Noona said. "He works for us. We pay him. So he does what we ask of him. What part of this fails to get through your thick skull, Junior?"

I felt like I was in horror movie where I was the only one who saw the monster and everyone else thought I was crazy. Though I had to give the monster credit for opening up the store so quickly: He pulled up the canvas curtains and secured the ropes on hooks like he'd been doing it all his life.

"Good job!" Father said. "You fast!" When Father saw that Alex didn't understand, he pulled on an imaginary curtain rope like a mime.

"Ah. I worked on my father's sailboat for many years."

At Father's request, Mother and Noona showed Alex how to dust properly. They both thought it was a stupid idea, but Father insisted, reminding them that Alex had little experience in retail.

"You want to provide him with sound fundamentals now," he said, "so he has a strong foundation upon which to build his skill."

It sounded like he was training for professional baseball. Of course, all this was communicated in Korean, so Alex stood in the background and shuffled his feet, waiting for his next set of instructions. When his eyes met mine, I gave him a steady, mean stare. *I'm watching you,* my stare said. *Your every move.* Thinking that I was joking around, Alex made a mock-serious face of his own, so I made even a meaner face, so then he made a more serious face. It wasn't working, so I gave up and started fixing up our Chinese purses showcase.

The whole dusting business turned out to be even more complicated. Though we had three dusters in the store, only one was made of real ostrich feathers. The fake ones had flimsy white plastic handles while the ostrich one was solid wood. It was Mother's favorite, but she was offering it to Alex.

To my surprise, Alex picked up on this. "Oh, I shouldn't use this one," he said.

"No, no, you," Mother said.

"Please, Mrs. Kim," he said. "I'll use this." He grabbed the one with neon green synthetic feathers, which was actually mine.

Mother gripped the wooden handle of her duster, smiled at Alex, and motioned him to follow her.

As I wiped down the showcases with Windex, I watched the ceramics section. Mother led with her ostrich duster and Noona showed Alex the proper mechanics of dusting. I couldn't hear what they were saying, but from the sound of it, Mother would say something and Noona would translate. Now they were laughing, all of them, as they moved from section to section.

"What did I tell you," Father said. "He's going to work out fine."

I said nothing. There was something funny about Alex. I wasn't exactly sure what, but in time I would find out.

By and large, everybody was happier. I say by and large because there was one exception: me. I'd woken up to find the family space shuttle gone, on its way to planet Joy, while I was still marooned at planet Misery.

Alex brought in more business. I don't know what made Father happier, the fact that he was right or that the money poured in. For someone without previous retail experience, Alex did just fine. He'd never used a cash register before, but by reading the manual, he figured out how to ring up the same-priced merchandise consecutively, something we'd never learned to do. Even Mother, skeptical Mother, approved.

"Did you see how he dusts *around* the small temple jars?" she said to my sister.

"And we only showed him once."

Then, of course, there was his selling. He did nothing special; didn't lie, didn't threaten, did nothing of the kind. I shadowed him on multiple occasions, trying to figure out his secret, what hypnotic spells he cast on people to buy things we hadn't sold since the store opened, items whose price tags were yellowed like old newspaper. All he ever did was go up to them and ask if they needed help, and then there was Father, ringing up the sale at the register with delighted fingers. Could Father actually have been correct, that because Alex was American, people felt more at ease about buying our stuff? It made no sense—wouldn't one be more apt to trust an Asian person selling Oriental goods? I knew I would, but then again, I was Asian and could only see from my point of view. Obviously I knew nothing about being American.

Not only did Alex increase sales, he also brought up the store status. "An American," Father would say over the phone, "that's what you need. I have one here, and boy, is he ever bringing in the business." My respect for Father, which had its ups and downs, was definitely on a downturn as he kept referring to Alex like a thing, an appliance. "Wasn't too tough to find one of these, either. Picked him over two others. Sure, just put out an ad in the newspaper and you'll get one, too."

But then as time went by, Father did more than brag, he abused, too: "Sure, he's a selling machine, and he's not even all that handsome! You should see this *kho-jeng-ee*'s huge head! Ha ha!" He said all these things right in front of Alex, and every time Alex heard his name being mentioned, Father winked and told him what a good job he was doing. I couldn't figure out then why he was being so mean, but of course now, I know better: because he could. For the first time, Father had the chance to be superior to an American, and the power went straight to his head.

Perhaps I should have felt sorry for Alex, but I didn't. On Saturday evenings, we had a tradition of getting a pizza pie from Eatza Pizza. When it was just the four of us, two of eight slices would always be left over (each of us had two, except Mother, who didn't care for it). Mother wrapped up the leftover and we took it home, and for Sunday breakfast I'd feast on cold pizza.

"Look! No leftovers!" Father exclaimed in English. He tried to speak as much English as possible in front of Alex. "Perfect!"

"Lucky," Mother agreed.

"Amazing," Noona said sarcastically, but it wasn't like her usual sarcasm that made fun of everyone and left her high and mighty. Instead, it was sweet, the way she rolled up her eyes and smirked at Alex, like she was saying *My parents, aren't they just too too corny?*

I said nothing. I was pissed. I wasn't getting my Sunday Cold Pizza Extravaganza.

"Thank you for the food, Harry," Alex said. "It's been a real pleasure working at your store."

"Not your store, no, no," Father corrected. "*Our* store."

Alex was embarrassed. "That's . . . no, Harry, this is not our store. This is your store."

"No, no," Father insisted. "Our store. Alex important, very important, VIP. Our store."

B y the second Saturday, Alex greeted us like this: *"Ahn-nyung-ha-sae-yo."* Then he bowed, just like a good Korean boy.

"Yea, ahn-nyung-ha-sae-yo!" Father replied. "Very good! How . . . ?"

"Mrs. Kim," Alex said, and when all our eyes went to Mother, she nodded with pride. In the two weeks Alex had been working at the store, Mother had surreptitiously taught him how to greet, thank, and count up to ten in Korean.

"He's a quick study," Mother told Noona and me later. "Just like the register, he learns fast."

"I learn fast, too," I said.

"Yeah, and you forget it even faster," Noona said.

"You *are* a very smart boy," Mother told me. She deftly deflected the subject at hand, dismissing me with generic "smart boy" praise.

Even though Mother no longer loved me as much as she used to, I was glad she was feeling better. Watching her teach Alex as they dusted the shelves, I tried not to be jealous. *"Noona,"* Mother said. "David, sister. *Un-nee* if David, girl." She was trying to tell Alex that depending on whether you were a male or a female, the Korean word for sister would change.

"Gahm-sah-hahm-nee-da," Alex said. He always thanked Mother after she taught him something new.

Playing the role of teacher brought great joy to Mother. Back in Korea, when she worked at the bag factory, she used to get excited whenever a new worker joined the company and she could instruct them on how to operate the equipment. That job had always gone to her because she was the best at it.

Every day, my parents came back from the store with more accolades.

Father: "He sold the monkey statue today. *The monkey statue.* Do you know how long we've had that damn thing?"

Mother: "Today he said *soo-gho-ha-sae-yoh* to Dr. Lee as he was leaving, and you should've seen the doctor's face."

I was having difficulty sleeping. How long would it be before Alex became the big brother I never had? Would he sleep in the living room? No, I'd probably be the one relegated to the couch and he'd take my bed. Though we'd better upgrade to a larger mattress, because that overgrown head of his wouldn't fit on a narrow twin.

'm in love with him," Noona said. "And I don't care who knows it."

"Have you seen the size of his head?"

Noona slitted her eyes at me. "Just like you, so stupid, so on-the-surface. You don't know a damn thing, Junior. There's so much more to a person than the way he looks."

"So you agree he's ugly."

"He's not ugly, and you say that one more time, I swear I'll gouge your eyes out when you're sleeping."

Considering it came from Noona, I thought her threat was distinctly possible.

Knowing how she felt, I had trouble watching Noona around Alex, how she tried to make eyes with him, laughed a little too loudly at his dumb jokes, and asked him about inane stuff just to get him to talk to her. Without Alex, Noona was certain her life would come to a cold, abrupt end. She overanalyzed his every move, torturing me to assess her latest contact with him. "Didn't you hear how he said 'Good morning' to me?" she'd ask me. "There was something else there, don't you think?"

"Uh-huh."

"I'm going to ask him out. I really am," Noona said. "I know girls aren't supposed to, but this is America. Girls have to be bold. I'm going to be bold."

"Good for you."

"You better be nice to him," Noona said, suddenly vicious. Then she softened, almost playful. "You never know what's going to happen. We might even get married."

That woke me up. Their offspring: a big red-headed loser who was meaner than Hitler, Genghis Khan, or Attila the Hun.

So began Operation Redhead, a systematic strategy to eradicate Alex Moyer from our lives. I took a hard-earned five-dollar bill, drew on the top right corner with red ink, and left it where Alex and only Alex would find it: right under the green-feathered duster. I watched him closely that morning. He dipped under the front desk, picked up the duster, did a quick double-take, and didn't even pause as he pocketed the fiver. So he wasn't perfect after all.

Now that Alex had my money, my plan was this: I'd mention to Father how I'd left the marked bill on the counter then stepped away for a moment, and when I came back, I saw Alex take the cash. Father would approach Alex, Alex would show him the money, end of story. It was rotten, but I had no choice.

That's not to say that it was easy for me to do this. If I were Alex and some punk kid got me fired, I'd be plenty sore. At least he wasn't the violent type—or was he? On TV, it was always the nice, quiet fellows who ended up chopping up little children.

"Excuse me," a woman behind me called. "How many times do I have to repeat myself to get service around here?"

I showed her the purse she wanted; of course, she didn't want it. "The color's all wrong." I wanted to throttle her; she couldn't see the color through the showcase window?

After she left, I was ready to head up to the register desk to put Operation Redhead into execution, but didn't. Alex was there, handing over the five-dollar bill. Words were exchanged. After Alex left to perform more dazzling dusting, I approached the desk.

"Isn't he something? Look," Father said, taking out my five-dollar bill. "He just handed this to me. He found it on the floor and thought that it might have belonged to a customer."

"He sure is something," I said. Father popped open the register and slid my five bucks into the money tray.

"He's smart, he's honest, and he can sell anything. We're so lucky to have him."

As realization dawned on me, the anvil of despair that had been crushing my soul floated off my chest.

"We are," I said, "aren't we?"

I felt like flying away, screw the family space shuttle. Because Alex Moyer, given enough time, would disappear on his own. Why would somebody with his talents stay at this crummy job? I searched for Alex and found him polishing our wooden jewelry boxes with a cloth and a can of Pledge.

"I am happy," I told him.

Alex squeezed a blast of aerosol onto the cloth. Fake lemony scent filled the space between us. "I'm happy you're happy," he said.

Two days later, Alex told Father that he found another job. "What doing?" Father asked, heartbroken.

"Computer programming," Alex replied. "It was my major in college." He was moving to Seattle before the end of the month. Wherever he worked, I hoped they had extra wide doorways to fit his head.

Everyone agreed to throw him a farewell party. "It's the least we can do," Father said. So at seven, after the store closed on Sunday, we were going to hold the "Goodbye Alex" party. Father would order pizza, Noona would get the cake from Marty's Bakery, and Mother would buy plastic dishes.

"I'm going to tell other people," Father said.

"Who else is going to come?" I asked. "He's our employee, and he's been here for all of three weeks!"

Father lowered his eyes, shook his head. "Alex is special," he said, and trudged to our cross-hall neighbor, Mr. McManus.

When seven o'clock came, I couldn't believe my eyes; there were at least thirty people in our store. Apparently they all knew Alex because he'd either helped them or talked to them at some point. There was the old guy from Wild at Heart, who had a broken boom box that Alex fixed for him. The owner of Wicker World was having knee issues, and Alex showed her exercises that made the pain go away. People literally lined up to shake his hand.

For his farewell speech, Alex read a poem by Robert Frost, "Nothing Gold Can Stay."

"Jesus," I muttered under my breath.

"Shut up, Junior," Noona said through her tears. "Just shut the hell up."

BOB MILLER

BOB MILLER WAS STANDING ON a chair with a hammer in one hand and a nail poised against the wall when he saw a black-haired boy scurry across the walkway and pivot into Cimmetri. He told the owner there something and walked out, and now that he was facing Miller, it was plain he wasn't a boy at all.

The short Asian man crossed the walkway and hurried over to HiFi FoFum, and flagged down the Jewish guy. They were too far away for him to hear their conversation, but from the way the man moved his hands, Miller knew he was delivering the same lines as before.

He went back to the task at hand, which was to hang up a sign on the wall:

MILLER DETECTIVE AGENCY
INVESTIGATIVE SERVICES

It was as plain as a sign could be, solid black letters against a white background, delivering both literal and metaphorical meaning. What people wanted when they came to see him were absolute results with no shades of gray. When a father wanted to locate his runaway daughter, he wanted her found. In a mystery novel or a movie, the detective would encounter morally ambiguous situations to complicate matters, but in reality, things were far simpler. Either Miller found her or he didn't. It was black or it was white, and either way, he got paid.

He repositioned the nail and took aim, but now he saw the Asian man approach, and Miller was glad.

"Good thing you're here," he told him. "Can you let me know if this looks centered?" When he saw the confusion on the man's face, Miller pointed to his sign. "I'm trying to hang this up, you see."

"Yes," the man said, but his tone was still unsure, and then it occurred to Miller that maybe his English wasn't too keen. He stepped down from the chair and lifted the sheet-metal placard to the wall, then moved it left, then to the right, then back to what looked to be the center.

"Understand?" he said, looking back.

"Yes!" he said, and after a few thoughtful advisory nudges to the left, Miller banged the nail into place and hung up his sign.

The man's name, it turned out, was Harry Kim, and what he wanted was to invite him to a party.

"A party?"

"Small party," Kim said, holding his thumb and index finger with a tiny space in between to show just how small. "Pizza and Coke and cake. Seven P.M."

"What's the occasion?" Miller asked, then immediately rephrased it. "Birthday? Wedding? Why party?"

"Ah, Alex. Alex my employee." He enunciated this last word carefully, as if he'd just learned it.

And that's why at a quarter past seven on this Sunday evening, when the empty walkways of Peddlers Town opened up as wide as a freeway,

Miller strolled two stores down to East Meets West. He wasn't usually fond of parties of any kind, tired of the whole small-talk thing, but this being his first day here, he couldn't think of a better way to meet his neighbors.

Kim's store was huge, at least ten times the size of his own space, and it was teeming not only with a ton of Oriental goods but with people as well. They were milling about, each carrying a blue plastic cup of soda in one hand and a red dish in the other. With the melted pizza cheese supplying the color white, it almost seemed as if they were performing a slow-footed patriotic dance.

It was a good thing Miller came when he did, because all that remained on the front counter were two slices next to a tower of empty pizza boxes. When he reached for one of them, another hand darted in to snatch the other.

"Hi," Miller said, loud enough to break through the background chatter surrounding them.

The Asian boy, probably Kim's son, said nothing. Instead he stared at Miller's hat, which was what kids usually did. He took it off and showed it to him. "You like it?"

"Nice hat," the boy said.

"That's right, it's a hat."

"Why the hat?"

Miller put his gray fedora back on his head, tamping it down so the brim just grazed the top of his ears, then tipped it slightly forward. The boy seemed impressed with the whole ritual. The hat was a conversation piece, an icebreaker. He often wore it to the occasional gathering because it usually made somebody curious enough to start talking.

"It's because I'm a detective," Miller said. "You know what 'detective' means?"

The boy asked him to spell it out, which Miller did; then he was off, weaving through the crowd. In a moment, beyond the thicket of human traffic, Miller saw him sitting on a stool and paging through a pocket dictionary.

The pizza was cold, but it was good and salty. He hadn't realized how hungry he was, and he finished the whole slice in six bites. Miller scooped some ice cubes into his cup and poured himself a fizzing cup of cola.

"Good taste?"

Behind him, Mr. Kim stood beside a tall, thin kid with what could only be described as a red Afro.

"Very good, Mr. Kim," Miller said. "And this must be Alex."

"Nice to meet you, sir," Alex said. "I like your hat."

Miller took a long sip, the bubbles tickling his throat. Alex was an unusual-looking guy with that big poofy hair of his, but there hadn't been a hint of sarcasm in his compliment. He was genuine, and Miller liked him immediately.

"I can see why Mr. Kim thinks so highly of you. It's too bad you're leaving."

"Yeah," Alex said, his eyes downcast. "I wish I could stay, but life goes on."

"Ah, Alex," Mr. Kim said, his hand on the kid's shoulder. Were those tears in his eyes? They must've been, because he turned away and excused himself.

"You must be like the best employee in the world," Miller said.

"It's not a very difficult job."

"Is Mr. Kim going to get somebody else?"

"I don't know. I suggested a friend to take my place, but he said it wouldn't be the same. But enough about me. What do you do?"

Miller told him that the bulk of his work bounced between pre-employment screenings and insurance fraud, though he did get the occasional missing persons case. Alex listened with such devoted concentration that Miller felt guilty for not saying more about his business, but the kid seemed to sense this, too. "I understand," he said. "Much of what you do is confidential."

"Or just terribly boring."

"Would you like to meet some of the other merchants? They're all fine people. I haven't been here even a month and they've all taken me under their wing."

With Alex at his side, introductions were a breeze, everyone greeting him with smiles and hearty handshakes. One by one, they offered their names and stores to Miller. The last one was the guy with the yarmulke.

"My name is Dmitri Popov," he said. "I own HiFi FoFum. And now there will be a test to see how much you remember." Everyone chuckled politely at Dmitri's joke.

Miller couldn't sing or play a musical instrument. He couldn't dance and he was terrible at any sport involving a ball. But he had one talent.

"Ted and Eileen McManus," he said, looking right at the couple. "Cimmetri."

"Big guy," he said, "Jake Martin, Hometown Grill."

Then Miller got even fancier by going out of order.

"Sylvia O'Dell," he said, who was a bit of a fox, with big blue eyes and Rockette legs. "Animal Attraction. And her daughter, Mindy."

"You pull rabbits out of a hat, too?" Sylvia asked.

Miller turned to the ugliest man in the room. "Ralph Woodford, A Second Chance."

And he continued right on, rattling off five more name-and-store combinations until the last one, back to Dmitri. He pretended to struggle with him because sometimes people got uneasy. It was good to relax them, to show that he wasn't a machine. He snapped his finger. "Dmitri Popov, of HiFi FoFum."

"A plus!" the Russian said, clapping wildly.

Miller basked in the applause, taking a dramatic bow, and it seemed entirely appropriate that from the back of the store came singing. Kim walked out cradling an enormous sheet cake with a lone flaming candle in the middle while another Asian man followed. "For he's a jolly good fellow," they started, and everyone followed.

GOODBYE ALEX, the cake read. The guest of honor blew out the candle and got busy cutting the cake into squares for speedy distribution. Miller looked around and saw how joyful everyone was, and he was glad he had came here tonight.

"Here you go, maestro," Alex said, cutting a piece and handing it to him. It was great cake, a rich buttercream frosting on top and a dark chocolate filling. He was almost done with it when he felt a nudge. It was Kim's son again, the little blue dictionary jutting out of his trouser pocket.

"I know detective," he said. "You really detective?"

The boy's tone was all serious, all business. Miller took one final bite of the cake. "I really detective," he said.

When Miller returned to Peddlers Town on Tuesday for his first day of work, he was faced with Frankenstein. At the party, the dimmed overhead lights had apparently cast favorable shadows on Ralph Woodford's face. Now, under the unavoidable flood of fluorescents, Ralph looked downright scary, what with his gigantic nose, Bugs Bunny overbite, and mismatched eyes—the left eye narrower and smaller than the right.

"Hi there, Detective Miller," he said. "We're neighbors."

Miller shook his outstretched hand and peeked around to see the hanging sign for A Second Chance. There was a picture of an open book underneath the words, so it was probably a bookstore, a used one.

"How ya doing, Ralph," Miller said.

"Just fine, fine," Ralph replied, and lingered. So this wasn't just a social call—he actually wanted something.

"Can I help you?"

Miller listened to Ralph's story, which involved a lady, eleven books, and true love. A week ago, a woman had rushed into his store with a backpack and slammed it on the counter. *I want these books out of my life.* That's what she'd said, almost screamed, her eyes red from crying.

In the middle of his inspired telling, Ralph jumped out of his chair and ran back to his store, got the other ten books, and splayed them out on the desk. He flipped to specific sections in the novels where the woman had scribbled what looked to be journal entries. Miller picked one up and saw a name and a year, DAPHNE MCEWAN '77, written on the top corner of the inside cover.

"Does this name appear on each one?"

"Sure."

"You couldn't track her down in the phone book?"

Ralph slowly shook his head. Looking up at him from this angle, Miller thought of those Easter Island statues, the slope of their foreheads. "I tried. I guess she's unlisted, but I don't even know where she lives."

"The notes in the books probably give some clues," Miller said, but Ralph wasn't listening.

"She's lonely, you see? That's why she did this, so somebody out there would find her. That somebody is me."

"Uh-huh," Miller said. "I'll need to study the books."

Ralph looked at him suspiciously. "How long are you going to keep them?"

"Long enough for me to read them, Ralph," Miller said. "I'll give 'em back to you, scout's honor."

"Right, right," Ralph said, still unsure. Then his face suddenly cracked open a smile. "Okay, you're my man."

When Miller informed Ralph of his fee schedule, Ralph opened up his wallet, took out a crisp hundred-dollar bill, and handed it over. "I just want you to find her. I don't care how much it costs, and I'm not just saying that to be dramatic." A hearty handshake, a profuse barrage of thank-yous, and Frankenstein walked back to his lair.

Miller stared at the money in his hand, the serious face of Benjamin Franklin like an accusation of his fiscal foolishness. He'd been working since he was thirteen, so that would make it forty years next September. For the last five, he'd been on his own, setting up his agency and running it himself, until he couldn't afford to pay the rent on his office. The first couple of years were good ones, probably because he was eager to start up his own service. The cases he had back then were no different than the usual, but it sure had seemed more exciting.

Downscaling from a real office with a real secretary to this dumpy strip mall hadn't exactly filled him with hope, and certainly dealing with people like Ralph didn't help any. Did they all have to be nutjobs? As Miller read through the scribble in *The Great Gatsby,* he wondered what was going through Ralph's head. His client earnestly believed that this Daphne McEwan was calling out to him through these journals—but what was she calling out? As far as Miller could see, these pages held nothing more than the confessions of a lonely college girl who'd left home for the first time. She had some bad dates, spent a couple of Saturday nights alone, nothing too alarming for a depressed freshman. Ralph picked up three more volumes and was not surprised to see that they also displayed nothing out of the ordinary. In the seventh book, Daphne was still without, as she put it, "a man of her own," but she was glad to have the company of her girlfriends Rebecca and Angie; during spring break of their senior year, the three girls drove down 95 South to Nags Head in North Carolina and it had taken them approximately eight hours, and taking account of the towns they passed on their way, that put her college around Upstate New York. In book eight, Daphne again felt out of place because she was in a new city, in a new job, and had no friends close by. Miller was amazed she had any friends—all she ever did in these journals was bitch and moan. The last book was like all the others, an endless diatribe about how she couldn't find her other half ("where are you? why won't you come to me? how shall i find you, you sweet bastard?"). Even her penmanship was irritating, especially the way she dotted her i's and j's with open circles.

Miller closed the book and set it down on his desk. *The Bell Jar,* by Sylvia Plath. On the cover was a dark red rose slipping out of a black-gloved hand. *The Heartbreaking Story of a Talented Woman Who Descended into Madness.* Yeah, whatever.

Next to the book was the hundred dollars, a pair of calm, unblinking colonial eyes staring back at him.

He didn't want to help Frankenstein find his bride, but as usual, he could use the money.

He found the college within a couple of hours. In her first volume, Daphne mentioned both the name of her dorm ("main") and the building of her English class ("long"); Frankenstein missed both of these references probably because she'd written them all in lowercase letters.

A closer reading of the subsequent volumes, which Miller grudgingly had to do, revealed a dock located across from the main campus, and although he wasn't sure, Miller had an idea that this was a women's college. It was a hunch, a feeling he got from reading the dining hall passages where no man was ever seen or heard.

He called up a couple of his contacts in academia, offered them his clues, and on his fifth phone call, he got what he wanted: "Why, that's Wells College, in Aurora, New York. A little girls-only college, upstate."

From directory service, Miller got the number for the college and dialed the main number. The operator gave him the numbers for Accounts Receivable and Alumni Affairs. He punched in the first number.

"Hi," he said, "is Mary there?"

The woman on the line said there was no Mary in this office.

"Mary Douglas? Hmmm . . . maybe I got the wrong department. This is AR, right? Who's this?"

Her name was Geraldine Faulk, and it didn't take long for Miller to realize she hated her job. Which was fine, because it made Miller's that much easier. He thanked her and dialed Alumni Affairs. He cleared his throat, got himself in the right mind-set.

"Hello, I need your help, boy do I need your help," he said. He sounded angry, fed up, helpless. "I'm sorry if I sound like I'm about to kill somebody. You know Geraldine Faulk?"

The voice on the other line, a woman, laughed. "I'm the one who should be sorry! You poor thing."

Miller told her that he was a temp stuck working with Geraldine to iron out some old accounts receivable. "I'm not kidding, in about two seconds, I'm gonna jump out the window. If you could just give me the address of Daphne McEwan, class of '77, I'd be eternally grateful."

He was briefly put on hold, then the woman came back on line and rattled off Daphne's last known address, it was good because the last mailing didn't bounce back, and did he want Daphne's telephone number as well? "God, you're a lifesaver," Miller said, copying down the area code for New York City and the seven digits that followed.

After hanging up with Wells, Miller wasted no time punching in Daphne's number. One ring, two rings, then a pickup. "Hello?" A nasal, weary voice.

"Hello there," Miller said, "may I talk to Daphne McEwan?"

"Speaking," the voice over the phone replied. So it was her after all.

"Good afternoon, Ms. McEwan. I'm calling from *The New York Times* Marketing Research Department and was wondering, can you spare two hours to answer some questions?"

"Two hours?"

"Yes, ma'am."

Daphne hung up the phone without another word. Miller took the piece of paper with Daphne's info, folded it in thirds, and slid it into an envelope. Then he piled up all the books, placed the envelope on top, and headed over to A Second Chance. He'd charge another hundred bucks for the legwork, and then he wouldn't have to talk to Frankenstein again.

"Already?" Ralph said, incredulous. "My goodness, you are a pro." He took out five twenty-dollar bills and exchanged it for the envelope. He held it in both palms of his hands, as if it were an offering to God. "Is it really here?" he asked.

No. I came over here in person, got your money, and there's nothing in there.

"Just open it," Miller said.

Ralph stared at the blank white envelope. "I can't," he finally said, shaking his head. "You open it. I'm too nervous."

"Ralph, I put it in there," Miller said. "I know what it is."

"Just please open it, please," he pleaded. Miller opened the damn envelope and took out the damn piece of paper he'd just written on and folded up. He shoved it at Ralph. "Here."

Ralph turned away and closed his eyes. "No, no, I can't. I can't look."

Before he lost it completely, Miller carefully laid the piece of paper on the counter and walked away.

Back in his office, he saw two Asians waiting for him, and he recognized them both from the party. He hadn't talked to the girl, but he'd exchanged several words with the boy, who once again brought his dictionary with him. They were seated in the two metal folding chairs he'd set up in front of the main desk.

"Can I help you?" Miller asked the girl.

"Yes," she said. She introduced herself and her brother as Susan and David Kim. Then the next couple of words came out staccato, like a badly rehearsed line from a play. "We wish you to follow my father."

"Follow your father."

"Follow my father." Then she shook her head. "Our father. He's brother, me sister."

"Where's your father now?"

"Store," she said, pointing to her right. "East Meets West."

"You want me to follow him and he's right here in this building?"

"No," the boy spoke up. "New York."

"And when does he go to New York?"

"All Monday, every Monday," the boy said.

"And why do you want me to follow him?" The brother and sister looked at each other, but neither spoke. "You don't want to tell me?"

The silence was broken by Ralph, who barged in, scrunched down next to Miller, and said, "I want you to go to New York, too."

"Excuse me?" Miller said, gesturing to the two sitting across the desk.

"What, them? I know them, they're Harry Kim's kids. Hiya, kids."

"Hello, Mr. Woodford," the boy replied.

"See?"

"And you were eavesdropping." He was going to have to shove some serious soundproofing material between the walls.

"I know, I'm sorry about that. But I figured, these kids want you to go to New York, and I want you to go to New York, so how about you go to New York?"

"Yes, go to New York," the girl and the boy repeated together.

"Look," Ralph said, dropping fifteen twenties on the desk. "You help us all out, huh?"

"Mr. Woodford," the girl protested nervously. "That is . . ."

"It's okay," he said, waving her off. "It's my treat." Like he was buying them ice cream. Back to Miller: "So what do you say, buddy?"

The Monday train to New York wasn't even half full at five in the morning, so Miller was able to stretch out on a three-seater by himself. All around him, as the dark blue sky ebbed toward daylight, early commuters from various New Jersey cities read newspapers, listened to music, or dozed lightly. Looking out his window, Miller yawned at the Hudson River, lit up gold by the rising sun. He opened his notebook and scanned his itinerary: take the N/R subway to Canal Street, where he was supposed to see Harry Kim drive up in a green station wagon and park next to a grocery store. The kids hadn't told him what it was about, but Miller had a feeling it had to do with a woman. It was either that or money, the two most popular paths of transgression.

After completing that task, Miller would grab brunch somewhere, maybe some crepe and yogurt, and then walk over to the apartment on

Houston where Daphne McEwan lived. He'd knock on her door, say a friendly good morning, and tell her that a gruesome monster of a man named Ralph Woodford was hopelessly in love with her, so would she please agree to see Frankenstein for a dinner date at the Four Seasons? In all the years Miller had been playing private detective, this was the first time he would ask out a girl for a client. For his half day in New York, he was able to squeeze another hundred bucks out of Ralph, but it didn't make him feel any better. In fact, seeing how easy it was to get money out of him made him feel like a crook.

Like the train, the subway was also deserted. Initially he had the entire car to himself, but with every stop, more people filed in. No one looked happy, which made sense. Who in his right mind would be glad to be up this early in the morning?

Certainly not him. Miller zipped up his windbreaker as he made his way aboveground, squinting his eyes against the wind. Autumn was definitely here, some of the trees already shedding their leaves. Most of the shops on Canal were closed at this hour, but not the grocery stores. They were just opening up, pyramids of red apples and bright oranges protruding out onto the street, and as Miller walked by one of them, he paused at the rich scent of coffee.

He got himself a cup and found a bench nearby to make sure his equipment was in order. He pulled out his 35mm, the roll of black-and-white film loaded and ready to go. All he had to was remove the lens cap, which he did. For this job, he'd shoot "from the hip," take a shot without looking at the viewfinder. It used to be a bit of an art, but now with auto-focus and a remote shutter release, it wasn't difficult at all.

Inside the camera bag were two more items, an eyeglass case and a Mets baseball cap.

"Master of disguise," Miller said to himself. Since there was a chance Kim might recognize him, he put on the pair of black-rimmed glasses and the cap. He checked his watch and saw that he should head over there; the Kim kids had shown him a couple of receipts that revealed the name and the location of this store, and the time stamp had been right about now.

He hurried over to Lucky Grocery, which looked no different than the other corner stores of its ilk he'd just passed. The only thing that stood out was that the Asian woman behind the counter was in a wheelchair. When their eyes met, instead of greeting him, she turned away. The shy type.

But she wasn't shy five minutes later when Harry Kim drove up and got out of the car. The little guy was fast, making a beeline to the counter. Luckily, Miller had his finger on the trigger and he snapped two shots. Like most SLR cameras, his Pentax made the familiar grinding noise when the shutter was depressed, but the hum from the huge industrial refrigerator nearby masked the sound.

Kim dipped down and kissed the woman. Miller took another quick shot, but he didn't have to hurry, as they locked lips long enough for him to take another five. After the kiss, they stared at one another silently, drinking each other in.

So Harry Kim was two-timing his wife, the dirty dog. He didn't seem the type, but you could never tell.

A few blocks down Canal, he found a diner, and as he sipped his coffee and cut into his apple crepe, he considered getting out of the business altogether. He'd take the easy five hundred bucks he just earned and buy himself some woodworking equipment—maybe a nice set of carving tools or a jigsaw—and start the carpentry business that had always been in the back of his mind.

Who the hell was he kidding? He could never make a living doing that. Besides, he'd just signed a one-year lease at Peddlers Town.

The waitress stopped by to drop off his check.

"Hey," he said, "think I could be a carpenter?"

"Karen Carpenter or Jesus carpenter?"

Oh, these New York waitresses—they were all comediennes in waiting. "The Jesus kind."

"Sure, why not," she said. "My pop was one, and he was a drunk, too, so I'm sure you could pull it off."

When he returned Tuesday morning to his office in Peddlers Town, he found neither David nor Susan Kim but rather another Asian, an older woman, waiting for him.

"Mrs. Kim?" he guessed.

"Picture," she said.

"Yes, I have a picture."

"Picture, please," she said.

"Are you sure you want this?" he asked her.

She was a tiny woman, and with each successive nod, she seemed to shrink even more.

He handed her a manila envelope.

"Thank you," she said, and walked away. Miller sighed, sat down in his chair. He never got used to delivering bad news to clients.

Ralph's face appeared at the corner.

"See how good I was? I waited until she was gone."

Miller recalled the moment Daphne McEwan had opened the door to her apartment, a short, anger-filled young woman with jet black hair choked into a ponytail. He'd initially thought she was scowling, but then he realized that she always looked like that. She was one of those people who was born with a particular emotion engraved on her face.

The Bride, in the flesh.

"She says yes," Miller said, closing his eyes, tired of this day already. "You can call her."

"Really?"

Behind the self-imposed darkness of his eyelids, Miller ran through a variety of sarcastic phrases to answer him with, but when he opened them, he saw tears running down his neighbor's long face.

"Oh, Christ, please don't cry. It wasn't anything."

Tears flew off in droplets and landed on his desk as Ralph shook his head fiercely. "No," he said, "it was everything."

"Come on, get outta here," Miller said. "Go call your girl."

"Robert," Ralph said before walking back to his store. "That's what we'll name our son."

"Maybe you should go on the date first," Miller said after him, but his cynicism was halfhearted. Those two were destined for each other. Would Ralph really name their kid after him? Probably. No, most definitely.

Miller touched a bead of Ralph's tear on his desk and rubbed the wetness between his thumb and index finger. He thought of the boy on the old black-and-white TV show, *The Munsters,* the little werewolf, his ridiculous widow's peak and his fake fangs, and it made him smile.

THE WOMAN IN
THE PHOTOGRAPH

 THEY WOULDN'T LET ME SEE the photograph, even though the whole thing had been my idea.

"You're too young," Mother said, sounding serious.

"Too young, Junior," Noona said, who did not. As usual, she took great pleasure in my pain.

Who talked to Detective Miller at our party? Who suggested that Father be shadowed in New York? So why was I the one who was left out?

When I returned home from school that day, I found them on the sofa, Mother sniffling and Noona consoling. Father was gone as usual, supposedly meeting with wholesalers, but that was obviously not the case. He was doing something else, and I had a pretty good idea what it was.

I dropped my bookbag on the floor and sat down next to Mother. Looking out of the balcony window, I wished I were still outside. As I'd walked home from the bus stop, wind dragged crispy October leaves across the pavement, and I chased after them as if they were giant bugs, squashing them and hearing the satisfying crunch underneath my feet. It was a game I used to play in Korea, and I was glad it still worked here.

"Is everything all right?" I asked, not knowing what else to say.

"What does it look like, Junior?" Noona said.

"Don't talk to your brother that way," Mother said. On the table was the photograph I wasn't allowed to see, facedown against the wood. That got me mad again, and Mother must have noticed because she started to run her fingers through my hair in the way that only she knew how. For the last month or so, the crow's feet at the corners of her eyes had etched deeper, and the silver strands on her head seemed to have multiplied in number, threatening to overtake her long black hair.

In the kitchen, a buzzer sounded. "Would you look into that?" Mother asked Noona, who awarded me a long, disgusted stare before complying. Then Mother got up herself and announced, "I'm going to freshen up in the bathroom." She pointed at the photograph on the table. "You can look at the picture if you want."

I was afraid. Even though I'd complained plenty about it, there was something nice about being protected. But what could be so awful about a piece of paper? Curiosity overcame me and I picked it up. It was an eight-by-ten black-and-white photograph, five people inhabiting the picture, three along the periphery walking away in various directions and two in the center, a man and a woman. The man was Father, his lips slightly protruding, his eyes closed, bending down to kiss a woman, his indiscretion forever frozen in time. The woman, whose body was obscured behind a stack of gray boxes, tilted her head up to Father, ready to receive his lips. She was a Korean woman, and she looked neither younger nor prettier than Mother.

On the bottom right corner of the photograph, a name and an address was written in blue ink along the white margin: Lucky Grocery, 189 Canal Street.

Noona snatched the picture away from me. "You're in big trouble."

"Mother said I could."

"That's because you're such a crybaby, throwing tantrum after tantrum."

I entertained the phrase "Am not" for a comeback, but thought better of it. When I said nothing in return, Noona sat down next to me and considered the picture herself.

"What do you make of it?" I asked.

I was expecting a put-down, but instead she surprised me with a genuine reply: "I don't know." Then she turned to me and met my eyes straight on. "You know, Junior, you're going to be a man, too, and you better realize that men do these kinds of stupid things."

"Are you saying that I'm going to be kissing another woman when I'm married?"

She sat stiff and upright, looking down at me. "It's possible."

"And that's why you're so mad at me right now."

"You think I need a reason to be mad at you?"

I picked up my bookbag and took out my books. "I have homework to do," I said, and got up and walked over to the dining room table, and before Noona could say anything else, Mother exited the bathroom and asked me if I was hungry, which, of course, I was.

When Father returned in the evening with the station wagon packed full of merchandise, he asked me to bring up a box. "Come on," he said, popping up the trunk. "It's really neat stuff."

As I helped him drag the box out from the trunk, I wanted to give him the benefit of the doubt. Maybe there was a sane reason for him kissing that woman, but I couldn't come up with one. I hated him, hated him for cheating on Mother, for making her feel bad, for making me feel bad.

"Where were you all day?" I asked him.

"Look at the car," he said. "Where do you think I was?"

The box was not heavy, certainly not heavy enough for him to require assistance; I supposed he just wanted some company. We carried the box up the stairs and Father nudged the door open with a pitch of his butt.

There were a dozen little black boxes inside the big cardboard box. I took one out and read the bold, white-lettered label: MAGIC BALLS. Next to the name was a drawing of a cubic frame that had five balls dangling on strings from two parallel bars, each forming a perfect V.

"What is it?" I asked Father.

"Open it," he said. "It'll sell like hotcakes, I know it will. Where's everybody?"

"Mother and Noona are talking," I told him.

"Oh," he said, looking at the closed bedroom door.

"There's food for you. Still hot."

"Have you eaten?"

I had, but the way he asked that question, I felt sorry for him, even if he was rotten. "No."

He muffed my hair. "My good son," he said in English.

The apparatus was half the size of a shoe box and had a funny, vinegary smell from the Styrofoam packaging. Made of chrome, its shine was bright, especially the five silver balls that lined up right after one another. Holding them up was fishing wire and some glue. It didn't look very impressive.

"Now watch," Father said, taking the leftmost ball and pulling it away from the pack, as if aiming a slingshot. When he let go, the ball struck the second one with a clap and the rightmost ball went flying up. And when that one came back down, the left one went back up, the pattern repeating until all five balls returned to stillness.

It was simple and clever. I mirrored what Father did, except I started with the rightmost ball. Clap clap clap, it went. I was hooked.

"It's cool," I said.

"Didn't I tell you?"

While Father ate, I played with the gizmo. I lifted two balls and let them go and was delighted to see two balls jump out on the opposite direction.

"Try three," Father said, his mouth stuffed full of rice. He ate like he was going to the electric chair. The woman in the photograph obviously didn't feed him very well.

Three balls resulted in three in the opposite direction; it was neat how the middle ball gave the illusion of switching sides. After three I tried four, and with that one, it almost looked as if the leftmost and rightmost balls were handing off the middle three back and forth, neither side wanting possession.

As the silver balls clacked back and forth, a curious thought crept into my head. "How can we sell this? This isn't an Oriental item, is it?" After all, our store was named East Meets West. There was no East meeting West here as far as I could see.

"Oh, sure it is," Father said. "Look at the tag on the bottom."

I saw the tiny red sticker: MADE IN HONG KONG. The man had an answer to everything.

That night, as Noona and I lay in our respective twin beds, I was fully prepared to put aside my pride and beg her to tell me what was going on, but it was my sister who surprised me by speaking first.

She told me that since Mother had gotten the picture from the Miller Detective Agency, she had been heartbroken. "First she was mad," Noona said in the darkness, "then she was sad, and now I think she's mad again." Mother had suspected for a couple of months that Father was doing more than wholesale-shopping during his Monday excursions to New York.

"How?" I asked.

"Women know these things. You live with somebody for a long time, and you notice things that are different."

"But Mother hasn't lived with Father for five years."

"That's why she didn't see it right away. It took her some time to figure it out. She knew it had to do with the grocery store because she kept finding receipts in his pants pocket, and last month one of Mother's church friends thought she saw him. He's so stupid."

"So why aren't they fighting?" On television, women screamed at men all the time. Sometimes they threw vases across the room; the man would duck, and the vase would shatter against the wall in slow motion.

And here Noona sounded afraid, which in turn made me afraid. "They are—just not like they used to."

"Are they going to get a divorce?" I asked. I knew a couple of kids at school whose parents were recently divorced, and none of them seemed very happy.

Our timing couldn't have been more perfect. A shout, a door opening, a door slamming shut. Heavy steps, the steps of a man, thudding past our door. "Go check," Noona said.

"Why don't you?"

"I don't want to see him."

I sighed, jumped out of bed, and stuck my head out the door. Father was trying to get comfortable on the couch and failing. He saw me and waved me off. "It's nothing, Joon-a," Father said.

"Then why are you sleeping out here?"

"I don't know, but I'm too tired to argue. Ask your mother and let me know, because I have no clue." He clicked off the lamp and all went black.

I whispered my findings to Noona, who said nothing. I figured she told me all she wanted to tell me, and that was that. I tried to go to sleep, but my bed seemed too cold. I tossed, I turned, I hugged the extra pillow extra tight, but still I couldn't sleep. What if I never slept again? What would become of me? I would look like Donald Sutherland in *Invasion of the Body Snatchers,* and once I thought that, I couldn't get that movie out of my mind.

"We're going to help," Noona said suddenly, surprising me to the point where I eked out a doglike yelp. "What was that?"

"Nothing," I muttered. "I thought you were asleep, is all."

"How do you think I can sleep when our family is on the brink of disaster?"

"Why doesn't Mother just chew Father out? She has the photo now, she has evidence."

Noona sighed one of her famous sighs. "Junior, you just don't understand. Maybe someday you will. For now, I have a plan."

I sat up and listened.

"Okay?" she said, after she finished laying it out.

I walked across the icy hardwood floor, sat on her bed, and licked my pinky. She sat up and licked her pinky, too. Then my pinky locked her pinky and I told her, "Okay," and when I went back my bed I was no longer cold and fell asleep immediately and dreamed of nothing.

The following night, it was Mother who stomped out of our parents' bedroom to sleep on the couch. Through the wall we could hear Father asking her why, but Mother said nothing. When their bedroom door slammed shut, Noona told me the one word that made it bearable: "Tomorrow." Tomorrow drained away the despair. Tomorrow was Wednesday, and tomorrow Noona and I were pretending to go to school. Earlier in the day, we made sure we wouldn't get in trouble by submitting written excuses to our respective school offices. I read mine over before handing it to Mrs. Croft, who knew everyone in school by their first name, even me. *Please excuse my son David Kim from school tomorrow. He has doctor appointment,* the letter read, complete with Father's signature, meticulously forged by Noona.

"I hope it's nothing serious," Mrs. Croft had said, her eyebrows furrowing with genuine worry.

I was all ready with the right answer. "A routine checkup. Thank you."

That Wednesday morning was like any other weekday morning, with Mother waking up an hour before us to make our breakfast. While she prepared rice-cake medallion soup, we emptied our bookbags and filled them with a foldout map of New York City, a leaflet of a subway map, a one-liter Coke bottle filled with water, and a half-dozen tray of corn muffins, all Noona's doing.

"Be careful and be good," Mother said as she saw Noona off, her standard goodbye, though she sounded different this morning, more forceful. There was no way she could have known what we were up to, so it was probably my guilt that made me think this way.

Twenty minutes later, it was my turn to leave. "Be careful and be good," she said again.

"Don't worry," I said, my standard reply.

She eyed my red windbreaker suspiciously. "Are you going to be warm enough?"

"I have a sweatshirt in my bag," I lied.

She nodded. Then she squatted down and held on to my hands. "It's all going to be fine, all right?"

"I know," I said. Then she got up, patted me on the head, and off I went.

It was a fine fall day, not a cloud in the high blue sky, the leaves on the trees so bronze they looked artificial. I breathed in the crisp morning air and walked away from the bus stop, the corner where East Robertson met

North Robertson. The usual bunch of kids stared at me but said nothing. Noona, who'd been waiting for me underneath one of the apartment entrances, grabbed a handful of my jacket and yanked me around.

"What took you so long?"

"Mother was just talking to me."

Noona seemed on edge, nervous, which was not good news. It meant she'd act more irrational than usual.

"You need to keep your mouth shut, Junior."

I hadn't realized what a trial this trip was going to be, having to deal with my sister all day long. The important thing, I told myself, was that we had a common goal—to keep our family together. I wasn't exactly sure how we were going to do that, but at least we had a plan: We'd take the bus to New York, go to the grocery store, find the woman. That's where the plan went hazy.

At half past eight, the city bus squealed and hissed to a stop, and it couldn't have been soon enough. We took the first available seats, four rows from the front. The seats looked old, parts of the blue fabric patched up with a brighter color, but they were surprisingly comfortable. Noona closed our window to keep the diesel smell from coming in. Sitting across from us was an Indian woman with two babies next to her, both fast asleep. She was wearing an orange sari and had a bright red dot on her forehead.

"Think they're twins?" I asked Noona, who had the window seat and was watching the trees blur by.

She leaned over to take a better look. "All babies look alike," she said.

"So what if the woman's not there?"

"She'll be there," Noona assured me, though she sounded uncertain herself. "If not, then we'll do this again."

"Write another letter, cut another day?"

She shrugged. "What's more important, school or doing this?"

We got off the local roads and merged onto the turnpike. We stayed silent and watched the roofs of cars pass by, the occasional convertible offering us a bird's-eye view of the interior. The last time I'd ridden a non-school bus was back in Korea with Mother into downtown Seoul to have a throbbing tooth extracted. "You'll feel better after, Joon-a," Mother had told me while holding my hand. She was right about that, and I hoped the same for us now.

My ears popped as the bus took us through the white-tiled tunnel. Noona informed me this was the Lincoln Tunnel, and that we were now going underwater.

"They should have made it out of glass, so we could see the fish," I said.

"It's burrowed through solid rock, dummy," she said, "though that would be kinda neat."

I squinted when we resurfaced onto the hustle and bustle of New York City. I'd been here just once before, when we all went to China-town. We ate at a Japanese-Korean restaurant owned by a friend of Father's, and afterwards we'd taken the subway over to the Empire State Building. It was closed so we couldn't ride the elevator up to see the entire city, so I had to be satisfied with just looking at the building from the street. I had almost fallen backwards as I craned my neck to see the tippy-top. Mother, vigilant as always, had kept me from cracking my head against the pavement.

The bus made a wide left at the second traffic light and we were on our way. Noona told me we would get off at Port Authority, and from there we would go a block and take the N train down to Canal Street. She unfolded the subway map and traced the route with her finger, a yellow line that ran dead straight to Fourteenth Street then eventually angled off to Canal.

"How come you know how to get around the city so well?"

"It doesn't take a genius to read a map," she said, and turned her body away from me to stare out the window.

A guy, no doubt. I figured he must've been something special for Noona to drag herself all the way up here. What worried me was her coming to the city all by herself, and I told her so.

"Little brother worried about his big sister, how sweet," she said.

"I'm serious," I said. "You know Mother would flip if she found out."

"I wasn't alone," she said, "I went with Lana."

Lana lived in the apartment complex, too, and I'd never seen her without a cigarette dangling out of her mouth or her frayed black denim jacket. "I didn't know you guys were friends."

"We're not. She just knew about getting around in the city, so we went. Twice."

"All right," I said.

After a moment of silence, Noona put her hand on top of my hand. "It's all going to be all right, okay?" Mother had told me the same thing, and now it felt more like a jinx than a reassurance.

The bus pulled to a stop. "Port Authority," the bus driver yelled, and we got off.

We rode the N train and talked, but not like we'd ever talked before. For whatever reason—I'd attribute it to nervousness more than anything else—Noona talked to me as if I were a peer. She never called me Junior as she described in detail her two previous excursions to the city, and I wisely kept quiet, enjoying the moment for what it was. At some point she'd turn on me and treat me like a baby again, but right now she was laughing and talking, about how she and Lana snuck into the Metropolitan Museum of Art and flirted with older men.

As Noona related her story, we were twice interrupted by panhandlers, one without legs and one without sight. They both had a paper cup, which they shook.

"Don't say anything," Noona said as she looked down at her feet. I followed suit, and the beggars moved onward.

As we neared the Canal Street stop, as if reading my mind, Noona took out two corn muffins from her backpack and handed me one.

"How did you know I was hungry?"

"Big-sister intuition," she said, pinching a piece and popping it into her mouth.

As I ate, I glanced quickly from one subway rider to the next. It seemed like every race and culture were represented here, and even though our parents had warned us of the dangers inherent to this big city, I wasn't the least bit afraid. The guy sitting next to me had hair longer than Noona's and fingernails painted black, and beside him, I felt almost normal. In school and at the store, I was the curiosity, the exotic one, but not here.

The subway came to a stop and the announcement came over the intercom, barely intelligible: "Canal Street—Chinatown."

Noona offered her hand and I took it, and we walked up the stairs to street level.

"What are we going to say when we see her?" I asked.

"There's no *we,* Junior. You're going to stay quiet and let me do the talking."

"What are *you* going to say?"

"It'll come to me when I see her."

I didn't like the sound of that, but I had little choice. I held my sister's hand tight as we threaded past the throngs of busy New Yorkers, trying my best not to look like a suburbanite from New Jersey.

The Korean word *byung-shin* has two meanings: Literally, it refers to a handicapped person, a cripple. Figuratively, it means a dumb person, a half-wit. We weren't sure if the woman in the picture fit the latter definition, but she certainly qualified for the former. When Noona and I entered the store, she was sitting behind the counter in her wheelchair.

"Good day," she greeted us in Korean, but as her eyes ran from my sister to me, her smile slowly retreated. A sound came out of her, something like a hiccup, and for a moment all was quiet.

I can't recall the exact details of what happened next, but I do remember the strong smell of fresh apples in that grocery store, apples in shades of red and green. They were everywhere, in half-opened boxes and little paper bags, looking like little heads of people watching, waiting to see what would transpire.

Noona tore into the woman in Korean, calling her names I'd never heard her say to anyone. As she yelled at her, my sister's face flushed a furious red and a network of pulsating veins popped out of her temples. It was as if she'd been nice all day, saving up her rage for this moment. Customers were fleeing the store, and from the back a man came out, maybe the woman's brother, and as soon as he uttered one word, "Hey," Noona grabbed a Red Delicious and hurled it at his head. If he'd ducked a second later, it probably would have broken his nose. Instead the apple grazed his hair, slammed into the wall, and exploded like a bomb.

"That's enough," I said. For this I received the hardest slap of my life, so hard that I almost lost my balance; it would leave an unnatural rouge on my cheek for the rest of the day. Noona and I had fought before plenty of times, but not like this, in front of strangers. My cheek burned with pain and I suddenly found myself crying.

"Not enough," my sister said, and turned her attention back to the crippled woman. "You leave us alone, you fucking whore. Because if you don't, I'm coming back." When Noona grabbed another apple, she cringed like a beaten dog.

"Please," the woman said, "please."

Noona dropped the apple to the ground, grabbed my hand, and dragged me away from the store. As we were leaving, I glanced back and saw the man trying his best to comfort the woman in the wheelchair. She had her face in her hands and was wailing over and over again, "It's all my fault, it's all my fault."

By the time we returned to Port Authority, it was half past noon. The next bus wasn't due for another twenty minutes, so Noona fished out a newspaper from the top of a full garbage can, pulled out two sections, and laid them on the floor so we could sit down. She opened her bookbag and offered me a corn muffin. I shook my head no. I'd decided that I wouldn't talk to her for the rest of my life. It might be difficult at first, but I knew I could do it. I'd answer her with either a nod or a shake, and that's how it would be from now on, even when she was eighty years old and had no teeth left.

"I'm sorry I hit you," Noona said, and she meant it. She rarely sounded this sincere. I didn't care. I saw my opportunity to hurt her back.

"Every day," I said, "you become worse."

Noona nodded, the tears running down her cheeks.

"I can't believe what you did back there. They should have called the police. You should be in jail."

She was crying hard now and for a moment I was glad, but looking at my sister weeping, I felt worse than ever. She hadn't planned any of this. She might have been my big sister, but she was only sixteen, and what did a girl of sixteen know anyway? Telling her that I was sorry seemed like a stupid thing to do, so I took out a corn muffin and stuffed it in my mouth. It was as dry as sand.

As we rode back wordlessly on the bus, watching the brilliant auburn foliage pass by, I couldn't decide if we'd made things better or worse. Noona had hurt the crippled woman, then she hurt me, and I hurt her back. Soon Father would get hurt by the woman and then what? Would the dominoes continue to fall? I had no idea. I was tired. I closed my eyes and tried to nap but couldn't; too many thoughts ran wild in my head, like the identity of the crippled woman, how Father got to know her, how long had they been together—but mostly I thought about divorce. If our parents were to split, that probably meant Noona and I would go back to Korea with Mother. Or would it? Could some crazy court-arranged agreement strand me here with Father instead? I didn't want to know.

I wished the bus would flip over and kill me so I wouldn't have to think about one more thing.

On Saturday, three days after our visit to the city, I found a letter in the apartment mailbox for Father. Since we were all at the store on Saturdays, we retrieved the mail at night. I stood under the front-door light and set aside the Korean newspaper and the supermarket circulars while scrutinizing the white envelope with no return address and a postmark of New York City. The handwriting was neat and curvaceous, the penmanship of a woman.

A myriad of possibilities ran through my mind—including steaming the letter open, throwing it away, writing "RETURN TO SENDER" and sticking it back into the mailbox—but in the end I did none of these things. I slunk into our room and called Noona over.

"It's from her," I said.

"No shit."

"What do we do?"

My sister didn't hesitate. "We give it to him."

"Aren't you afraid about what might be inside?"

"Not really," she said. "Want to know why? Because he's wrong and we're right, and he might be brainless as all men are, but he knows the difference between wrong and right."

"How can you be so sure?"

"Come on," Noona said. I followed her out into the living room, where Father was reading yesterday's newspaper. From the kitchen we heard water running and glasses clanging, Mother doing the dishes left from the morning. Father peered up at us above, his eyeglasses perched at the end of his nose.

"What is it?" he asked.

Noona handed him the letter. He read the envelope and looked at us, then looked back down at it. The envelope vibrated like a strummed string in his hand.

"It's for you," Noona said.

We waited for him to reply, but Father couldn't get his eyes off the letter. Then without a word, he rose from the armchair, walked into his bedroom, and closed the door behind him.

I thought I wouldn't sleep a wink that night, but surprisingly enough, I was out cold. If it wasn't for Noona shaking me awake the next morning, I would've slept the day away. I stumbled out to the bathroom and almost ran into Father, and the previous night's encounter shocked me fully awake. He wore large black half-moons under his eyes and dragged his feet back to his room, as if he were in slow motion.

After we got to our shop, Father announced that he had to help

Mr. Hong with something, but a couple of minutes after he left, Mr. Hong came by and asked for Father.

"I thought he was helping you," Mother said.

"Oh, right, that's why I should be getting back," Mr. Hong said, but he was a terrible liar. He apologized and excused himself on the double.

I'd screwed up enough to draw Mother's wrath on many occasions. When mad, she never yelled or screamed; instead, it was a quiet, simmering kind of anger that was far scarier, for it seemed as if she was in full control of her fury. Looking at her eerily calm face was like staring at a stranger.

When Mother told us that she was going to go find Father, we realized it was time she knew what happened. Noona detailed our Wednesday trip, minus the part where she slapped me. I almost corrected her but decided against it. Even though I felt slighted, I did my best impression of a maturing young man by telling myself that the focus of the situation was not on Noona or me, but on Father and Mother.

Mother said nothing for a while. She took out her handkerchief and dabbed at her eyes. "You shouldn't be involved," she said. "I shouldn't have shown you the photo."

Back in Korea, she had close friends she could confide in, but here, we were all she had. As I listened to Mother's quiet weeping, I thought of only one thing: *ee-hone*. That was Korean for divorce, and if that word could speak, it would probably sound like this.

Father returned an hour later. He looked tired, incredibly tired, and fell into his chair behind the front desk gratefully. He saw us sitting behind the showcases, and started to say something but stopped. Instead he propped his elbows on the desk, closed his eyes, and rubbed at his temples. My guess was that he'd probably shut himself inside one of the pay-phone booths in the new wing of Peddlers Town and talked to the woman in the photograph.

The store got busy; it was just what we needed to free our minds from the ugly situation at hand. It felt good to get involved in the simplicity of work, to wrap and box and bag and say "Thank you" and "Have a nice day" a thousand times. I was sorry to see the day end so quickly; I dreaded the ride back.

We drove home under the scarlet spread of autumn twilight. A jazz saxophone flowed out of our station wagon's single speaker, and as we left the highway and ramped over to the town streets, I thought maybe we were in the clear. I hoped Father and Mother would go quietly into their room and talk things over like normal people.

Father cleared his throat and said, *"Yeuh-boh,"* addressing Mother with the familiar term of endearment. It'd been at least a week since I heard Father and Mother talk to each other.

Seeing that Mother wasn't about to acknowledge his existence, Father continued anyway. "I think we need to make a change," he said.

"Go ahead," Mother said, her voice as flat as a tabletop.

"I want you to come with me to New York on Mondays," Father said.

Those words were the antidote to the poison that had seeped into our lives. Everything was going to be all right after all.

"I think it's too late for that," Mother said.

It wasn't so much what she said but the way she'd said it. There wasn't a shred of hope in that dead voice of hers; it was the brutal sound of a final disappointment, and I wished I'd never heard it.

JULIE

 THEY CAME IN WAVES, they always did. An hour would go by and not a single customer would jingle the bell on the door of Lucky Grocery, and then in a matter of minutes, a line would snake from the cash register to the back wall of refrigerated cases full of soda and beer.

"Just moment," Julie said to the woman standing at the register. The customer looked like a lawyer, a burgundy jacket fitted tight over a white blouse, her leather briefcase standing upright next to the pack of cigarettes she wanted to buy.

The customer crossed her arms. "What is going on?"

Julie pointed to the final piece of pink-streaked receipt paper sticking out of the machine, curled like a scroll. "It's out," she said. "Just moment, please."

"Jesus Christ," the woman said, glancing at her watch.

If there was one good thing about being in a wheelchair, it was how it extended most people's level of patience. Julie rolled away from the register to holler down the basement stairs at her brother. "This line's not getting any shorter," she said in Korean.

"It's here somewhere," Doug echoed from below, also in Korean. "Ha! I found it."

Her handicap now fully visible, Julie noticed the customer looking away. She was pretty, especially her legs, her calves long and toned. Julie stared at her own set of useless limbs, her feet clad in a pair of olive-green slippers. It wasn't that long ago that she walked the streets of New York like this woman, her toes sardined into uncomfortable high heels. What she'd give to feel that sharp pinch at the tip of her toes. It was really true: You never knew what you had until it was gone.

"Thirty second!" Doug announced to the crowd, and flipped the receipt slot open and went to work. "Hello, dear sister," he said.

"Hello, dear brother," Julie said.

"Are you having a good day, a great day, or a fantastic day?"

As usual, Julie felt sorry for Doug, for having the burden of keeping up her spirits. And she constantly felt Doug's pity for her, for being bound to the wheelchair for the last nine months. Nine months, Julie thought. The time for a baby to be born, this was her baby, her goddamn worthless legs.

But that wasn't true, and she had to stop thinking so negatively because she was getting better. Inside her slippers, she wiggled her two big toes as a reminder of her steady but slow recovery.

Doug was three years her junior, two years shy of hitting his thirties. He used to talk about his plans—to sell this grocery store of his and pack his bags for Europe. It wasn't fair, none of this was fair, and it still amazed Julie how her life was only one unfair accident away from becoming a mess, how everyone's lives, every single person in this store—the lawyer woman with her cigarettes, the guy in the Jets cap with a fistful of beef jerky, the two teenagers sipping from their shiny cans of

Coke—they were all a single incident removed from utter disaster. How did people go on knowing this? They couldn't. Everyone lived in a delusion of safety.

"Julie," Doug said, gesturing to the door, "he's here."

She could set her watch by this man. Every other day at three o'clock, Mr. Paik would come in, snap her a quick bow, and wait for her to roll over to the back door that led to the apartment upstairs.

"Hello, Mr. Paik," she said.

He greeted her and the rest of their encounter fell in step like a ritual. Mr. Paik set his rectangular bamboo case on top of the box of cabbage. She opened her arms to him and he crouched and met her embrace like a lover. As she wrapped her arms around Mr. Paik's neck, he slid his left arm underneath her knees and lifted her out of the wheelchair.

He pushed open the back door with a gentle kick, and Julie reached out and picked up the bamboo case. Mr. Paik climbed slowly, one step at a time, his breathing becoming labored as they ascended. Julie felt the dampness around his neck, smelled the hint of lavender on his shirt, and closed her eyes. She thought of her childhood home in the Korean countryside, the stream that ran through their backyard, the porch that overlooked the neighboring farm's rice fields. Her mother and father had liked sitting on the floor of that porch, and every chance she got, Julie nestled herself between them, her legs hanging off the ledge, swinging free.

A month ago, Julie had received her first acupuncture treatment.

"Okay," Mr. Paik had said at the top of the stairs. His arms were shaky from the effort of carrying her up.

"There," Julie said, pointing to the flower-patterned couch against the wall. Like the rest of Doug's furniture, this, too, was a purchase from the Salvation Army. Even though it had been in the apartment for as long as Julie could remember, the couch still retained the clinical odor of the hospital it had come from. Her brother had tried everything to get rid of the smell—various upholstery cleaners, a lime and juniper-leaf solution from Heloise, even a basil and ginger concoction from his neighbor Mrs. Yoo. Now, as Mr. Paik laid her down on the cushions, Julie found comfort in the faint scent of rubbing alcohol and disinfectant that surrounded her.

"Breathe," Mr. Paik said. "Into your belly, like this." He puckered his lips into an o and drew in a magnificent lungful of air, his hands palm side up and rising. It might have been more of a performance than an actual intake of air, but Julie couldn't deny what she saw, his chest and stomach expanding like a balloon. His eyes bulging out, Mr. Paik held the air like a tenor holding a note. Then he exhaled, the release accompanied by something like the deep growl of a lion. It was an impressive, funny, and slightly scary demonstration.

"Now you do it," he said, "just like that. I'm serious."

Julie did as she was told, even though she figured this was Mr. Paik's attempt at distraction. While she tried emulating his breathing technique, she watched him open up his bamboo case and bring out a shallow red box.

Inside the box were needles, no doubt, hundreds and thousands of needles, and now Julie did take a deep breath, so deep that it almost hurt. The idea of having ten, twenty needles piercing through her skin—Mrs. Yoo, a devotee of acupuncture, told her that she regularly had at least twenty on her—made her stomach lurch.

Mr. Paik collected the scattered magazines on the coffee table into a single pile and sat down. The red box lay next to him, and as Julie looked at it up close, it seemed more malevolent than ever, the paint on the tin a perfect, brilliant crimson, the trim around the edges glinting silver like a knife.

"Are you hungry?" he asked.

"No. Why?"

He rubbed his hands together vigorously, then rested them both on her stomach. "Your tummy's growling."

He had small hands. Everything about him was small—the tiny mole above his left eye, a slight piggy nose, ears that reminded Julie of the little pork dumplings her mother used to make. Mr. Paik rubbed her belly in a slow, circular motion, and the ache subsided.

"Your brother—what's his name again?"

"Ki Duk."

"No, his American name."

"Doug."

Mr. Paik chuckled. "Makes sense. So Eun Joo becomes Julie, right?"

She said nothing, just stared at him, her Korean name ringing in her ears like an echo. "Say it again," she said. "My name."

Her name was composed of two syllables, like most Korean names. "Eun," he said slowly, "Joo."

It wasn't his voice but the way he'd said it, the questioning lilt at the end of "Eun," the full extension of his lips as he said "Joo." All week she'd tried her best to push Min out of her mind, but now here he was, her memories running a slide show of him in various poses: smiling Min standing under the Statue of Liberty, mirroring its pose with his ice-cream cone; laughing Min sitting next to her in the Korean restaurant, telling her a raunchy joke; weeping Min at the foot of her hospital bed, his hands clasped in prayer.

Mr. Paik handed her his handkerchief. He wore the expression of lost tourists who sometimes came into the store.

"I'm all right," Julie said, but she wasn't. Everything that happened that day rushed back at her—the girl and the boy barging into the store, the girl shouting horrible things to her and hurling apples at Doug. Even if Min hadn't shown her a picture of his children, Julie would have known who these two were, especially the boy. The resemblance between the son and the father was strong. The encounter had lasted no longer than a minute, but as Julie played the scene back in her mind, it was in ridiculous slow motion, the sharp screams of the girl elongated into howls, the widening of Doug's eyes as he barely ducked the apple aimed for his head.

Mr. Paik slid down from the table and kneeled on the floor. He took her hands and turned them palm-side up, revealing her wrists. "Doug told me you didn't like needles," he said, applying slight pressure to her pulse, "but there is nothing to be afraid of."

Did he actually think that she was this upset over acupuncture? Julie didn't know whether to be amused or annoyed. "Yeah," she said. "Thanks."

Closing his eyes, Mr. Paik touched her wrists lightly. "Your pulse," he said finally, "it's wiry. Fast and light."

She didn't know what heartbeat had to do with sticking needles into someone's body, or for that matter her tongue—now Mr. Paik asked her to stick it out and say "Ahhhh"—but she couldn't argue with his prognosis. He asked her if she hadn't slept for the last few nights. He asked her if she was irritable.

"You're a little dizzy right now, with a headache more on your left side than your right?"

"Did my brother tell you all this?" Julie asked.

Mr. Paik chuckled. "Flaring up of excessive liver fire," he said, picking up the red box and opening it. He removed a clear cylindrical vial, a bag of cotton balls, and a brown bottle of rubbing alcohol, and placed them on the table. "That's what your pulse and your tongue tell me."

He didn't wait for Julie to ask what he meant. Mr. Paik told her about fire, earth, metal, water, and wood. The idea was to keep these five elements in balance, and right now, her kidneys and liver—water and wood organs—were severely off.

The last item he extracted from the box was a matching red notebook. He flipped it until he found the right place and returned to sitting on the table. "We'll get your gallbladder running good, too. But before we start, can you tell me what happened?"

Min's daughter had called her a whore. A fucking whore. Was there any other kind? The boy had stood still during her tirade, looking just as frightened as Julie. When he asked his sister to stop, she whipped around and slapped him so hard on the cheek that he almost collapsed. The apple the girl was squeezing in her other hand was bleeding with juice.

"No," Julie told Mr. Paik, "I don't think so."

He looked up from his notepad. "You don't have to tell me every detail, but the more I know, the better I'd be able to help you. I know Doug brought me for your legs, but the principle of five elements acupuncture is not about treating specific areas, it's about moving you back into harmony with yourself, your emotions, your life as a whole."

And suddenly Julie was furious. Why was Mr. Paik doing this to her? Why was he making her remember? What gave him the right? She stared at him and said nothing and welcomed the uncomfortable wall of silence that formed between them.

"Okay," Mr. Paik said. There was genuine hurt in the single word he'd just spoken, and Julie found pleasure in jabbing this man with a shard of her personal pain.

Mr. Paik said nothing as he prepped her for acupuncture, and watching him, Julie found her satisfaction slowly turning into guilt. All he wanted to do was help her, and she was doing the exact opposite for him. But she couldn't tell him about the attack; she couldn't talk about it with anyone, not even Doug, and he had been there. Not only was it the most embarrassing moment of her life; thinking about that incident was a harrowing experience: the girl's mad eyes, her arm loaded like a slingshot, her lips trembling with hate.

After pumping a squirt of alcohol onto a cotton ball, Mr. Paik stood up and surveyed her like a painter planning out his canvas. He started with a needle between her eyebrows and worked his way down: four needles on her arms and hands, another six needles on her legs. She enjoyed this moment, feeling the initial cool touch of the alcohol before it evaporated into nothing. Julie wondered if Mr. Paik saw her body as a network of points, like those connect-the-dots drawings she used to do as a kid.

"You are 'wood,'" he said.

She answered immediately, glad he was talking to her again. "I'm what?"

"Breathe in," he said, so she took in a breath. Mr. Paik's right hand flew out of nowhere, partially covering her vision, then it was gone again. "Now breathe out. How was that?"

"How was what?"

Mr. Paik pointed to the mirror on the far side of the room. In it, she saw the glint of the acupuncture needle sticking out of her forehead.

"Didn't feel a thing, did you?"

Now she saw what was in his hands: a tiny strawlike tube and a metal needle. He loaded up the needle like a blow dart and tracked her left hand with the tips of his fingers. When he located the point, a fleshy area between her thumb and index finger, he again told her to breathe. He tapped the end of the tube and it shot right in.

That one hurt, and she told him so. Sometimes they did hurt, he admitted, especially when he gave the needle a slight twist, like he did now.

"But it's only for a moment," he said, loading up another one. "It'll fade within seconds."

He was right. Even when it did pinch, it always dissipated into a dull thudding. As he moved from point to point, he explained that each person was closest to one element. Wood was the element of spring and was associated with anger. "When out of balance," Mr. Paik said, "wood people tend to have a sense of hopelessness."

Julie gestured at her legs. "I don't have a right to be hopeless?"

"Sure. But it isn't healthy. I know things may seem bleak right now, but you'll get better. You will. The best thing you can do for yourself is to let your anger go."

Jesus Christ, now she really was getting mad. "Will you please stop telling me how angry I am? You keep saying that, and I'm not, but you know, now I am! Okay? Are you happy?"

Mr. Paik said nothing, just nodded. He moved down to the end of the couch to work on her legs.

Maybe she was angry. Maybe she was angry at Min, but that wasn't fair. He'd never lied to her about anything, not about his kids or his wife. She'd always known what situation she was getting into. So if Julie was angry at anyone, it was at herself.

She watched as Mr. Paik treated the last four points, two on her ankles and two on her feet, the needles shooting in one after the other. It was like watching somebody else's body, and suddenly Julie felt heat rise to her face, her hands tightening into fists.

Her legs, her worthless, lifeless legs. She wanted to take a hammer and bash them into a bloody mush.

Mr. Paik took one last needle and poked it into the webbing next to her right big toe. "Nothing?"

Julie shook her head.

He got up and stared at her like a specimen, which she supposed she was. "Five weeks."

"Five weeks what?"

"You'll feel something in five weeks."

He had been wrong, and Julie couldn't have been happier: It only took three. She never thought she could receive such joy from the sharp prick of a needle.

It was an ordinary day, nine months ago. The sky was a clear cobalt blue, finally cloudless after three days of steady snow. New Yorkers, fluffy and fat in their long winter coats, carefully negotiated the slushy streets of the city. That morning, Julie was shoveling out Lucky Grocery's sidewalk with Doug, the two of them working side by side, heaving away two feet of snow while they listened to Christmas music blaring from their neighbor. It was an electronic interpretation of "Rudolph the Red-Nosed Reindeer," the song reduced to computerized beeps and blips. Even though no words had been exchanged between them, Julie knew Doug hated these songs as much as she did. Maybe she knew it by seeing how hard he drove his shovel into the snow, the way he flung the white mound up and over his left shoulder, like he wanted to get rid of something toxic. Or maybe it was because she was his sister and he was her brother, a bond of blood and time that led itself to a certain kind of familial, genetic assuredness.

As she watched Doug scoop up another shovelful of snow, Julie wanted to tell him how good it was to be here with someone she'd known all her life, how valuable this intimacy was, and how it could be replicated with no one else, but she said nothing. Instead she shoveled next to her brother, choosing to partake in the experience instead of verbalizing it. Because talking about something was always less than actually doing it, wasn't it?

That's what she and Min had agreed on last night after another argument, which was the usual progression of their weekly encounters. He took her out to dinner where they ordered enough drinks to get a buzz, then back at the empty apartment, with Doug politely having vacated the premises, they stumbled into her room and made love on her twin-sized bed. And then they fought.

"Please," Min said. "What's wrong?"

Julie wanted to shout at him, *I'm with a married man. I'm the other woman.* She didn't shout at him, but she did tell him her feelings, and he listened.

Underneath the covers, he interlocked his fingers with hers. "You do know that we always fight about the same thing, right?"

She pulled her hand away. She stepped out of the bed and walked up to the window and gazed at her half reflection. She wasn't a beautiful woman, she knew that, but she wasn't ugly, either. People often complimented her naturally wavy hair, an anomaly for Koreans. She had just turned thirty, a spinster if she were back home, but she was here in the United States of America. If Julie wanted, she could find somebody else, but that was the problem: She didn't want anybody else. The man she wanted was in her bed, staring at her nakedness with a smile that made her blush.

"Come here," Min said. Sometimes these fights ended well, and Julie could tell this was going to be one of those occasions.

Min greeted her with three kisses, two on her nipples and a full one on the mouth. "Talking about something," he said, "is always less than actually doing it, isn't it?"

It wasn't brilliant, what he said. It hardly ever was. What gave her hope was how he seemed to genuinely believe what he was saying, a childlike optimism that led Julie to think that next time, she might be able to avoid the guilt, the shame, the self-hatred. It was possible, wasn't it? It was possible, and that sliver of possibility meant everything. It saved her.

"Salt. Julie. Salt. Julie. Salt. Julie."

She hadn't noticed Doug standing beside her and dangling the empty bag of rock salt. MELT-AWAY, the outside of the bag read. A grinning snowman was pouring salt onto the ground.

"I'm sorry, I just don't get it. Can you be more specific?"

"Salt. Julie. Salt. Julie. Salt . . ."

She snatched the bag out of his hands.

"Just get a little bag? Duane Reade has them on sale, I think."

"Little bag," Julie said, and remembered the McDonald's on the way to the drugstore, the tiny white packets of salt in the plastic bins on the counter. She'd grab a handful of those and present them to Doug. "You said little bags," she'd tell him with a straight face.

At Duane Reade's checkout line, Julie stood behind a girl and a boy. Both had blond hair and identical eyes, obviously siblings. Before he left last night, Min showed her a photograph of his two children, brother and sister like these kids in front of her. They and his wife were due to arrive by January—which meant what, exactly? She had no idea, and she was afraid of asking Min, because she already knew the answer: He didn't have a clue. How was it that they continued to have this relationship when they knew nothing, planned nothing, were nothing? Sometimes it seemed as if the only reason that they kept going was inertia.

The kids in front of her paid for their packs of gum. The boy, strangely enough, turned around. "Bye," he said. The girl, embarrassed, yanked him out the door.

"Goodbye," Julie said.

Two blocks down the street, after stopping in the McDonald's for her packets of salt and waiting for the light to change, Julie continued to revel in the boy's unexpected farewell. He had no reason to say anything to her, but he had; it was a good omen. She recalled Min's photo and zoomed in on his son. "Dae Joon," she said to herself, wanting to permanently imprint his name in her head. In the picture, he'd stood with his left shoulder slightly lower than his right, a posture she'd often noticed in Min.

The light turned green, and the WALK sign lit up. Julie cradled the bag of salt like a baby and rocked it back and forth as she made her way across the street.

At some point in the future, she would meet these two kids of Min's, she was certain. "I'm Julie," she'd say, and give the girl a hug and shake the boy's hand.

"It's nice to meet you," the boy would say.

Then something would pass between all three of them, some silent, beautiful feeling, and this was what she was thinking when the taxi slammed into her thighs, pitching her into the air and throwing her down onto the pavement.

Before blacking out, she saw snowflakes, which was strange because it hadn't been snowing, but she was glad they were there. What she actually saw were the packets of salt that had flown out of her left hand, cresting before their inevitable descent.

On their second date, he told her he was married with two kids.

"Oh," Julie said. "I see."

If they hadn't been in a restaurant, surrounded by four other dining couples, she would have cried. Not because he'd lied to her, but because he wasn't hers to have.

Julie could almost hear her brother's exasperated voice: *It's only your second time together, your second time!* She knew there was no explicable reason for her to feel this strongly about Min, but so what, wasn't that love? *No, it's just foolishness. You do this with every guy you meet. You give them what they don't deserve, and that's why they hurt you.*

Julie picked up her chopsticks and stared at her half-eaten bowl of rice, tinted pink from the *kimchi*. *At least he came clean with it,* Julie thought. *At least he had the decency to end it quickly.* She looked up from the dinner table, expecting to see a familiar expression on Min, the solemn, serious face men reserved for letting down stupid girls like her.

"What are we going to do?" he asked her, and seeing the distress in his eyes unlocked her tear ducts. Min followed suit. It didn't matter that the diners around them had turned silent. She and Min, holding hands across the table, wept together until the owner came out and asked them to leave.

Later that evening, as they strolled through Washington Square Park, Min put his arm around her shoulder and she looped her arm around his waist. It was the end of spring, white and pink flower petals scattered over the grass like confetti. As they walked, they realized that their strides matched exactly, like a pair of metronomes tuned to the same beat.

"This is it," Min said. "This is all that we have to do." Seeing that Julie didn't understand, he pointed to their feet.

Was it that simple? Why not. She was young, she wasn't even thirty yet. She had time to make this work. All she needed to do was put one foot in front of the other.

THANKSNOTHING

 I CELEBRATED THE EVE of my first Thanksgiving by moving Father out of our parents' bedroom and into mine. At the same time, Noona was moving into what was once Father's side of the room—filling the top drawer of his dresser with her frilly underwear and lace-top socks, placing her Mickey Mouse alarm clock on the side table where his glasses used to be.

"How long?" I asked my sister. After a month of unbearable silence between my parents, nothing surprised me. They were beyond repair, and this move was in keeping with the inevitable regression of their relationship.

"You'll have to ask Mother," she said. "I have no idea." She wasn't thrilled with what was going on, either, but like me, there was little she could do.

I had no plans to ask Mother anything. In Korea, she'd always put us ahead of everything, especially herself, but that was no longer the case. Lately, she was able to function in one of two modes: brooding or bitter.

Father was the bad guy in all this, but it surprised and frightened me that Mother could be so unforgiving.

Father hardly had anything to move, just his clothes and a couple of books. We were done way ahead of Noona, who wasn't even halfway finished by the time everything of his was out of our parents' bedroom. We watched her come and go until all that was hers had vanished.

"I could just sleep out on the couch," Father said, sitting on Noona's bed. It was strange to see him there. It was strange to see him in my room, period.

"No," I said. "This is fine."

"You sure?"

"Yeah."

"I'm sorry about all this."

Seeing that I would be offering him nothing more, Father fell back on the pink and baby blue sheets and closed his eyes. He went to sleep like that, in his regular clothes and not in his usual pajamas, not bothering to brush his teeth or wash his face.

I met Noona at the hallway as she was exiting from the bathroom. "Good night," I told her.

"Good night," she said. I couldn't remember the last time we didn't sleep in the same room. Noona hugged me and slipped two small foamy cylinders into my hands. "He snores."

The earplugs offered some protection but not enough. Not only did he snore, but he muttered in his sleep continually, a broken stream of gibberish leaking out of his mouth throughout the night. I couldn't make out what he was saying, but they sounded like apologies. At some point fatigue must've overpowered my sense of hearing and I fell asleep, because I woke up on Thanksgiving morning feeling groggy and tired, hoping this day would be better than the one before.

Father had gotten himself cleaned up and was wearing fresh clothes, a red sweatshirt and a pair of jeans that made him look like an ancient teenager. He'd made his bed and was now sitting on the chair and desk set we'd rescued from the Dumpster. There was nothing wrong with either one, except that they were bruised and cheap-looking. The wooden desk was made out of particle board and its laminated surface was bowed. The chair's cushion was patched with duct tape and its legs squeaked with every movement, now more than ever because Father was nervously shaking his feet.

"How did you sleep?" he asked.

"Okay," I muttered. I didn't like the pitch of his voice, slightly high, one he used whenever he had some plan he wished to pursue.

"Let me ask you something," he said. "What do you think about us getting a turkey for dinner?"

"Mother's not going to cook?" I wondered if that was next on her agenda, to stop cooking altogether.

"Well, of course she will, but maybe we can, you know, help out."

Having turkey on our first American Thanksgiving wasn't a bad idea, but two things kept me from agreeing. One, what if Mother took this the wrong way? Maybe we would be offending her somehow.

"I wouldn't worry about that, Joon-a," Father said. "I asked her yesterday, and she didn't mind."

"I thought she wasn't speaking to you anymore."

"She nods or shakes her head," he said. "She nodded."

The other thing that bothered me about this turkey venture was that I would be working with Father. Frankly, I wanted to distance myself from him as much as possible. It was already bad enough that I bore the stigma of sharing living quarters with the sinner, and I didn't want to give Mother the impression that I was supporting him in any way.

But I also felt sorry for him.

"All right," I said.

Father leaped from his chair and ushered me out. Noona and Mother were already up and preparing in the kitchen. Mother sat on the lino-leum floor with a big green bowl cradled between her legs while Noona stood at the counter with a bag of flour next to her. We would be having *mahn-doo,* the traditional dumpling dish that was served during the Korean equivalent of Thanksgiving, *Chu-suk.*

"We'll be back with the turkey," Father announced.

Noona stopped kneading the dough to look up. "What turkey?"

"We're having turkey with *mahn-doo* tonight," I said. "Father said he talked to Mother about it yesterday."

"It's what he wants, so I guess we'll have both," Mother said.

"It's not what I want," Father said to me, and I didn't want to play this stupid game of being the go-between, so I opened the door and pushed him out.

"Did you sleep okay last night?" I asked Noona before leaving. She had it tougher than I did, since she had to sleep in the same bed as Mother. It was a king-sized bed, but still, I wondered how anyone ever managed to sleep with someone else tossing and turning next to them.

"I'll live," she said, and went back to the kneading. When I looked to Mother, she dropped her gaze, looking into the mishmash of ground beef, diced onions, and chopped spinach in her bowl.

On the way to our neighborhood supermarket, I finally found the courage to ask Father about the woman in the photograph. I figured this might be the best time, since we were roomies now and I was doing him a favor.

He said nothing for a good while, and just when I'd given up hope, he said, "She's someone who kept me company when you weren't here."

"What kind of company?"

"Things you're probably too young to know about but know anyway."

"But why her? Why someone in a wheelchair?"

Father snorted. "She wasn't always in a wheelchair. She was in a car accident. She hurt her spine."

"Is she going to walk again?"

"She doesn't know yet," he said. We pulled into the massive parking lot, which was just about deserted. "You want to know her name?"

I shook my head. Even talking about this woman in these round-about ways was making me feel like I was betraying Mother somehow. "So what now?"

Father turned off the engine and yanked out his key. "I'm not seeing her anymore, if that's what you're asking. I wasn't really seeing her even then—after you all came, we were just friends."

"Friends kiss like that?"

He was starting to get angry. "She just hasn't been the same since the accident." He paused, gathering his own nerve to say what he'd wanted to say. "What you and your sister did there at her grocery store, that wasn't right."

I was about to inform him that what he'd been doing every Monday behind Mother's back wasn't right, either, but I stopped myself. He knew that already, so why bother? I looked into his face, a face that until this January I'd seen only in photographs, and now I wished it could have stayed that way.

It was cold in the meat aisle; I could see my breath. We found shrink-wrapped turkeys of all shapes and sizes carelessly thrown together in a frosty grave. Had some of them been friends before the ax fell, sharing the same batch of seeds, drinking from the same trough, yelling at one another in their quavering voices?

"Hong?" Father said behind me. Mr. Hong was smiling uncomfortably, and with him was Yun Sae.

"Just picking up a couple of things," Mr. Hong told Father. Anticipating Father's next question, Mr. Hong said, "The missus is feeling a bit under the weather, so us two dumb men are trying to buy the right things for dinner." I peered into their shopping cart: a dozen flat boxes of various frozen meals, a jug of apple juice, and margarita mix. "What are you guys doing here?"

"Us two dumb men are going to cook up a real American turkey," Father said.

"How come your wife's not here?" Mr. Hong asked.

"She's busy cooking," Father said quickly. "In Sook, too," Father said to Yun Sae, who smiled at the mention of my sister's name.

I left them talking amongst themselves while I went in search of the perfect turkey. They all looked identical, except the Butterball turkeys had the neat button that popped up when it was done. Considering we'd never cooked one before, I thought we should make it as easy as possible. There were only four of us, so I found the smallest one at the bottom of the pile, a thirteen-pounder, and dumped it into our cart.

"See you later tonight," Father said to the Hongs. They waved and I waved back. "That's gonna be too small, Joon-a," he said, and chucked the turkey back into the bin. He picked out one roughly twice the size.

"Did you just invite them to dinner?"

"Yes," he said. "We're going to have too much food, and since Mrs. Hong's sick, it's the least we can do."

Had he lost his mind? "Don't you think you should've cleared this with Mother first?"

"They're friends, it doesn't matter," he said, but I knew the real reason behind this maneuver. With company, everyone had to act cordial.

We rolled through the aisles to pick up the rest of our Thanksgiving essentials, according to Mr. Hong: celery, carrots, onions, a can of gravy, a can of cranberry sauce, and a box of Stove Top stuffing. Apparently he knew something about making this American feast because they'd done it last year.

We made our final stop at the frozen section, where Father found a stack of Mrs. Smith's Pumpkin Pies. There was half an inch of frost stuck on the boxes.

"What's that?" I asked.

"Pumpkin," he said. "It's like a really big *ho-baak*."

"Squash pie?" I made a face.

"Hong says it's good," he said, but he didn't sound sure himself.

When we came home, I thought the first thing Father would do was tell Mother and Noona that we would be having company, but he said nothing. Instead, he went right into the kitchen and started preparing the turkey, telling me to prepare the stuffing. For a little while all four of us were crammed into that tiny room, and although it was crowded, I enjoyed the atmosphere of our family working toward the simple, common goal of eating a good meal.

The directions to prepare the stuffing were straightforward, and in ten minutes I had a beige mound of . . . something. I wasn't exactly sure what, but it smelled kinda nice, if a bit fake.

"Smells like medicine," Mother said from the floor. I was glad she was talking. It was her standard response to Western cooking, and I hoped I'd be able to convince her to have a little sliver of turkey breast.

"It's the stuffing," I told her. "You eat it with the turkey over gravy."

Mother nodded, and went back to making the *mahn-doo,* picking up one of the round flour shells and dropping a spoonful of filling in the middle. There were two styles of making these dumplings: One was a semicircle, where you folded the shells in half and made a serrated crust by pressing the edges together between thumb and index finger at exact intervals. The other style also involved folding the shell in half, but instead of making a pattern, you left it plain and drew the two corners together to form a round dumpling with a hole in the middle, like a misshapen doughnut. I preferred the round over the serrated, because that's the way Mother made it. Noona made the other kind, and hers never tasted as good.

When Mother and Noona finished assembling the dumplings, they moved out to the dining room to make their other dish, *jahp-chae,* clear noodles with shiitake mushrooms, shredded carrots, and spinach mixed with sesame oil.

"Aren't you going to tell her?" I whispered to Father.

"Sure," he said, his hand and arm shoved deep into the turkey, pulling out the white bag of entrails and neck. "I will, just as soon as I put this in the oven."

He washed the turkey inside and out, salted and peppered the skin, and spooned my stuffing loosely into the neck and cavity. He asked for a needle and white thread so I got them for him. He sewed the opening shut with five quick stitches, dropped celery, onion, and carrot pieces into the pan, and placed the turkey carefully on the bed of vegetables. Using his hands, he coated a layer of melted butter on the skin. I was impressed and told him so.

"I'm just following what Hong told me." He lifted the pan with a grunt. "Open the oven, please, Joon-a!"

I pulled open the door and dragged out the rack with a ladle, then guided him to it. He gave me a potholder and we both pushed back the rack, flipped the oven door closed, and watched our bird sizzle through the oven window while arguing quietly.

"*Now* are you going to tell her?"

"Joon-a," Father said, then in English, "my good son."

"No."

"She won't be so mad if you tell her."

"But it was your idea!"

"Do you wanna have a nice Thanksgiving or a rotten one?"

As I watched the rings of onions turn brown and the liquid boil out of the chopped celery, I brooded over the unfairness of the situation, of this family, of the world.

"I'm sorry," he said, and he really sounded like he meant it, which pissed me off even more.

I left him in front of the turkey and marched into the dining room to get this over with. "Father invited the Hongs to dinner tonight," I said.

"Why?" Noona said.

"Mrs. Hong's sick." To Mother, I said, "With the turkey, I think we have enough food."

"Fine," she said, and I was glad she looked more tired than angry. "This was your idea?"

"No."

"Coward," Noona said, loud enough for Father to hear.

Mother put a hand on her arm. "We'll make extra noodles, and we still have some shells and filling left, so we should be fine."

I sat down next to Mother and dragged the cutting board and knife in front of me. "I can chop whatever you want me to chop," I said.

"That's all right," she said. "We can handle this. You go on and cook your turkey."

"I don't want to help him anymore," I said.

She handed me a pile of carrots and showed me how to slice them thin enough to see through. I screwed most of them up, but Mother didn't care. Whatever didn't turn out right she shredded, turning my mistakes into thin orange threads.

"I'm sorry that you have to share your room with him," Mother said. It was the first time she had acknowledged her regret over the changes in the household.

I wanted to be strong like my sister and say what she'd told me earlier in the day, that I'd surely live and go on living, but what came out of my mouth instead was desperation and fear.

"Let's just go back home," I said.

Mother kept on chopping. "Don't be stupid, Junior," Noona said, but without malice.

"It was good when we were there," I said.

"We have enough now," Mother said, speaking of the carrots. "You go on."

I left the table and sat down in front of the television in the living room but didn't bother to turn it on. I stared at the empty gray screen for a while, then lay on the couch and closed my eyes, wondering if our lives would ever go back to normal. They might not, and the hopelessness of admitting that very possibility left my chest heavy. Of course, even then I knew that happy endings weren't always possible in life, but I never thought reality could be so cruelly contrary.

In spite of all this turmoil, I fell asleep.

What woke me up was the heavenly scent of roast turkey and Korean dumplings. I smelled it no matter where I went in our little apartment—behind the shower curtain in the bathroom, even inside the medicine cabinet. After I washed up and changed into my black sweater and brown corduroy pants, I went into the kitchen to find Father tending his turkey. He peered through the oven window.

"How's it going?" I asked.

"I think it's almost done," he said, "I think."

I checked it out and saw the problem. "Doesn't that thing pop when it's ready?"

"I know," he said. "I don't know what's wrong. It should've popped half an hour ago according to the instructions, but maybe it'll never pop. Hong said that nothing's worse than an overcooked, dry turkey."

"Maybe the popper's broken."

"Maybe," Father said. This was getting us nowhere, so I knocked on Mother's door and asked her to take a look at it. She was also dressed up for the occasion, wearing her white silk blouse and an ankle-length woolen brown skirt.

"But I've never cooked a turkey before," Mother said.

"But at least you've *cooked* before," I said.

Father stepped back to give Mother room. She said nothing to him, just went right to the oven, opened it up, and took a long look. She got a metal chopstick and shoved it all the way through the breast, then pulled it out quickly. She looked at the stick like a doctor examining a thermometer.

"Take it out," she said. "It's done."

"What if it's not?" I asked. "I've heard you have to make sure to cook turkeys all the way through."

Mother turned the oven's dial to zero. "We'll live," she said, and grabbed the pair of oven mitts on the counter.

"I'll do that," Father said. "It's very heavy."

She dropped the mitts back on the counter and walked out. Father sighed.

"It'll get better, Joon-a," he said as he heaved the aluminum pan off the oven shelf and onto the range, but like with everything else he'd been promising lately, his words sounded empty and defeated.

The doorbell rang at seven o'clock sharp. All the dishes were ready by then—the golden turkey steaming on the table, two huge plates of dumplings and noodles, and various little sides surrounding the main course. Noona, wearing a hunter green sweater and a knee-high pleated skirt, opened the door to greet our guests.

"Where's Mrs. Hong?" Mother asked as Noona took Mr. Hong and Yun Sae's coats. Mother and she weren't close, but they usually found things to chat about in each other's company, and I could tell that Mother was disappointed. The two men sat down on the sofa.

"She's sick," Yun Sae finally said.

"We know that," Father said. "But I don't understand why she's not here."

"She's very sick," Yun Sae said, meeting our eyes—Noona's first, then Father's, Mother's, and finally mine. His were hard and angry, not at us but something else.

"I don't— What the hell's going on, Hong?" Father said.

"She's got ovarian cancer," Hong said, and I heard Mother suck in a quick breath of air. "We should go, Yun Sae, we should've never come, spreading our bad news around. It's bad luck." He got up but Father put a hand on his shoulder, then he hugged him.

"I'm so sorry," Father said.

"No symptoms," Hong said. "You know? I mean she said she felt bloated and she felt tired, and her back's been bothering her for months, but how the hell are you supposed to know that's cancer?"

"You can't," Mother said. She sat down next to Yun Sae and held his hand. "How is she doing?"

"Not well," Yun Sae said. "They're doing chemo, so she feels nauseous all the time."

"Is she okay right now? I mean, is somebody with her?"

Hong nodded. "Her sister is there. She told us to go. We've been going there every night for the last three weeks."

"My aunt may look like my mother," Yun Sae said, "but she doesn't cook anything like her."

Hong laughed softly. "She's a terrible cook. We're afraid to eat anything she makes, so we're buying prepared stuff."

"We haven't eaten a real home-cooked meal in months."

"Well, you've come to the right place," Father said. "Come on, let's eat."

So we ate. We ate American turkey and Korean dumplings, two distinct cuisines melding into one as the evening progressed. We dipped the dumplings into the gravy, and mixed the clear noodles with the stuffing. The cranberry sauce went well with slices of Mother's steamed pork, and it wasn't half bad with the turkey, either.

"You got this turkey out at the perfect moment," Mr. Hong said to Father as he helped himself to a third serving.

"It wasn't me," Father said, "it was my wife."

"I should've known," Mr. Hong said.

Mother gave Mr. Hong a small, tight smile. If the Hongs weren't here, she wouldn't have even done that much.

When we couldn't possibly eat another bite, Father brought the pumpkin pie fresh from the oven and Mother made coffee and tea. I liked seeing them together, even if they weren't speaking. It gave the illusion that things were okay after all.

Mr. Hong took a big, long whiff when Father put the pie in the middle of the table. "Ah, *ho-baak* pie! Give me a big slice, Kim, would you?" He was a little man, but he could eat.

Yun Sae, who sat next to Noona, was telling her about the part-time job he had in the law school while he attended UConn. They'd been talking by themselves throughout dinner, and Noona was enjoying it, even asking him questions. She'd never been so friendly to him before, but maybe it was because she felt sorry for his mother. Or maybe she was finally realizing that he was a pretty good guy. I'd always liked him.

"So they call you William at work?"

"I wonder if I'll ever get used to it," Yun Sae said.

"I'm Susan at school. I kinda like it. I like the shortened version, too, Sue."

"You know what that word means, right?"

"Yeah, it's what you do for a living."

"Whoa! Not me, my bosses. I spend all my time in the library, I'll have you know."

"Okay, whatever." She picked a tiny corner of the pie and tried it. Then she took another bite, a bigger one. "This is good."

It surprised me, too. I thought it'd taste like a vegetable, but it was sweet and soft inside like thick cream, and it tasted like nothing I ever had before.

She turned her attention back to Yun Sae. "I don't see you as a William. You're more like a Billy." She pulled herself back from her chair, as if to capture a complete, overall view. "Yeah, Billy."

"I don't know," Yun Sae said, laughing. "Well, you can call me Billy."

"And you can call me Susie." Then she said in English, "Hello, Billy," while offering her hand.

"Hello, Susie," he said. He took her hand and kissed it, and then they both cracked up.

Empty plates, turkey bones, leftovers. I carted the dishes from the dining room table as Mother and Noona formed a washing and drying team. The rest of the turkey I carved to the best of my ability, which wasn't much; I developed a mild blister on my hand from all the sawing.

I placed the cut-up meat in four flat Tupperware containers, crammed the stuffing into a round container, and covered the gravy bowl with plastic wrap. There was enough here for another two meals, even though we gave the Hongs two huge chunks of breast meat and a drumstick. Coupled with the Korean leftovers, Mother wouldn't have to cook for at least three days.

As I stacked the containers on the bottom shelf of the refrigerator, I thought about Mrs. Hong. She was probably the same age as Mother, and going on my parents' reactions, it seemed certain she wouldn't recover. What would it be like to not have a mother? I'd lived without a father for years, but I couldn't imagine a world without my mother. She hadn't been acting like one lately, but I'd still take that over no mother at all. I watched her rinse dish after dish, her wet yellow gloves slick in the light of the kitchen, and I was glad that she was physically fine, though it concerned me that the cancer in Mrs. Hong came without warning. But there had been warnings—Mr. Hong had said she'd been bloated and tired.

I closed the fridge door and stood next to Mother. "You're feeling okay, right?" I asked. "Not bloated? Or tired?"

Mother was rinsing the suds away from the chopsticks and laying them on the drying rack. "I'm fine, Joon-a."

"You should go see Dr. Choi."

"It wouldn't be a bad idea," Noona said, apparently thinking the same thing. "You should get a physical. We all should."

Mother turned off the faucet and removed her gloves, hanging them to dry on the handle of the oven. She squeezed a dollop of lotion and rubbed it into her hands, releasing the familiar scent of aloe. "I'll be just fine," she said. "I'll live a long time, don't you worry. Now I think I'll go lie down. This has been one long day." Like most older Koreans, Mother believed checkups were a waste of money, especially since we didn't have health insurance. Though if we all got one, she'd have to go, too. I followed her out of the kitchen and sat down next to Father on the couch, who didn't look so good.

"Maybe I ate too much," he said, rubbing his belly. "My stomach hurts." I brought him a Pepto-Bismol and he gladly chewed on a pink tablet. Then I got a can of ginger ale and poured it into a glass for him. "Thanks, Joon-a. I don't mean to be unappreciative, but why are you being so nice to me?"

"I'm always nice to you."

"Oh, I get it, you want some money?" He took out his wallet and pulled out a dollar bill.

"I want all of us to go for a checkup."

Father put away his money and his wallet. "After Christmas. We'll have enough money for all of us to go see Dr. Choi."

"Okay."

"Though from the way I'm feeling, I think I might have to go see him tonight. Will you bring me a heating pad? Sometimes putting heat on a tummy ache helps."

I got the heating pad, put it on his stomach, and even got a blanket for him.

"My good son," Father said in English.

First came the bellyaches. Then came the farts. These were deadly farts, the kind that make you wonder how something so vile could come out of your body. If this were a race, Father had ten laps on us, though I was closing in. Whatever this was, it didn't care what sex you were. By the time Father and I were taking turns in the bathroom, the women of the house were at the gaseous stage.

"Maybe it was the turkey," Noona said, her hands massaging her stomach. She dashed into the bathroom.

"Maybe it was the combination," I said to no one in particular, "putting Korean and American food together."

When the clock rang midnight and Thanksgiving officially came to an end, we all sat in the living room, nursing our mutual pain. The runs had stopped, and the bellyaches were slowly ebbing away.

"Oh jeez," Father said. "Poor Hong and Yun Sae."

"We need to check up on them, apologize," Mother said. "I don't think it's too late, they're probably up like us."

Noona volunteered to make the phone call, which came as no surprise to anyone who noticed the way she and Yun Sae were carrying on during dinner. She went into her room to make the phone call, and a little while later she came out. "They're fine."

"Did you apologize?" Mother asked.

Noona laughed. "You don't understand. Nothing happened to them."

"They must be being polite," Father said.

"Yun Sae would have told me if they really got sick. It was just us."

"How could that be? They ate everything we ate, didn't they?"

In the ensuing silence, the answer came to me from, of all places, my health class. "Family bacteria," I said. I elaborated that each family has a group of bacteria that they share without ill effect, even though the microbes might be harmful for people outside the family.

"Doesn't explain why we got sick," Father said.

"Sure it does. It was Mr. Hong and Yun Sae who brought their family bacteria to us. And because we're a family, we got hit with it all the same."

"That's the stupidest thing I've ever heard," Noona said, and both Father and Mother chuckled, and for moment we'd achieved familial harmony, but only for a moment. When Mother realized Father was laughing with her, she stopped immediately and cleared her throat. "Good night," she said, and kissed my forehead before retiring to the room she shared with Noona.

I didn't care if my answer was stupid; I knew I was right. Like it or not we were still a family, and if it took a mess of wicked germs to prove it, that was just fine.

There was only one way to appease my stomach after a night like that one: chocolate.

"I'll be back," I said. It was Friday, my evening run to the candy shop in Peddlers Town, Candy Lane, a habit of mine lately. They sold a hundred different types of chocolate by the pound, though I always ended up getting the same thing.

"You're gonna rot out your teeth," Noona said, something that Mother would usually say, but Mother was sitting at the back of the store, in the clothing section, where she spent all of her time now. It was the furthest distance away from Father.

"They're good for you," I said. "Raisins are healthy."

"Not if you slather them with chocolate."

"Maybe I'll also pick up some chocolate-covered cherries?" They were Noona's favorite, and that shut her up momentarily.

"No, thank you," she said, but I could tell she wanted them.

On the way, I envisioned the chrome tray heaped with Raisinets that waited for me, the thrust of the silver shovel into the mountain of round chocolate pebbles, the weighing and adjusting on the electronic scale. I never got very much, just a quarter pound, though whenever it went a little over, I never had the guy take the excess out. It seemed like a gift, and I was eager to pay the extra few cents.

As I neared the shop, I thought less about the candy and more about

Mindy. I was anxious, then happy, then back to anxious again. What if she wasn't there?

But she was.

"Hey," Mindy said, semi-nonchalantly.

"Hey," I said, supplying the other half of the nonchalance.

Last spring, it was Mindy who had scared the hell out of everyone in our store when she screamed at her mother, but it turned out that she wasn't so scary after all. When we'd first met up at Candy Lane a month back, it was a coincidence, but maybe it was fate, too.

"Hi, David," she had said, in her usual chirpy way.

"Hi, Mindy," I replied.

Our chance encounters always ended at this point, but that evening, we kept talking. She and I ordered the Raisinets, and our mutual love for their chewy sweetness triggered the mysterious process of friendship.

I don't know why we circled the mall that evening, why we stopped at stores that never held any interest for me before, like the pawn shop and the jewelry store, but that's what we did. Oddly enough, it felt utterly natural to have her by my side, and she must've felt the same way because the only reason we eventually parted ways was because it was closing time. When I finally returned to our store, a little dazed and fuzzy from all that walking around, Father chided me for making him worry, but I told him I was hanging out with a girl and he forgave me instantly, happily clapping me on my back.

Now, as we stood in front of the vast array of candy behind the glass showcase, I suddenly longed to be physically closer to her, so I scooted over a little, and to my delight, Mindy leaned toward me until our shoulders touched.

"You two guys are back again, huh?"

Sometimes the owner of Candy Lane was behind the counter, and he knew us.

"Hello, Mr. Singh," I said.

"The usual?"

Each showcase displayed eight trays across, five trays high, and there were six showcases surrounding the small store like a bunker. Every time I came here, I felt as if I should try something new, but in the end, I always got what I loved. Why risk it?

I watched the ritual unfold in front of me, the shoveling and the weighing and the bagging, gleeful when the total weight came to 0.28 pounds.

We thanked Mr. Singh and walked over to the bench across the arcade, where we untied our respective bags. We made it into a game, this opening and eating, making sure it was a synchronized effort.

I pulled out a single Raisinet, and so did Mindy. Her green eyes always seemed to shine brighter before our ceremony. I knew she wasn't pretty like girls on TV or in magazines. It was entirely possible she was even ugly. But the more I saw her long face and freckled cheeks, the more I got used to her, and the more I missed her when she wasn't around.

"Ready?" she asked.

The first one was always the best, so I took my time. I cleared my throat and took in a long, deep breath, and breathed out.

"Ready," I said.

My life was crappy at the moment, but for a little while, everything was sweetness and bliss.

YUN SAE HONG

 HE TOOK ANOTHER HIT, full of sweetness and bliss, his throat on fire, and the telephone rang.

"Fuck," Will said. He didn't want to pick it up but he had to, because the only person who'd call at one in the morning was his father.

"Oh no," Robbie said, then started crying, which wasn't out of the ordinary. Pot had a melancholy effect on his roommate, often moving him to tears when he heard a sad song from the radio or saw a sappy commercial on television.

"Yeah, okay, no, everything's fine, that's just the TV," Will said into the receiver. He didn't know why he was speaking so softly; it wasn't as if Robbie understood Korean. He put his hand over the mouthpiece and told Robbie to shut it, but that made him cry even harder. "I'll be there tomorrow, Dad, all right." Will hung up the phone and glared at Robbie.

"Man oh man," he said, "I'm so sorry."

Robbie had no right to be sorry. It wasn't *his* mother in the hospital stricken with ovarian cancer, it wasn't *his* father sounding like a fucking robot, it wasn't *his* life rotting like roadkill on the shoulder of a highway, but there he was, tears streaming down his stupid face, and Will wanted to scream at him, and tell him he was being an asshole. But suddenly the lamp in the corner of the room flickered like a candle, and Will found himself staring at it. As he waited for the next flicker, he felt every single strand of his wool sweater tickling him. It felt good, and he felt calm, and Will knew the pot was kicking in again.

He sat down on the beanbag chair in his dorm room, closed his eyes, and let Pink Floyd take him away.

The next morning, after dropping a liberal dose of Visine into his eyes, Will visited the dean. It was a Saturday, so he met him at his home at eight o'clock. In the two and a half years he'd been attending UConn, Will had never seen the dean outside of his suit and red bowtie, and today was no exception.

"Come on in, Will," Dean Palmer said at the door, his face grave, obviously prepped to receive him.

Will walked in, following the dean's lead into the living room, and sat down in one of the two distinguished chairs by the bay window, the kind of antique furniture that Will always envisioned the dean to possess.

"I know you've been under a devastating amount of stress," Dean Palmer said.

Will nodded, but he couldn't meet the man's eyes. Most likely the dean would interpret this as further evidence of Will's suffering, which was fine. All Will knew was that he had to act the part and get out of there.

"So you've had a chance to read my letter?" Will asked.

Dean Palmer nodded. "As you know, this is a crucial part of the fall semester. You have a final exam and a term paper due, both of which will count for half of your grade."

He hadn't even begun the Jung paper, and he was four chapters behind in his reading for the other class. If the dean didn't grant him his leave of absence, he would fail those classes, no question. Which would mean he would lose his scholarship, be put on academic probation, maybe even be kicked off campus.

Will's hands felt damp and cold, but regardless, it was time to put the skills he'd learned from Intro to Acting to good use. Time to think about his poor, sick mother, get those "method" juices flowing, time to face the dean with the heaviest heart imaginable.

"The fact is, Dean Palmer," Will began, "I can't get my mother off my mind." And as he piled on lie after lie and saw the dean believing every false word, Will realized one thing for sure: He was going to hell for this.

Will led two lives, and the minute he got into his Subaru and started driving on Interstate 84 West, heading toward home, he assumed the role of the good Korean son. At UConn, the only biweekly evidence of his alternate identity was on his paycheck, and sometimes he would gaze at his full name printed in capital letters, YUN SAE HONG, and wonder just who the fuck he was.

To his parents, he was a source of great pride. He'd gotten a free ride to attend a good university, and his mother never forgot to let every friend know that he'd been waitlisted at *Hah-bah-duh,* the butchered Korean mispronunciation of Harvard. He was eventually rejected by the esteemed institution, but his mother deftly left this off in her conversations.

The problem was that Yun Sae had no clue what he wanted to be, and time was running out. By the end of his sophomore year, he was supposed to know his future profession, and he was already halfway through his junior year. Psychology was his declared major, but the more he got into the subject matter, the less it interested him, and as he advanced in his study, the courses became more difficult. He was carrying a full load of five classes, and although he managed to maintain a B average in three of them, the two core psych classes were killing him.

And to think, he'd used his mother's cancer as an excuse to save his own failing ass. Could he have sunk any lower? He had been distracted, it was true, but her situation was hardly the reason for his academic malaise.

Yun Sae floored the accelerator and dove over to the passing lane, glancing at the loser in the minivan, idiotic enough to actually obey the speed limit. It was an Asian man who resembled his father, and even though Yun Sae glowered at him, the man remain oblivious, his eyes straight ahead, both hands on the steering wheel.

He dreaded having to see his mother after what he'd done. At least he could look forward to seeing In Sook, the only bright spot to his homecoming. Since Thanksgiving, they'd been talking almost every night, which had frankly surprised him. It started with her calling him after the big dinner, because everyone in her family had gotten sick, and somehow that single conversation managed to sustain a bond between them. He didn't know whether he could call her his girlfriend, or if she considered him similarly, but then again, he was never good at identifying the point of a relationship when those labels could be affixed.

The last thing he needed was a traffic ticket, so he switched back to the right lane and reduced his speed to a steady sixty. It wasn't even two in the afternoon but it seemed later, the sky low with thick, dark clouds. The forecast had called for snow, but you never knew with these meteorologists, always sounding like the storm of the century was coming.

He tried to find something palatable on the radio, but the only station that came in was a minister imparting his views. "Ask the Lord for help," the man was saying. "Because only through Him will you achieve absolute forgiveness." Yun Sae had no desire to speak to God, but he did hope to tell In Sook about all his troubles. He wouldn't want her to say anything, just to listen, so he could unburden himself before visiting his mother. He wondered if that was wise at this point in their courtship. Wouldn't it quite possibly push In Sook away from him instead of bringing her closer? Could he take that chance? But who else could he talk to?

"Fuck!" he yelled out to no one but himself.

The drive took three hours as it always did, though it seemed much longer. When he finally pulled into the lot at Peddlers Town, next to his father's black Corolla, Yun Sae wanted nothing more than to tilt back his seat, close his eyes, and go to sleep, but he did what was required of him, which was to open the door and push himself off into the cold December air.

The Gucci knock-off purses that resembled bowling-ball bags were lined up on two shelves with rulerlike precision. The black Samsonite luggage set, which his mother had equated with their household ("father suitcase, mother suitcase, baby suitcase," she used to say with affection), was displayed like Russian dolls, one inside the other. Even the large barrel that was heaping with clearance items—canvas wallets, irregular belts, out-of-fashion coin purses—even this looked like it had been sifted through and organized.

He had the urge to kick it all down, turn the barrel sideways, and roll it down the walkway until it spat out every last cheap wallet.

"The store's looking good," Yun Sae said, unable to suppress the accusation in his tone, but his father didn't notice.

"It's not the same," he said.

Which was true. If anything, it was looking better, but before Yun Sae said anything he would regret, he paused to study his father. Unlike the store, he looked awful, his eyes dark with fatigue, one of his shirttails pooching out, two large shaving nicks on his cheek. He was doing his best to keep it together, but a part of Yun Sae wished for a complete meltdown, the store in embarrassing disarray, his father a blithering mess.

The UPS man dropped off a large box shortly after Yun Sae's arrival, which was good. It was easier to talk about things while they performed some sort of physical action, so as they unpacked an assortment of canvas gym bags, he attempted to get his father to open up.

"So there's no improvement," his father said. "They have her on this new radiotherapy treatment. I don't know."

"Sure," Yun Sae said. "And how are *you* doing?"

His father unwound the shoulder strap and snapped it onto the two triangular rings at the ends of the bag.

"I'm fine," he said, and hung it on the hook above.

"You're fine."

"Yes," his father said. Like a machine, he unzipped yet another gym bag, stuffed wads of newspaper inside to give it shape, attached the strap—then on to the next one. "I mean I'm ready, for whatever happens. I'm a strong person, so I'll be strong."

Yun Sae knew it was his father's way of dealing with this situation, but still, it annoyed him. At the Thanksgiving dinner, he'd broken down when Mr. Kim hugged him, but with his own son, there was no sign of that man in anguish.

What was strange was that last spring, his father had shared with him a very personal incident that'd happened at the store, when he had purposefully tripped a boy out of anger. As he heard his father's confession, Yun Sae had felt like an adult for the first time. It was one of the proudest, happiest days of his life, and he looked forward to their future together as father and son with great hope.

But now here was his dad, his emotions tucked away, sequestering himself inside this house of indifference. There were no doors to knock on, no windows to crack open, but Yun Sae knew he had to try.

"Dad," Yun Sae said.

His father looked up, and Yun Sae saw how his grip on the gym bag tightened, how his entire body stiffened, as if to brace against a powerful gust of wind. He didn't do this often, but Yun Sae had seen it enough to know there was no use speaking to him. It was funny, but seeing his father dig in his heels like this reminded Yun Sae of himself as a child and the stubborn, silent tantrums he had thrown. Back then, his father had stared down at him, but now it was reversed because Yun Sae was a foot taller.

"I'm gonna stop by and see In Sook before I go see Mom, all right?"

"Of course, of course," he said, returning to the task at hand. Yun Sae turned back before leaving, and it seemed as if his father was now working twice as fast.

Everywhere he looked, there was Christmas: twinkling lights and golden tinsel tacked around a doorway, a full-sized robot Santa yelling, "Ho Ho Ho!" as shoppers walked by its motion sensor. Peddlers Town was drowning in a sea of green and red and silver and gold, and the merchants couldn't be happier. Christmas was three weeks away, the day of financial salvation for retailers everywhere.

East Meets West, on the other hand, wasn't decorated in the least, and Yun Sae was grateful. After being inundated by everyone else, it was nice to have a store in its normal state, an oasis in the middle of a vast desert of Christmas.

"Oh no, it's coming," In Sook said. "Lights, signs, all that crap. We're just late, that's all. It's just a matter of putting them up."

They sat behind the cluster of showcases, she on the aluminum stool while Yun Sae occupied the wooden one. In Sook looked good, as she always did, even if she wore something he found unattractive. But today she was wearing a tight pink turtleneck and a white skirt, and he couldn't keep his eyes off her.

"You're staring," she said.

"I certainly am," he said.

She nodded approvingly, then turned serious. "I'd like to come with you to the hospital, if that's okay."

Yun Sae took her hand. This was a surprise, and a sweet one. "I'd like that very much. It's okay with your parents?"

"They don't give a shit," she said, and he supposed it was true. The last time they spoke, In Sook had informed him that she and her mother were now sharing her parents' bedroom, and from the look of things—Mr. Kim sitting behind the front counter and Mrs. Kim all the way on the other side of the store—the war was still on.

He shook Mr. Kim's hand before taking off.

"I'll have her back in a couple of hours at the latest."

"That's fine," Mr. Kim said. He had dark pouches under his eyes just like his father, but at least he wasn't masking his tiredness. He plopped back down into his chair and sighed. "Please give your mother our regards."

They walked toward In the Bag, holding hands. She looked even prettier in profile, the sweater outlining her gentle curves, the skirt revealing her calves.

"You're still staring . . ."

"You're still beautiful . . ."

She giggled at that, and for a moment, Yun Sae felt like he could lift a thousand pounds, fly an airplane, wrestle a gorilla.

"Where's your brother? I didn't see him at the store."

In Sook stopped short. "What time is it?"

When he told her it was a quarter past noon, she pulled him in the opposite direction. "You'll have a good laugh, believe me."

They hurried down the walkway, heading for the new section of Peddlers Town, then suddenly In Sook slowed down. Like a spy, she cautiously led him to the candy shop, then flattened herself against a wall, so Yun Sae did likewise.

"Look over there, at that bench. And try not to laugh."

He didn't have a great angle, but he could see her brother sitting next to a blond gawky girl, and they each held a bag of candy. After watching them for a while, he thought they were trying to imitate one another, but that wasn't it.

"They're eating their candy simultaneously," Yun Sae said.

"Is that not the dumbest thing you've ever seen?"

He said he agreed, but he wasn't sure. It was silly, but there was something innocent about it, too, their desire to share their experience.

They stopped at In the Bag before going to the hospital so Yun Sae could tell his father that In Sook would be accompanying him. But before leaving, he realized he hadn't told his father that he would not be going back to school for another month, until mid-January.

"I took a leave of absence," Yun Sae said.

"What?" his father asked.

"It's fine, the dean okayed it. He's letting me take the final exam in the beginning of next semester, and I can work on the term paper over break."

His father said nothing, then for some inexplicable reason, he seemed angry. "Why did you do that?"

Yun Sae hadn't expected an onrush of gratitude, though maybe in the back of his mind, he had. Still, outright hostility had not been a part of the scenarios he'd imagined, and he didn't quite know how to reply.

"I think he's just trying to help, Mr. Hong," In Sook said. Most girls, especially Korean girls, wouldn't dream of speaking at a moment like this, but this was what made her special, her boldness. "It probably isn't a bad idea, anyway. School's hard enough, and with all that's going on . . . right?"

Hearing the explanation coming from In Sook softened his father, and he nodded. "Of course. His mother's sickness has been very hard on him."

And what about you? Yun Sae wanted to say, but he stayed silent. Instead, he watched In Sook hold his father's hands and tell him they would return in a short while.

In the car, she leaned over and planted a quick kiss on his lips. "You're a good son, you know that?"

This was the time, the segue he'd been waiting for. *No,* he'd say. *I'm not a good son at all, and let me tell you why I'm a total fucking loser.* And as he admitted his awful secret, she would hold him and love him and tell him it was okay, everything would be fine.

All he had to do was say the words, but he couldn't do it. He couldn't let those admiring eyes of hers look away from him, not right now.

As they drove toward the hospital, Yun Sae thought back to In Sook's brother and his girl, their quiet simplicity. Did they know how lucky they were? Of course not. *Just you wait,* he thought. *Ten years from now, you'll be just as miserable as I am.*

How foolish of him to think that In Sook could save him. After all, this was between him and his mother, no one else. And with her, there would be no hesitation. He would say what had to be said, because that's the relationship they'd always had.

Mom, I'm sorry, but I used you.

She would be let down, but Yun Sae also knew his mother. She was the kind of woman who would tell him that at least her disease was good for something.

Yun Sae signaled right and slowed down at the hospital entrance.

"This is the same hospital that your father went into after the fire, isn't it?" In Sook asked.

"Yeah, that's right," he said. Both of his parents had spent time here this year, and that made him sad.

The visitors' lot was full, so they drove up to the parking garage, where they still had to snake around twice to find a spot.

"There's never a shortage of sick people, is there," Yun Sae said.

"Especially in a hospital," In Sook said. It was a joke, and it was funny, but he didn't feel like laughing, and she didn't expect him to. She was so perfect.

They rode the elevator up to the third floor and the lady at the reception desk greeted him. He told her they were here to visit his mother, and she asked him to identify themselves.

"I'm her son," he said, "and this is my girlfriend."

In Sook gave his hand a reassuring squeeze, and he squeezed back.

When he was here two weeks ago, they'd just started the chemo, so his mother still had hair. His father told him it was all gone now, so he'd tried to imagine her bald and couldn't quite do it. His mother wasn't a vain woman, preferring to have her hair permed for the sake of convenience more than for looks, but still, she often fooled with it in front of the mirror, humming and teasing at her curls with a pick.

"Here it is," Yun Sae said. "Room 314."

"I overheard your father talking to my father yesterday," In Sook said. "He said it's bad. Okay? So hold on to me." She took his hand.

He held on, thinking she was being melodramatic, and realized the moment he entered the room that there were no words that could possibly prepare him for what he saw. Because the woman in the bed could not possibly be his mother.

He knew ovarian cancer was deadly, he'd heard the doctor's quiet words, and now it was plain what had happened: He hadn't really believed. His mother may not see him get married, he'd known that, but certainly she would see him graduate, see him in his cap and gown, stand next to him as his father snapped a few photos.

He thought back to the morning, his drive down from UConn, when he'd considered his unknown future. Time was running out, that's what he'd said to himself. But was it really? Not for him, it wasn't. Because this, right here, this was time running out. This was the end, and suddenly his own problems seemed very small. In fact, they weren't problems at all. They were merely a part of his life, because here, here was death.

"Yun-Sae-ya?" his mother croaked.

He laid his hand on her forehead. It was dry and cold.

"It's me, Mom," he said.

"It's good to see you."

"You too," he said.

"And is that you, In Sook?"

"Yes," she said, coming over, her voice quiet.

"You guys shouldn't be here," his mother said.

"No," he said. "This is exactly where we should be."

His mother laughed, and it was ghastly. It was a disgusting joke, a skull opening its jaws, the muscles underneath the skin of her face pulling tight like ropes. She gestured at the window. "It's snowing out there is what I mean."

Yun Sae looked out the window and saw the sudden blizzard, the snowflakes swirling, spinning into each other. If only it would keep snowing, snow forever and ever, until the Earth was covered and there was nothing at all.

TIME OF THE YEAR

 ON A SNOWY MORNING IN DECEMBER, Father gave up trying to fix things with Mother. There was no drama: No dish flew across the dining room in a spinning rage, no door got slammed hard enough to fall off its hinges. Instead it was a quiet, subtle shift in the way he greeted me in the morning. Since we'd been rooming together, I heard a tinge of sorrow and shame every time he said, "Good morning, Joon-a," but on this day it was gone. This day, he was perfectly happy to tell me that this living arrangement, where a father and son shared a room while a mother and daughter shared another, all under the same roof, could constitute a good morning.

"It's not normal," I told my sister. "Normal people don't live like this."

"Then I guess we're not normal," she said. The old Noona would not only have said that with a sarcastic bite, but followed it up with some other nasty remark. The new Noona, however, delivered the line with compassion and understanding. Since Yun Sae started calling every evening, Noona had become unrecognizably calm; it was as if Noona and Mother had switched places. Maybe I just wasn't aware of a curse on our family where one female was required to act irrational at all times. "Be patient," she cooed. "Things will be right again." Then the phone rang and she was gone.

I doubted things would be right again. They might improve, but they weren't going back to the way they were. Not that our lives before were so spectacular, but they sure beat this mess.

On the day Father officially quit on Mother, I woke up to piercing brightness. It was the first day of the two weeks when Peddlers Town, in preparation for the Christmas season, opened daily with extended hours. The sun, unencumbered by clouds, reflected itself every place where there was snow, the front yard sparkled like a field of diamonds. From my window, I saw only the tippy-top of the ruler I'd stuck in the snow heap on the balcony last night, a foot.

I saw the clock: 6:55. I wondered why I was up so early. Last night they'd already closed the schools because of the snowstorm, so somebody must've woken me. I vaguely recalled being shaken awake, but it could've been a dream.

"Good morning, Joon-a!"

Father stood at the foot of my bed. He was wearing his boots, his big black coat, and mittens. He even had the furry hood of the coat over his head. It all seemed very strange, very unreal.

"Wha . . . ?"

"Did you fall back asleep?"

"Yeah . . ."

"Well, brush your teeth, wash your face, and help me clean off the car. We're going tree hunting!"

Tree hunting? Maybe this was still a dream. Why weren't my parents at the store? I crawled out of bed and stumbled to the bathroom. Splashing cold water on my face cleared my head.

Over toast and cereal, Father explained that a water pipe had burst in Peddlers Town overnight, so the whole building was closed for the day. This was apparently good news, because all the merchants were covered by insurance for the lost day of potential shopping. Through some complicated calculation involving the rent, the size, and the tenure of our store, we would benefit $850.

"Considering the amount of snow we got, that's probably eight hundred dollars more than we would've sold if we had opened the store," he said.

So not only did Noona and I get a snow day, my parents did as well. But instead of doing nothing like I'd hoped, I now had to shovel out the car to go get a Christmas tree.

"Is it just you and me?" I asked, seeing the closed door of my old bedroom.

Father crunched on the last bit of his toast, then wiped his buttery fingers on a napkin. "Unless you want to wake *them*," he said. He was using that word a lot lately, *them*, whenever he referred to Noona and Mother.

I shrugged. I didn't want to wake them. What I wanted was to be a girl. If I were, then I would be in that room, too, snoozing and dreaming underneath the warm covers.

Shoveling wasn't bad. There was a lot of snow, but it was fluffy and powdery. A plow had already come through the apartment parking lot, so we only had to move enough snow for our station wagon to get out. By the time our car was free, I had to unzip the front of my winter coat to cool down. After scraping the windows, I jumped into the passenger seat.

"My good son," Father said, tapping his hands to the song coming out of the stereo, "Jingle Bells." The "Jingle Bells" refrain was in English, but everything else was in Korean, which, when I thought about it, was really stupid.

The local roads were rough, but the highway was clear. Staring out the window and seeing every tree and bush white with snow, I almost couldn't tell that I was in a different country. The last big winter storm we had in Korea was about this time a year ago. Noona and I had built a snowman at our neighborhood park, a short and stout one like a fat grandmother. How long before it had all melted away? It stayed bitterly cold until we left for America, so maybe it lasted until the spring thaw. And maybe, by some cosmic coincidence, somebody else had built a snowman in our old spot, and she was back there right now, taking in the scenery through a pair of coat-button eyes, the cold sunshine turning her snowy skin into an icy crust.

Our eventual destination was Herman's Garden off Route 35 South, a nursery with a deceptively small entrance. Once you drove in, the place stretched back for maybe half a mile, just rows and rows of potential Christmas trees waiting to be chopped. There was nobody there, not even Herman. Instead we were greeted with a hurried cardboard sign written in black magic marker:

> *Good morning. I might be running late, so if you want a tree, take it and deposit $25 into my gray box. Scout's honor.*
> —*Herman*

In the barnlike structure that stood before the field, there was a machine to net the trees for easier transport. A stack of bow saws hung on the wall. Father picked one out, a thin rusty sawtooth blade with a bright orange handle.

"We should cut our own," he said.

I pointed at a canopied cluster of precut trees leaning against the barn. "Don't you think that's a better idea? The trees out there have a lot of snow on them."

"Come on, Joon-a. We'll shake the snow off. Don't you want the whole experience?"

And off he went, strolling down the main path to pick out the perfect tree. I sprinted to catch up with him. It was windier out in the field, my nose was running almost instantly. My cheap yellow boots not only looked unfashionable, they did little to keep my feet warm.

We found our tree on the eighth row, a perfectly conical six-foot Douglas fir. Its sharp needles poked me like a torture device. Father handed me the saw and I started cutting, the fresh scent of pine bursting with every stroke of the blade.

"Want me to give it a shot?" Father asked after I'd sawed about a third. I was glad to let him take over; it was tough work. In half the time I had taken, Father cut down the tree. We shook off as much snow as possible and dragged it over to the netting machine. Though neither of us had ever used one, it seemed fairly straightforward.

"Push in and pull out," Father said, pointing at the mouth of the machine.

"Sounds good."

The tree came out squeezed and shrunk; it really was just that simple.

We were less sure of tying down the tree to the roof of our car, but luckily, a truck pulled in and an old man with bulldog cheeks stepped out of it.

"Need any help?" he asked. He was wearing overalls with a name tag that read ERMA. The H and N were covered up with red paint.

He was a pro, looping little nooses at each end and running a line through them all. He cinched that line and tied our tree flush against the car, like magic.

"When you get home, all you need to do is release the main line," he said, handing it to me.

Father gave him twenty-five dollars. "Merry Christmas," Herman said.

With the tree mounted on top of our car like a green warhead, we swung by Kmart and picked up a tree stand, two sets of white lights and two sets of colorful flashing lights, two dozen round glass balls in various metallic shades, and a box of plastic icicles. Just when I thought we were finished, Father put the brakes on the cart and turned it around.

"We need to get an angel for the top," he said.

By this time, I was beyond tired. Waking up early, shoveling, sawing, shopping—all against my will, and what for? Back home there was nothing but silence and hate, and a fully decorated tree wasn't going to remedy any of that. In the middle of the automotive section, I simply stopped. When he realized I wasn't following him, he rolled the cart back.

"Should I get a star instead? Why don't you pick?"

There were boxes of motor oil along the wall, so I sat on one. I closed my eyes and leaned back against the hard concrete. I didn't want to go home and I didn't want to stay here.

"All right," Father said, "I won't be long." He left the cart with me and shuffled off in search of his angel, his star. I watched him as he walked up and down the aisles, and at one point, I saw one hand raise his glasses away from his eyes while the other quickly wiped away tears.

On the way home, he said, "You know, I've lost everybody else. You're all I have."

I said nothing. He hadn't realized he'd lost me, too.

When we got home, Mother and Noona were in the kitchen, and they were surprised to see the tree, but not angry. In fact, Mother seemed glad to see it, even if Father was the one who'd brought it into the house.

I assembled the stand and Father placed the tree in it. When it stood up straight, he tightened the bolts and sat in front of it, no pride or joy in his eyes, just weariness.

For lunch, Mother and Noona made *bi-bim-baap,* egg-fried rice with kimchi and soy-marinated spinach on the side. They didn't realize that they'd unwittingly used Christmas colors for their meal.

"It's red and green," I said, but no one seemed to care.

After he finished eating, Father went into our bedroom and closed the door.

"What's his problem?" Noona said.

"I think he's just tired," I said.

A string of lights didn't work out of the box, so we had to fiddle with it until all fifty lights were lit. With the three of us pitching in, it took less than an hour to hang up all the ornaments. Noona dragged one of our dining room chairs to impale the sweet-faced angel on top of the tree. She had a halo on top of her head that lit up with the rest of the lights when we flipped the switch. We stepped back and took it in, our fully decorated Christmas tree.

"It's beautiful," Mother said, walking around the tree, admiring it from different angles. "Where did you get it?" I related the morning's events to her, and for the first time in a long while, her face resembled the one I'd known all my life.

It didn't last long. Next morning, we discovered that sometime during the night, the tree fell.

"It must have slid against the wall," Noona said. "Otherwise, we would've heard it."

"My fault," Father said. I'd never heard him sound so thoroughly defeated. "I must've not tightened it enough on the bottom."

No one was more shocked than Mother. The tree looked dead, laying on its side. She picked up the broken ornaments (luckily, most were fine, cushioned by the carpet) while Father heaved the tree back on its feet. Noona got three big towels from the closet and tried her best to soak up all the spilled water. That's all the time we had, because they had to go to work and Noona and I had to go to school.

When Father and Mother came back from the store that evening, we'd just finished redecorating the tree. The most time-consuming part was getting all the lights to come back on: this time, two of the strings had gone out. Noona put her artistic touch to work by replacing the broken ornaments with little winged angels she drew on cardboard cutouts.

"We think the tree was too heavy on one side," Noona said.

"It's even prettier than last night," Father said, but it was obvious he was just saying that to make us all feel better. The tree looked like crap.

Father turned off the lights in the living room and brought in the "Jingle Bells" tape from his car. We sat around the tree until the tape played the last song, "Rudolph the Red-Nosed Reindeer," which, like all the other songs on the album, was in Korean except for the title.

"Why do they do that?" I asked Father. "Sing just that part in English?"

"So they can pretend to be where we are, in America," Father said.

"Really?"

"Who knows. That's my guess."

"It just sounds weird, is all."

"Didn't you ever dream of being here?"

"No," I said. "I was happy where I was." I didn't care if that hurt him; it was the truth.

Father unplugged the lights and the tree went dark with the rest of the room, but the full moon illuminated the nighttime sky with its steely glow. As we headed to bed, the morning's horror was forgotten, chalked up to uneven weight distribution and a smidgen of rotten luck.

Next day, as we stood around the once-again fallen tree—this time on the other side, leaning against the left wall—no one said anything. Father looked at the tree as if he wanted to chop it into little pieces and burn it up. "Wait until I get back tonight," he said before leaving. It wasn't accusatory, the way he'd said it, but Noona and I still blamed ourselves.

When our parents returned that evening, Father went to work immediately. He twisted four hooked wall screws around where the tree would stand, paired near the top and bottom, then looped a thick, green cord around the trunk then tied it to a hook. He repeated this with the other three, and when he was finished, the tree was strapped at four corners.

The tree didn't fall again, but it looked odd all bound up, especially during the day. Father thought the twine would be camouflaged, but under sunlight, the color was weirdly off, reflecting a lurid, fluorescent green.

"It looks like a hostage," I said.

"Now it's stuck here," Noona said, "just like the rest of us."

For Mother, I bought a canary-yellow dress with short-sleeved arms and a scooped neck. She wouldn't be able to wear it until the summer, but it was a quality dress, according to Mindy, who found it for me. I thanked her and whipped out the little red box I'd been hiding inside my back pocket. It was Christmas Eve, so I wouldn't be seeing her until the holiday was over.

She looked surprised more than happy, which both mystified and concerned me. I hoped I wasn't doing anything to offend her.

"You open the box?" I asked her.

"Of course," she said, flipping the velvet-covered case until it clicked up with a pop.

It was just a dumb necklace we sold at the store, a gold chain with a jade pendant in the shape of a curled-up kitty. "I love it," she said, and kissed me on the cheek. I was hoping for one on the lips, but we were in the middle of the clothing shop and people were everywhere.

On the way back to her store, we passed by A Second Chance, where she yanked my hand and pulled us both to a stop. "Wait here," she said, and jumped into the store. I saw her take a white hardcover book from the front display, but its title was too small to read from where I stood, and then I got it: She was getting my present. She hadn't thought of it in advance like I had, which peeved me somewhat.

"What is it?" I asked.

"Nothing," she said. At Animal Attraction, Mindy found a roll of gold-foiled wrapping paper underneath the register counter.

"What's shakin', Dave?" Sylvia, her mother, asked. Since she'd come to know me, she no longer simply said hello or hi—it was always whether something was shaking, cooking, up, going down—I could probably fill a notebook with her numerous variations. I liked the way she called me Dave in her easygoing drawl; it made me feel as if we'd been friends forever.

"Not much, Sylvia," I said, my usual response.

"Looks like you're about to get a nice Christmas gift."

"It *is* a nice gift," Mindy said.

"Oh, honey," Sylvia said, seeing Mindy struggling with the paper, "you don't need to use that much."

"Will you just leave us alone?" Mindy said.

"Fine, fine," Sylvia said, retreating to the rear of the pet shop. She picked up a cylinder of fish food and sprinkled the top of one of the aquariums. A kaleidoscope of tropical fishes gunned for the surface, and Sylvia watched them eat with motherly satisfaction.

Mindy was doing a terrible job of wrapping; she'd cut off too much, so now she had to shear another little piece of wrapping paper to patch up the bottom of the book from jutting out. She wasn't a very graceful girl, which had been Mother's biggest complaint when she still cared enough to have opinions about someone besides Father. She said Mindy was too tall and compared her to a horse, citing her big, flaring nostrils and long face.

"She does not," Noona said, and for a second I'd foolishly thought she was defending me. "She looks more like a . . . giraffe! You know, with all her spots on her skin!"

While she and Mother had a good chuckle, Father took me aside. "Don't listen to them, Joon-a. They're just jealous."

"You don't think she's too tall?"

"American girls, they're big. You're small right now, but you'll get big."

Looking at my father didn't exactly make me a believer. If I took after him, I'd be doomed to a life of gazing up at people.

Mindy had a long neck, and her skin was littered with brownish freckles, packed all over her face and arms, a mosaic of brownish spots that, up close, broke apart into a myriad of strange shapes and sizes, but I still liked her fine.

"Merry Christmas," Mindy said, handing me my gift.

The cover of *The Little Prince* featured a blond kid with spiky, un-kempt hair standing on top of what looked to be a ridiculously small planet. There were illustrations throughout—an elephant stuck underneath a hat, a bright star over a barren landscape, a single rose against a lonely moon.

"I love it," I said, because that's what she'd said about the necklace. In actuality, I felt uneasy—because even from the little I saw as I flipped through, I skimmed by a bevy of words I didn't know.

"We can read it together," she said, as if reading my mind. "If you want to."

My Mindy, my giraffe.

Ten minutes to closing time, Mr. Hong walked into our store, his face ashen.

"I'm leaving for the hospital right now," he said. "I just came by to wish you a Merry Christmas."

"Hong," Father said, but didn't know what else to say. He just nodded and wished him the same.

As we pulled down our canvas curtains for the day, Father asked me, "Don't you think we should be there, Joon-a?"

"It's Christmas Eve and I want to go home," I said. I dropped the last curtain and picked up a handful of locks. I crouched down at the farthest curtain and started chaining and locking up the ends.

Father picked up the remaining locks and followed me. "It won't be for long, just to stop by and wish her a good Christmas, too. Don't you think she deserves that?"

I kept silent, concentrating on the sound the locks made as they snapped shut.

"I mean if you were really sick, wouldn't seeing your friends cheer you up?"

I couldn't take much more of this. With every passing day, my respect for Mother's level of patience grew: How had she been able to live with him without picking up a baseball bat and bashing him until he stopped talking?

"If you want to go, then go!" I said. It was almost exactly what I'd heard Mother say to him a hundred times.

Hearing my outburst, Noona walked over. "What's going on?"

"He wants to go to the hospital," I said, pointing at Father. "He wants to spend Christmas Eve there."

"We're not going to be there all night," he said, making it sound like I was crazy. "I just said we'd stop by."

"We'll be there all night," I muttered to myself. It was then that I felt a hand on my neck, it was the hand of my mother, her tenderness—in the dusk of her almond eyes, the warmth of her palm, the quiet sag of her shoulders.

"We'll go," she said. "It'll be all right."

We closed up the store and left at seven.

The hour and minute hands of the round clock on the wall of the ICU waiting room were about to converge into one solid black line on the twelve. I waited until the red second hand completed its circular journey.

"Merry Christmas," I whispered to Noona. She said nothing, just sat there with her arms crossed, her eyes closed.

In this drab gray room lined with hard gray plastic chairs, we sat with the rest of the bleary-eyed families, watching the ceiling-mounted television screen, flipping through outdated magazines, picking at our fingernails. The room was poorly lit, some of the fluorescent bulbs either missing or burnt out. There were only four other people besides us: two Latino men who looked alike, one white-bearded old man thin enough to be on a hunger strike, and a chain-smoking twentysomething girl who constantly had some part of her body in motion—a tapping finger, a shaking foot, a bobbing head.

Since we weren't immediate family, none of us was allowed to go into Mrs. Hong's room at this time of night. Every hour, Mr. Hong pushed through the large double doors to give us an update. It was obvious he didn't want to do this, but Father wouldn't leave, despite Mr. Hong's insistence, so he felt as if he had to keep us in the loop.

"I don't think her condition is going to change," Mr. Hong told Father. "You really should go home. Look, it's past midnight, it's Christmas."

"We're staying right here," Father said, squeezing his shoulder.

Mr. Hong gestured to the three of us. "I think they want to go home."

"We'll wait until Yun Sae gets here," Father said. Yun Sae was driving up from Maryland with Mrs. Hong's sister; they were due to arrive at any moment, or at least that's how the story went.

"I bet you every cent I have that even when Yun Sae arrives, we won't go home," I told Noona, who had dozed off.

Ten minutes later, my claim was put to test, for Yun Sae arrived. He woke up my sister with a peck on the cheek.

"Why are you guys here?" he said.

"Support," Father said.

Yun Sae nodded. "How is she?"

"We're not allowed in," Noona said. "Because we're not family."

He flagged down the attendant and spoke to her quickly. He grabbed Noona and whispered quickly into her ear, and she nodded. The three of them talked for a bit more, then the attendant came over to us and apologized.

"What did you say to them?" I asked Yun Sae.

"I told them In Sook's my fiancée and that I'm a lawyer. Come on, let's go."

What hit me first was the smell of the room, the smell of death, a low, rotting scent of a body on the brink of passing. Nothing could prevent this odor from surfacing—not the bouquets of flowers, not the bowl of potpourri. Mrs. Hong was dying.

"Yun-Sae-ya," Mr. Hong said, embracing his son.

"I drove as fast as I could," Yun Sae said.

"You got them all in?" When Yun Sae told him the story, Mr. Hong managed a laugh. "We can get more chairs." Mr. Hong and Father went to the empty room across the hall and brought four folding chairs. Mr. Hong, Mrs. Hong's sister, Yun Sae, and Noona sat on the left side while Father, Mother, and I sat on the right.

Yun Sae kissed his mother on the forehead. "She doesn't look good."

"The doctor says . . ." Mr. Hong had trouble getting it out, but he got himself under control and continued. "The doctor doesn't think she'll make it through the night."

Two clear plastic tubes ran into Mrs. Hong's nostrils and a yellow tube burrowed into her arm. She wore a blue cap to hide her radiation-induced baldness, and her bony face was completely drained of color. Three months ago, which was when I last saw her, saying she was leaving for Korea to visit her relatives, Mrs. Hong had been a short, plump woman with a perm who liked to read, and now here she lay, unrecognizable, her face a skeletal mask. To her left was a heart monitor, the green line doing the familiar jump as it made its way across the screen, beeping softly with every heartbeat. *When she's dead,* I thought, *that's going to flatline.* What then? Mrs. Hong would be here one second, and in the next, she wouldn't be, never to return, her soul detaching from her lifeless body and rising, invisible.

Mother walked up to her and touched her cheek.

"Hello, Jenny," she said.

"Hello, Emma," Mrs. Hong said.

Then Mother turned away quickly, hiding her face from everyone.

At 1:14 A.M., Mrs. Hong stopped breathing. The EKG fell silent, the dot running from right to left in a straight green line. Everyone put their heads down but me. I kept alert for something, anything—a sudden flicker of light, an inexplicable chill in the air, the ringing of far-away bells—but nothing. There was one less person in this world and nobody outside of this room knew or cared.

We all took turns hugging the Hongs, then we drove home.

Usually it took a serious amount of yelling or shaking or even water splashing to wake me up in the middle of the night, but for whatever reason, when Mother tiptoed into our room, I woke up instantly. I didn't feel even a hint of grogginess; it was as if I hadn't been asleep at all. Maybe it was because I'd gone to sleep so late, my body rhythm out of sync.

I heard her walk past me to Father's bed. *"Yeuh-boh,"* she said as she shook him awake, *"yeuh-boh."*

"What time is it?" Father whispered, his voice thick with sleep.

"Four-thirty."

"You couldn't sleep?"

"We should talk."

After they left for the living room, I slunk out of bed and opened my door a crack as quietly as possible, just enough so I could hear. My bare toes curled against the icy floor.

"Don't say you're sorry," Mother said. "I know you're sorry. You kept seeing her. I can somehow deal with you and her when we weren't here, but how could you? When we, when I, was here, right here?"

A minute, maybe more, passed by before Father answered. "I just didn't know how to break it off. I know I should've, but I just . . . didn't know how."

Another long pause. "I'm giving you another chance," Mother said.

"Why?"

"I don't know. Maybe it was seeing Mrs. Hong tonight. I can't believe she's gone."

"She's younger than both of us."

"It's just . . . not fair."

The next moment of silence was so long that I thought they were done, but then Father spoke. "So does this mean we go back to the way we were?"

Mother didn't say anything, but she must have nodded, for Father let out a long, thankful sigh.

"I think Joon-a hates me," he said.

"This has been hard on both of our kids," Mother said.

"So tomorrow we move back?"

"Yes," Mother said. Then she added, "are you going to fuck up again?" It was the first time I'd heard her say that particular curse word, and I felt stung. Coming from Mother, that word seemed especially harsh.

"No," Father said, "I won't fuck up again. I won't."

As I slipped back into bed, I wished I felt happier than I actually did. In my mind, I'd expected their reconciliation to be more loving than what I'd just heard, with both Mother and Father apologizing, running into one another's open arms, pledging to each other they'd never do something so cruel again.

On Christmas Day, while Mother and Noona slapped lunch together, Father went to work on the living room coffee table.

"Come on, Joon-a," he said. "You can help me count." He opened up a pouch and out came stacks and stacks of twenties, like he'd held up a bank. I'd never seen so much cash in my life. "A lot of money, huh? It was a pretty good Christmas."

I sat down on the floor next to him and sorted the piles in decreasing denominations, starting with the hundreds and ending with the ones. There were so many twenties, we had to make five pillars of them. Even though my fingertips were turning dark, I loved every second of soaking in the rich scent of paper currency.

"Let's count," Father said, so we counted. We counted three times, coming to a grand total of $24,984 for the two weeks leading up to Christmas, an average of $1,800 of gross sales per day.

As we were snapping rubber bands around the bills to take to the bank, Father raised his eyebrows, his best conspiratorial look. "You wanna know a secret?"

If I didn't hear another secret for the rest of my life, that would've been just fine. He must have seen this in my face as he cleared his throat and said, "It's nothing bad, in fact it's something quite good."

It probably had to do with what I'd overheard last night, so I nodded, but Father changed his mind. "I'll announce it over lunch," he said. "It's worth waiting for."

We washed up and sat down at the dining table. "Why don't you sit over there?" Father suggested, leaving the chair open for Mother, a seating configuration we hadn't used in a while. It was Father and Mother on one side and Noona and me on the other, all of us busily digging into our respective bowls. When we were finished, Father spoke.

"We're going back to the way things were," he said, which wasn't exactly true. All he and Mother would be doing is sleeping in the same room again. "And Joon-a," he added, "you're going to have your own room."

There was no way I could have another room, unless they shoved a bed into the bathroom. Unless, of course, we were moving. Looking at the cash on the table, twenty-five thousand dollars of cash, the idea suddenly didn't seem so preposterous. It would be enough for a down payment on a small house, not around here because houses were too expensive, but the next few towns over weren't so bad.

"Are we getting a house?" I asked, looking from Father to Mother and back to Father.

"That's not what he meant," Mother said, trying her best not to sound annoyed. "We're going to set up half of the living room as your space."

"It's almost like a room," Father said. "We'll move the piano to the other wall. We have a plan, you'll see."

"Did you know about this?" I asked Noona.

"Mother told me when we were making lunch."

Of course, I was always the last to know, even when it came to things that directly affected my life. "When?" I asked.

"Soon, I guess," Mother said, looking at Father. Father shrugged, disappointed at my disappointment.

After lunch, he took me aside and explained that on our coffee table was a quarter of what we earned for the whole year, and it would have to last us through the slow winter, like squirrels depending on their reserves of gathered nuts. How retailers survived before Jesus Christ died on the cross, nobody knew.

"A good chunk of that also goes to the rent, and of course, to our wholesalers for the goods we sold," Father said.

I nodded, but I wasn't really listening. My mind was on the living room, how it could be configured to accommodate me and my stuff. It made the most sense to move me into the corner by the sliding balcony window, maybe get one of those vertical blinds to block the sun.

"You'll get your own room," Father said, "a real one. Business is good, and we're saving some money. The houses in Neptune aren't too expensive."

Again, I nodded. His predictions and promises were full of good intentions but rarely came true. I saw no reason why this would be any different.

Instead of walls I had rice-paper screens, two standing side by side and one perpendicular, framing me into a rectangle. They transformed the corner of the living room into a place of my own, where I slept, read, and dreamed. At first, it was strange to not have anybody else in sight, but it didn't take long until I looked forward to stretching the screen across my "doorway," bathing in the milky-white translucence of my room. With my earplugs in, it was as good as being alone.

I was alone a lot after Christmas, when Father and Mother moved back in together and I got my space. Two weeks of quiet and harmony was all I'd get, as they soon resumed their usual bickering about money and everything else. I was learning to hate them in that special way only an adolescent can hate his parents. I missed being with Noona, but she was different now that she and Yun Sae were together. We were growing up and growing older, whether I liked it or not.

I told all this to Mindy as we sat in her pet store, surrounded by chirping birds and barking dogs. She usually put things in perspective, but today she said nothing to comfort me. Instead, she had this to say: "We're moving."

I almost choked on the Raisinets I'd popped into my mouth. "Where?"

"Vermont," she said, snapping the book shut. We'd been on the second chapter of *The Little Prince,* where the author meets the prince for the first time. The prince wanted him to draw him a sheep, and that's as far as we'd gotten.

"When?"

"I don't know," she said, then bitterly, "ask Mom. I hate her."

"Why you moving?"

She munched on a handful of Raisinets, washing them down with a Coke. I sipped on my lemonade, which tasted way more sour after the sweets. "I don't wanna go," she said, but we both knew she had no choice. She explained that her grandmother was retiring from the bed-and-breakfast she owned and ran, and it'd been agreed for a long time that her mother would take up the reins.

"When?" I asked her again, because I thought she knew but just didn't want to tell me.

"A month," she said. "Maybe two weeks."

"We will write?" I asked. It was stupid. I knew how to construct simple sentences, but what would I say?

She nodded quickly and dabbed her eyes with the sleeve of her fuzzy pink sweater. "I wish I could grow up," she said. "Like really fast, you know? So I could make my own decisions, go where I wanna go, and stay where I wanna stay."

It was a slow Saturday evening, the dead time of dinner when only the restaurants get business. On the counter were a pair of rubberized chew toys for dogs, in the shape of a moon and a sun. Faces were painted on their round surfaces, and initially I'd thought they were both smiling,

328 SUNG J. WOO

but upon closer examination, they looked more like expressions of concern than good humor.

"You know what is today?" I asked. Mindy shook her head. "One year before today, I came to this country, on the airplane."

"I didn't know that," she said, sounding hurt. She must've felt left out that I hadn't told her in advance. "Well?"

"Well, what?"

"What do you think?"

"About?"

She rolled her eyes, punched me on the arm. "Don't be smart. You know, do you like it here now?"

It would suck when she left, and I didn't want to think about that. Instead I thought about now, right now, being here with a girl I liked, who liked me back.

"Could be worse," I said.

It was the truths that made the people grotesques.
—*Sherwood Anderson,*
Winesburg, Ohio